Mark Dawson was born in Lowestoft in 1973, and now lives in Hackney. He was formerly a resident DJ at the Hacienda in Manchester. His second novel *Subpoena Colada*, is also published by Pan Macmillan.

Mark Dawson

The Art of
Falling Apart

PAN BOOKS

First published 2001 by Macmillan

This edition published 2002 by Pan Books
an imprint of Pan Macmillan Ltd
Pan Macmillan, 20 New Wharf Road, London N1 9RR
Basingstoke and Oxford
Associated companies throughout the world
www.panmacmillan.com

ISBN 0 330 48499 0

1 3 5 7 9 8 6 4 2

A CIP catalogue record for this book is available from
the British Library.

Typeset by SetSystems Ltd, Saffron Walden, Essex
Printed and bound in Great Britain by
Mackays of Chatham plc, Chatham, Kent

To Mette

Nothing in excess.

– Inscribed on the temple of Apollo at Delphi

I still have the art of falling apart.

– Soft Cell

part One

Part One

Jared

Jared stirs as the mechanical rumble of the unfolding undercarriage resonates with the bulkhead that he is leaning against. His cheek is creased from sleeping against the lining of the complimentary pillow and his limbs are rigid, his quadriceps cramped despite the generous acreage in First Class. He flicks aside the curtains and gazes out into the night. The black seems more total than London's night and he wonders if this is an American phenomenon or just the absence of the sodium pollution that bleeds into the night around major cities. He presses a button and his seat quietly exhales, muffled servos bringing it back through the full ninety degrees and into the upright position. The black cowl of the Mojave Desert prickles with the occasional lights of vehicles running the desolate expanse during the cool hours. They have already passed over Lake Mead and the Hoover Dam; Jared missed the wide footprint of the water, dark and glassy from thirty thousand feet. They pass to the north of Boulder City and Henderson, their twinkling gloaming no preparation for the blazing cascade of light that explodes as Las Vegas comes into view.

The others are sleeping and Jared decides not to wake

3

them. He presses another button to kill the overhead reading light and watches as the plane commences its descent.

Airport

Their passage from the plane through Customs and into the limo company's waiting room at McCarron International Airport takes less than ten minutes, point to point. This is one of the benefits of flying First Class, the express dis-embarkation procedure accelerating the rich and famous through the mundane chores of international arrival as smoothly and effortlessly as a needle through silk. Those poor unfortunates flying in Business or Economy have their endurance tested by interminable and inevitable delays at the whim of Immigration and Customs and the pre-Vegas roulette at the baggage carousel. Not so for Dystopia. Smoking his third Marlboro Light since leaving the cabin (ignoring the No Smoking signs plastering the walls), Jared wonders if Customs have even checked his luggage. It appears to have been delivered straight from the cargo hold, ferried the short distance from the runway to the arrival lounge by a caddy in blue-and-white BA livery driving a bastardized golf buggy.

Jared idly picks at the destination label fixed onto his thousand-pound Louis Vuitton suitcase by one of the flunkies at Revolution Records back in London: LONDON HTR-LAS VEGAS MCR, it says, hand-printed in careful script with obsessive, anal exactitude. Not that losing his luggage would be a disaster, not now when he could afford to replace every item in it from the roll of notes in his wallet: his small change. Bored, he opens the case and lazily roots around, a cursory examination. True enough, his stuff has not been touched; everything is folded neatly away, just as Gretta packed it. He knows sniffer dogs have probably been over it but he curses Alex anyway.

Alex is the band's manager and he forbade them from bringing their own stash with them into the States, telling them that, regardless of who they are and how important they might think themselves to be, they could be arrested, charged and then deported, never to return. This self-importance barb was aimed at Vid, who was the most likely to contravene international law by transporting large quantities of Class A narcotics which were, however improbably, exclusively for his own personal consumption. As this was Dystopia's first US tour, and the one that all the critics were saying would break them, Jared was prepared to play along. But that didn't mean he hadn't resented the ten-hour flight and the chemical embargo that restricted his range of artificial diversions to the complimentary alcohol supplied by the airline.

They are all slightly frazzled from the combination of lack of sleep, lack of narcotics and too much alcohol consumed at altitude. Jared's throat is dry and sore and it hurts to unstick his tongue from the top of his mouth, and a headache is throbbing behind his eyeballs and against the top of his skull. He rubs his eyes and looks around the room: Astrid, lounging lengthways across an upholstered banquette, toying with the leaves of a rubber plant with one hand (manicured: electric-blue nails today) and splaying a copy of *Fear and Loathing in Las Vegas* with the other; Vid pacing the lounge, his hands shaking, on the barren outskirts of cold-turkey city; Damien, his tattooed, muscular arms as dark as the sagging bags beneath his eyes. Alex is the only one who looks normal, haranguing the limo company's clerk for the tardy arrival of their car.

'Hey, man, where's our chariot?' asks Vid, a filigree of red weave tracing the whites of his eyes. Vid is wearing a wide-brimmed cowboy hat he had a roadie pick up from the Harrods concessionaire at Heathrow. He is tugging at the frayed sleeves of a KMFDM T-shirt decorated with Brute's artwork: a picture of an Aryan-esque man holding a pistol to a girl's head. He is wearing it because – and not despite – the shootings at Columbine. Vid is a sucker for controversy; he said he wanted to join the NRA.

'Fuck this waiting shit,' Vid says. 'I'm tired and I need a joint. Sort it out.'

'There's a jam on the Strip,' sighs Alex, pissed off with Vid's childish bouts of pique. 'The car's on its way but it's been held up, OK? We just have to wait, so be patient. Be cool.' Vid has been like a petulant brat during the flight, making trouble for the stewardesses and annoying the other passengers in First Class by singing extracts from the band's songs as well as selections from the back catalogues of Marilyn Manson, Coil and the Machines of Loving Grace. And then he trashed his personal movie viewer because the 'movies were way too fuckin' bogus, man'.

'You all see Bono in the arrivals lounge?' asks Astrid, putting her paperback away in a tote bag that costs more than most entire sets of suitcases. 'Where'd he come from?'

'He was on the same flight as us,' says Jared. 'He was sat up front.'

'There's further up than First Class?' asks Vid.

'Yeah. Ultra First Class,' confirms Damien. 'Über First Class. For very, very important people. V-VIPs.'

'Can you believe *that*?' Vid interjects. 'Fucking guy's yesterday's news, man. You didn't suck his cock, did you? You didn't ask for his autograph? Please tell me you didn't—'

'I didn't ask for his autograph—'

'—'cos that dude oughtta be asking for *our* autographs. The crest of the new wave. The New Power Generation. That's what we are.'

'—and I didn't suck his cock.'

'Can you restrain your ego for a nanosecond, Vid? Please?' pleads Alex. Vid sneers at him. 'Christ, I thought Billy Graham was going to spontaneously *combust* when you started up with *Antichrist Superstar*.'

'He deserves worse: like Satan's trident up his arse.'

'Does Satan have a trident?' asks Jared thoughtfully. 'Isn't that Neptune?'

'Stuck-up prick,' Vid says, spiking a can of Red Stripe he has taken with him from the plane. He downs half of it, his Adam's Apple bobbing cartoonishly. 'No, man, not you, Jared – Billy Graham. He just doesn't recognize natural, God-given talent when he sees it. He should've been rejoicing, not complaining. I am the truth, the way, and all the rest of that John 3:16 bullshit. I need to score some blow.'

'You wouldn't have wanted to distract his attention for too long, would you?' suggests Jared, settling into a seat and lighting up fag number four. 'His special link to the Creator was in serious jeopardy for a moment back there.'

Vid once heard a comedian explain how it is that aeroplanes manage the miracle of flight. The comedian posited that God watches our pathetic attempts at the physically impossible in a paternal, sympathetic light, and humours us by performing feats of celestial juggling to keep the world's aircraft in flight. A jumbo here, a single-seater there, a helicopter over here. Like all the best jugglers He occasionally drops a ball to demonstrate His fallibility and to heighten the sense of awe for the rest of the act.

Vid has elaborated upon this thesis: according to him, God pays special attention to those planes carrying clergymen, preachers and other men of the cloth. To fly in holy company is to ensure that your plane has a special beacon protecting it from divine misidentification and possible accident. Vid's thesis has been extended to cover – depending upon who is flying with them, and the apparent severity of the predicament – Buddhists, Humanists, Confucianists, Shintoists, Taoists, Satanists, Unitarian Universalists, Zoroastrianists, New Age Spiritualists. In moments of clear-air turbulence that charade as life-threatening descents, those members of the band in particularly pious mood (i.e. those not drunk/high/fucking groupies) have also been mistaken for shining astral beacons.

'He might be a conservative, reactionary prick, but he certainly got the old man upstairs' attention. Smoooth flight – nice one, Billy.' He screws the hat tighter onto his head. Jared realizes he looks like Hank Williams just before he died: skinny, haggard, about the same age. 'What happened to that fake, silicone-implanted, zero-talented, nul-point girl band . . .?'

'All Saints?' suggests Astrid. 'They got into their limo. Five minutes ago.'

'What the fuck? Alex, man – *Alex*! Please explain to me how the All *fucking* Saints' limousine is here right on time but we're still here waiting for ours? There must be some kinda misunderstanding going on here, right? I mean, surely they took our ride? How else would a bunch of no-account, talentless, fuckwit feminists get away from here before us? And what happened to the jam on the Strip? I want answers, Alex. Give me *answers*!'

'What can I tell you?' Alex looks weary with Vid's tantrums but he is trying not to show it. Vid can be unbearable, but he is the frontman, the vocalist, and he is allowed a certain leeway. Jared resents Vid sometimes; he is a man of large ego and only a little talent, and his antics sometimes obscure the fact that it is Jared who writes Dystopia's songs and Jared who lays down their distinctive – he would say revolutionary – sound.

'Why are All Saints feminists, Vid?' asks Astrid. 'And if they were, what would be wrong with it?'

'When I want an opinion I'll rattle your cage.'

'And when I want any shit from you I'll squeeze your head. It wasn't an opinion, arsehole. It was a *question*.'

Astrid pauses quizzically. 'Do we say *ass*hole now or can we still say *arse*hole?'

'Vid's an arsehole in any language,' offers Jared, ducking as the half-empty can of Red Stripe flies over his shoulder and hits the wall. A pool of yellow beer spreads out on the polished pseudo-marble floor, like a puddle of urine. The concierge regards Vid with a disapproving glare. Vid eyeballs him back, staring him out. Jared has seen this before: inevitably Vid will become rude with the authority figure that fails to recognize his greatness, and will then become aggressive. In England this has led to several nights cooling his heels in custody; part of Jared would enjoy seeing Vid try his luck with American lawmen. The same part of him hopes the Las Vegas Police Department uses long, brutal night-sticks.

Limo

The dry slap of the desert heat weighs upon them as they traverse the short distance between the waiting room and their replacement limousine. He watches the shark fins of airplanes jostling for position, sprinting out to the concrete tongue of the runway. The heat is completely, utterly, arid, without even a degree of humidity. Jared imagines his skin bubbling and bursting like the basted skin of roasting chicken. It makes him swoon and his vision swims, registering the rippling heat haze rising up from the tarmac. An illuminated thermometer, by far the most sober piece of neon they will see in Vegas during their stay, flicks between the time and temperature: it's still 94 degrees Fahrenheit, even this late. As Jared watches, the digits blur and a 5 replaces the 4: 95 degrees.

A fleet of white and black limos is swooping in and out of the airport; Jared has never seen so many. Their own ride is an oversized white Lincoln Towncar. The air-conditioning is blowing fiercely as they slide inside, and the difference in temperature is startling. The car is upholstered in distressed black leather, the rumpled kind of material that Jared would find hideously tacky on a World of Leather sofa; here, in the car, he thinks the look is classy and sophisticated. There is a minibar and two TV sets built into the side panels of the interior. There is plenty of expensive-looking mahogany. The windows are tinted. The moon roof is open and the sounds of the Strip are dimly audible in the pauses between planes taking off and landing. Tom Waits is on the sound system. Jared's first ride in a limousine was an experience, perhaps gilded retrospectively by the signing en route of their half-million-pound contract. That lustre has faded now, but he still gets a thrill as they roll past other travellers marooned in their garish yellow taxis.

Vid is still fuming about the missing limo which he is convinced was appropriated by All Saints. 'What's the plural of pudenda? Pundendi?' he asks, as they hustle off the speeding Las Vegas Boulevard and nose into the slower-moving traffic on the Strip.

'What?' asks Alex, wearily.

'Fannies?' offers Jared.

'Yeah, exactly,' replies Vid. 'I rest my case.'

'No one understands you,' says Alex, articulating the obvious. 'Welcome to Vid-town. Population: one.'

'Yeah, yeah, whatever,' says Vid. Then, muttering, 'Get with the programme, party people.'

The towncar cuts across Tropicana and onto the slip-road to their hotel, cutting through verdant green borders and stands of palm trees, fronds whispering in the breeze that has picked up. The car rolls to a halt outside the awning of New York New York, where Alex has hired six penthouse suites, comprising almost half of the top floor of the hotel, at a cost of twenty thousand dollars a night. Bellhops appear to disgorge their luggage from the second limousine pulling up alongside them in the wide forecourt. Even their suitcases get executive treatment. The crew is staying in the Luxor, down the Strip, because it is less expensive and because Alex does not want them – with a less restricted access to drugs and the other assorted bad influences a town like Vegas has to offer – to be in full-time contact with the band.

Alex has already built into his mental profit-and-loss account for the trip the instances when the band will slip outside his ambit of influence; these moments are unavoidable, and all he can hope for is to limit such exposure. He wants *regulated* turpitude; the band's reputation is one of the reasons for their burgeoning success, in much the same way as Marilyn Manson exhuming New Orleans graveyards and smoking human bones allowed him to ride a right-wing wave of moral outrage to the top.

He has a press officer with him for this tour and intends to leak a few stories to the hungry media: drop the ravenous pack of dogs a hunk of meat here and there, keep them interested. They are already salivating on titbits that have preceded the band over the Atlantic: Vid's 'suicidal' heroin addiction (true); Astrid's rumoured lesbianism (true); Damien being a 'convicted felon' guilty of 'second-degree murder' (false: manslaughter). And then there is the music itself: Jared's industrial pop music, 'anthems for generation why?', a thunderous tumult that has seduced tens of thousands on both sides of the Atlantic. 'MR ZEIT-GEIST' was the headline in *Q* over his favourite interview, a copy of which he keeps framed at home.

'Who's up for hitting the tables?' asks Damien, who has been studying websites devoted to blackjack and roulette technique on his PowerBook during the flight over. 'I fancy blowing some cash.'

'Uh, hello, McFly? The aim is to *win*,' suggests Vid.

'Bollocks it is. What do I need *more* money for?'

'Why not,' says Jared. 'I'm game.'

'Not me,' says Astrid. 'Not tonight. I have an appointment in the bath with Hunter S.'

'Can I come too?' asks Vid. Astrid sneers at him and he gruffly changes the subject back to Vegas. 'I'm keeping my powder dry. You go. Speaking of powder, I'm going to score some blow.'

'Take it easy, OK?' Alex pleads. 'We're on MTV News tomorrow, remember? Let's do it sober.'

'Is *sober* my style?' asks Vid. 'Do my fans expect me *sober*? They don't want me sober. They want me a-rockin' and a-rollin'. I can't disappoint them.'

'What a martyr,' says Astrid.

'Just don't go nuts,' warns Alex. '*Please.*' Jared thinks he looks more on edge than he usually does.

Vid spreads his arms mock-helplessly. 'Can't fight nature,' he says.

The Mirage

The night is so balmy that Jared and Damien pass up the limousine waiting for them in the forecourt. After negotiating the five-acre frontage of the hotel, crowded with palm trees and monumental fountains splashing plumes of silvered water into the night air, they reach the Strip. They can walk the streets here in comparative anonymity; were they to attempt to relax in this fashion in London, fans would mug them within seconds and paparazzi within minutes. Their obscurity is despite the enormous canvas advert for the gig that stretches over the Strip itself, suspending their sullen publicity shot overhead as they walk beneath it.

The sidewalks are choked with hundreds of Vegas revellers: mostly Americans but with large contingents of Japanese and European travellers. The Americans amuse Jared's Darwinian leanings. He has read anthropological papers demonstrating how the American population (male and female, old and young) is the most obese sociological group anywhere in the world. He wonders whether the fieldwork for this study was undertaken in Las Vegas or, if it was not, whether an additional Nevada analysis would add a few pounds to the median. Every second person seems to be struggling with ponderous rims of spare flash – sloppy wedges of fat quivering like jellies from exposed shanks. The gruesome freak show is accentuated by the utterly inappropriate choices of clothing on display: these suburban monoliths waddle past in Hawaiian shorts, garish shirts undone to the navel, and always, *always* white socks.

Jared looks over at Damien, smiling, enjoying himself more than he expected. Damien looks fabulous, his lustrous skin a harlequin counterpoint to the outfit he has changed into: a blinding-white Issy Miyake suit, cut off at the elbows, with a white Kenzo T-shirt. The black skin of his arms, bulging with coiled muscle, is decorated with oriental script. Selected extracts from *Das Kapital* are tattooed on both arms, down his chest and across his back. Both he and a junkie he used to see were Communists, *Marxism Today* subscribers, with a bust of Lenin in their kitchen as a hatstand. He thought that the coolest way to espouse his creed was to inscribe it indelibly on his body. Since Dystopia's rise to fame the needle gauging his political leaning has jerked to the right; with the obscene amount of money he is given (none of them believe they *really* earn it, except maybe Vid), and his disinclination to invest it in establishing proletarian communes in Somerset, a re-evaluation was inevitable – for internal balance if nothing else.

The tattoos are too freakish, too Ewan McGregor in *The Pillow Book* for Jared's taste, but he often finds himself debating whether he would swap places with Damien. It is a hypothetical question: Damien's HIV renders serious contemplation moot. His junkie ex-girlfriend gave it to him on a needle five years ago. They all know about that now. The band takes a private physician with them on tour, who takes bi-weekly T-Cell counts to monitor the infection's progress. He also administers Damien's drugs, a prototype Hoffman La Roche cocktail that costs eight hundred pounds a week and will not be generally available for another three years. The HIV has lain dormant since it was detected eighteen months ago, when Revolution insisted on testing them before offering them a contract. Damien has never displayed any resentment towards his illness, but since his diagnosis he has abstained serious alcohol and Class As. He smokes enormous amounts of pot and takes the occasional herbal trip, but that's it. The rest of his time is spent drumming or reading or in the gym. Of Jared's immediate friends, Damien is the cleanest, the sorted one.

They cross Tropicana and head into the Mirage, past the illuminated banner advertising Siegfried and Roy's Albino Tigers and the new Tom Jones show, *Green Green Grass*. Still no one has recognized them, and Jared has completely relaxed. The noise of Las Vegas – a compound of voices and the clatter of machines ingesting coinage or ejecting it – can be heard all along the wide pavements of the Strip, from the Fremont Street Experience in the North to the Luxor in the South. As they walk through the fibreglass-covered entrance under the splashpool of the Mirage's man-made waterfall, the noise intensifies, solidifies, until the cacophony slips inside the skull and settles, muffled like an alarm clock under the pillow.

'What's with all this water?' asks Damien. 'We're supposed to be in a fucking desert, man.' Damien is right:

Jared has never seen such an overwhelming display of pointless ostentation.

'This is the American way,' posits Jared expansively, accepting a lei from a hula girl. 'They do it because they can. We see desert: they see oceanariums, water parks, reservoirs. You know they built a new Italian-themed hotel over the road.'

'Yeah. Alex said it was full when he tried to book.'

'They're going for the whole Renaissance thing there. I mean culture. Something else the Americans don't have.'

'Along with class and grace?'

Jared nods, continues: 'They built a gallery in the reception and filled it with art. They've got stuff by Botticelli, da Vinci, all those guys.'

'Cultural raiders,' Damien adds in agreement.

'With very bad taste.'

'When I lived in Chicago, I went out to this crazy theme park they had, out on the outskirts. They'd built a replica of a Scottish castle and they simulated fights, jousts, banquets, everything. It took a while to figure out why they bothered. And then it clicked. This place – this *continent* – is only, like, two hundred years old, or something. The only real history belongs to the Indians; you know the Algonquins sold Manhattan to the Dutch? And the Yanks hate that 'cos they can't do anything about it. That's why they love Europe, 'cos we've got so much of it. And it's why they build joke casinos like the Italian place over the road.'

Jared nods solemnly in agreement, sure they have divined a fundamental truth. A lounge band is entertaining an audience of well-heeled women as their husbands wager their mortgages on the tables and wheels that stretch around the three acres of covered gambling space.

A middle-aged waitress in a micro-skirt hands them complimentary Buds, and they each buy a thousand dollars' worth of chips, drawing the funds from their platinum AmEx cards. They circle the periphery of the high-roller tables where Japanese businessmen (with their college-girl American whores) compete with Mid-West oil barons (with their mistresses) and the Silicon Valley nouveaux-riches (with their PAs). And all of them are competing against the house, against the croupiers, dour-faced professionals flown in here to win and paid five hundred dollars an hour to do it. The Mafia may have been run out of the Strip but the casinos still pursue their trade with the same single-minded determination.

They decide to play blackjack and take seats at a table with a one-hundred-dollar minimum per hand.

'You think Vid's over his little, uh, problem?' asks Jared, watching without paying attention as the croupier's hands blur, leaving face-down cards in front of his players, and one for the house.

'Fuck knows,' replies Damien, inspecting his cards, 'but I doubt it. He only ever calms down when he's high.'

'Which is the state of being he's trying to arrange now, of course. Fuck, I wish I had an easier life.'

'Alex has to keep him in check. Simple as that. The guy's a prick, I'm not arguing, but he's a valuable prick. Everyone associates us with him, for better or worse. It's like Culture Club, or Wham!, or Marilyn Manson – who remembers the other guys?'

Jared's hands are clenched on the table and his knuckles are whitening. 'Andrew Ridgely.'

'You what?'

'He was in Wham! With George Michael. Played guitar. Like me.'

'Course,' Damien nods.

'Zim Zum's in Marilyn Manson. Uh, then there's that guy who formed Spear of Destiny after Boy George shagged him. Allegedly.'

'Yeah, I stand corrected but, like, my point is this: if he ends up on some mortuary slab because he's had another overdose, we've lost *everything*. He's *become* the band. I mean, right, sure, he couldn't do this without us, but right now we need him a whole lot more than he needs us. The record company could fit him up with stooge session guys, and he'd get by for a while until the public realized he can't write songs for shit. But we'd be straight back down the chute. That's the truth.'

Jared grits his teeth and concentrates on his cards. He has an eight and a three. Eleven. 'You know that time when Vid had his stomach pumped? After Wembley?' Jared knows a little about blackjack and blackjack etiquette; he taps his finger twice on the green felt table. The dealer spins him another card from the top of the deck. It is a three. Fourteen. Hit or stand?

'Yeah. Not easy to forget.'

'When he was drunk last week, Alex told me what they

pumped out of him.' He hits. An eight? Bust. The dealer scoops up his cards.

'I know already. Two bottles of bourbon, two Es, plus he was doing Panama Red *and* he'd been mainlining, right?' It's like a recipe: booze plus ecstasy plus weed plus brown makes an appointment in casualty with a tube down your throat. Damien has eleven: an eight and a three. He hits and gets a queen. Blackjack. He leans back on his stool. 'Am I right?'

'Yeah, plus half a bottle of sedatives.'

'No shit?' This is an autopilot response; he doesn't really sound surprised. For Vid, this is not beyond the realm of the expected.

'Half a bottle of Seconal, or Quaaludes, whatever. He washed them down with the whisky and then shot up to go out on a high.'

'Fuck.' Damien is annoyed. This problem was supposed to have been cured. '*Fuck!* What happened to his counselling?'

'No idea. Maybe he doesn't go. Maybe it doesn't work. Maybe it was a story to keep us quiet. "He's got an addictive personality, you know?"' This is Alex's half-hearted justification for Vid's compulsions, but even he knows where Vid's headed. (Alex just hopes he can make enough money off him before the toxins in his liver achieve their critical mass.)

'Does Astrid know?'

'Not from me she doesn't. She'll go ape. She's saving up for a penthouse in Knightsbridge. I don't want to be around when she finds out her earning potential is, um, precarious? Shooting the messenger and all that.'

'Selfish prick.'

'He's got *serious* problems,' Jared agrees, swigging from a fresh Bud that has replaced its half-finished predecessor. The beer helps him change the subject and they talk about their new album, the tracks that Jared has laid down already, the ideas he has for others. They are planning to have the album written by the end of the trip, so they can take a couple of months off and then hire the Marlin on Ocean Drive in Miami Beach and record it, like U2 did.

They bet some more. Jared wins a couple of hands but stakes what's left of his stash on the roulette wheel and loses the lot. The croupier is impassive as he marshals the three thousand dollars' worth of plastic chips back into the house's corral. Jared doesn't care – it's only money. The croupier wishes them a good-night as they disengage from the table.

They get back to the hotel at three-thirty in the morning, pissed and down four thousand pounds between them. It means nothing. The crew has been over and trashed the corridor that runs between the suites. Alex is pacing, his tiny mobile pressed almost into his ear.

'Have you seen him?' he hisses at them.

'Who? JFK?' Jared slurs. 'He's alive! He's in the lobby checking out.'

'Or Elvis? We've seen Elvis. We've seen hundreds of fucking Elvises. If he wanted to hide out, this is the place he could blend in.'

'Vid – he's gone missing.'

'Oh,' says Jared, his anger bubbling again. 'No.'

'Well, if you see him, let me know? We're on fucking MTV News tomorrow morning.'

Jared rolls a jumbo roach and lets the zephyrs waft him into a thick sleep. He is thinking of Gretta as he goes under. He vaguely remembers two groupies waiting for him as he steps out of the bathroom and takes off his shirt.

Jared's suite

Jared is naked, waking up slowly on a bed sodden with sweat and sex and the jets of air from the air-conditioning printing goose-bumps onto his hot skin. A girl, also naked, is curled into a fetal ball on his left, her head on his chest and her long hair pooled over him, over his chest, his face. Jared lets wakefulness complete its slow infusion. The backs of the girl's legs and her buttocks are bruised in blacks and browns, and slashed with scarlet welts. Jared remembers his fingers peeling condom wrappers, but is that memory last night's or any other night from this last six months? He claws himself to the edge of the bed and rolls off and onto the floor. The girl's eyes flick open and she stares dumbly at him for a moment, lost in the unfamiliar room, before recognition blooms.

'I love you,' she says.

'No, you don't,' he replies. He feels empty, hollowed out.

The scalding water in the shower sloughs off the grime

and he stands under the steaming surge, slugging from a bottle from last night, and eventually he feels less soiled. The sound of the water splashing against the glass shower door muffles the sounds from the bedroom. He listens at the door of the bathroom until he is sure that the girl is gone.

Empty suite, the interview

The MTV people are already setting up their kit in the suite when the band, minus Vid, make their appearance. The furniture has been pushed back against the wall so that a vivid red sofa shaped like a pair of lips can be fitted into the space. This is MTV's sofa, the prop which has become the trademark of their 'MTV On The Couch' feature, and their set-dressers had to carry it up the twenty-five flights of stairs, since it was too big for the lifts, even the service lift. Although MTV have a fleet of fake sofas that they ship around the continent to film these five-minute features, this is the mother lode. A plate fastened to the back identifies it as the original, the prototype: this is the sofa on which Kurt Cobain gave his final interview for Italian TV before he blew his brains out. MTV bought it for half a million dollars while his corpse was still warm. It was also the sofa that Courtney Love, with Frances Bean on her lap, used for her first interview after his death. Karma, thought Jared.

Now, the sofa is being brushed off, sitting in a pool of ultra-harsh light cast by the four 600-watt klieg lights

23

spaced, out of shot, around it like the floodlights of a football stadium. An S-VHS Panaflex Platinum camera is set on a tripod in front of the sofa and another two handheld broadcast-quality Sony Walkcams will provide the station-defining jolt pans and zooms. The veejay, Kevin Correlly, is talking to his producer as a make-up girl dusts his cheeks with anti-glare powder. The producer, in his mid-twenties and with multiple nose, ear and eyebrow piercings and a tongue-bar, spots Alex as he clears the obstruction of the black background screens.

'Alex, man, so *great* to see you,' he says, oozing bonhomie as he takes Alex's hand. 'It's been . . . how long? Too long!'

'Woodstock '99. Remember?'

'You're right, Woodstock. Man, was *that* something? You guys weren't playing, right?' He still has not released Alex's hand from his grip and is pumping it on automatic.

'We're not into festivals,' says Jared, taking an instant and profound dislike to him. 'People come to see us for *us*, or not at all.' In Vid's absence, he almost feels obliged to adopt the mantle of hostility. 'Festivals are, and let's face it, an excuse for exploitation. They've been hijacked by corporate-hospitality fuckers.' Self-satisfied, he stores the line. He can almost hear the beep being inserted into the sentence.

'And we have a problem with being on the same bill as festival prog-rock dinosaur wankers,' says Astrid.

'Like the Manics,' adds Damien.

'They do *suck*, don't they,' agrees the producer.

'Hey, what about your tour deal with Nike?' asks the

veejay, a frown of earnest concentration wrinkling his olive-brown forehead. 'Isn't Nike an abbreviation for exploitation?' He must consider this an adroit response to the impression of being railroaded onto the periphery of the conversation.

'Isn't MTV an abbreviation for chart-friendly talentless wank?' asks Jared, equally earnestly.

'Hey, nothing too heavy for this early in the morning,' Alex interrupts, faux-laughing, finally freeing his hand. 'Guys, what do you want from us?'

'It'll be completely painless, trust me. Kevin'll ask you some questions, nothing contentious, fifteen minutes tops. We edit it up in the truck, add some video clips of you guys in action, do the VO, and get it to LA for broadcast this evening, ta-da. And there you have a feature for MTV News.'

'Sounds great.'

'And if you rock tonight, we'll put clips out on tomorrow's show.'

'Double exposure. I like it.'

'So, let's see. We've got Astrid, Jared, Damien . . .' He's counting them off on his fingers. 'Where's Vid?'

'Vid's, um, been delayed. He's going to try and get along in a moment.'

'Oh man, not good, not good.' The producer turns to consult with the director, a surfer-dude with ratty white dreads that look like they have been soaked in Coke, and an antique Ocean Pacific T-shirt. They have a grim exchange before the producer turns back to them with a wry smile: 'Yeah, OK, no problemo, kiddos. We were kind of keen to get a quote from Vid, but we can catch him later and interlace something. We'll go ahead, but you might find your piece slips down the pecking order a little, depends on the edit.'

'We had you slated for the opening five minutes,' says the director, 'but we may have to bump you for Aeyilah doing the catwalk show in Paris, and Coolio's NASCAR team. We'll raincheck until we've got something in the can.'

Although Jared cares little for whether Dystopia open MTV News or not he feels a burn of annoyance that Vid is doing his rock-star routine again. He is enjoying fronting the band again in Vid's absence, like it used to be when they started, but Vid's increasingly frequent pouts confirm what they all suspect: that he sees himself as the crucial component in their success. Jared wonders if he feels obliged to live up to this petulant, irascible model despite it being a prosaic and predictable cliché, or if he actually thinks the guitar-smashing routine is original. He is not sure which would be worse. He finds the whole pretence childish and, since he has a perfect recollection of what Vid was like when he was plain Christopher Driscoll before joining as their singer and before they broke through in England, more than mildly contemptible.

The cameramen take their positions and someone pulls heavy industrial fabric over the windows, shutting out the burning sunlight. Kevin Corrally sits down in a director's chair in front of the sofa, and the band take their places on it. The director checks over his crew and counts them in.

'*Three. Two.*' The *One* is silent. He chops with his hand and the cameras roll.

'I'm Kevin Correlly and I'm here with the biggest band from England since, well, the last big band from England. They're in the States to tour their new album, *Plastic People*, which has b-b-b-burned up the English charts for sixteen weeks. They're playing the Las Vegas MGM Grand Garden Arena tonight. The first show on their US tour.' He's speaking to camera, one of the handhelds turned on its side, and now he's speaking in staccato, chopping his sentences like an MC at a fight. 'The show is sold out. They're big. They're loud. They're coming to an amphitheatre near you. They're . . . Dystopia.' The last word is murmured, a counterpoint to the crescendo of the preceding blurb, and he swivels to face them on the sofa. The cameraman peels away and settles into a position where he can zoom comfortably onto whichever band member he wants.

'You're not comparing us to the Spice Girls, are you?' asks Astrid with venom.

'Or the Beatles?' asks Jared. The lights are hot but his bloodshot eyes are protected by the Ray Bans he is wearing, their lenses cut into ovals to look like the saucerplate eyes of an alien. It co-ordinates nicely with the T-shirt from Custard House he has on, with a luminous alien face staring out of it. The banner says: We're the Aliens. 'We're the Aliens' is the final, hidden track off *Plastic People*. It closes out the album with a tsunami of syncopated, raw industrial chic.

'Or Oasis?' asks Damien.

27

'Because we're bigger than all of them – put together.' Astrid is in Tank Grrrl mode, smoking a Lucky Strike between magenta nails.

Thrown off the scripted path of the interview, Kevin Correlly laughs nervously, receives mild inspiration, goes with it and risks an ad-lib: 'You know when Liam Gallagher said Oasis were bigger than Jesus? You remember? Are you bigger than Oasis?'

'Jesus does our laser show,' answers Jared. 'He's a big fan.'

'Yeah, he runs our fan club,' adds Astrid.

'And it was Noel,' Jared adds.

'What?'

'Noel Gallagher said Oasis were bigger than Jesus.'

'Yeah, my mistake.'

'You probably thought he was cribbing from Ringo, right?'

The uncomfortable pause will be excised during the edit. Jared knows this but still enjoys the brief, despairing look Kevin Correlly gives his director.

'What do you think of our album?' asks Damien, helping him out.

'It rocks?' answers Correlly, with a tremulous upturn that indicates a question rather than a statement.

'What's your favourite track?'

He is becoming increasingly nervous. 'The opener rocks hard, real hard. It's a cool track. Like Crystal Method doing Filter doing Metallica. Early Metallica? Like, you know, maybe?'

'And what's the name?'

'Come again?'

'The first track. The name of the first track?'

'Let's get back *on* track, guys. We're getting diverted. How are you finding Las Vegas?' It is the plaintive cry of a trapped animal. Damien applies the *coup de grâce*.

'"Sound and the Fury"?'

'Excuse me?'

'"Sound and the Fury". That's the name of the first track of the album you've never listened to.'

'Right. We're straying, guys, and time's not with us. Can we move on now?'

Alex leans over Correlly's shoulder and rolls his hands around one another, indicating they should move on. But he is wearing a grin. He knows this will make great TV and great TV makes great publicity. And this is totally free publicity, courtesy of MTV and their vapid Muscle Beach air-headed veejay.

A scuffle breaks out at the back of the room as Vid tries to force open the door to the suite that is being secured by two grunts from the casino. He has caught them off guard and has managed to fit half of his skinny frame into a narrow gap between door and doorframe. The guards are trying to shut the door on him.

'Hey, call these neanderthals off me, will you!' he yells. 'This is your lead singer calling. Get these motherfuckers off me, like, *now*!'

The director indicates that they will keep rolling. One of the handhelds peels away so that it can shoot the door where the producer is letting Vid inside. He looks wasted. He is holding a three-quarters-full bottle of Jack Daniels by the neck, and golden liquid splashes up his arm as he staggers forward. He is wearing the same clothes as he wore for the flight: the KMFDM T-shirt, now ripped at the neck as well as the sleeves, baggy dun-coloured skateboard pants, the same cowboy hat with a packet of Strikes wedged inside the band around the crest. He looks as if he has gone without sleep, and his skin is slick with sweat and grime. A track of dry blood runs down from the crook of his elbow. He sits down between Jared and Astrid in the middle of the sofa and the cameras swivel to him. He swigs from the bottle. He is completely without expression.

'We've just been joined by Vid Danton,' explains Correlly off camera. Jared watches the output through the Sony monitor on the floor to his right. Under the lights Vid's skin looks almost translucent. His limbs are twitching like a zombie's.

'Hey Boy, Hey Girl,' says Vid. '"What Time is Love?"'

'Guys,' the veejay says, hastily, nervously, 'you've never played the US before. A lot of people won't have heard your stuff.' He pauses uncomfortably, the script re-exposing his ignorance. 'What makes you think that you can make it over here? I mean, it's not like there's any shortage of industrial popsters in this country, is there?'

'Define "industrial popsters",' slurs Vid.

'You know: Marilyn Manson, Rob Zombie, whatever Trent Reznor's doing at the moment.'

'You think we have anything in common with *them*? Like, those guys are even fit to suck my cock?' Vid is slurring badly. He turns to the camera and stares down it, pointing; on the monitor he looks like a grizzly caricature of Lord Kitchener doing a pastiche Presidential address. His nails are crusted with blood. 'Listen to me, America: we are the most original, the most powerful, the most *fucking* important band ever to tour this country. If you have the *privilege* to hear us play, you'll know where I'm coming from. Until then, I don't think I have anything more to say.'

'Vid from Dystopia, eloquent to the end,' says Correlly, indicating with a slice-motion across his throat that he is out of patience and he wants the cut. Before the cameras stop running, Vid has leapt across the space between them and, holding Correlly into the chair with one hand, has tipped half of the remaining Jack Daniels over his head. The canvas seat of the director's chair is pliant and he is wedged into it, unable to fight against even Vid's meagre weight.

'Cocky arsehole,' Vid says, fetching a Zippo from out of his trouser pockets. He strikes it and lets the flame dance in front of the veejay doused in alcohol.

'Vid, back off,' barks Alex, not able to translate the bad thoughts burning up his synapses into physical action. But Vid has already backed off. He is facing the sofa, with a feral grin exposing his yellowed teeth, and he tips the rest of the bottle out onto it, soaking the golden-brown whisky into the red felt. The others don't need prompting; they abandon the sofa like rats fleeing a sinking ship. Vid lights the Zippo again and drops it. A conflagration engulfs the material and spreads up and over the back as frantic staff search for a fire extinguisher.

'That's the last sofa Kurt Cobain ever interviewed on!'

shouts the producer over the crackle of the flames. 'Have you any *idea* how much it cost?'

'Is this still on tape?' someone asks the cameramen. He nods, yes. And it is. Jared watches on the monitor as the sofa burns, inky smoke heaving a cloud of soot towards the ceiling of the suite. Someone has finally found a fire extinguisher and white foam is spurting over the blackened fabric and soaking into the carpet.

'Have you got any idea what that sofa *means*?' shouts the producer.

'Yeah,' says Vid. 'It's the sofa Vid Danton from Dystopia set alight when he was pissed off with the lack of fucking respect he got from MTV. When he had a really, *really* bad hangover. That's what it *means*.'

Sotto voce, the director says to Alex: 'You can take it as read that you'll be opening the show again.'

A klaxon sounds in the corridor outside and the sprinklers drizzle a fine shower into the room.

'Lovely,' says Alex.

The limo, en route to soundcheck

They're in the limo on the way to the arena. But Vid has just purchased a 1975 Harley Davidson and insists that he will ride it across America for the tour. Right now, he is buzzing the limo, opening the throttle and gunning the tiny gaps between the car and the raised barrier of the central reservation. The chauffeur is jittery, one eye on the road and the other on his mirrors. Although he is unsure as to the identity of his passengers, he has driven these kinds of arrogant shits before. He knows that it would be a terminally bad career move to be the driver that ran over the cocky British kid on the Harley.

'Where was he last night?' Jared asks Alex.

'I'm not sure. The police found him. He had his room key on him, so that's how they ID'd him – just rang the front desk. They picked him up from a strip club a mile out into the desert.'

'And they let him *go*?' Astrid asks, with a curious combination of incredulity and ennui.

'Well, for one thing he was too paralytic to go for them when they brought him in. And, hard as this is to believe, he was clean when they frisked him. Seems that this was one of those rare alcohol-only binges.'

'What about the . . .?' Damien points to the inside of his own elbow, where Vid's blood had been. They'd all seen cuts like that and knew what they meant.

'That was this morning,' Alex says. 'He cut himself shaving.'

'He shaves his *arms*?' Astrid asks.

'Apparently so.'

'Ugh.'

'He shaves all over, I think: arms, legs, chest.'

'Double ugh.'

'Baxter had to bail him out of custody at four this morning. They've charged him with some sort of drunk-and-disorderly equivalent, but I've taken care of things.' I've paid the people I needed to pay, legitimate or otherwise. Alex types into the open PowerBook on his lap and then looks up again, intent. 'Incidentally, do you know how much the record company is paying to insure him? One hundred thousand pounds a year. Minimum. They reckon he could croak at anytime from an overdose. And they don't know about *that*' – he gestures outside to where Vid is now shooting the gap between their limo and an oncoming juggernaut – 'yet.'

Jared notices beads of sweat rolling down Alex's forehead and patches of moisture blooming underneath his armpits.

Arena, soundchecking

The arena is usually reserved for the great boxing bouts that helped Vegas cement its reputation in the global consciousness. The main hall is a shallow amphitheatre with one flat end, seats descending in stepped circles towards the front and a wide expanse of space where the ring would usually be. Tonight, the space will be jammed with Dystopia fans who have spent thirty dollars on a ticket, fifty dollars for one of the branded T-shirts, maybe five dollars for a programme, another five bucks for a hot dog and a polystyrene cup of four-fifths diluted Coke. The band has hired two accountants to keep a track on the income from their merchandising; Alex believes it will outstrip the ticket sales by two-to-one.

The stage is still being constructed as they are shown around by the manager of the facility; there are three emptied articulated trucks outside and roadies are swarming over the disgorged scaffold like worker ants over a hive. None of the band has seen the set in its constructed state before. Anton Corbijn designed it on computer and built a miniature model with tiny fibre-optic lights, but it has only ever been test-assembled once before, in a hangar in Swindon, where the band were rehearsing for a gig on the Jo Whiley show. The skeleton is nearly complete; the next stage is to hang the curved sheets of lightweight steel onto it, like the segments of an armadillo, and to suspend the three hundred different lights and strobes. The Marshall stacks are in place, a gargantuan set mirrored on either side of the stage, and the auxiliary rig halfway down the arena.

Vid is talking to one of the roadies, a grizzled veteran called Baxter. Baxter has worked on all the major UK bands' US tours during the past twenty years: the Stones, Depeche Mode, U2, Oasis, Primal Scream. He is a bull of a man: enormous shoulders, enormous arms, enormous legs. He has a ZZ Top beard with the wispy tip reaching down to the distended mound of his belly. Today he is wearing a sun-bleached T-shirt that says 'MECHANICAL' on one side and 'ANIMAL' on the other. Baxter knows everything there is to know about touring the States and has a contact in every town, able to supply whatever he needs. Vid knows this, which is why he insisted Baxter lead the crew. Jared knows this, too, and wanders over to where they are talking.

'I don't care what Alex says,' Vid is saying. 'He needs to

unwind a little. You know? Let off steam. If I don't get what I need, this tour is going to last one gig and then I'm fucking off on the Harley.'

'What's going on?' asks Jared.

'You want to add anything to Baxter's shopping list?' Vid has Astrid's copy of *Fear and Loathing in Las Vegas* in his hand.

'What's on it at the moment?'

'Well, let's see.' Baxter spreads open the book and thumbs pages. 'Hmm, here we are: page four, and I quote: "Two bags of grass, seventy-five pellets of mescaline, five sheets of high-powered blotter acid, a salt shaker half full of cocaine, and a whole galaxy of multi-coloured uppers, downers, screamers, laughers . . ."'

'That's pretty extensive.'

'Uh-huh, there's more: 'A quart of tequila, a quart of rum, a case of Budweiser, a pint of raw ether and two dozen amyls."'

'Sorry, *very* extensive.'

'And *I* want some reds,' says Vid, 'some yellows, some blues, a couple of bags of brown – the whole fucking rainbow, I guess – some Librium and Valium, plus some pick and mix in a paper bag. A handful of E, some LSD, some mushrooms, some crank.'

'What is there to add? Aspirin?'

Jared was wearily familiar with Vid's appetite but had harboured the faint hope that his spell in detox might have abated it. Obviously not. With the kind of cocktail Vid was planning – with his blood as the soda water, and his stomach as the cocktail shaker – they could have been in

London six months ago, just before he stopped his heart for two minutes with a speedball after their gig in Brixton. Jared knows all about the barbiturates – sodium secobarbital (reds); sodium pentobartital (yellows); sodium amobarbital (blues). Jared himself has taken plenty of barbiturates before – if they were good enough for Hendrix they were good enough for him, he figures, enjoying the cliché – but he has always managed to control his appetite and can regulate his intake.

Vid, with his 'addictive personality', is something else. These were the drugs of the seventies making a nostalgic comeback, in much the same way as flared trousers, floral shirts and lava lamps have all enjoyed comebacks. Vid isn't into them because of their kitsch appeal – he's into them because they are downers, because they are manufactured for suicides, because he can find peace when he fills himself with them.

'The only way I'm going to get that kind of stuff is to have someone bust open a chemist's,' says Baxter.

'Then have someone bust open a chemist's. I'll make sure they're well paid.' Vid reaches into the pocket of his shorts and takes out a thick doorstop of folded notes. 'Here, this'll be a start.' He hands the wad to Baxter.

'OK, man, so long as I can partake. I'm gonna need some R and R tonight.'

'Goes without saying, Baxter, my man. What's mine is yours, dude, you know that.'

Jared knows that he should intervene, on commercial if not moral grounds. He wonders whether he should tell Alex, but he finds that the prospect of Vid overdosing again fills him with black apathy rather than the urge to offer assistance or seek prevention.

Soundcheck never changes. The band line up on stage, chainsmoking from a carton of Camels that one of the roadies picked up at Heathrow. The stage is covered with dog-ends by the time the sound engineers are ready to get going. Astrid's keyboards have developed a glitch, and the sequencers have to be unplugged and logged into a laptop so that the diagnostic software can be run. They sit on the stage and smoke. Someone brings out a crate of Fosters from the rider of booze supplied by the organizers, and Damien shears off the polythene covering with a six-inch serrated hunting knife Jared has never seen before.

'Spread the wealth, baby,' Jared shouts out. Damien tosses him a warm can. He spikes it and lets the tepid beer slake the desert dust from his throat.

Jared takes up his guitar and strums out a few chords; they reverberate back at him from the monitor, and then, as the stacks are juiced, echo around the empty cavern. Damien punches out a beat on the drums, circling through them to ensure every one is miked properly. They have hired a session musician to lay down the live bass, a gaunt Bowie-a-like who insists on being called Torquemada and who has worked with Beck and Jurassic 5 and a dozen American bands Jared has never heard of. He plucks out a scale of fat buzzing notes that fray at the edges until the engineers refine the sound.

'Why can't we hire someone to do this boring shit for

us?' complains Vid, toking from an enormous roach someone has put between his fingers. 'It's not like we're adding
value, is it?'

'We *could* hire someone to do it but they wouldn't be
using the instruments in the gig, would they,' Alex ration-
alizes patiently, 'and no one wants to deal with *your* tantrum
when your guitar isn't just as you like it.'

'Fuck off,' Vid says, bored.

Now that her keyboards are fixed, Astrid lays down a
tune she wrote on the plane coming over; Jared likes it and
resolves to incorporate it into a new track he is working
on: 'Black Heart'. Vid is the last to soundcheck, slipping
his guitar on and picking at the strings. A roadie brings
him a mike and he sings out, in his strong, hoarse voice, a
compound of Eddie Vedder's throaty power and Brett
Anderson's effeminate versatility, a verse from 'Truckin'',
off *American Beauty* by the Grateful Dead.

The roadies clap his performance when he is finished
and Jared knows why, is almost impressed enough to join
them; every time he hears Vid sing he forgets a little of
what it is about him that pisses him off: the tantrums, the
ego, the supercilious arrogance, the way the media flock to
him like moths around a light or flies around shit. Even
this choice of verse, with its overbearing faux-ironic self-
references, does not bug him as much as it should.

Vid does some scales, then booms out a reproach to the
engineer on the levels to amp up his guitar in the mix.

New York New York, waiting

Soundcheck finishes at three. The gig doesn't start until seven-thirty and they are not due to take the stage until nine-thirty, after a couple of minor league up-and-comers have teased the crowd's patience. Their support bands – a New York three-piece called Apogee, and an avant-garde duo, Razor's Kiss – are halfway decent and Jared plans to catch them at sometime during the tour, but not tonight. He remembers what it is to play support, filling that null zone between the crowd and what they want to hear. He remembers it well enough to empathize with them.

They are all in Damien's room, the windows are open and the night blows in through the fine transparent drapes. Alex is pacing. 'Block Rockin' Beats' from *Dig Your Own Hole* is playing at high volume from the minidisc player that Damien bought when they played in Frankfurt last year.

'You might have brought some decent stuff,' Astrid complains, shuffling through Damien's minidiscs. 'I mean, Jesus Christ, Damien: Jeff Beck; Leonard Cohen; Bob *fucking* Dylan. I thought you'd got over all that manic-depressive bullshit.'

'I might have some kd lang,' offers Jared, purely for the entertainment value of rattling Astrid's cage, 'or some L7.'

She throws a minidisc across the room at him like a high-tech Bond girl. Jared is too strung out to care.

'Has wardrobe sorted out your costumes?' asks Alex.

'We're about ready to rock – steady,' says Vid, mimicking the Chemical Brothers' sampling.

'That's so fucking depressing: *costumes*,' says Astrid. 'Like the music's just an adjunct of what we do.'

'Caution: imminent danger of disappearing up your arse,' says Damien. '*Adjunct?*'

'Can I come too?' Vid asks.

Astrid just sneers.

'You know that's not true,' Alex says, 'it's just that the whole of our merchandising ties in with what you wear. It's product unity, we need *convergence*. Don't forget Dystopia's got the potential to be a big brand out here. Look at the Manson T-shirts: they fly out of the shops. It'll make you a lot of money.'

'It'll make *you* a lot of money, you mean,' says Jared.

'You're proving my point,' Astrid says. 'It's all about branding and merchandising and all that shit. It's getting too U2 for my taste, that's all.'

'The moment Vid calls the Pope up on stage, that's the moment I leave.'

'Astrid, Damien – noted and taken onboard,' Alex says, discarding their conversation as he does so.

Vid is sitting cross-legged on the bed, tapping into Damien's PowerBook. They have all checked their hotmail accounts. Jared had a message from Gretta, which he didn't feel able to read right now, and some others from zealous fans who have already discovered his new address. He will have to change it again. Vid is laughing to himself.

'Come see,' Vid says, turning the laptop around so that

the others can see the screen. He is logged onto the website of the *Evening Standard* in London. He is reading from a story from the paper's late edition. He reads it out – it tells of a couple in Hyde Park who got killed by lightning while sheltering beneath a tree.

'Wow,' says Astrid. 'What a way to go.'

'What a *stupid* way to go,' says Jared. 'I mean, sheltering under a tree during a thunderstorm? How brainless is that?' He taps his knuckle against his forehead.

'And check this,' Vid says, clicking over to the weather forecast. '"Five inches of snow have fallen in London this afternoon and a heavier front is moving south now." Can you believe that? I could've got some 'boarding in.'

'And here we've got one hundred degrees of dry desert heat,' says Damien.

'Is that better or worse?'

'It's hot.'

'If you want to go 'boarding we could stop off in Aspen after the Denver gig?' offers Alex. 'The scene out there is pretty wild. Lots of rich college girls.'

'Yeah, whatever. Cool.'

Baxter clatters through the door. He is drunk. Alex moves to show him out, but Vid springs from the bed and ushers him to a chair.

'Whoa, tiger, what have you got for me?' he asks.

'You might want to close your eyes at this point,' Astrid suggests to Alex.

'Got some choice gear, people – *choice*. I got some Es, all kinds of downers, some speed, some coke, some dope on a rope. Rope-a-dope?' He pauses, confused, before something triggers inside his head and he continues: 'I couldn't get any scag, but I did get some crack. That do you?'

'Crack? Oh fuck,' says Alex.

'That will more than fulfil my requirements. You are a gem, Baxter, a gem. How much do I owe you?' Vid takes another roll of high-denomination notes out of his pocket and fans them at Baxter, who takes five or six, and then the rest.

'That should cover my expenses,' he says, rolling out again.

'*Please*,' pleads Alex.

'Just a little,' says Vid. 'I just need a little. I need to find my edge. It'll be a flat show if I'm not on the edge.' He fishes around inside the bag and withdraws a small, transparent bag with two or three grams of coke inside it. Vid pulls out the coke spoon he always wears on a chain around his neck and opens the bag.

'Ah, my dear Charlie, where have you been all my life? All right, party people, we have a stereotype to fulfil. Let's get high.'

Backstage

From backstage, Jared can see that the arena is heaving. He knows that the capacity is around twenty thousand and the place looks choked. He is getting the buzz from the roar of the crowd as Spin, their deejay, segues the playlist that he and Jared compiled for the UK leg of the tour. Nothing too predictable, laying in all sorts of unusual licks from big beat to motown to Elvis. They could have recorded the mix on a DAT tape but Jared insisted that Spin came along with them to deejay live – to cover the possibility that Jared might want to adjust the playlist to meet some unforeseen set of circumstances. (Spin has changed tonight's playlist to include 'Viva Las Vegas'. Only the most sure-footed would dare such corniness and Spin is the best.)

Apogee left the stage fifteen minutes ago and the deejay set is scheduled for another fifteen. Spin will gradually harden the sound, throwing in early Ministry, some Skinny Puppy, some Finitribe, whatever else he fancies. Their cue is a cut from a cheesy electro-tack version of the *Star Wars* theme, which also signals the start of the video playback on the giant twenty-foot screens suspended from way above them. Two space-walking astronauts – floating upside-down against the void – open the film. Then Astrid goes out onstage and plays the thudding electro-overture that Pedro Almodovàr commissioned for his new movie, *Excision*. The tune made the charts on its own merit when they decided to release it under a pseudonym: 'Terminus'. For many of tonight's crowd this will be the first time the connection between the biggest underground hit of the year and Dystopia is made.

Jared finishes the bottle of Evian he is drinking from and goes back into the dressing room.

'It's a big crowd,' he reports. 'Looks full.'

Damien nods solemnly, getting his usual pre-gig nerves. His sticks are wedged into his belt. Vid has his forehead against the cold brick wall of the dressing room. The remains of the rider lie on the floor, decimated.

'Ten minutes,' says Alex, sticking his head through the open door. 'Get yourselves juiced. They're going crazy out there.'

Vid turns away from the wall and slams the heel of his hand against his temple. His make-up has been applied, white face paint with black eye-liner and black lipstick. His pupils are tiny, completely pinned by the coke, and the veins on his neck are bulging. He slips his oval-lensed shades on and pulls his leather trenchcoat around his shoulders. Following his lead, the others check themselves over in the full-length mirror. Jared is wearing a waist-length fur coat dotted with half-inch plastic spikes, a pair of leather shorts and knee-high leather boots. Research has demonstrated that the best market penetration is achieved by this particular look: shades of glam; shades of S&M; shades of goth (which encompasses both, anyway). Gretta says they look like the Village People for the millennium.

Onstage

The final bars of Astrid's orchestral crescendo waft across the rabid audience, suddenly plunged into darkness, and the band pick their way across the stage and take up their instruments. The fans in the front spot them, dark wraiths against the flickering lights of the set, and raise the word. The cheer is a wave fanned by strengthening winds; it starts at the front and layers are added as those further and further towards the back realize what is happening. By the time Jared has slipped the strap of his guitar over his shoulder, he can only barely hear Damien as he taps out the countdown to the opening song on the rim of the snare.

The lights are still down as Vid sings out the a cappella couplet of 'My Dead Life' from their eponymous first EP and the song they have opened with these last six months. Even though this song is not on the album and is not one that most of these fans are likely to recognize, the roar intensifies to a corporeal force, battering down against them. Vid has his arms spread wide in the crucifixion pose as the lights burn up, Jared's eyes adjusting slowly behind his shades. At the same moment, Jared fires out the song's repetitive central riff, Astrid replays the sampled introduction, De Niro to Pacino in *Heat*, and Damien fires out a syncopated blast like gunfire. A sound like a dozen jumbos rips open the fabric of the arena.

Images burn out of the giant video screens looming behind them: a series of fuzzy jump-cuts between close-up shots framed by luminous red, green, yellow and blue backgrounds, showing Damien's foot pumping the pedal of the bass drum, on red; Astrid's fingers on the keyboard, on blue; Jared's hand around the neck of the guitar, on green; Vid grasping the mikestand, on yellow. Then, interspersed, nanosecond-long symbols and icons: an ankh; an ampersand; a swastika (Hindu); a swastika (fascist); the Greek letters alpha and omega; a pentagram; a cross; a raincloud;

obscure national flags; a stop sign. Manga. Animé versions of themselves flying against a jet background.

Jared hides behind his shades and marshals the stage. He is into this from the start, this is where he is meant to be, this feels correct. He thumps his distortion pedal mid-riff, and opens up a whole new soundscape to play with. A ripple goes up in the crowd as they figure out which song is coming next. Vid is leaping in time with Damien's beat and, as they segue straight into 'Desolate Me', he leaps onto his monitor and reaches out over the crowd, like the figurehead on the prow of a ship. Hands sprout up for him but he is too high, out of reach; the spotlights catch fire behind them and track around until he is caught at their intersection, a glowing, angelic icon.

He never really addresses the crowd, but then he doesn't need to, not tonight; he already has them in the palm of his hand and he can manipulate them with a gesture: a shrug, a clenched fist, a thrust of his hips. The only girls that Jared can make out, grey spectres mashed against the barriers, wail for Vid as if he is the only man in the world who could make them feel complete. And when Vid leaps into the pit, Jared thinks the barriers will buckle from the surge, yellow-shirted security rushing in to plug the burst-ing barriers.

Fucking sing, thinks Jared, sweat pouring off him under the lights even though they rarely settle on him. *Sing my songs like I wrote them.* Vid is slurring and he starts to leave lines unfinished, more interested in breaking away from the mikestand and prowling the front of the stage. Astrid has to put more into her backing vocals as Vid loses interest in the songs. A ripple and Jared's vision blurs; he fights back and focuses on Damien's pounding beat. Vid flings his guitar into the middle of the crowd as 'Suffocation' ends, and a roadie scuttles out, hunched low to the ground, to replace it with another. The roadies bring in dozens for him; his guitars are only props, Vid is a terrible guitarist and Dystopia's power is provided by the three straining musicians sweating sewers behind him.

As the chemical stench of the dry ice clots in Jared's throat, he steps towards the crowd, riffing hard, his slick hand slipping on the fretboard. He reaches the front of the stage, the narrow pit patrolled by security seeming a thin slice of calm compared to the sea of faces morphing into a blurred mess beyond the definition provided by the stage lights.

Fourteen- and fifteen-year-old kids are body surfing, held aloft and then dumped the five feet down into the pit where they are thrown back by the guards. Roadies spray the front rows with water hoses. A strobe explodes, Vid has taken his shirt off, the place erupts. Jared stands in a shaft of light, lit up for a moment as a spot is aimed his way, and puts together a perfect solo, the gilded decoration atop the magnificence of their aural edifice. No one is looking at him. Someone throws a plastic bottle full of water that glows amber as it passes through the shaft of a spotlight; it wobbles towards him, misses, skids across the stage, and bursts open along the way. The water spews out, sprays onto his legs. Another bottle, and then another, are flung towards him. He retreats back into the fog as they land, his stomach knotting. A darker song is forming, the origins of a black elegy.

Jared is never able to keep an accurate track of time when they are gigging. They mix the songs on the album with some old stuff, test out the new stuff they have already written and rehearsed, and toss in two covers for good measure: 'I am the Walrus' and 'Professional Widow' tonight. They finish with 'Dispossessed'. Torquemada is right up against the front of the stage as they crescendo, and Vid fly-kicks him into the pit. He half-lands on the metal restraining fence and his back jackknifes unnaturally before he is greedily devoured by the mosh pit. Jared edges forward again, drawn towards the hundreds of raised lighters like a moth. Vid whirls around; he has lost the shades and his pupils look as big as saucers. The veins on his neck are standing out like cords. Before Jared can react, Vid locks his wrist in both of his sweaty fists and pivots, his entire weight impelling Jared towards the pit and the lurching crowd.

As he reaches the lip of the stage Jared leaps, arching over the barriers like a high-jumper clearing the bar. Dozens of hands sprout below him as he thuds into the heads and shoulders of the mosh pit. The acrid funk of sweat and dry ice is everywhere. The crowd bellow out the final couplet, 'Doesn't matter what you want / We don't care any more', and Vid and Astrid and Damien leave the stage. There is no encore but they keep singing it anyway, even after the house lights are brought up. As hands pull Jared down to the ground, so that the pack of ripping, tearing hyenas ready to scour the flesh from his bones can get at him, he sees a yellow-shirted phalanx of security surging towards him. But Vid has come back onstage and he flings his second guitar out over their heads, and Jared watches with something approaching clinical distance as the crowd recoil from him as if he were leprous, and scurry, as one, for the instrument. He is left on the floor in a sticky slick of sweat, piss and beer.

Backstage

'What the fuck were you playing at?' Jared shouts, shoving Vid up against the wall.

'What you talking about, man?' The words are garbled; Vid is speeding. A dusting of powder is still around his nostrils.

'What am I *talking* about?'

'Yeah, man? What?'

'You threw me into the crowd, you twat,' Jared says, clawing his hand around his throat, the other cocked and ready. Damien pulls him off him, puts himself between them. Jared presses against the muscles fanned out across his back.

'It's traditional,' Vid says, arms apart. 'It's *expected*.'

Jared surges up against Damien, but Damien is too strong to get past. 'Since when have we been Status *fucking* Quo, you arrogant cunt? I thought you were going to hold the mike out for a crowd singalong.'

'Fuck *you*, man. They loved it. Listen to them' – the

crowd is still yelling for the encore they won't get – 'they fucking loved us.'

Astrid is paying only vague attention; she is halfway through the second litre of Evian from the rider, looking for some coke.

'Us? Do you know what "us" means?' Jared is livid.

'What is this? Paranoia, man?'

'"Us" does not mean Vid Danton.'

'Your point?'

'My point is I am seriously losing it with you, man. This is a *band*. We do this *collectively*. This isn't a vehicle for your ego.'

Vid juts his head forwards, leering. 'Jealous?'

Jared barges Damien out of the way and lands his fist square in Vid's face. His nose explodes in a splash of blood. Damien heaves Jared off and tosses him away.

'Maybe you ought to look for a new singer?' suggests Vid, trying to stem the blood. ''Cos you are one jealous motherfucker.' He is laughing hysterically and the blood is dripping down his face.

'Calm down, guys,' says Alex, coming in, intervening with palms up, placating them. 'Jesus, *why* are you *fighting*? That was *awesome*. Vid, man, you are so *zeitgeist*, it's not true. And Jared ... whoa, Jared, baby – you *rocked*. Ab-sol-ute-ly. That stage-dive at the end ... man, I had goose-bumps. What a touch.'

'It wasn't a fucking stage-dive.'

'Whatever, it was so cool. They, like, *loved* it.'

'Fuck this calming-the-waters bullshit, Alex. This has to

be said: I can't keep doing' – he gestures around the room – '*this*. Not like this.'

'Listen, you're tired, it's been a hard couple of days. We're *all* tired. This is going to seem trivial tomorrow, you know it.'

'Will you just shut the fuck up, Alex? You're supposed to be managing this fucking menagerie. And all you can do, as Vid unilaterally changes the spirit of this project, is stand there and tell me that I'm pissed off because I'm *tired*? Ah, fuck it.'

'This project?' sneers Vid. '*Project?*'

Jared gives up. His hand is aching and he knows from bitter experience that it is pointless to rail against Vid when he is in this kind of indestructible mood. He can be intractable. And Alex's sycophancy, his *hypocrisy*, is too much for him to handle. He glares at him before going to the wings to watch the crowd filter away.

Party, in the desert

The after-show party is held in the desert on the outskirts of the city. The crew have built a bonfire and set up a sound system that is playing the bootleg remix version of *Plastic People*. Spin's mix of 'Power and the Glory' is playing, the tense undercurrent of the original track augmented by the addition of choppy drum and bass percussion. Drugs are being dispensed from the back seat of a Thunderbird that has been acquired, a mobile pharmacy. There are forty or fifty fans and some journalists, all here on a strictly invitation-only basis. Security guards are patrolling the perimeter, the demarcation point where the light from the fire stops and the darkness of the desert begins. MTV are here again, looking for Vid. *Rolling Stone* are here, looking for Vid. Vid is out in the desert somewhere on his Harley, Jared doesn't know where.

Jared punches his mobile phone to life and hits the fifteen numbers necessary to connect him to the flat in Islington. He waits as static hisses back at him. The call takes ten seconds to connect and then another five as the answerphone is triggered. The answerphone is recorded to play an acoustic version of 'Dispossessed' that Jared recorded with Vid just after he joined the band, back when Vid was still Chris and when they were called the Indigo Violets. Gretta always thought it was an ostentatious and self-aggrandizing gesture, but Jared liked the corniness of it.

'Hi, Gretta,' Jared says. 'It's me. Pick up.' The answerphone message continues. Vid's voice rolls back at him: *Doesn't matter what you want / We don't care any more.* 'It's, what, nine your time? Where are you? Pick up.' She is not there. He does not leave a message; he cuts the connection with a stab of his finger.

Jared spikes a beer and takes a pensive sip. He looks over towards the bonfire. Astrid is being chatted up by a girl with severely cropped, bleached hair. Damien is sitting with the crew, cooking skewered beefburgers in the flames. Jared does not feel like joining them. He wonders how many people are buried out in the desert in shallow graves where no one will ever find them. He lies back in the sand and gazes into the sky. There are so many stars. There must be hundreds, like a sprinkling of sugar over velvet.

'Hey,' says a girl he does not recognize. 'You're Jared Melchior, aren't you?' She is eighteen, nineteen maybe. She leans over him, close enough so that he can't help looking along her smooth legs and up into her skirt. She sits down next to him, close enough for her outer thigh to brush against his.

'Yeah.'

Her hair is held back in bunches fastened by silver metal rings that glint against her dark tresses. She is wearing dark eye-liner around her eyes but the neat circles have been smudged and the edges are indistinct. Jared thinks it makes her look vulnerable, even a little cute. He banishes this thought.

'I *knew* it was you. I'm Jolene,' she says, smiling with vacuous emptiness or innocence.

'Hello, Jolene,' says Jared.

'Just *loved* the show. And the album's my all-time favourite. Well, maybe just a tad behind *Portrait of an American Family*, but then that's a classic, right?'

'I guess. But thanks,' says Jared, faux-enthused. It's vacuous emptiness, he decides.

'Your security guys picked me out of the crowd. They asked if we liked to party.'

'Must be your lucky night, I guess.'

'I told them we *lived* to party.'

'Good for you.'

'You landed near me when you stage-dived,' she says.

'Yeah?'

'Yeah. Then Vid threw his guitar. He's such a natural, don't you think?'

'Oh yeah. Definitely.'

'Man, this is unreal, to meet you like this. It's amazing.'

'Like I said, must be your lucky night.'

'Is there anything I can do for you?' she asks, shuffling closer to him so that the whole of her torso is pressed against his. He can feel her firm arse against his hip. 'I mean *anything*?' She lies down next to him, propped up on one elbow so that she can look at him, and drums her fingers against his breastbone.

'No, I'm fine – really. But a moment to myself would be nice, if you wouldn't mind.' He sits so that her fingers fall away. A lone car is cutting through the desert miles away, its headlights lancing ahead.

She continues as if she doesn't hear him. 'My manager says I give the best head in Vegas,' she says with a faraway look. 'But I'd do a lot more for you. I'm a dancer, by the way. At Caesar's. You want me to dance for you? I love dancing. Maybe you'd prefer something else? You can do whatever you want to me. It'd be cool. You could do me up the ass, or wherever. I'd be cool with that.' She has shuffled closer still, so that the inside of her thigh is half leveraged off the sand and onto his leg. 'Or I could just blow you here? We could go into the desert and you could let me blow you? That'd be cool, too.'

'No, really. Thanks, but no. Bye.' He stands to leave, brushing the sand off his jacket and trousers.

'Are you sure?' she asks. Looking down on her, Jared

can see her flat stomach through the tunnel between her breasts. 'I wouldn't normally be so forward, it's just that your manager Andy . . .'

'Alex?'

'. . . sorry, yeah, Alex, he said that you could do with some company. He said you looked miserable. My friend Layla's over there, she could come too, if you liked.'

'Alex asked you to come over here?'

'Yeah. Like I said, he thought you might like some company.'

A film of darkness washes over Jared's eyes. His nails are digging into his palm. 'Maybe that's not such a bad idea,' Jared says. 'Maybe that *is* what I need. I am a little down, I guess. You said you had a friend?'

'Sure. Layla. You want me to get her?'

'Why not. Go and get her and we'll head back into the city.'

Jared's suite, early morning

With his nose to the mirror Jared's face looms back at him in a foggy morass of pinks and blues.

The coke swims through his bloodstream, dissolving throughout it and stimulating a surge of norepinephrine that would usually have been reabsorbed immediately, the chemical kick imperceptible under everyday circumstances. But the cocaine is amplifying the stimulation, preventing reabsorption of the chemical, capping the nerve endings so that it gathers in larger and larger quantities, like water that will eventually engulf a blocked sink. His nostrils burn briefly, and the fleshy join between teeth and gums tingles like children's sherbet tingles; this is where he rubbed what was left of the coke after he had snorted the two jumbo lines. The fatigue that ached in his bones sloughs away. His muscles feel fresh, energized. His blood pressure increases. His heartbeat accelerates. His pupils dilate. Then the 'freeze', the cocaine shrinking the mucous membranes and clearing the sinuses. This coke is a pure cut, expensive and of a ridiculously high quality; the laxatives or sucrose that usually dull the edge are absent, and this is only a gram – one gram doing what it would take three grams of cut Soho coke to do.

Jared opens his eyes. He feels powerful, immense, in all places at all times. He staggers to the windows and flings the drapes aside, welcoming in the kaleidoscopic craziness of the Strip. The lurid neon counterbalances the sombre contrast of the flat desert, petering away into the foothills of the mountains. He opens the window, sixteen storeys up, and lets the warm air suck greedily at him, cloying and close compared to the frigidity of the AC inside the room.

He is not tempted to jump.

Alex

7 January
New York New York

Alex pads down the corridor barefoot, only half-dressed and munching on a salted-beef bagel he had room service deliver with a jug of OJ and the international edition of the *Guardian*. He is semi-awake; he didn't return from the party in the desert until three. They were driving up the semi-deserted Strip with the street lights etiolating the black into a grey fuzzy haze. The limo was crammed with drunks and dopers and the AC pumped back the overheated fumes and alcohol mist until a thick miasma, almost tangible enough to touch, settled against the ceiling and then sank back down.

He snatched an hour of sleep, par for the course on tour.

Alex steps over vampiric bodies slumped in the corridor, some dressed, some not, all sheltering from the cold eye of the dawning sun. He passes a broken guitar, the strings bending back against themselves, quivering. Empty beer cans. Empty wraps of coke, speed. Cigarette butts: dozens of them. He knocks on Damien's door, calling for him to awake, and feeling like a teacher supervising a dormitory full of undisciplined children. This is not a new sensation for Alex. His time with the band has taught him not to try and close the distance between himself and his charges. He feels marginalized by them. They are younger than him, richer than him, more attractive, more talented and more successful than him. And, although his contract with Revolution does not reflect this, he knows that in reality they are his employers. With their star so much in the ascendant, Alex is under no illusion that if they wanted a change of manager, all they would have to do is ask.

Keeping the band happy and still securing his position: it makes his job more difficult than he would sometimes like. Balancing the need to cut Vid enough slack with the rest of the band's need to have Vid kept under control is no mean feat but, by and large, Alex considers himself fortunate. He is able to tour the world, he is paid a fortune to do it, and occasionally he is able to seduce ridiculously good-looking girls who are labouring under the misapprehension that he wields the influence necessary to propel them on the path to fame and fortune, or reward them with a date with one of his charges. Like the girl he has left sleeping off the effects of the Rohypnol he doped her Stoli with last night. She will awake with no memory of what he was able to do to her. Anyway, the contract is up in a month and he has his own ideas of what should replace it. He has a plan, and his plan has backing.

Damien grunts an acknowledgement, but Alex keeps knocking until he hears him swing out of bed and plod to the bathroom. The muffled hiss of the shower is his green light to move on. They are leaving Las Vegas later in the morning for the long drive south to Phoenix. They are playing a gig there in two days' time. From there, the bus will take them north to Los Angeles, and a spot on Jay Leno, then north again to Seattle. They'll cut north into Canada for a gig in Vancouver, then fly to New York for a gig and join the second bus which will take them to Washington, Philadelphia, Miami then home. They could fly instead, but Alex insisted on the bus. It just seemed right, natural, at the time. Better to be a traditional touring band on the road, as it was meant to be. Before then, they have a photoshoot in the desert for a clutch of newspapers and magazines from all over the world. He knows enough to wake them with plenty of time to spare. It's five now, and they'll need hours to rouse themselves and get ready, get made-up.

He passes Jared's room. There is no need to knock. Jared stuck his head through Alex's door earlier, telling him that he couldn't get back to sleep and that he was going to go down to the hotel café for a jolt of caffeine and a Danish. It's not unusual for Jared to arise earlier than the others. He parties as hard as the rest but suffers the least from burning the candle at both ends; he seems to need only a narrow margin of sleep. Alex envies him as his own hangover throbs.

He reaches Vid's room.

There is no reply to Alex's knock. He tries again; still nothing.

Preparing himself for the worst, inured as he is to the excesses of Vid's post-gig behaviour, he turns the unlocked door handle and opens the door.

Alex drops the remains of the bagel onto the floor. The crumbs splash into Vid's suite.

Vid is half-sitting, half-lying against the side of the kingsize waterbed he insists he has to sleep on whenever they are on tour. His eyes are open and he is staring at the door, straight through Alex, unblinking. His face is freeze-framed in a moment of intense ecstasy or pain; the rictus of his curled lips and bared teeth is impossible to interpret. He is naked from the waist up, and his pale skin is taut over the sharp ridges of his ribs. Alex's eyes are drawn first to his tattoos: a Celtic band around his left bicep and an elaborate phoenix in flames on his left breast. From there, they follow the line of Vid's shoulder down his arm to where a Gucci belt is fastened tightly at the elbow. Below this tourniquet his arm is discoloured, beginning to show a mottled blue-green, the tincture of mould. A line of crusted blood has snaked down from just below the belt, over the raised bluffs of his radial and ulnar arteries, then through his clawed fingers and into the fluffy shag-pile of the carpet. His face and body is covered in a shell of dry mud, dust, sand – mottled grey and breaking away in scabrous flakes.

Fuck, thinks Alex. *Fuck!* He has seen these before, Vid's overdoses. The last time was after the breakthrough gig, Brixton last summer. Astrid found him unconscious in the bath of his hotel room, the after-effects of a speedball. The paramedics said his heart stopped on the way to the hospital; he was dead for two minutes. They had to pump adrenalin straight into his heart with a foot-long needle, like that scene out of *Pulp Fiction*, but a million times worse because Alex was in the back of the ambulance with him and it was really *really* happening. After that, Alex has always carried a hypodermic primed with artificial adrenalin. He fumbles in his trouser pocket for it now as he stumbles over the detritus strewn left and right – clothes, beer cans, a syringe, a bottle of Jack Daniels, instruments, an elaborate bong – to get to the bed.

As he kneels, scuffling in his pockets for his mobile, his eye is drawn to the mirror on the open door of the wardrobe on the other side of the bed. Framed in the glass is another person, a girl with freshly dark bruises and welts on her naked body, and a dried crust of blood running from her nostrils and mouth down to a puddle of snot and blood in her lap. Her head has been bent backwards and it juts out from the column of her neck at a crooked, aberrant angle. Hair the colour of claret is fanned out in loose fronds; it does not hide the mushy pulp of her temple. What the fuck has he done now? What if she is dead? Alex briefly contemplates taking her out into the desert and burying her. He rejects the notion; it does not present him with a moral difficulty, but then he is not paid enough to take risks like that. His hand closes on the tiny phone and he flips it open, dials 999, corrects it – 911 – and calls for the paramedics. There is enough adrenalin in the syringe for one shot. Alex loosens the belt and sinks the needle into Vid's cold dead arm.

Jared

Jared is in Broadway Joe's, the themed all-day café set into the cavernous ground-floor complex of cafés, bars and restaurants inside the hotel. The place is half-empty with late-night gamblers returning to recover and early birds readying themselves for another stint: the changing of the guard. Jared has the *Las Vegas Tribune* spread out on the formica-covered table in front of him. The early editions of *USA Today* and the *Nevada Sun-Herald* are also on the table. A plate of pancakes doused in maple syrup weighs down one corner of the paper against the desert breeze that rustles through the café every time the door to the street is opened. He is rereading a review of the concert last night.

Imagine **Nine Inch Nails** cleansed of the corrupting influence of tune or lyrical structure, reduced to fiercely mechanistic riffs and, well, pure rage, and you're close to how this breathtaking, terrifying gig sounded. Vid Danton, the demi-rockgod fronting the UK's next *next* big thing, **Dystopia**, hates being pigeonholed ('Sorry we're late,' he apologized onstage, 'I've just had **Marilyn Manson's** cock in my mouth') so we won't try. But if you absolutely *have* to

63

genre-tag them, you will borrow from the schools of glam, rock, industrial, trance, big beat; the whole shebang. Danton's sound is a mathematical exercise in repetition and brutality that often seems designed to shake off the whiffs of banality that floated across the crowd when the insipid (by comparison) support was doing its thing. From the mountainous weight of the album-opener 'Sound and the Fury' to the contemplative thuggery of 'Dispossessed', Danton's songs run the emotional gamut and leave mental scars and psychological bruising. Danton has that rare combination, critical acclaim and unthinking public adulation, to back up his boasts. The Bible Belt will hate him because he has the depth and artistic credibility Manson would kill for. The band lay the bricks for Danton's elaborate constructions, they provide the grunt, but there is no doubt who's carrying this outfit all the way to infamy.

Jared sweeps the crumbs of a bagel from the picture of Vid, his arms held aloft like Christ on the cross, opening the show. He takes another spoonful of pancake, wipes it around the syrup and chews it down, swallowing as he reads the review once again.

The review in the *Herald* is much the same as the one in the *Tribune*: a reverential, passionate ode to Vid, and fuck the rest of the band. Jared takes his knife and carefully draws the tip down the page, circumventing the border of the story and then cutting left to slice underneath the picture of Vid, this one showing him dry-humping the speaker stack. When he is done, Jared carefully removes the excised portion and slips it into his wallet, next to the review from *USA Today*. He signals the waitress's attention and asks for the tab.

The Strip

Outside Circus Circus, the digital clock set into the crotch of the forty-foot-high billboard of Tom Jones thrusting his hips flashes 8.33 a.m. It is already 92 degrees. The Strip is as quiet as Jared has yet seen it; perhaps a moment of reflection is needed to freshen up before the dizzy cycle is booted up and restarted. The outdoor escalators keep up their twenty-four-hour momentum even when there are no passengers to ride them. Muzak, spliced with adverts for the casino shows, continues on its never-ending, eternally zestful loop. And some time soon the twenty-foot volcano outside the Luxor will start up with its fifteen-minute eruptions and the full-scale sixteenth-century Spanish galleon in the Mirage's pool, complete with full crew in historically accurate costume, will engage the full-scale English warship in battle, sink, and then resurface, on the half-hour. Jared knows that Vegas is a hollow pastiche of life, but he finds himself drawn into it, sucking up the sights and smells and tastes, immersing himself in the best and worst of Americana.

Frazzled croupiers on the graveyard shift are blinking into the hot light as their stints end; teams of Mexican and Puerto Rican immigrants scrub down the sidewalk with mops and buckets, polishing away the desert's grit. He passes one crew with their boombox tuned to KROQ and the deejay is playing the radio-friendly remix of 'Sound and the Fury', the first cut off the album to get a single release. One of the cleaners says something in Spanish and the radio is clicked off. Jared feels like interrupting them and introducing himself but he strolls on, enjoying himself too much to be worried about such minutiae.

Jared thinks he could get used to living in a place like this, as he plugs in the minidisc player the Sony rep gave him when he was in New York last month. He thumbs PLAY on the in-line controls, and Radiohead's *The Bends* starts up. The sidewalk is comparatively empty as he strolls northwards, wondering if there will be time to take a trip up the Stratosphere, look out over the desert from five hundred feet up. He figures that they won't be leaving Vegas on time, that the police will want to interview them all. He corrects himself: the tour *must* end here. It cannot continue. This prospect doesn't concern him and he stops at an open-air espresso bar to order a *café au lait*. The blue-and-white handpainted sign says 'DENNY'S ESPRESSO – DON'T GAMBLE ON QUALITY'. The vendor, a white-bearded old-timer with a blue-and-white striped apron that matches his sign, says, 'You're *welcome*,' dumbfounded, when Jared thanks him for the coffee. One of the little things Jared likes about Americans is that moment of wonder when they encounter common courtesies. So quaint.

There's no rush. He has time yet before they need to set out for the photoshoot. Plenty of time. He takes a seat and lets his mind wander back to the previous night. Jared is coked to the eyeballs but with clarity of purpose, focus, clearer than ever before. He fucks both Jolene and Layla, slowly and dutifully, preparing the ground for an alibi, covering all his bases. He waits until both have fallen into hazy narcotic sleep and then untangles himself from the nest of arms and legs. He dresses. He does another line, finishing the coke. He feels invincible.

Then to Vid's suite. Vid, helpless on his bed in the grip of the speedball he has just injected into his arm. Heroin and cocaine dusting the fibres of the deep carpet. A red-haired groupie, naked and unconscious, bloody, strung out on the floor. Vid stares dumbly at him as he takes the empty syringe from his fingers. His mouth moves as if to speak, but there is no sound. There is plenty of heroin to spare from his ready-cooked supply and Jared kneels, draws back the plunger and fills the barrel with clear liquid. Specks of Vid's blood are prised away from the inside of the barrel and float in the fluid like the globs in a lava lamp.

Vid's arm is already pumped up, his belt tight around the crook of his elbow. Jared picks a plump, juicy vein, runs his forefinger along it, imagines sliding the needle in: the razor point pressing against the tight skin and then puncturing it, a drop of blood bubbling up around the needle. Vid will be too far gone to respond. Threads of his blood will leak into the barrel. Jared imagines gently increasing the pressure on the plunger, depressing it, and sending the blood back down into the vein, a solvent with fatal narcotic solute. Sliding the plunger down until it runs up against its buffer, draining the barrel. A thread of spit trails down Vid's chin as he slips into his coma.

Jared gets up, leaves a ten-dollar bill under the saucer, and walks the short distance back to the hotel. The bus is waiting by the side of the hotel, the livery exactly as he expected it would be: the name of the band written in huge script across both sides. The driver, a fat man swaddled in his blue uniform, half-moons of sweat under his arms, has already loaded Jared's luggage.

'What time are we kicking off?' he asks.

'Round 'bout eleven, eleven-fifteen,' says the driver.

'Right,' says Jared.

part Two

Damien

**15 April, previous
Service Station, M62**

A steamy, sweaty garage shop, dug into the embankment at the side of the northbound M62, encircled by a horseshoe of tall dark firs. Neat rows of provisions for car and driver fill the shelves and cabinets: oil, sponges, chamois leathers, cleaning products; crisps, chocolate, middle-of-the-road mainstream tapes and CDs, bottles and cartons in ordered ranks. A dozen customers circulating, dropping items into wire-mesh baskets and miniature trolleys.

Damien waits as the queue to the checkout slowly unravels. He is listening to the Chemical Brothers on his Walkman, to muffle the dreadful piped muzak version of 'Eleanor Rigby', and is cradling the provisions for the final leg of their trip to Manchester: a crate of Fosters, two packets of Rizlas, two Cornish pasties, three steak sandwiches, six bars of chocolate. Chris is flicking Vs at him through the windows in the back doors of the knackered Transit, and Gabriel is pissing into the bushes at the side of the slip road leading down onto the motorway. Damien smiles a taut smile, wondering how he has ended up where he is now, stuck here fifty miles from Manchester. Rain is falling steadily – a dirty insipid drizzle, rain you only ever find north of the Pennines. It drips in fat blobs from the roof over the pumps, and in a fine spray out on the road. Windswept, it streaks down the fume-tinted windows of the garage in a greasy film, like oil.

The other customers in the shop have swung gawking double-takes his way at least once. This is to be expected, he figures, given his appearance: big, black, a wide stetson and his arms and neck – his exposed flesh – covered in Chinese script. What a life! He sighs, patting his pockets for the fags he smoked two hours ago.

The queue winds down and Damien's attention is drawn over the shoulder of the guy with white dreads and friendship bracelets standing in front of him, onto the newspaper he is reading. It looks like the *Melody Maker*. As his eye lazily scans the open page, he notices a small box with a black-and-white picture in the live section. Wait a minute.

'Sorry, excuse me,' he says, dumping the provisions on the ledge in front of the cashier, and jogging back to the newspaper racks in the sanitized mini-mart. He picks up the *Maker*, and the *NME* too, just in case.

'Sorry about that,' he says, shouldering his way through the queue to pay the bored-looking cashier with the collection of coins he cups in his hands. 'That pump next to the big white van, please – and all this stuff.' He slaps the coins onto the counter.

Van, M62

They have followed the main arterial route running out of London and up the backbone of the country, up the M1 to Birmingham and over the Pennines into Lancashire and the M62. They set off three hours ago, everyone piling into the back of their van with their equipment and their rucksacks and all their other paraphernalia for the road. They will be away for a week, playing gigs in Manchester, Birmingham, Coventry and Wolverhampton. Mostly to students.

Damien hates students.

The van is one of the old-style Transits that are hardly ever found on the roads any more, the ones with rounded curves instead of the abrupt, modern lines. The headlights nestle in moulded round mountings, and the door handles used to be gleaming chrome fittings rather than this oxidised debris that stains the hand. Alex bought the van from a friend who works in a breaker's yard, for two hundred quid and his collection of classic *2000AD* annuals. It is unlicensed, Alex is uninsured, and the creaking, moaning wreck is held together only by its scabrous skin of rust and dirt, together with wrappings of gaffer tape. Spray from the back wheels of the coach in front is thrown up over the van. The windscreen wipers screech over the cracked glass, and Damien watches as red tail-lights blur into wet smudges.

The back of the van is a heaving, sweating scrum. Chris, Jared, Damien and Gabriel sit leaning against the metal wall-panels, flung left and right as Alex veers the van across the lanes of the motorway in search of the optimum route through the evening traffic. They are running late and, this being the best support slot they have ever managed to secure, they cannot afford to screw up. Beer cans roll with the tilting suspension of the van, a clattering tin wave spilling the dregs of the beers they have already finished. Roaches litter the dirty floor of the van like confetti; Chris managed to score eighty quid's worth of dope from a bouncer before the gig at Club 169, and they have made excellent progress into that aromatic wad. Jared's industrial-sized glass bong is seeing plenty of use – the back of the van smells like a hippie squat, the underlying odour suggesting a squat fed on baked beans.

Water drips down into a gathering puddle from a hole in the roof. Their equipment is stacked precariously along one side of the van – every time Alex slaloms into a fresh lane, Damien's drum kit wobbles, threatens to collapse onto them, settles. Gabriel has already had to lash his keyboards more securely to the hooks studding the wall of the van. Jared's boombox is wedged between Damien's snare and high-hat: 'Doll Parts' by Hole is blasting out.

This isn't so bad, thinks Damien. They grumble and whine all the time – he does too – but, at the end of it all, this is not such a bad life. They get to travel around a bit, earn just enough to keep pumping fuel in the tank, play their clutch of songs almost every night, get to look almost desirable to the slutty rock chicks that come to their gigs. This is better than sacrificing his life in an office, or doing time on a shitty McJob with no prospects of escape. When they formed the Indigo Violets six months ago, they breathlessly toasted the beginning of a journey together, this great liberating adventure. And so what if the journey ends here, or in Manchester, or after tomorrow's gig in Birmingham? It's been fun. He'll enjoy it while it lasts.

They play cards for a while, blackjack and poker and then, when they tire of that, porno-star top trumps. Chris plays Tetris on his Gameboy. Damien finishes his copy of *A Farewell to Arms*, watches the road unravelling through the foothills of the mountains, a misnomer for these stunted dwarves, reads placenames fuzzed by the drizzle, counts roadkill and looming sodium lights flicking on as the dusk falls, feels the van shuddering up and down the hills. They change CDs, taking turns to choose: Jared's was Hole; Gabriel picks Kraftwerk; Chris takes Throbbing Gristle; Damien's is Metallica – James Hetfield singing 'Master of Puppets'.

He remembers the *Maker* and reaches into the plastic bag of provisions to fetch it out, flicking through the pages to the live reviews. There they are, three short paragraphs of closely knit text and a postage-sized photo of Chris fellating the microphone. Skinny Chris, all fierce angles and spiky hair. Three weeks ago, before he quit his job for the tour, he was working at the delicatessen counter of a supermarket in Primrose Hill. He looked ridiculous in his white smock and clear plastic gloves. Damien wonders if he looks any less ridiculous in the split sarong he is wearing in the photo. Damien reads it aloud:

INDIGO VIOLETS
Club 169, London

Korn are number-one in America. Your parents can sing word-perfect renditions of **Marilyn Manson's** back catalogue. What is the state of the music industry coming to when talentless drivel like this is peddled as art with a millennial message? And what could be worse than four middle-class rich boys from the posh bits of London pretending to be the Riders of the Apocalypse? Things are worse than we first suspected.

This gig reeks of four desperate men trying to cling on to their youth as it beats a hasty retreat. Admittedly, the band attack their instruments with great gusto but the screeching cacophony they produce sounds more like a cat in a blender than any kind of sonic artistry. Only **Kris Driscoll**, the pseudo-enigmatic sub-Iggy front man managed to stir anything other than bored yawns from the Spartan crowd.

Thankfully, it seems that the **Indigo Violets** are only ever destined to play to half-empty pubs and clubs like this. The rest of the world will be spared the full-on apathy fest they stirred up tonight, with as much wit and energy and anger as a bowl full of lumpy custard. They are worse than embarrassing. Still, at least your parents will like them.

'Phew,' says Jared after Damien has finished reading. '*They* liked us.'

'All very constructive,' says Gabriel.

'What a load of wank,' says Chris. 'Wait a minute: check how they spelt my name?'

'With a "K," just the way you like it.'

'Well, it's not *all* bad then,' suggests Jared sarcastically.

'We just got nuked by the *Melody*-fucking-*Maker* and it's not all bad?' says Gabriel.

'I was *joking*,' says Jared.

Alex swivels in his chair up front and shouts back into the van: 'Jared's right. It's not *all* bad. At least you got noticed. Think of the hundreds of other bands playing that will never get into print like that. This is a breakthrough. Pass me a beer, I need to celebrate.'

'Alex. I . . . was . . . *joking*,' repeats Jared.

'You're setting a very bad example, Mr Tour Manager,' says Damien. 'Drinking and driving is a dangerous activity.'

'And there's a fucking misnomer if I ever heard one,' says Chris. 'I mean, this is hardly a "tour", is it? This is four mates – well, four blokes who know each other a bit – plus a leaching parasitic "manager" shuttling around the country in a shitty, stinky Ford Transit to play to tiny crowds who don't give a flying fuck about them. Someone remind me why I'm doing this?'

'Because the alternative was selling sliced sausage to old ladies?' says Gabriel. 'Or to sign on? No, sorry, I forgot – you're still doing that, right?'

'Come on guys,' shouts Alex. '*This* is not just another gig. This is a big chance. The Kitchen Bitches are a big act, and tonight sold out ages ago. I repeat: *sold out*. There'll be scouts there tonight, hiding amongst the multitudes. I know at least two who're going, and they *loved* the EP. Loved it. We can start generating some proper interest.'

'Excuse me while I die from excitement,' says Gabriel.

'Whoah!' Alex screams out of the window as the back of the van starts slithering towards the central reservation. 'Fucking use your mirrors!'

'We're all going to die,' moans Chris.

Happy Chef, M62

Damien's toasted teacake is soggy, dripping gobs of icky margarine onto his plate. Jared and Chris have gone into the gents to share the dusting of coke that they have left from the wrap they managed to score from a dealer in Dalston last night. Alex is comparing the two pieces of artwork they are considering for the cover of their first album, if they ever get the deal they need in order to release it. Alex's girlfriend, Nadia, an art student at St Martin's, has provided one, and a dope fiend that Jared knows the other. Both are beyond terrible.

'What do you think?' asks Alex, holding them both up. 'Do we go medieval or post-modern? I kinda like the Rothko meets Van Gogh in space on acid angle in this one, but then the whole swords and sorcery thing going on here is kinda interesting too, don't you think?'

'Isn't this a cart-before-horse situation, man?' suggests Damien. 'Doesn't this business go: contract – album – peripheral shit?'

'Doesn't hurt to be prepared,' he replies. 'Let's go with the swords. Chris'd look pretty good in that chainmail outfit, don't you reckon?'

Hard shoulder, M62

'Ready,' says Damien. 'One, two, three, *lift.*'

Cars stream past in the dusky gloaming, leaving parabolas of spray in their wake, dozens of white faces swivelling to stare as they brace themselves to lift the dead weight of the crippled van. The right rear tyre exploded noisily when Alex clipped the curb on the central reservation during a daring dash up the inside to overtake an ambling eighteen-wheeler. The van lost control at once, the remaining three tyres screeching their displeasure at having to bear the entire brunt of the load, with a background of horns and screeching brakes as they slid from right to left. Long tracks of rubber have been inscribed onto the tarmac, describing the crazy route the van took before it settled safely onto the hard shoulder. The burst tyre has been shredded into razored shards. They sent it freewheeling down the slope of the embankment and into a field of perplexed cows. The restraints in the back snapped in the confusion and they were all covered by an avalanche of their equipment. Damien rubs a fresh bruise swarming over his thigh from where Jared's guitar spiked him.

They heave at the back of the van and Damien slides the jack under the wheel arch. He somehow finds a stretch of metal not crumbling with powdery rust and the van settles back down, groaning with displeasure and metal fatigue.

'*OK*,' says Damien. 'Part one accomplished. Part two: pass me that spanner.'

Jared tosses it over. 'Always make sure your drummer is also an ex-mechanic,' he says. 'The first rule of gigging.'

'No,' disagrees Damien. 'The first rule of gigging is to ensure your manager stays well away from the steering wheel when there are kerbs to be mounted.'

'Whatever,' sighs Alex wearily.

Boarding house

Alex has booked them into the cheapest accommodation he could find close to the venue. The boarding house, 'Happy Valleys' according to the wooden sign swinging over the gate, is two adjacent houses in a terrace a mile inside the perimeter of Moss Side. Other houses on the street have windows boarded over with pieces of plywood daubed with adolescent graffiti. Several of the parked cars are derelict, windscreens and windows staved in, all saleable parts scavenged. Some rest on brick crutches and others are missing panels and bodywork, the cavities left by their plunderers standing out like dirty scabs. One has been gutted by fire. A couple of baleful youths sit kicking their heels on a crumbled brick wall at the junction, coldly staring as the band makes sure the van is secure.

'Nice area, Alex,' says Jared.

'I've always fancied a visit to Sarajevo,' says Gabriel.

'Why didn't you tell me where you were booking us in?' Jared asks. 'I used to live near here. I could have warned you.'

'OK,' says Alex. 'I forgot, OK?'

'Is the gear going to be safe here?' asks Damien.

'Probably not,' Alex admits.

'Probably not? How do we play a gig with no instruments?'

'We'll, um, have to keep watch?' he suggests. 'Who's for first watch?' They stare at him incredulously. 'That'll be me, then.'

Manchester Academy

The dressing room is more of an afterthought located at the back of the venue behind the stage. It is underground, and the damp from the wet earth above is creeping down the walls. The room smells of old, stale sweat. Kitchen Bitches' crew are scurrying around their equipment with anxious efficiency, tuning and testing, thwapping the drums, plucking out fat throbbing bass lines and show-boating solo riffs. The Indigo Violets still haven't been able to get onto the stage to install their own gear, and now the first tendrils of the crowd are extending into the wide hall from the bar. No roadies for them tonight – such luxuries they cannot afford – and so they do all the set-up them-selves. If they have time to soundcheck, it will be terribly abbreviated.

Damien has returned from a sortie outside. A long queue stretches from the venue, past the Holy Name Church, past the labs of the University's science department and all the way past the Students' Union. Swarthy touts are swarming along the line with fanned tickets, growling that they are buying and selling. Damien has bought a can of Diet Coke from a shop in the Union and gone straight back to the venue. No one recognized him. Not that they should.

They are crammed inside the dressing room to work on the meagre rider the management has provided.

'We've got A&R guys from three decent labels here,' says Alex enthusiastically. 'Not *big* players, but still pretty decent.'

'Who?'

'ClearTone, Grabbing Hands and Revolution.'

'Never heard of them.'

'Like I say, they're *decent*. Certainly good enough for us.'

'No,' says Gabriel. 'Good enough for *us*. Indigo Violets and their blood-sucking parasite tour manager.'

'Funny guy,' says Alex. 'You'll be grateful when I land a recording contract for you.'

'You'll be waiting a long time for my gratitude, man,' Gabriel replies. 'After that review you think we're gonna get anything but an embarrassed silence out there?'

Alex appeals to the others: 'Jesus, don't let this *negativity* put you off,' he says, glaring at Gabriel. 'Do you think I'd drive halfway around the country in a van full of farting musicians if I didn't think you stood a chance? Huh? Do you?'

'You want an honest answer or an answer to shut you up?' asks Jared.

'I have even *more* good news,' says Alex, pouting, ignoring him. He waves a fax. 'The EP has gone back *up* again in the charts. You've gone up two places to number ninety-six.'

'Gimme that,' Jared says, swiping the fax. 'Let's see. Ninety-six, ninety-six – *here* we are. Just above the Rodean School Choir's charming rendition of "Grandad We Love You" and just below "Satan Loves Cindy" by the delightfully named "Eternal Motherfuckers".'

'Pretty auspicious company we're keeping these days,' says Damien.

'We can't even bow out of the chart gracefully.'

'We've sold precisely three-hundred-and-ninety-one copies. Wow. Big time.'

'At two pounds ninety-nine a copy. We're rich, *rich*!'

'We're on *fire*. A runaway train destined for the top,' shrieks Gabriel.

'You have to start *somewhere*,' says Alex helplessly. 'What happened to your *enthusiasm*?'

Gig

The crowd is already raucous when they slink on stage. The lights are never dimmed properly for support acts, and

Damien can still make out the faces in the grey front rows as he slips behind his drums. Damien hates support slots, just filling time until the crowd get the act they've paid to see. There is a mixture of apathy, tedium and hostility as Jared strums out the opening acoustic chords of 'Suicide Isn't Painless', the only song they all really like and the only one they haven't screwed up live (yet). Damien bangs out the stutter-step beat, his sticks flashing from snare to cymbals and his right foot squeezing out the bass. The others pick up the beat and keep his time, Jared's chords drifting a little, Gabriel's decorative keyboard wobbling as the song crashes through into the first verse. Chris launches into the vocals, his redundant guitar slung over his shoulder, and pulls the stand close enough to brush his lips against the mike. You can say many things about Chris, and most of them would be true, but he knows how to do this. His awkwardness, his gawkiness: he masks them well on stage.

Sweat is already pouring, little cascades glittering like jewels in the lights, as Damien pounds out the beat. A stick shatters and he discards its shards, his empty hand plucking a spare from the pouch with a gunslinger's speed. He looks up into the crowd, blinking sweat out of his eyes. A few are dancing, the real enthusiasts, but the rest are drinking and talking and smoking, some sitting, some gathered in tight groups, mostly treating this as background noise. The levels are all down at half-strength – the main act always gets the full power; their own deafening entrance must never be diluted by the support band. The familiar surge of anger he gets during these dead slots – all this effort, giving the music everything, all absorbed by the crowd like so many drops of water soaking into a soggy sponge.

Listen to us! Look at me!

Into the third verse, and Chris's vocals start to drift and flutter. Damien thinks it's the mix but then sees the look of concern on Jared's face as Chris starts to sing the vocals for 'Stigmata', two songs too early, shoe-horning the couplets into a song they weren't written to fit. Damien stretches his neck for his background mike, starts to sing out the right words, repeating the refrain. Jared is up at the front of the stage, singing hard, trying to mask Chris who is still singing the wrong words. 'Shut the fuck up,' mouths Gabriel but Chris doesn't see him, his face clenched by confusion.

Alex's face pokes out from the wings, concerned, then glances out at the crowd. Damien thinks they have fooled them, but then the first bottle wobbles through the gloom and skitters across the stage. There's another, aimed at Gabriel, and another skidding to rest at Jared's feet. (Damien remembers their gig way, way down the bill at a festival near Epping Forest, when the bored crowd pissed into empty plastic coke bottles and threw them onto the stage like grenades. The lids careened off the bottles as soon as they thwacked the stage, and great gouts of piss splashed everywhere. Gabriel caught one splash full in the face and threw up there and then, all over his keyboard. The biggest cheer of the day.)

The spitter-spatter of bottles has become a shower and Chris is at the mike telling the crowd that they suck and then he unhooks his guitar and brings it down like an axe across Gabriel's keyboards. Gabriel had kept playing on, and now jerks his fingers away as the black and white keys shower upwards with a rending electronic buzz ripping through the speaker stacks.

'Fuck you and good night,' says Jared, sprinting into the wings as he becomes the target for dozens of bottles and cans and coins. Damien scurries after him, as Chris sends his broken guitar looping into the middle of the baying crowd, now surging against the yellow-shirted cordon of bouncers. Someone throws it back again, unwanted; it skids into the drum podium. The boos follow them all the back through the bowels of the venue and follow them through the door and into the dressing room.

One song – *half* a song – and they couldn't even finish that. What was he thinking earlier about this being fun?

Party

Gabriel did not stop to finish off the rider; he collected his jacket and the rest of his stuff and went to get a taxi to take him to the station.

'I'm finished,' he said, slapping away Alex's placating hand. 'I can't do this any more. I've got standards, you know, and that, like, *sucked*. *We* suck. Anyway, that was my only keyboard that Chris just fucked up to make himself look like Roger Daltrey and I can't afford another one, so you can find yourself another keyboard player.'

'I'm getting seriously bad vibes here, man,' said Alex. 'Remember George Best. You're just going to give yourself something to regret for the rest of your life if you quit now.'

'*Pete* Best,' corrects Jared, rolling his eyes.

'You're comparing this sorry shower of shite with the Beatles? Fuck me, Alex, you're more deranged than I thought. I'll be seeing you all,' Gabriel fumes.

'You're just, like, quitting?' Chris asks. 'Just like *that*?'

'Have a nice life,' Gabriel says. 'I'll be sending you the bill for a new keyboard.'

None of them had the appetite for it, but Alex persuaded them they should stick around for the after-show party at a nightclub just down the road, put in an appearance. It took ten minutes to persuade security to let them inside.

'I'm going to change my name,' says Chris as they sit around a table drinking beer and smoking.

'You've already changed it once, man,' says Jared.

'Yeah, but I still don't like it. It's still too *suburban*. I need something else.'

'Like what?'

'Like, um, Vid Danton, I think,' he says.

'Vid Danton?'

'Yeah. Vid. Punchy, no?'

'Great,' says Jared, sighing.

'What does that, you know, mean?' asks Damien.

'Doesn't mean nothing,' says Chris. 'Just sounds cool.'

Alex says: 'Don't look now, but the Kitchen Bitches are coming over. Just, like, act cool, guys, OK?'

Two of the Kitchen Bitches walk over to the table and

each of them has a young-looking student-type hanging on to his arm. The girls are drunk or drugged, walking unsteadily, glassy eyes, with ultra-short leather skirts and black eyeliner running and smearing around their eyes. The bassist, Flick, takes a chair and spins it around, straddling it and facing their table. The other one, Monkey, the drummer, taps out a fag from the half-empty packet on the table, and lets his girl light it for him. Both of them are wearing Ray-Bans, both have short-cropped haircuts dyed platinum blond, and both are wearing skin-tight, shining silver tops.

'The Indigo Violets,' says Flick, giggling. He looks younger than both the girls. 'Hey, we've been fans of yours for like forever, man.'

'You have?' asks Alex.

'Fucking yeah. You've been, like, a real influence on our formative careers.'

'Really?' asks Alex.

'You guys are the best,' says Monkey sarcastically. 'Loved that *Maker* review, by the way.'

Flick laughs, says, 'Hope our fans didn't treat you guys too rough?'

'We've had worse,' Alex says with a nervous laugh.

'How many songs were you like planning on playing tonight?' asks Monkey, a stud glinting on his wet red tongue.

'Four, maybe five,' says Alex. 'Hey, let me just say, you guys really *rocked*. You've got that whole androgynous thing going. Punk meets metal meets ska. Madness meets Metallica in a Green Day influenced kinda way.'

'Green Day suck,' says Monkey. 'They, like, *suck*.'

'They do suck, don't they?' Alex backtracks. 'But you guys don't suck. You rock.'

'Yeah, we rock,' says Flick, puffing smoke rings over the table. 'That's what we do: we *rock*. Isn't that right, you little bitch?' Both girls, not knowing which one he is talking to, laugh cautiously, then intensely when Flick and Monkey laugh too.

'So, like, how old are you boys?' asks Jared. The girls are still giggling, one of them nuzzling the back of Flick's neck.

'Young—' says one.

'—and fucking talented,' finishes the other.

'You've got a great future,' agrees Alex.

'Why don't you just get on your knees and lick their arses for them?' mutters Jared, tensely.

'What's it like to get bottled off the stage after just one song?' Monkey asks him.

'Yeah, tell us, 'cos we'd love to know. It's never, like, happened to us.'

'Past your bedtime, boys,' says Damien, flexing a bicep demonstratively. His tattoos bulge and stretch.

'Can we get you a drink?' asks Alex. 'A beer, or something?'

'Nah,' lounges Flick. 'We're not stopping. MTV are waiting to do an interview with us.'

'Yeah, that whole red-couch deal – the one Kurt used that one last time before he blew his brains out. They've put it on a barge on the Manchester Ship Canal or something. We got interviews lined up from now until next month.'

'Neat,' says Alex.

'Have you guys got any coke?' asks Chris.

'Oh sure,' says Flick, leaving a heavy pause where he is supposed to offer them some.

Chris, confused: 'Could we, um, have a couple of lines?'

'What do you reckon, girls, do we let the losers have a little of our blow?'

Both girls giggle inanely, like puppets.

'Nah,' says Monkey. 'I don't think so either.' He straightens his shades. 'You like these girls? We've got a roomful of them back at the hotel. We're going to feed them cocktails of different drugs and see what happens. We've got a whole pharmacy's worth of stuff. It's gonna be a crazy experiment. Flick's going to write a thesis on the effects.'

'Wow,' says Alex, confused. 'Cool?'

Flick stands up. 'Listen, guys, great to see you and everything. Thanks for warming up our fans. You need anything signed, an album or something, you just gotta ask, OK? Anything for you guys.'

'We'll be seeing you.'

They smile sweetly as they saunter back to the bar.

They order another round of drinks, Alex paying on his card because they ran out of cash buying kebabs in the café outside the venue. They had to queue with fans steaming with sweat and spilt beer. No one recognized them – probably a good thing. The Kitchen Bitches are doing another set on the club's small stage, and they watch dozens of guys in suits around the bar watching them, nodding their heads in time, exchanging appreciative glances, some holding up mobile phones so that other executives in London and New York can listen as the band play their songs. MTV have four cameras here, recording the gig so they can splice footage into the interview they will film later. The lead singer, a guy who looks like a junkie Cameron Diaz wearing black lipstick and a pink fur coat, is thrusting his groin at a camera, pseudo-masturbating and yelling 'motherfucker' over and over again, but still looking like he's fifteen, maybe sixteen. Twenty or thirty young girls are moshing in front of the stage, a couple pulled up onto the stage with the band every now and again, and then thrown back down into the pit.

'Arrogant little shits,' moans Jared.

'Yeah,' Damien agrees.

'Keep your cool,' says Alex gloomily. 'There're some pretty influential people here. You see that guy over there, with the beard, smoking the cigar? That's Michael Kaiser. *Grand fromage* at Revolution.'

'Tonight might not be the best time to make a play,' Damien suggests.

Alex nods disconsolately.

'Got a light?' asks a girl who could be a model, with short, spiked red hair and a nose-ring through her left nostril. Her T-shirt says 'KEEP BRITAIN CLEAN' in a big, brash font with a picture of a stickman dropping a swastika into a dustbin.

'Um, sure,' says Jared, cracking his Zippo.

She feeds the tip of her cigarette into the flame and

sucks, her cheeks hollowing. 'I'm Astrid,' the girl says. 'And this is Frosty, my brother.'

'Hi,' says Frosty, a wiry, ratty guy wearing a fake-Nike AIR JESUS T-shirt, Jesus swooping at a basket like Michael Jordan, with wraparound semi-opaque amber shades. He has a host of nervous tics and twitches and his eyes dart behind his pellucid shades like a lizard's. Damien recognizes him: the guy from the garage shop, the one reading the reviews.

'We, like, saw the gig,' Astrid says. 'And I love your stuff. I've got your EP.'

'Congratulations,' says Chris. 'You are one of only—'

'—three hundred and ninety-one,' supplies Jared.

'—three hundred and ninety one nice people to have bought a copy.'

'Like I said, I really like it.'

'Really?' says Alex, shouting a little to be heard above the noise of the band. 'You really like it?'

'Yeah, I do. Really. All that bleeding-heart angst thing – pretty fashionable right now.'

'You like these guys?' asks Damien, gesturing up at the stage.

'Nah,' says Astrid. 'They're just clones. They'll have a couple of hits and then get dropped. They'll be on the pub scene in a couple of years.'

'Like the Farm,' offers Frosty.

'Or the LAs,' suggests Damien.

'Exactly,' says Astrid.

'I loved the Farm,' Alex says semi-wistfully.

'That's because you have nil taste,' says Jared.

Astrid sits down, sucking smoke out of the fag and blowing a long jet between her black-glossed lips. 'I saw your keyboard player after the gig. He looked unhappy.'

'He's a prima donna,' moans Chris. 'What was it you said, Alex? He's like . . .?'

'Pete Best,' Alex supplies. 'The fifth Beatle.'

'Chris was thinking of George Best,' says Damien.

'Funny guy,' sneers Chris.

'I have my moments,' admits Damien.

Astrid interrupts. 'Listen, I don't mean to be forward or anything, but I'm wondering, given the situation, whether you've a vacancy for a young, gorgeous and, quite frankly, fucking talented keyboard player. If you don't, fine, just say. I won't be offended, but I just can't let you go without asking.'

'Well,' Jared says slowly, 'maybe we do, you know, maybe. How good are you?'

'She's fucking good, but she's way too, like, modest to say so,' says Frosty. 'She was in Cheap Trick for a while and then in the Orchids. And Toilet Duck.'

'There's a band called Toilet Duck?' asks Alex.

'Um, yeah,' Frosty stammers, 'they're, um, really big in Scandinavia. Or, like, somewhere.'

'I dunno,' she says. 'I guess I'm OK. And I love the stuff you're playing. The influences are just right for me: Skinny Puppy, Coil, Foetus. A little late Soft Cell in there too, if I'm not mistaken? Am I right?'

Damien is impressed. 'Sounds pretty much on the same page,' he says, and Chris is nodding.

'I heard the Orchids, once,' says Jared, screwing his face

up, trying to reach back into his memory. 'I think I liked them.'

'Cheers, I hope,' Astrid says.

The Kitchen Bitches are playing their number-one single, 'Fruit', and the girls scream as they recognize the opening chords playing out. The lead singer has taken a long draught of beer and spits it out over them. He has his shirt off now. He has a tattoo of the sun on his midriff; all very Aztec, Damien thinks.

'Listen, we'll give you a chance to play, see what we all think of each other. Get down to London next weekend, we'll set up the studio and see what comes out.'

'OK,' says Astrid, 'that sounds great. Perfect.'

'But we're pretty shit,' says Chris. Jared and Damien and Alex glare at him. 'I just thought she should know, is all.'

Suzy

From: DystopiaFan3@hotmail.com
To: Plastic-Person@aol.com
Date: Wednesday, December 15, 1.35 P.M.
Subject: Hi!

Dear Jared

    It's pretty hard to believe I'm actually doing this, writing to U, knowing that this will get through to U at your home, wherever home is, but here I am, listening to *Plastic People* on my Walkman in my lunch break and drinking herbal tea, typing out the letter to U I drafted last night, desperate to finish so I can press Send and fire it away. *Please* don't be offended with me for writing. I know how annoying spam mail can be, I mean it annoys me as much as anyone else, but this isn't spam. At least I *hope* it isn't spam! It's just a dedicated fan taking her chance to say 'HI' and hoping that U R feeling happy and good. So don't flame me, OK! (If I'm invading your privacy just say so and I promise I won't mail U again. But I hope U don't feel like that. It'd be great if U could reply so I know that U have read this.)

    Brief facts about me: my name is Suzanne Abbott (my

friends call me 'Suzy'), I am twenty-seven years old and I am a *huge* Dystopia fan. (If U don't believe me, check out my email address – how's that for dedication! Three others had already registered the email address before me but none of them love the band like I do.)

I guess I'm just mailing to say 'HI!' and that I hope U will find a moment to reply.

Love

Suzy

PS: Is it OK if I call U Jared? I got your email address from a website that publishes the addresses of famous people. I don't know how those guys find this stuff out! I have attached a 'delivery receipt' and a 'read receipt' so I'll know that this gets through safely. Just so U don't think I'm checking up on U or anything!

From:	DystopiaFan3@hotmail.com
To:	Plastic-Person@aol.com
Date:	Wednesday, December 15, 1.55 P.M.
Subject:	Hi Again!

Hi again! It's just me, Suzy. Just mailing to check if the last one got through OK. The delivery receipt didn't come back to me but that sometimes happens and mails still get through I think. Anyway, I've attached another one to this mail.

Keeping my fingers crossed!

Love

Suzy

From: DystopiaFan3@hotmail.com
To: Plastic-Person@aol.com
Date: Thursday, December 16, 1.37 P.M.
Subject: Hi!

Here I am again! I'm writing this from work again and I am *seriously* bored so sorry if I ramble a bit. My friends say that this is one of my worst vices (writing long emails) but I think it is one of my best strengths. I mean, if I was born in the last century instead of this one I reckon I would have been really popular! I love writing emails and letters and writing was bigger then, wasn't it, before the telephone and TV and stuff like that? I've read loads of Jane Austen etc and I know that people wrote letters then more than they do now. I think I prefer proper letters to actually read, getting something U can touch and look at again and again is much better I think, but the snailmail is so *sloooow* compared to email. One button and whoosh 'U have mail' as the computer says.

    Well, both of my earlier mails got through OK I'm glad to say. Why am I telling U this since U know already? U read them after all! I hope U don't mind but I also attached 'read receipts' so I could see if U read them. Sneaky, eh? When they came back and told me that U had read them and the time U did and everything I think I actually punched the air and shouted 'YEAH' or something. It's not like I am keeping tabs on U or anything creepy like that, it's just that it means a lot to me to know that U R getting my mails. It's great to know U R reading them and that I am not completely wasting my time doing this. Even if U don't have time to reply knowing that U have actually read them is more than enough for me. Even so, it would be *fantastic* if U could just send me a couple of lines, saying 'HI SUZY' or something. But I know U R really busy with promoting the album and planning for the tour, so I'll understand if U don't, OK? I'll be cool!

I should tell U some more things about me. U already know my name. I live in London like U do. My birthday is on 25 November, which makes me a Sagittarius and means I have 'a positive outlook on life' as well as being 'honourable, trustful and truthful'. I know that U R a Scorpio and U know what they say about Sagittarians and Scorpios! Maybe we should get together! (Just kidding!) I am 5 foot 4 inches tall with bluey-grey eyes and dark curly hair. My sister says that I am pretty and wasted doing what I am doing, which is being a market researcher for a company in the West End. I'd really love to be able to do something more glamorous, like be in a band or on the television or something like that. Pipe dreaming again! Only the lucky few get so that they R rich + famous and the rest of us just have to accept what we have.

I must be the world's *biggest* Dystopia fan. I went to five Dystopia concerts this year (the two in London, as well as Sheffield, Manchester, Cardiff) – I would have gone to them all but my train to Glasgow broke down for FOUR HOURS and I was late when I was travelling up (don't worry – I wrote a really *nasty* letter to the train company and got all my money back plus the cost of my wasted ticket. It didn't make up for the disappointment of missing the concert though).

I don't think there's anything U could tell me about U that I don't already know! I always buy every magazine or newspaper that U and the others appear in. My little sister Christie is also a massive fan (she is 15 – she says 'HI' by the way) and she helps me to keep an eye on the papers and stuff so that I don't miss anything. I have about a million scrapbooks full of cut-out stories and pictures! And my prize possession is a vinyl copy of *Plastic People* (vinyl is so quaint!) with a gatefold cover that U and the others signed. Do U remember signing that for me? The signing was in HMV on Oxford Street and I was the fourth person in the line and I slept out on the pavement for two nights with these other really *freaky* girls, including two Japanese girls who said that they had slept with Vid and U even though I knew they were lying. U signed my copy 'To Suzy – Jared', which was just the most wonderful personal message I could ever have wished for and I couldn't stop looking at it and touching it for days afterwards. I told U how great I thought U were and how it was really incredible to meet U. Do U remember? U said, quote 'Yeah, glad you like us, thanks.' That was so cool of U! It's great that U have the personal touch with your fans, not like certain other bands I could mention. What a fantastic day! My flatmate (a French girl called Monique who is doing an English course over here and who is really pretty but a bit vacant) saw my collection of Dystopia stuff the week she moved in and thought it was, quote 'creepy'! I think it was all a bit much for her – but I guess I do have rather a lot of stuff, my little 'shrine', and until U know me U might think it was a bit 'OTT'.

Sorry, I know I've been going on for far too long *again*. Hope U R not too bored with me already? Anyway, gotta run, my boss hates it when we go online and I can see her doing her 'rounds', as she calls it. Hope U R well – mail me?

Love

Suzy

From:	DystopiaFan3@hotmail.com
To:	Plastic-Person@aol.com
Date:	Friday, December 17, 1.35 P.M.
Subject:	Christmas and other things.

I'm going to visit Brighton at the weekend. I am finding all the preparations for Christmas R getting me down. I know that it's silly, but whenever I see parents and so on queuing up in the toy shops at this time of year to buy their children Christmas presents it just makes me feel sad + lonely. It's not that I feel like I am being 'left on the shelf' or anything like that, but it does make me sad. I wonder why? They say that Christmas is the time when the most people commit suicide, don't they? Anyway, having a break will do me good and I am looking forward to it. Christie is coming too so it will be fun. I'll tell U all about it next week.

What R U doing for Christmas? R U having it with your parents or with the rest of the band? I'd love to know what your plans R. By the way, could U email me with your snailmail address so I can send U your card. If U R *very*

lucky I might even get U a little present but we'll just have to
see about that!

Anyway, time for me to get back to work. Even though
we R nearly at Christmas it never dies down for a second!
Love
Suzy

Alex

20 December
Liverpool Street, London

The pretty oriental girl in the Vivienne Westwood grey wool suit (complete with school-style tie: very cute) shows Alex into an anteroom decorated with a blatant and ostentatious disregard for expense. This is industrial minimalist chic, but even with nothing much in the room Alex knows it would take him a lifetime on his salary to afford even these meagre furnishings: walls made of granite slabs with the floor and ceiling black, cut from something like obsidian or marble; tall fronds of palm fanning out from Ming vases in the corners; one wall sliced in half by an aquarium, an eel hovering in the backlit turquoise water.

'Congrina Aequoreus,' says the girl.

'Excuse me?' says Alex.

She points at the aquarium. 'The eel. Also known as green conger eel.'

'Oh,' he says. 'Nice.'

A window as narrow and long as an arrow-slit offers a wide-screen panorama of the London skyline outside. Head down reverently, he watches his own reflection in the polished floor as the girl guides him across the room. She disappears through a door set so seamlessly into the wall that Alex wonders if he would be able to find it, let alone open it, if he had to.

Alex sits down on a long leather and chrome banquette and toys with a quartz paperweight that is pinning a glossy brochure to the Arne Jacobsen slate-topped table. There is also a metronome-styled clock, its arm swinging left and right with an hypnotic cadence. He listens to its ticking for a moment, trying to slow down the jackhammer thumping in his chest where his heart ought to be.

Keep calm. Keep cool. This is important.

Everything is so *understated.* From the sober entrance at the foot of the newly constructed glass-and-steel cuboid on Bishopsgate, to the inaudible whisper of the elevator's motor as he was whisked up twenty floors, to the tiny black-and-white sign fixed behind the desk in the elegant reception: THE POUND MACHINE. The receptionist, wearing a Star Trek earpiece and microphone, tapped his details into her keyboard; the details played out on a plasma screen as thin as a slim paperback.

'Ah yes, Mr Culpepper,' she said. 'You're a little early.'

This was true. Alex had been pacing the backstreets around Spitalfields for half an hour, rehearsing his pitch, breathing long hard breaths.

It is the obsession with fine detail that sets this place apart from other offices he has visited. Comparing this to the brash exuberance on show at Revolution Records is like comparing a Beethoven concerto with an Iron Maiden gig. Sitting in the tranquil anteroom, Alex is put in mind of a chapel.

He stands up and straightens his tie. He spent two hours

making sure he looked his best this morning. He had his hair cut at Toni and Guy's, had fifteen minutes on a sun bed, then into a new suit and shirt from Hugo Boss on Regent Street. He felt good when he left the flat this afternoon, but now he feels fraudulent, as if there was a sign stuck onto his back that said TRYING TOO HARD. Is it as obvious to everyone else as it is to him that he is out of his depth?

He walks over to the smaller hand-table underneath the window. A laptop has been left open and switched on, and a miniature slide-show runs on the screen. Images of projects into which the fund has invested slip and slide into and out of one another: one shot has builders swarming over the skeleton of a skyscraper in Times Square; another shows a white cruise-liner cutting through a Norwegian fjord; this next one shows a train bulleting into the heart of Munich airport. Serious money is at stake here, and these are serious players. How has this all come to pass? (He knows, of course. An opportunity has come to him that he cannot possibly refuse. No one could refuse it. A once-in-a-lifetime opening that does not brook rejection as a possible response.)

The oriental girl brings in a pot of steaming lemon tea and a cup on a silver platter. 'Mr Bratsky and the others will be ready in a moment, Mr Culpepper,' she says, all deep green eyes and dimples. 'I thought you might like some tea while you waited?'

'Yeah,' says Alex, 'that'd be great. Thanks.'

The porcelain handle slips in his sweaty palm as he raises the cup to his lips. Why is he so nervous? He has been to dozens of meetings like this before; dozens. In his previous life, before the offer to manage the band came along, he worked for Kramer & Lewis, the monolithic city law firm with offices just down the way. He did the corporate stuff mostly: contracts, refinance, flotations, MBOs. How many times did he sit in on completion meetings, a footsoldier amongst the competing regiments of lawyers and accountants trying to annihilate each other in the frenzy of testosterone and bravado that deal-time always seemed to engender? How is this any different? And, anyway, it wasn't as if he was casting any kind of final die today. All they would be discussing was a little pre-contract contract, almost a pre-nuptial if the truth be known. Just setting down some rules of engagement before they cast their lots together and enter the field for the bigger prize.

(But he knows how this *is* different. This couldn't be *more* different. The sums involved before were all abstract concepts, money floating between corporate entities as insubstantial as wraiths, or mist. Make the paper trail and the money will follow. But he has made *himself* a part of this transaction. This is not fantasy. He has staked his future on the outcome. He stands to gain an obscene amount of money should the scheme succeed; if it fails, he'll lose his job, his flat, his cars, his lifestyle. Stark opposites. His investment is immense.)

He wonders whether he should have brought his own lawyer with him. Is this arrogance to rely upon his own legal experience? After all, it has been – *think* – two years since he resigned from Kramer & Lewis? He is bound to be rusty, vulnerable to the blind-side shenanigans he loved pulling when he was in the game. Would they do that to him, lull him with soothing words before clipping him? Of course they would.

This is business.

This makes him even more nervous.

Another door that Alex had not previously noticed opens in the wall behind him.

'Please step this way,' says another girl, this one with skin the colour of milk chocolate, and as maddeningly beautiful as the first. 'Mr Bratsky is ready to see you.'

He is led through a second reception area, complete with a miniature waterfall and furnished with the very best décor that an alliance of feng shui and unlimited resources can procure. The girl opens a semi-transparent door and ushers him inside.

If he was in any doubt before, those doubts are instantly erased. Now he knows he is in the big-time.

The conference room is on the top floor of the building, set into the slope where the wall ends and the glass roof begins. The entire west-facing wall is made of a solid pane of glass, with no obvious signs of buttressing to support its unquestionably immense weight. The winter sun is setting behind the bulk of the offices that crouch over the squat railway station, and the clear cold sky has been burnished with gold. Points of light glisten from reflective surfaces like icicles. A jet lays down a trail of fluffy cloud as it crosses the sky. Ragged pigeons wheel in the thermals, gliding past the window on stiff wings. Alex's view is drawn to the streets below and to the buses and cars and trucks that look like toys and the swarm of people being sucked into the wide concourse of the station. He feels as if he has scaled the slopes of Mount Olympus.

The conference room is equipped with a large oval table around which sit five people. Each has a crescent of papers fanned out before him or her, red whorled amendments swirling over the documents. Bratsky he recognizes; the big American, as solid as a linebacker, has his jacket slung across the back of his chair and is supping from a cup of black coffee. He is wearing a pair of black braces with dollar signs embroidered all the way down them.

The others are strangers to Alex. They all turn as he enters.

'Alex, *Alex*,' booms Bratsky, getting up to shake his hand. His grip is ultra-masculine, firm, and Alex feels his finger joints compressing. 'Just great to see you again.'

'Yeah, good to see you again, too,' Alex says, trying to match his bombast and hiding a wince of discomfort from the handshake.

'Sorry to keep you waiting,' Bratsky says. 'What do you make of the offices?'

'Amazing,' Alex says truthfully. 'Stunning.'

'The building's only been up a couple of months. An interesting fact: when the foundations were being excavated, the builders discovered an ancient Roman crypt. They found a sarcophagus with some kind of Roman chick inside. They dug up – what was it – one hundred bodies in all?'

There is a murmur of assent.

'Neat,' says Alex, confused, uncertain of himself. 'I liked the eel.'

'Isn't she great? I'll leave you to figure out the rather crude symbolism.'

'I think I get it. James Bond, right?'

Bratsky laughs. 'Close. It's terribly blatant of me, but I like to think it symbolizes what we do here at the Pound Machine. Little bits of bait are dropped into our tank every now and again. If the bait is of a sort we like, we snap it up. You needed someone with an eye for the main chance, right? Someone with some *appetite*. And when it comes to deals like this, we're *famished*.' He laughs again and claps his hands together. 'Listen, before we get started I should introduce you to these unfamiliar faces.' The others are all on their feet, aiming broad grins at Alex. 'This is Mohammed Rafiq – Mohammed is the director of our finance department. Over here is Lynette Supperstone, legal director. This is Mark Rafael, my accountant, and here is Alice Brooks, PR director.'

'Nice to meet you,' Alex repeats as he shakes the row of proffered hands.

'Now, you take a seat and let me get you something to drink. You fancy a beer?'

'A beer? Oh, um, yes, that'd be great. A beer would be just great.'

'Excellent.' Bratsky thumbs a button on the space-age device on the table that looks like a spider, evidently a communicator of some description. 'Six beers, please, Michelle, and maybe a couple bottles of champagne too. I'm hoping we might have cause for a little celebration later.'

Alex sits down, breathing long and slow. This is it. He has to keep his composure; a sign of weakness here and a predator like Bratsky will devour him. He's seen it happen so many times before. These big carnivores at the top of the food chain know exactly when to pounce on their frail prey. But every other time Alex has been outside the cage looking in.

'We were just going over the fine detail of the deal you suggested,' says Bratsky. 'I wanted to get the minutiae straight in my head before we got into the nitty-gritty proper. I have to say, right at the get-go, that I'm pretty enthusiastic about the proposition you've put to us.'

'That's great,' says Alex, sweat dampening the patches of skin behind his knees. 'Like I said, I reckon this could be a licence to print money.'

'Well, we've done some initial market research and we're inclined to agree. Not that we needed to research for long – I mean, everyone at the table knows something about the product that you've got to sell.'

The door opens again and a chilled bottle of Budvar is delivered to each of them. Alex wraps his hand around the cold glass, letting the chill sink into his palm and into his hot blood. Little bowls of tortilla chips and salsa are dropped into the middle of the table.

'We'll have a proper celebratory dinner later, don't worry,' jokes Bratsky, indicating the chips. 'I've booked a table at Pont de la Tour for seven.'

Alex can feel the whiff of money going to his head. He has to ground himself, keep it all together. He will drink this beer slowly, can't afford to be light-headed.

'So, let's cover the bases here. You think you can deliver the product at a minimum price and with minimal hassle?'

'Oh yes,' says Alex, sloshing beer in his hurry to speak. 'No question. All it will take is some kind of compensation payment to Revolution, low six-figures I'd have thought, given their contractual position.'

'You said that the current deal runs out in three months' time?' asks the lawyer, Lynette.

'Uh-huh,' affirms Alex. 'They've got them on a one-album deal only. That's it. I remember at the time telling them how stupid and short-sighted they were being, but they were adamant about that. They've been buzzing me for a while to see what the score is with renegotiating but I've been able to put them off. I've already seen draft contracts with strings of zeroes but none of the band know anything about it yet. They just know that another contract'll have to be sorted before the next album comes out.'

'No need for compensation then, I'd say,' corrects Supperstone, scribbling on a yellow jotter.

'OK,' says Alex, blood in his cheeks.

'You said that the next album is nearly finished?'

'It's progressing. I know that Jared's got six songs he thinks are pretty fantastic. They're planning to write the rest while they're in the States on tour.'

'Great, great,' says Bratsky, a little distracted. 'I just need to know when we might start seeing a return on our investment.'

'It'd be soon,' says Alex. 'Really soon. And the return itself should be massive. You know what sales have been like for the album?'

'We do,' says Alice Brooks. '*Plastic People* shifted two

hundred and fifty thousand units in the first three weeks. That's faster than the Oasis album managed.'

'It went platinum three times on advance sales alone,' says Alex, keen to deploy the spiel he has rehearsed at countless industry parties.

'It's on track to become the fastest-selling début album of all time. The band will contribute around eighty-five per cent of Revolution's turnover this year, once merchandise and endorsements have been factored in. If they lose them, Revolution's in big trouble.'

'Not our problem,' says Bratsky, with a dismissive wave.

'I think we can safely say that the market is baying for a follow-up.'

'That's a fairly safe bet,' says Alice.

Bratsky dips a tortilla chip into the salsa and crunches down on it loudly. 'Excellent. And what about the protagonist himself? What would his view of all this be?'

'I've kept them in the dark as much as possible,' says Alex. 'Like I said, they don't know that Revolution have been screaming at me to renegotiate. They're closeted away in an apartment in Barcelona at the moment, rehearsing for the tour. And I've made sure Revolution don't know where they are.' He sips his beer, focuses again around the cold jolt that scampers down his throat. 'I know exactly what the terms of the deal they're on at the moment are. I mean, *I* drafted the agreement in the first place.'

'We've checked it over,' says Supperstone. 'A fine piece of legal drafting.'

Alex smiles, despite himself, at the flattery. 'I reckon

that if we can offer them fifteen or twenty per cent more than they're getting now, they'll swallow it.'

'It's not a question of what we can and can't do,' says Bratsky. 'If the deal is a profitable one, we could double his present return without too much bother. Or triple it. No, the question is this: we must make sure that we do just enough to have him pull the trigger, and no more than that. We can leave ourselves the scope to renegotiate should need arise in the future.'

'I agree,' says Rafiq. 'Judging the level of offer is the most crucial consideration.'

'And you have a unique insight into that, Alex,' says Bratsky.

'Yeah, I understand,' says Alex. 'And, yeah, I know the level to set the offer at. I've been feeding them the line that they should be looking at a ten per cent raise from the next deal. They all trust me implicitly. If you come in and offer twenty, I'll tell them it's the best deal they'll ever get in their lives, and they'll bite our hands off.'

'I have no doubt that you're right, Alex. None at all.' A ray of sunlight has been slowly moving up the wall as the sun sinks down further. The colour of the light has worked through the amber of honey to the red of a watermelon's insides. Bratsky's shadow looms large against the wall.

'Revolution can shout and scream as much as they want,' Alex continues. 'And if the band do find out what they were offering, I'll tell them the deal was heavily conditional or something.'

'We've taken the liberty of establishing a shell company to own the rights to the recordings,' says Supperstone. 'It's called Epsilon Limited, at least for the moment. Here's what I'm thinking: we get Vid on board, and have him sign up with Epsilon. The agreement will be between that company and Vid, and the company will be responsible for paying him his artist's fee and royalties. We then negotiate with the major record labels and broker the best deal we can.'

'Epsilon will stand as an intercessor on his behalf,' says Bratsky. 'But the cash will come straight to us. Oh, and by the way, I've had some very interesting conversations with the chief executives of some very important record labels in the States and the Far East. I think we can assume that a deal will not be difficult to strike.'

'Like I said,' embroiders Alex, 'this is a hot property we're dealing with. They can name their price at the moment.'

'Luckily, Vid doesn't appear to realize that.'

'Oh yeah,' he agrees. 'They've got the whole artistic integrity thing going. They're pretty naïve and they tend to leave the business side of things to me.' Alex finishes his beer. A realization blooms. 'Wait a moment,' he says. 'Did you say "Vid"?'

'We did.' Bratsky rifles through a tan folder on the table and withdraws a memorandum, studies it. 'Vid Danton is the lead singer, isn't he?'

'Yeah, but I thought we were talking about the band. As a whole. Dystopia?'

'Ah,' says Bratsky. 'I forgot we hadn't mentioned this before. Alice, would you explain?'

The blonde, slight PR director takes off her glasses and

addresses Alex directly. 'We commissioned extremely extensive market research to find out exactly what it was that has made the band as popular as it is at the moment. It's on the table in front of you there.' Alex picks up a thick, bound report headed 'PROJECT EPSILON: MARKET FEASIBILITY STUDY'. She continues as Alex flicks through the data-rich pages. There are graphs, charts, spreadsheets, pie-charts, tables, pages and pages of figures. 'These pop phenomena are ephemeral things, by and large, and we needed to know as much as we could about what makes this one tick before we took your offer any further. We did some pretty intense focus grouping across almost the entire demographic spectrum that has been or could be exposed to the band. We did Manchester and Birmingham last Saturday and Edinburgh and London on Sunday. The US report is due in next week, but I understand the results are the same.'

Alex is sweating and his beer is nearly finished. He clenches his fist, trying to wring out the gloss of moisture between his fingers.

'It's fair to say that the testings put up some quite *remarkable* results. Apart from the expected conclusions (the over-fifties are not going to be converted, even if the band covers "A Whiter Shade of Pale"), it's also fair to say that there were some big surprises.'

'Surprises?'

'What we found was that it is not the band *per se* that has struck a chord with the music-buying public. Vid Danton has had the *real* impact. Our test sample shows consistently that Vid is the reason for the band's success. Not the songs, not the collective image of the band, not even the videos (even though they all rated extremely highly) and certainly not the others. No, what came back almost every time, in both sexes and across all age ranges and social groups we tested, was that Vid has been selling these records, not the band.'

'Whoa,' says Alex.

Alice nods. 'There is a very high degree of probability that rather than assisting in making the Dystopia *concept* so successful, the other members of the band might actually be holding Vid back.'

'Whoa, whoa,' says Alex, palms facing towards the table. As if oblivious, she flips to a tabbed page in her bundle of papers.

'Astrid tested *horribly* with men between the ages of fifteen and thirty-five. They just don't *get* the whole lesbian thing – guys just seem to have this image of their female pop stars, and she just isn't it. No sexual frisson, despite the undeniable great looks. It's that whole "look but don't touch" thing. It's very worthy, very admirable, but it's death insofar as selling records to a key, key market is concerned. As soon as the test group were confronted by that issue, they just went away in droves. And that male negative isn't balanced by any great appeal to the same female cross-section: all we detected there was extreme jealousy and a healthy dose of spitefulness. And Astrid hasn't helped herself with all the posturing on gay rights. The public don't need another angry young lesbian.'

Alex is shifting preconceptions in his head, altering priorities, running calculations to scope exactly how far he is prepared to go.

'Damien rated only lukewarm in the marketplace he ought to have cornered: women between the ages of twenty-five and thirty-five. That whole "I don't need drugs" thing he has going? Too *boring*. These women might not *approve* of drug-taking and rock-star excess, but that's what they still expect their rock stars to *do*. The tattoo thing is passé, also. Finally, the rather pious HIV revelation he came out with a couple of months ago? The public just *hated* it. If he had any sex appeal before, that just about sent it through the floor. Now he looks like a bleeding heart and a hard-luck story all rolled into one. Bad combination. Damien is damaged goods.' She sips at her beer and angles a glance at Bratsky. He nods, impelling her onward.

'Jared Melchior. Hmm. Jared is the biggest liability of them all. He tested negatively across the board, the whole demographic. And the worse thing is none of the test subjects were able to posit accurately why he pissed them off so much. I guess he just has one of those irritating personalities, or something. An example: in the video for the band's first big song—'

'"Power and the Glory",' supplies Alex, as she fumbles for the name.

'Exactly, he appears on screen in either the foreground or middle-distance for fifty-nine seconds. Thirty-three per cent of the test subjects found this video to be either "unsatisfying" or "deeply unsatisfying". Now, compare that with the second video—'

'"Broken Down and Beautiful".'

'—precisely, when Jared is in shot for longer, one minute thirty-three seconds. This time, sixty-seven per cent of the test subjects said they thought it was "deeply unsatisfying". In other words, Jared looks pretty irredeemable.'

Bratsky is doing a slow, continuous nod.

'Now – Vid Danton,' she says. 'His approval scores are *off the scale* in just about every demographic. We're talking adolescents, twentysomethings, thirtysomethings, gays, straights, marrieds, singles, all social groups, all castes, he even made some conservative inroads into test subjects who professed no enthusiasm for this kind of music. It's *him*, Alex, he's doing this. It's not the band.'

'I'm finding this all a little hard to take in.'

'This is all in the report,' Alice says, riffling her tabbed version. 'There's more, too, but I think that serves as a useful indication of the content.'

'Alex,' says Bratsky, 'what we are saying is this: Vid has a chance to be a big, big star. An astronomically successful star. We are talking Madonna and Michael Jackson combined, and then add some more on top. We don't know quite how, but he has somehow tapped into a defining, universal constant that is making him popular across almost every statistical bracket that it's worth being popular in.'

'Are you saying we should ditch the others?'

'Yes,' says Alice. 'This company has a duty to its shareholders to ensure that any investment it makes is in their best interests. The research we've commissioned has demonstrated beyond doubt that if the band stay together they have a shelf life of one, or perhaps two, extra albums.'

'We think the second album will be successful, not a patch on *Plastic People* but still selling decent numbers, before the third just scratches the surface.' Rafiq finishes the sentence with a smug flourish of his pen, underscoring some fact or another in the report.

Alice continues: 'But if Vid Danton is allowed to pursue a solo career, there is *no* discernible shelf life. And no ceiling on the prospective earnings we stand to make. He is, as you say, a licence to print money.'

'But it has to be a move he makes soon, while he's firmly in the public eye,' says Rafiq. 'While his escape velocity is at an optimal level. We think he's got six weeks, tops, to get out. If the US tour even skips a beat, he's lost it.'

'But you do realize that Jared has more musical ability in his little finger than Vid has in his whole body? Vid can't play his guitar, for example? And besides that he is, well, um, a little *unstable*? You know, like, substance abuse?'

'As far as his musical ability is concerned,' says Bratsky 'we'll just make sure he has the best session musicians money can buy in the studio with him. And as for your second point, that's where *you* come in. It will be your responsibility to keep him sober when he needs to be sober, and safe when he doesn't.'

'I'm assuming we're talking deal-breakers here?'

'I'm afraid so. To use clumsy analogies, he is our cash

cow,' says Bratsky, 'or the goose that laid our golden egg. Or eggs, plural.'

'Do the band have any form of contractual agreement between themselves?' asks Supperstone.

'Um, no, I don't think so,' says Alex. Then, with more certainty: 'No, I'm sure they don't. They never thought it was necessary.'

'Well, that's a plus,' says Supperstone. 'No compensation payments to structure either.'

'The others won't get anything?'

'Not from the looks of things, no. That's not a problem?'

'Uh, no,' says Alex. 'Not at all.'

'You're happy doing this?'

'Sure. Sure I am.'

Supperstone produces a contract. The agreement will be between Alex and the new company, but is conditional upon Vid agreeing to sign up along with him. Alex scans the recitals, and then pauses when he reaches the section headed FINANCIAL SUMMARY.

'These figures correct?' he says, too stunned to berate himself for sounding like a novice.

'Quite correct,' says Rafiq. 'If our financial projections bear up, we might even be getting a bargain. But you'll see there's an upwards-only review clause further on, should certain thresholds be reached.'

'Is everything OK?' asks Bratsky.

Bratsky did just ask him whether an annual salary of £1,500,000, *after* tax, was 'OK'?

'Hmm,' says Alex, trying to stop the dollar signs kachunking into his eyes. 'I'd say that was more than generous. I mean, with the review clause and everything. It's, um, fine.'

'Well, I see no reason why we shouldn't put ourselves onto a formal footing now,' says Bratsky. 'The non-refundable signing bonus will be credited to a bank account of your choosing as soon as you get Mr Danton on board. Or, if you prefer, we could have it paid to you in cash. It's really up to you.'

Signing bonus? Alex scans the contract again. God. They want to pay him £500,000 just for Vid signing his name?

'Non-refundable?' he says.

'Completely. As a mark of our gratitude, and our confidence in you.'

'Let's get it over and done with,' he gulps. 'Anyone got a pen?'

'Excellent,' says Bratsky, handing him a chunky Cross. 'Alice, why don't you crack those bottles of champagne. I've never invested in the music business before. Film finance, of course, you knew that already, but this is different. A new frontier. And I have to say I'm rather looking forward to the experience.' He raises a glass.

'Here's to Vid Danton.'

Suzy

From: DystopiaFan3@hotmail.com
To: Plastic-Person@aol.com
Date: Monday, December 20, 1.53 P.M.
Subject: Brighton and other things

Hi again. I feel kind of awkward writing this mail because I'm guessing U must be annoyed at me for something. R U? Listen, if U think I went on for too long in that last mail it wouldn't surprise me. People R always telling me I go on too much! I have this tendency to get carried away with myself sometimes. I'm just really worried that U R pissed off with me, that's all, and that would be awful cos all U have to do is tell me to keep it brief and I will. That'd be fine, it's not like I'd be mortally offended or anything. (U wouldn't be the first person to tell me to shut it!)

Can U believe this weather? They say that it's already the coldest December on record and that it's going to get worse. Can U believe that? Something about arctic winds and stuff like that, that's the latest explanation on the TV. Maybe we'll get a white Xmas! I'd love that. (Have U seen the new all-day weather channel, 4-CAST 24, yet? Pretty sad, I know, but when I go home I like to leave it on, not to watch, just cos it's really soothing, kind of. Do U know what I mean? Am I making any sense here?)

Like I said, I went to Brighton at the weekend, which was pretty cool but a little weird too. It's really strange going to a seaside town when it is out of season. U know when U think of places like that U automatically think of thousands of tourists and music and hotdog stands and tacky shops and everything? Well, try and imagine that kind of place when all of those things R gone. It's just really bizarre. The pier was completely empty and everything was shut down with shutters. Even the seagulls looked miserable. Even though the wind was incredibly cold I still had an ice cream and a stick of rock just because that's the kind of thing U do when U go to the seaside, isn't it, even though I had to walk for miles to find somewhere that was open and selling them. I had to go on my own in the end cos Christie was busy which made me kind of sad too. U can get really lonely in places like that when there is no one around, even though I'm not the type that gets really lonely any more. (The trip was worth it in the end – I found a bootleg CD of the concert in Manchester, the one where U were wearing those silver spandex shorts and your right nipple was pierced and where Vid threw his guitar into the crowd at the end. That was an *amazing* concert, completely amazing, and I was pissed off with *Select* when they said U were, quote, 'a cynical money-making machine hell-bent on milking the fans for all they're worth'. I mean, why bother writing negative stuff like that? Does it make them feel *special* or *superior* to slag off the favourite band of loads of people? It makes me mad. It's so *selfish*.

R U interested in this kind of stuff? Me going on about my life? I hope U R. I know it can't be anything like your life but I also know U R not the kind of star who forgets where he came from. (Wilmslow, Manchester, born 25 October – I know all the details!) Maybe U could use it as inspiration for a song? U write about ordinary people, don't U? U can't imagine what that would do for me – it would make my whole life!

Did U get my last mail? It's just that my 'read receipts' haven't been coming back like the other two did. Maybe U R too busy or maybe something happened with the internet. Oh well. Hope U R feeling good. Will U write to me?

Love
Suzy

From:	DystopiaFan3@hotmail.com
To:	Plastic-Person@aol.com
Date:	Tuesday, December 21, 1.31 P.M.
Subject:	This winter!

The weather keeps getting colder. I ask myself 'Is this possible?' The weatherman on 4-CAST 24 seems to think so and he said yesterday that the temperatures R still dropping. Can U believe last night the temperature was minus 15 degrees? *Minus 15?* That's *so* cold. It was actually warmer in places like Reykjavik + Moscow + Oslo.

It makes me really sad to think of all the people in London who live on the streets with no food + shelter. How on earth do people survive in these kinds of temperatures I ask U? I always make sure I leave the homeless person at the tube station my change in the evening, especially at this festive time of year. It's just a little thing, isn't it, but every little bit helps or so they say.

Still nothing back from U – R U definitely getting my emails? I called my ISP's helpdesk last night to see if there was a way they could confirm my mails R getting through but apparently there isn't (even though the guy I spoke to was really unhelpful and I wouldn't be surprised if he just wanted to get rid of me so he could play Quake or something). So I'll just have to keep hoping, I guess. I'm not going to give up that U will reply.

How is the new album going? R U still working on it? I can imagine U hanging out at some really cool bar with your guitar strumming out the chords to a new tune that U had buzzing around in your head for weeks. Is that how U compose the songs? Or do they come to U in a blaze of sudden inspiration, like in the middle of the night or something? I know this is crazy of me but I worry so much that U will never release another record and all the world will ever have is *Plastic People*. Not that that would be a bad thing, it's just I sense U have much more to say to us all. I worry about crazy things like that and I know it's stupid of me, but there U go. Shoot me! I guess it must be so easy to burn yourself out with all the pressure U R under – it must be easy to lose your creative spark, just burn out.

I saw my doctor today (why am I even telling U this?).

He said that the condition I had is better now the medicine has started to have an effect. (It works OK apparently even with my regular prescription which was kind of worrying me and why I went to see him again in the first place. U hear stories of drugs reacting badly with one another, don't U.) I'm not a depressed person usually, it's just that sometimes life kind of gets me down, U know? Crazy things make me sad, like when I'm out with my parents and I look at them and think they've had over three-quarters of their lives already and that in 15 years time they probably won't be around any more. Yes, I know that's a stupid morbid thing to think and it's probably really unhealthy but there we go, I can't help it, that's me. But the medicine does help. I've even stopped listening to The Smiths + Morrissey (only kidding!). I heard that Vid Danton is taking Prozac although I know that can't be true cos he's such a fun guy and what with the kind of life U R all living. People like me can only dream about the opportunities U must have. U must be having an amazing time being in such a great + amazing band.

Do U want to know something that has really been bugging me? Why is it that there is a fan club for the band and a fan club for Vid Danton but no fan club for U? That is the most ridiculous thing ever! I can understand Vid Danton having a fan club cos he is a talented and popular individual and I am sure there R a lot of people that would really like to know more about him. But if he has one, why don't U? That's stupid. Everyone knows that U R the really talented one in the group and that Vid Danton just sings the songs that U have written for him. And yes, I suppose he is good-looking, but then U R really handsome too. So what's going on? When I realized this, I wrote straight to Revolution Records to tell them I thought this was a really bad decision and that something should be done about it. I offered to run the fan club too, by the way. We'll just have to wait and see if anything comes of it, but I just wanted U to know that the whole thing is really bad and that if U had a fan club I am sure the thousands of fans that know about U would join it at once. I would!

Big news! I have a 'blind date' tonight! His name is Simon and he is a friend of my boss here at work. She and her fiancé Andy R going out to see that new British movie *Vaudevillian* – she says that it is on special preview tomorrow night at a cinema in Soho. Andy has this friend, Simon, and he doesn't have anyone to take along with him. That's where I come in! I have to say I am quite excited about it because I haven't had much luck with men recently and from what I've heard Simon sounds like a really nice person and someone I'll probably like a lot. So I said I'd go along with them all. Now I have to worry about what I should wear and everything but that's a nice problem to have, isn't it, better than sitting at home on my own watching the weather channel. Anyway, wish me luck and I'll tell U all about it tomorrow.

I know U R busy and U don't have to do this if U don't want to but it would be amazing if U could send me a note or something in the snailmail, maybe a copy of a track list or something else from a gig that U have signed, something I could frame and put up next to the signed album? (Let me know and I'll send you my address.) That would be so cool!

Anyway, better run, lunch break almost over too soon again! I just hope U R feeling good about yourself and that U R happy. And if U get a moment I would be really happy to get a mail from U, even just one word.

Love
Suzy

Vid

21 December
Bethnal Green

The sky is grey, the colour of granite, shot through with livid seams of red as the sun dissolves into the darkness. An aeroplane overhead smokes a milky vapour trail behind it. Vid watches it pass across the windscreen, from left to right, as he waits at the junction for a green. The signal lights on the nose and on each wing tip of the plane beat out an ordered beat: *one* two three, *one* two three, *one* two three. Vid thumbs through the tracks of *Plastic People* on the in-car minidisc until he gets to track three, 'Suffocation', one of the ones he has not been able to memorise.

He parks in the lee of a tenement block off the Old Bethnal Green Road and heads up stairs that stink of piss. Frosty's flat is at the end of a long passageway cut into the side of this crumbling block. Satellite dishes hang like giant mushrooms on the soiled walls. Scabs of paint have peeled away from the walls; the discoloured plaster squares of the adjacent block look like a slice of mouldy Battenberg cake.

Frosty's is the last doorway off the passageway, separated from it by a heavy metal grille, and then an iron lattice fixed around the entrance to the flat. Frosty gets a lot of unwelcome callers. He insists that his customers leave with their purchases, little clingfilmed wraps of powders and pills, pressed beneath the tongue or inserted up the anus, but even if his patrons are frisked Frosty will still be secure. By the time the police have clattered up the six flights of stairs, broken through the remains of the first gate and brought their blowtorches or boltcutters to bear on the second, he will be watching the remnants of his stash dissolve into the whirlpool of the flushing toilet and observing their ham-fisted attempts via the CCTV camera he has fixed to the ceiling of the walkway.

Vid feels eyes following him as he tramps towards the flat. The sodium striplights beat down harshly, casting his shadow like a long stain on the concrete. Curtains twitch as he passes them, and yellow faces with hollow eyes slink back behind the opaque glass. He stiffens his collar and fixes his shades more snugly to his face.

At the end of the walkway a gaunt junkie with weeping abscesses pocking his face and neck and hands sits with his back propped against the damp parapet. A trail of snot and spit has wriggled down from his nose and is clotting in the cold. Vid instinctively shuffles over against the opposite wall as he passes. The man's teeth are jagged and sparse like the stakes of a crooked fence, yellowed with mould and decay. Matted friendship bracelets too wide for skinny wrists. White tracks on his forearms. He is missing a boot. His legs are splayed and twisted like the tree roots in the car park below. The eyes are those of the helpless junk fiend, glassy and dead; the pupils don't even twitch as Vid steps past him, hung in their web of bloody strands.

He buzzes the intercom and waits. He imagines Frosty

clomping impatiently across the bare floorboards of the front room and into the murky tunnel of the corridor.

'Yeah?'

'Hi.'

'Yeah?'

'There's a dead junkie out here, man.'

'That's Arthur. He's not, uh, dead.'

'He's not moving.'

'He's been mainlining all day. He's, like, uh, resting.' The speaker crackles with static, then clicks off.

Vid feels something brush against his shoe, then something crawling up the leather and onto the bony nub of his ankle. The junkie is on his belly now, wriggling towards him like a withered zombie and looking up at Vid with his desert eyes.

'Got any pills?'

'Fuck off me!' Vid yelps, kicking the hand away. An abscess has spilt frothy pus over the shiny cap of his Docs.

Vid buzzes again urgently. 'Can I come in?'

After a long pause: 'Yeah?'

'Can I come in?'

'Who goes there?'

'It's me. Vid.'

The speaker clicks off again and Vid has the itchy sensation of being observed. He turns to face the pocked façade of the twin tenement opposite. Something glints in a fourth-floor window, before orange curtains are swished across. He watches his reflection in the black lens of the camera. A clutch of small children has gathered at the end of the walkway. They are giggling and pointing at the prone junk fiend. One of them throws a small rock that clatters into him.

Then: 'Why didn't you say, man?'

The lock on the gate is buzzed and Vid pushes it aside. The second gate opens outwards and a succession of locks and bolts are unfastened, one by one, until the door is left to swing outwards. Vid follows the corridor into the depths of the dismal flat.

Heavy black curtains undulating in the breeze from broken windows. Feeble light in the front room from little clusters of candles fixed by their own spilt wax to the naked floorboards. The acrid tang of burning wick; the more pervasive undercurrent of weed and crack. The candles casting only cramped pools of jaundiced light and most of their glow devoured by the darkness. Faces cast in sallow shades by the flickering as the flames, briefy cowed by the breeze, right themselves again. Other dark figures flitting through the fringes of the candlelight like shadows passing through deep Atlantic trenches. A stereo playing the Dandy Warhols.

There is Whitey, cooking up in a spoon over a candle flame – 'Whitey' because of his hair the colour of milk. He looks up balefully and the flame of the candle catches his eyes, tranquil pools set in his junk-ravaged face. They are lizard's eyes: calm, placid, lifeless. Crumb is slouched against a wall, his knees drawn up tight against his chest and his forehead on his knees. His used works are on the floor beside his feet. A blob of blood has gathered in the crook of his elbow. Crumb is a pimp who works a couple of girls on the Great Eastern Road. His hands are the size of shovels. He is schizophrenic and prone to violent outbursts.

Vid squints into the gloom until he sees Frosty. This squat is Frosty's business premises. Vid has heard that he has a big flat over in Shoreditch, and other dealing flats like this all around the fringes of the city – his business empire. He is crouched over a kettle, holding a whisky miniature in the jet of steam rising from the spout. Inside the bottle a solution of acetone, water and powdered cocaine, together with whatever bulking agent the coke has been cut with. Vid watches reverentially as Frosty dips a long thin metal rod into the neck of the bottle. A large crystal coalesces around the end of the rod. With the circumspection of a child playing a fairground game of skill, Frosty slowly withdraws the rod without touching the side of the bottle, holding it steady so as not to dislodge the crystal. When it has been safely removed he shakes the crystal onto a pad of blotting paper to dry with a row of others.

'Hey, man,' Vid whispers, without realizing that he is whispering. No one looks up. Frosty finishes counting the crystals. There are eleven. He pours another measure into the bottle from a flask at his side.

'You want?' he says, offering him an empty Diet Coke can with a hole punched through the side. 'On the house – the taste of a new generation.' He is giggling somewhat crazily. Vid takes the can and fishes out his lighter. The can has been used before; the tin is warped and buckled from heat exposure and the base is blackened with scabrous ash. Vid plays the flame of the lighter onto the base and waits until the crack inside begins to deliquesce and melt and the thick white smoke begins to puff out of the hole. Vid greedily lowers his mouth to the hot hole and gulps in a mouthful.

'You doing all right?' asks Frosty.

'Yeah . . . No,' says Vid, confused. 'I don't know.'

'Christian can't make it tonight. He says he's kicking.'

'Yeah?' A head rush, tilting the floor on its side.

'Really. Like, can you even *believe* that? Like he'll last four hours with his habit. I have his prescription ready for when he comes to his senses.' Frosty takes another can and heats it up. 'Dr Frosty.'

'Listen, man,' Vid's voice echoes internally, his head aches, 'before we get started I need to place an order for some stuff.'

'Relax. The package'll be waiting at the usual time.'

'Yeah, sure, but I need something else.'

'Name it.'

Vid pauses, his forehead crinkling. 'Smack?'

'Yeah? Really? Smack?'

'Yeah.'

'Hmm, that's some serious raising of the stakes, man. You know what H can do to you, don't you? Look at *these* fucking junkies.' He indicates the derelicts in the room.

'I know. I need it. I need something to give me a *push*, you know? I've got, like, writer's block,' says Vid. 'I need something to break me out of it. I want to write my own songs, instead of singing stuff Jared's written all the time. But the words don't come. Nothing comes.'

'And some super-shamanic industrial-strength hallucinogens will do the trick? That's what you're thinking? That's the direction you want to go?'

'I-I-I don't know,' Vid stammers, unsure of the words; the can is smoking and his head hurts. 'Maybe. Smack's the only thing I haven't tried. The stuff I've been writing when I'm high on the other stuff – you know, the songs I told you about – it's just embarrassing, just worthless. I haven't even got the nerve to show them to the others, you know? It gets me down. I need, like, serious *help*.'

'You've been reading too much, man,' says Frosty. 'Way too much Burroughs and Thompson in your diet.'

'Can you get me some?'

Frosty pauses. 'Sure I can. How much do you want?'

'I'm not sure. A grand's worth, maybe? Enough for a decent supply.'

'*OK*,' Frosty says, nodding, clucking his tongue. 'That'd be a decent supply. I'll see what I can do.'

'I need it soon.'

'Soon?'

'Yeah – I don't want to lose any time.'

Vid unplugs a long stoppered tube from his jacket pocket and tips out two tablets. They each swallow down a tablet dry. He squeezes his eyes closed and watches the explosions of colour bloom against his eyelids, the stereo sounding as if it is playing underwater. Someone has changed the CD: Nine Inch Nails are playing. White noise and distortion, a massive weight of static that batters its way inside his head, he is tipping back on his haunches and sprawling in the dust and grime on the floor, his back propped against the peeling paint of the wall. He sees the room through acid eyes, closes them again, patterns of light exploding on the lids. The heavy beat of the drums echoes, a meaty thud followed by the patter of tinny repetition. The line between reality and delusion is blurring, the music might be playing backwards, he doesn't know, someone screams or doesn't scream.

Alex

21 December
Restaurant

The table is at the Oxo Tower looking down onto the cold brown waters of the river as it sludges its way through the city towards the sea. Tug boats are guiding a Scandinavian cruise ship, a space-age behemoth, through the deeper channels to its berth deeper into the city. The gunmetal sky is darkening with encroaching black fingers. The restaurant is full – a Christmas party is taking place in one corner, everyone wearing paper hats and popping crackers and getting drunk.

Michael Kaiser is in his early middle-age but dresses younger, always in black, always – whatever the weather and time of year – with Ray-Bans on or in his pocket. Today he is wearing a black suit from Prada with a plain white ribbed T-shirt. His shades lie on the chequered tablecloth between them, next to the bottle of Perrier and his half-finished plate of potato terrine, the flaky potatoes topped with tar-coloured coins of salty fresh truffle.

'I appreciate everything you've done with the band,' he is saying, a loaded forkful of potato hovering over his plate. 'I mean, we all know how *temperamental* they can get, sometimes. We've all seen the tantrums.'

'Yeah,' says Alex. 'Sometimes it's hard but, you know, it's worthwhile. I get a kick out of it.'

'And when they shift the units they shift, *I* get a kick out of it too,' Kaiser half-jokes, slotting the forkful into his mouth. He has an unusually shaped face, Alex thinks. His jaw is so wide and his chin is so square that his face is narrower at the top than it is at the bottom. He is made up of hard straight-edges, completely lineal, the shape described not oval or even square, but trapezoid. Little black nuggets for eyes are inset beneath the glowering ledge of his brows. Below that chunky nose, his face is covered by a furze of beard, neatly trimmed.

He scares Alex.

'Alex,' Kaiser says. 'We ought to get onto the business. The contract with the band expires in three months—'

'Ten weeks,' Alex supplies quickly. Then, 'I think.'

'Ten weeks, yes. We really have to get around to sorting out a new one. Something a bit more permanent. Something that would reward the band for their success. It's clear they are being undervalued at the moment, but then we could never have guessed six months ago how successful they were going to be. Not even in our wildest dreams.'

'Mmm,' Alex says, trying to hide his nervousness by concentrating on a piece of bruschetta.

'I've spoken to the board and the parent company and I've got some indicative numbers I'd like you to cast your eye over.' He reaches into his briefcase and pulls out a sheaf of papers. 'You'll have to have a think about this, of course, but the headline figures go like this: twenty-five per cent for the band over a three-album deal, plus a signing bonus of one million each and an equivalent slice of the merchandising revenue. Sound fair?'

'Jeez, yeah,' says Alex. 'More than fair.'

'I know you're in a slightly invidious situation here, Alex, what with your friendship with the band and your professional obligations to the label. I know it's a difficult one to handle, but I guess it's my duty to the shareholders to remind you that you are employed by Revolution.'

'I know,' Alex whimpers.

'I'm not trying to get heavy – it's just that Dystopia are crucial to the label's future. We've made some pretty big investments after the album's done so well. If anything happened—' he slices a hand across his throat '—we'd *all* be down the dole office together.'

Alex laughs, nervously, and pours out the rest of the Perrier.

Suzy

From: DystopiaFan3@hotmail.com
To: Plastic-Person@aol.com
Date: Wednesday, December 22, 1.42 P.M.
Subject: Ice!

The blind date last night was a bit of a disaster. Simon and I didn't really get on so great. I spent ages getting ready and my flatmate said I looked great and that Simon wouldn't stand a chance. Me and Simon spoke a bit at the beginning of the evening while we were waiting for Andy to get some drinks and my boss to come back from the toilets but after that he didn't really seem to be interested in conversation. Even when he was speaking to me I was wondering if it was just because silence would be more embarrassing. I even tried to start him talking again but there was no persuading him. So it's back to the drawing board again I suppose. I try hard to keep a positive outlook on these things but I'd be lying if I said it didn't get me down. I mean, whenever U go shopping U see all these couples walking around hand in hand and they all seem so happy. And there's me, wandering around the precinct on my own, usually listening to Dystopia on my Walkman and shutting everything else out.

When I got back last night I saw the show on TV about your tour to America and that was great for cheering me up. The whole thing sounds so amazing! I taped the show of course and I'm going to watch it again when I get home. I'm wondering at the moment if I can afford to fly out to Las Vegas so I could watch your first ever concert over there. It's quite expensive I think but I have lots of holiday left and it would be the most incredible experience to be there that one special time. And money is no good just sitting in the bank, is it! I'll let U know if I decide to go. I'm thinking that I will, if I can.

Did U notice U have been in the papers a lot this week? Don't tell me, stupid question – U probably have a press officer who tells U all about when U R in the papers and on the TV and stuff like that, right? If U missed it, it was mostly the usual stuff – complaints about the videos being too graphic or the bad influence the music might have on children. But there was this one story in VOX about 'Stars' Other Halves' that supposedly was all about the less well known partners of famous people who R in the spotlight. It was such salacious gossip, completely *rubbish*! How do these stories get printed? I wonder if papers have any dignity at all any more, even the proper papers like the *Guardian* and the *Independent*. There were all kinds of celebrities from the worlds of music and TV that were mentioned. U were in there too – there was a picture of U holding hands with a girl they said was called 'Gretta Conroy'. The picture was obviously taken when U weren't expecting it – U were both next to your car and there were plastic Tesco bags with shopping in them on the floor. She looked pretty average which was the first clue that she wasn't your 'celebrity other half'. U know, it's these kind of false stories that give the British press such a bad name in the rest of the world. It almost makes me *ashamed*. Journalists just have no integrity these days. (Need I remind U what they did to Princess Di?) And to think I wanted to be a journalist when I was a girl. I don't know *what* I was thinking. I think U should sue them like Elton John so that they know U won't take that kind of BS lying down.

My boss has just told everyone that we can all go home. The temperature in the office is now officially zero degrees (!) (cos the boiler is broken) and she says that the office will be closed until the boiler has been fixed. That won't be until after Christmas, apparently, so I hope U have a really MERRY CHRISTMAS! I don't have email at home so I can't email for a while. I'm not exactly sure when I'll be back here so I hope U can survive without my messages for a few days!! But maybe U'll find time to email me a reply? I really hope so. That would be about the best Christmas present anyone could ever possibly give me I think!

Love

Suzy

Frosty

22 December
Night bus

What is he doing here? First thing in the morning that car goes straight to the garage for whatever scraping and gouging it needs to get it started again. No, better than that, first thing in the morning it goes straight to the scrapyard where it belongs, and he goes straight to a decent garage to buy himself a new motor. The last week has been profitable. His debtors have paid up on time, more or less, and his creditors seem to be happy with the structured repayment plans he has suggested. But this relief is short-term and the demands will soon start to pile up again. All he ever does is tread water.

Two-thirty a.m. and the bus is choked with zombies, a proper legion of the damned. Zombies retching up viscous chunks dyed by the colour of their last cocktail. Zombies sleeping on the shoulders of other zombies or with their noses squished flat against the sweaty windows. Zombies singing, or talking in yells to their neighbours. The zombie next to Frosty is, thankfully, only a Sleeper although Frosty's perch at the front of the bus is within close proximity of both Retchers and Yellers.

Why is it so difficult to find a cab going east from the

city at this time of night? Don't all the cab drivers live in places like Woodford and Forest Gate? They sped past him with their yellow lights switched off. Even the minicabs have vanished. He would have gladly accepted the furtive offer of transport from those shady types at the top of Charing Cross Road, even with their notion of the red stoplight as an abstract concept, and their disdain for other traffic akin to the downhill skier's attitude to slalom flags. But he received no offers of transport as he zigzagged through the back streets and, much later, broke through onto Bishopsgate. The best carrion was obviously elsewhere.

And what persuaded him that having that first hot dog outside the Bank of England was such a good idea? He wasn't even hungry, but the smell of the meat and onions frying on the grill was too appetizing to resist. Never mind the fact that the thin red tube wedged between the doughy bap was probably comprised of the bits of a cow that no right-minded carnivore would deign to touch: hooves, brains, innards, genitals. Never mind his previous experiences with these revolting victuals, usually entailing stomach cramps and the squits the following morning. You would think that the weight of this previous damning evidence would have been enough to steer him away from the smoking little cart and its Armenian attendant. You would be wrong. The smell of the sizzling food, the indeterminate wait for a bus, and the sub-zero temperatures all contrived to force him to purchase not one, but two, of the noisome articles. The tilt and canter of the bus, worse than a cross-Channel ferry in a force-nine gale, is already conspiring with the contents of his stomach to make him feel wretched. And meanwhile he is as sober as a judge. He had to be to do what he has just done.

The zombie wedged tightly in the same seat with him is dribbling onto his shoulder. This may not have been a recent development, since the shoulder of Frosty's Gestapo-esque long leather jacket is slick with spittle. Juddering with revulsion, Frosty brings his arm sharply up and the zombie's head flops through ninety degrees, now dangling into the aisle. He does not stir a jot. Frosty is feeling progressively worse.

A party of Yellers boards the bus at Liverpool Street. The bus is already cramped, and these additional passengers tip the balance from hardly bearable to absolutely untenable. The Yellers are clearly City types with too much disposable income and too little sense of how to spend it constructively. Frosty numbers a few such types amongst his best clients. Usually only for coke, though; the prospect of mainlining turns most of them white with fear, although one of his longest-serving junkies is a banker at a major City bank. The party decides the top deck is where the action is at, and they troop up the stairs and circulate into the few empty seats, the rest of them standing with arms wrapped around one another, surfing as the bus sways around the corners. One of them plumps down into a double seat that everyone else – even the most thoroughly inebriated – has scrupulously avoided. A previous tenant has puked his guts out onto the worn fabric. The natural dent in the seat has served as a shallow reservoir, holding a thin puddle of the red goop that looks like chunky soup, and the rest has splattered onto the back of the seat in front and down into the treads of the floorboards. The vomit splashes noisily as he lowers himself into it. His sensate neighbours explode into fits but he is already asleep, dribbling, the icky fluid already soaking into the expensive thread of his Armani suit. The nascent Retchers on board blanch as sympathetic bubbles of bile burst in their throats.

This makes Frosty feel considerably worse.

The City types start up a lusty chorus of 'Swing Low Sweet Chariot'. One of them is harassing a pretty French girl. The bus slowly crawls up the Bethnal Green Road. There are still miles to go, and on a night bus the miles seem to take an eternity to unwind. The bus swims along the dark channels like an infirm whale, the cars and vans and bikes swarming around it like pilot fish.

Previous night

Earlier: Frosty swallowed up by the tube and shuttled into the city. City suits, hiding the worn lines of their fatigue behind the day's papers, sitting in ordered rows as their trains stagger back east. Frosty pitied them. He did not envy the stale routine of their lives.

He had cleared his customers from the Bethnal Green squat and hidden his stash back under the floorboards, knocking the nails back in and spreading the mangy carpet across. That squat is an almost perfect place to deal from. The council can't evict him without serious legal effort, and even if the police were to break in, they'd probably miss his stash. Even if they did find it, they'd never prove it was *his* stash. They could suspect as much as they liked, but they'd never prove it beyond reasonable doubt. And he'd get the best brief money could buy; his father would make sure of that. The only consequence would be the financial hit he would take, and even that would be easy to absorb. Roll with the punch; bounce straight back through his other operations.

Vid wanted the gear quickly. Frosty had shaken his head and tutted like a mechanic addressing the symptoms of a sick car, and said that it would cost him more at such short notice. A lot more. As soon as Vid was jolting into the grip of his dream/nightmare, Frosty called Zorba to ask whether he could help. He could: he knew a man who knew a man.

Despite his familiarity with the area and the contact he had arranged to meet, Frosty was nervous as he rode the escalator out of the subterranean depths at the Angel. He was straying into a market for goods that he was not completely accustomed to and the uncertainty, for some-one who trafficked in a business such as his, was enough to make him shiver.

Zorba arranged to meet in the Brigstock Arms, a small pub located off the main drag of Upper Street. It is a quiet pub; not frequented by the wealthy inhabitants of the area who prefer the busier bars on the main road. Inside: a pool table with faded baize; brass fittings fixed to the wall; over the bar a photograph of the pub football team, now disbanded; a draping of tinsel and other Christmas deco-rations; the pub's prized artefact – an old-fashioned Wur-litzer jukebox, the sort where you can watch as the seven-inch records are plucked out of a vinyl cylinder by a jolting mechanical arm and slapped down onto a platter to be played. Meat Loaf's 'Dead Ringer for Love' is playing as Frosty steps into the pub's smoky, garish atmosphere.

Zorba has an interest in the freehold and uses it as a front for his illegitimate businesses, of which there are many. Zorba is sitting at the bar supping a pint when Frosty walks in, one shovel-like hand clasped around his Guinness, his fat sovereign ring glinting gold against the sooty beer.

'Hey, Zorba,' says Frosty.

'Mmmm,' says Zorba, wiping froth from his nose. Zorba is pale, the dark half-rings under his eyes seeming to throb beneath his pasty, semi-translucent skin. He is a fat man lacking the fat man's hearty aspect; bearing his weight like a burden, his cheeks sunken and sallow. His teeth are always grimy, little patches of gunge sticking into the crevices between his incisors and creeping out like mould. Zorba is wearing his usual business uniform, an unwashed red Adidas tracksuit from the seventies, complete with the three-line white action stripes running down the arms and legs. His distended belly wobbles through the fabric and swings out over his groin like a fleshy cowl. He is smoking a fat joint down to the last scruffy nugget; he skewers the end between long fingernails crusted with half moons of scum.

'Have you got it?' Frosty asks. He wants to be here for as little time as possible.

'Yeah,' says Zorba. 'Highly fucking irregular request, this amount. But I got it.' He pats a bulky A4-sized Jiffy bag on the bar, which is underneath his copy of the *Standard*.

'Great. You want to go somewhere else to do the business? A little more discreet?'

'My motor's outside,' Zorba says. 'Lemme just finish this joint.' He puffs away the last millimetre and flicks the roach into an ashtray.

The transaction takes place in the seats of Zorba's Mercedes, right outside the pub itself.

'Not easy to get hold of this much H these days,' he says, handing over the jiffy bag. 'H is pretty elusive.'

'I'm sure,' says Frosty. Another car passes in the quiet street, its dipped lights filling the Mercedes's interior as it rolls by.

'The Met are keeping a careful eye on it, so I had problems finding a reliable source.' Zorba fiddles with the radio and tunes into a station playing a Dystopia number that Frosty likes. He wonders what Vid is doing just now. 'What d'you need H for? Bit outside of your usual game, innit?'

'It's not for me,' says Frosty. 'And I've no idea what it's needed for.'

'You got my cash?'

Frosty drops a sealed envelope into Zorba's lap. 'Don't spend it all at once.'

The pubs have called time long before he makes his way back down to the platform and the southbound train. Mice scamper between the tracks. The open doors of the carriages suck in the throng from the platform, and Frosty is pressed between two drunken lawyers barking out the intricacies of a demerger they are devising. One clings onto the overhead rail, his sopping armpit inches away from Frosty's nose. The carriage is hot, and the frantic atmosphere is underpinned by a sense of imminent panic.

Frosty abandons the Northern Line at Bank, and reluctantly eschews the last Central Line train heading east. The freezing air slaps him as he emerges into the clear dark night. He walks through the quiet canyons of the Square Mile to Spitalfields, where he leaves the package in a carrier bag in the same industrial bin they always use. A heavy bank of cloud is shouldering its way over the city, and a thin slice of moon emits a sickly light. The city is unnaturally quiet, as if holding its breath, waiting.

Suzy

From: DystopiaFan3@hotmail.com
To: Plastic-Person@aol.com
Date: Monday, December 27, 8.30 A.M.
Subject: Why R U ignoring me?

The boiler was fixed faster than we thought. I got in this morning and still no email from U. What have I done? Have I upset U in some way? If so, please tell me. I know that U have received mail from me at *least* twice, so why haven't U replied? I was really looking forward to getting back into work so I could check my mail because I was so sure U would have sent me something and now I feel stupid and my whole day is ruined. I understand that U R probably busy right now, getting ready for the tour and doing everything else that U have to do, but is it too much to ask to receive just a short email, even if it is to say 'Sorry Suzy I'm too busy right now?' I don't think that's too much to ask even if U R busy. Is it?

I'm too angry to write any more. I just hope U have an excuse for ignoring me, that's all. It's not like U, or at least I think it is not like U.

From: DystopiaFan3@hotmail.com
To: Plastic-Person@aol.com
Date: Monday, December 27, 1.30 P.M.
Subject: FWD: Why R U ignoring me?

I got in this morning and still no email for me from U. What have I done? Have I upset U in some way? If so, please tell me.

<SNIP>

I've just reread the email I sent U this morning and I'm really sorry if I sounded mad. I was just disappointed, that's all. I just had this idea that U were going to mail me, I don't know why, just a premonition or something. I've been looking forward to checking my mail over Xmas and I guess I mailed U when I still had the 'red mist' in front of my eyes. I know U R busy and I shouldn't expect to receive mail from U but it still hurt when there was nothing in my in box this morning. I guess I *am* sensitive – like everyone says.

Anyway, sorry again, OK? R we still friends? I hope so.

I need cheering up. Christmas was a pretty depressing time for me. I went to my parents for our usual Christmas meal on Christmas Day and that was great, them stuffing their faces with turkey (I had veggie nut loaf) and then watching the Queen's Speech and everything. V. traditional. Christie was there too and we had a talk about stuff which was nice as we haven't spoken for a while. My parents seemed older than I remembered them but they were happy and full of laughs and my Dad even got out a bottle of whisky from his cabinet after the Queen which he only ever reserves for the most special occasions, so that was great. But then for the rest of the time I stayed at home in my flat. It was cold and my flatmate wasn't there so I spent most of the time listening to *Plastic People* and staring out of the window. Despite being so cold there was no snow. For a weird reason that really upset me. I guess I had kind of built up my expectations too much.

I'm going to go now because I'm having a hard day with pretty much everything and I don't much feel like writing now. I'll write more tomorrow.

Love
Suzy

From: DystopiaFan3@hotmail.com
To: Plastic-Person@aol.com
Date: Tuesday, December 28, 1.37 P.M.
Subject: Anyone out there?

Still nothing from my mysterious email correspondent. Where could he be? What is he doing? I'd love to know. I'm still waiting for that email . . .

I'm sitting at my desk staring at my screen thinking of what I can tell U. What has been happening in my life since the last time I wrote to U? My doctor has prescribed more new pills for me to 'take the edge off my anxiety' as he put it. I had one just before my lunch and I'm feeling comfortable and relaxed right now. The snow is falling really softly outside the window and the road is empty because of the ice.

I had a dream about U last night. I was at the concert at Wembley Arena last year but I had a backstage ticket and I was watching U from the side of the stage. U were concentrating on playing your guitar + singing and U didn't notice me there. I watched for the whole set, just standing there quietly, watching + enjoying the show.

The office is cold again today. I have gloves on and it is difficult to type. I'll go now and email more tomorrow.

From:	DystopiaFan3@hotmail.com
To:	Plastic-Person@aol.com
Date:	Wednesday, December 29, 1.38 P.M.
Subject:	Gretta Conway?

There was another picture of U yesterday that was in a lot of the papers. It was taken before a première, I think, or something like that. The story said it was last weekend. U were there with this strange + mysterious 'Gretta Conway' person. She was holding on to your arm with a weird half-smile on her face and U were just staring at the camera with this blank, cold expression. U obviously know who this girl is since U have now been pictured with her twice and the papers R all starting to say that she is your girlfriend. I don't believe that for a second. Yes, she is really pretty (if U like skinny girls) but I know that just cos someone has a pretty face that doesn't mean that U will automatically like them. U R a deeper person than that I think. I have been thinking about Gretta Conway since I saw that second picture and I reckon she must work for Revolution Records and that she is your personal assistant or something like that. She was helping U with your shopping in that first picture and maybe U needed an escort for that premiere and she was available. There R a lot of possible explanations and I'm not going to believe the rubbish in the papers. But what's the news from the 'horse's mouth', as they say? Am I right? Am I wrong?

Please write. I want to hear from *U*. Please?

From: DystopiaFan3@hotmail.com
To: Plastic-Person@aol.com
Date: Thursday, December 30, 1.55 P.M.
Subject: FWD: Gretta Conway?

There was another picture of U yesterday that was in a lot of the papers. It was taken before a première, I think, or something like that.

<SNIP>

Another theory! I know that U have a sister and I realized that although I have pictures of U (hundreds!) and your mother and father (a few) I have never actually found a picture of her. I'm wondering if these R pictures of her? Maybe she has decided to come out into the public eye now? Maybe 'Gretta Conway' is just a code-name for her, her 'pseudonym' (sp?). This sounds a lot more plausible than the nonsense in the papers. Am I on the right track?

Alex

2 January
Barcelona

A hotel, ten paces from the throng of the Placa de Catalunya and its whirlpool of traffic and tourists, the seething angry roil of humanity. The building is a mangy paperback in the bookshelf of the narrow street, crouched between antiquated tall hardcovers and shiny squat new editions. The room on the fourth floor is bland, nondescript furnishings, walls painted a grey shade of beige; his clothes pooling from his open suitcase like spilt guts. Pyrenees rain is battering down against the single window, an insistent thrumming at first and then a rushing, tumbling hiss as the storm breaks. A peal of thunder unfurls directly overhead: it sounds like a firecracker and Alex twitches, startled, on the bed. Car alarms are triggered and start wailing. He gets off the bed, dressed only in his boxer shorts, and takes a bottle of Evian from the minibar. He takes a deep draught as an upside-down tree of lightning spreads its branches out from the furious darkness. The peal of thunder is immediate, the window rattling in its frame. He looks out into the street below: cars crawling into the choked delta of the square; people scurrying for shelter, some with umbrellas blown inside out, others with maps and guidebooks held over their heads.

Alex decided not to stay with the rest of the band. He needs time to think. He has disconnected the phone in case Kaiser calls.

He returns to the bed and settles back down inside the cordon formed by the pages of the contract he has spread across the blankets. He compares the figures with the spreadsheet that Kaiser gave him. Revolution's offer dwarfs what Vid would earn with the new company – and if he goes to them the others will get nothing.

He sips the water.

Astrid

3 January
Barcelona

The studio in Barcelona, freezing cold, a ten-room mansion in the Barri Gòtic – well away from the tourists and pickpockets and street artists and pimps choking Las Ramblas and its snaking tributaries – complete with stucco façade and with ceramic mosaics decorating the walls and ceiling and chimneys. A single room on the top floor of the mansion, walls white-washed and framed posters, one of a girl exposing huge cleavage leaning out of a window with the line ROOM WITH A VIEW underneath and another displaying the artwork for *Plastic People*, hung on nails driven into the bricks. The floor is dark polished oak, ending with open French doors, with gaps where the glass should be, leading onto a stone balcony, overlooking the narrow street below which is still sweating out last night's rain – narrow enough to make it possible to touch the balustrade of the balcony opposite.

There are the following items in the room: three tall palms, a cactus, window boxes full of blooming flowers; a widescreen TV, with muted sound, playing a DVD of *Enter the Dragon*, Bruce Lee screaming silently at the camera; a laptop computer linked to a mixing desk by a nest of wires and cables, blinking lights and gauges like a flight deck; three guitars (two acoustic, one bass), a bank of keyboards, a set of drums, a 1960s-style microphone on a stand, four Marshall amps; a deck of Tarot cards, an old ouija board, three books by Aleister Crowley; a stack of CDs and minidiscs and DAT tapes; bottles of Evian and Cava and Bud; some empty, food-splattered pizza boxes from Dominoes and take-out cartons from an Indian; an antique hand mirror dusted with tracks of cocaine, some poppers, several bongs, a large polythene bag of hash hanging from the door handle.

A DAT tape of the band rehearsing is playing on the stereo. The band are listening to it, while lounging on leather sofas and pouffes: Jared, wearing a sleeveless vest with the word 'SPUNKY' written across it and creased red leather trousers, his hair gunked into daggered spikes by means of a pot of ultra-expensive French hair gel; Astrid, skintight ribbed top and short skirt, red knee-length boots, feeding olives and scraps of Catalan sausage to her chihuahua Keith (Keith is wearing a diamond necklace glinting in the noon sunlight. He yips and totters excitedly on his back legs till she flips another slice of sausage at him); Vid doodling on an A4 tablet with a magic marker, Ray-Bans clamped around his eyes, looking perplexed, a half-finished bottle of Cava in his hand, picking at a plate of paella; Damien sitting out on the balcony, swinging his legs over the alleyway, a spliff dangling from his lips, plucking a tune out of the bass in his lap.

'I mean, just *listen* to that,' Jared is saying suddenly, getting up to pace across the floor, frowning.

'Hey,' says Alex, putting his head through the open door.

'It needs some work,' mutters Astrid, scrubbing her forehead. Vid sounds bored on the DAT, like he is only partially concentrating on the song. He gets only about half of the lyrics right.

'Hey,' repeats Alex, moving further into the room, more cautiously.

Jared stabs his finger on a remote and kills the playback. 'It's like, what does this have to do with the song I wrote?' He picks up a sheaf of sheet music, waves it accusingly. 'Like, where do these extra lyrics come from, exactly?'

'Hey, Alex,' says Vid, looking up from his pad. 'Jared's just complaining that my spontaneousness is, you know, bad for his precious music or something.'

'*Spontaneity*,' corrects Jared. 'And spontaneity has its time and place. But this isn't a jamming session, man. We are rehearsing. These songs are *finished*. They're on the *album*. Now we just have to make sure they show at least a passing resemblance when we play them live. This is why we're here.'

Alex holds up his hands. 'Sounded pretty good to me,' he says and then, by way of an explanation, 'I was listening from out in the street. The windows are open.'

'There aren't any windows,' says Damien, pointing at the empty spaces in the wall, the shutters locked back.

Alex clears a space on a low table with a skyline of bottles and glasses spread out over it, and sits down.

'Remind me again why we put up with you,' Jared says to him, ejecting the DAT tape and tossing it onto a pile of other tapes. It slithers down the slope and onto the floor. 'I mean, you know *nothing* about music, do you?'

'Because I get results, maybe?' suggests Alex, querulously.

'Oh yeah. I keep forgetting,' Jared gibes. 'All those results you get.'

'Shall we try it again?' suggests Astrid.

'I saw a mime artist today. He was called Toni Macaroni,' offers Vid, ignoring the suggestion.

'Yeah,' says Jared. 'From the top.'

'Is anyone interested in Toni Macaroni?' asks Vid, pacing. 'I thought we could hire him for the tour. A warm-up act or something. What d'you think? Pretty, like, original? Like, far out?'

'Great idea, Vid, just great. You're a genius,' sighs Jared. Damien has walked back out onto the balcony, sighing with boredom.

'Shall we do it again?' repeats Astrid, trying to maintain the shreds of her enthusiasm.

Vid sighs, a long expulsion of breath. 'Nah, I'm too bushed,' he says, lounging deeper into the sofa. 'Later maybe?' He flicks on the television: a Spanish gameshow where the house band plays songs and the contestants have to dance to them.

'Come on, man,' prompts Jared, picking up one of the acoustic guitars, slipping the strap over his shoulder. 'We've gotta play this until it's perfect. And right now it's not, you know, perfect.'

'Not even close,' agrees Astrid.

'Work, work, work,' mutters Vid, muting the TV. There are adverts playing: something about sanitary towels blends into a Budweiser plug.

Damien resets the drum machine, a neat black box with a hand-written label saying DOKTOR AVALANCHE on top, then fetches the bass and plugs it into his amp – a clatter of feedback; Vid slouches to the mike stand and brings the mike down level with his throat so he can hunch over it; Astrid shoos Keith into an adjoining room and plays a scale on her keyboard; Alex drops onto the vacated sofa and rests his feet on a pouffe.

They pump out 'Disappear Here'. Jared strumming out the chords, harmonizing the backing vocals; Doktor Avalanche playing out a perfectly timed beat, neatly ordered bars that Astrid decorates with keyboard noodling; Vid singing the lyrics from a sheet in his hand, getting them largely right, his voice sounding powerful with an edge of hoarseness in the upper registers; Astrid's fingers stabbing down on the keyboard, layering textures and ambient effects (whale-song played backwards; an industrial drill; distorted explosions; feedback). Alex is tapping his foot and nodding his head, an expression of deliberate concentration on his face. Contrived, thinks Astrid, feeling like laughter – what does Alex know about music? He likes Celine Dion and Mariah Carey, for crying out loud. He liked the Kitchen Bitches, with their three-second half-life. Who remembers *them*? He's not qualified for this.

'That's it,' Vid says when the song is finished. 'I need a break.'

'OK,' Jared agrees, shutting off the recorder. 'We'll meet up here again at, say, five? Enough time to get some lunch, some sleep, whatever.'

'Anyone want to get a bite to eat?' Vid asks.

'Why not,' says Astrid, bored.

'Me too,' says Alex. 'I'm starved.'

'Follow me,' says Vid, leading them down the stairs and out into the narrow streets. The temperature is cool, still wet from last night's storm; the sun fills the thoroughfare only briefly when it reaches its apex. For the rest of the day the tall tenements on either side reduce the sky to a thin, wispy ribbon between the roofs. Vid leads them through a maze of backstreets until they enter a broad plaza deep in the residential heart of the city, cafés and bars around the periphery. Vid picks a bar and they head inside.

'Any news on our new contract?' Astrid asks as they take a table, ordering beers.

'Nah, not really,' Alex lies, looking at his fingernails. 'Revolution say they'll get round to it eventually, but I haven't seen anything concrete yet. It's no problem.'

'What do we do? Wait? Look around?' Their meals arrive: calamari rings, strips of rabbit, salads, sausage, salami, bottles of Cava.

Alex munches a hunk of crusty bread dipped in olive oil. 'I think we wait. There's no rush. We don't want to appear, you know, too *keen* or anything. We have to look a bit aloof, like we've got other offers to think about – the secret of negotiation. Anyway, it might not hurt to play this out a bit. You *could* fish for a better offer.'

'Leave Revolution?' asks Astrid. Vid is paying no attention, absently staring into his salad, then up to the TV supported on a bracket in the corner: a plump housewife dancing to a cheesy version of 'La Bamba' on the quiz show.

'Why not?' Alex says. 'We're not tied to them after this album. We just want to get the best deal we can get. If it's with them, fine, if not . . . we'll just go elsewhere.'

'I guess,' Astrid says. 'It's just . . . well, it's just I guess you feel a sense of loyalty and everything. You know, them being the first label to show an interest in us. Tough to just leave them now we're making it.'

'Made it,' corrects Alex. 'And, anyway, you can't live your life like that. You got to look out for number one in this business. You think if the next album bombs they'll show *you* any loyalty? That's not how this industry works. Trust me, I know.'

'Yeah, I guess. I can't help feeling we owe them, though.'

'It's natural,' Alex says smoothly. 'Look, just wait a week or two and see what happens. We'll, like, cross whatever bridge needs to be crossed when we get to it.'

Astrid nods, thinking. 'Aren't you supposed to work for them?' she asks.

'Technically, yeah,' he says. 'But I've got your best interests at heart, don't I? Anyway, if you get a better deal I'm counting on being invited along too. You know?'

'Goes without saying,' says Vid, munching and staring, not concentrating.

'Good squid?' asks Alex, pointing at Astrid's plate.

'Yeah, it's good,' she says, slicing a bit with her knife.

Suzy

From: DystopiaFan3@hotmail.com
To: RockGod4@hotmail.com
Date: Monday, January 3, 1.38 P.M.
Subject: Why so cruel to me?

When I tried to send emails to your old address my delivery receipts bounced straight back to me and said that the address was not recognized. I was really *devastated*. I thought that something must have happened to U, then that maybe my emails have never been getting through to U and that I've just been wasting my time with all these messages. Then it came to me – I realized that U must have changed your address. Why would U do that? I mean, that's so *cruel*! I emailed the web master at the celebrity email site and asked him if he could check out the link and see if it had been broken. He told me that it was broken and that U had changed your address. He has been searching for U for the past FOUR DAYS and he has finally found U again. That's FOUR DAYS when I haven't been able to email U. Do U know what that FEELS like? He also told me that U were emailing a lot just before U changed addresses so I also know that U have been on-line and that U must have read my other messages. What does it feel like to be found out?

Why would U be so mean + cruel to me? What have I ever done to U to deserve this kind of treatment? All I have been doing for the last six months is thinking about U and the band and telling everyone how amazing U R, doing my bit to help U get the break U deserve. I must be your best fan. I think I have contributed in my own small way to your rise to fame + fortune so WHY WHY WHY have U decided to be so heartless to me? All I wanted was a simple 'HI' from U, how many times have I told U that? And now I feel as if my whole life has been ruined and I am feeling worse than I did before the doctor gave me the Prozac. I felt so low that I thought about swallowing a whole bottle of aspirins cos the whole world seemed like it was against me again. Do U even care how I feel? Do U care that I can't listen to your music any more cos it just makes me angry + mad?

It just makes me mad that a person who says that he does everything for his fans could behave in such a SHIT way like this. Excuse my language, but as U can tell I am SERIOUSLY upset. I am upset enough to wonder if my last six months haven't been wasted completely on U. I NEVER thought I would hear myself saying that.

I'm going to give U one last chance to show me that U R a nice guy and that everything U say about your fans being important to U is true and not a load of show-business lies and double-talk. I'm going to skip work tomorrow and be at the Aroma coffee shop outside Liverpool Street station between three and four in the afternoon. I know U R busy but I think U owe it to me to tell me in person that U R sorry and that U didn't mean to hurt my feelings. I was going to send U a picture of me so U will know what I look like but I think I'll wait until U can see me 'in the flesh'. I obviously know what U look like and I will keep my eyes peeled for U.

I probably shouldn't be giving U another chance after the way U have treated me (the story of my life!) but I'm the forgiving type – another of my better qualities. I'll be at Aroma tomorrow and I hope U R too.

Frosty

Frosty wakes at twelve and surfaces at four. The afternoon crackles with cold. Long icicles hang from the eaves of the roof and stretch down outside his bedroom window like the bars of a cell. The feeble sunlight is not even able to make them drip. A bank of clouds frowns over the city, the grey deepening like a bruise into the east. It looks like rain, or snow.

The answerphone is blinking with a message. As he prepares a pot of black coffee his father's voice is unwound and replayed, a reminder of their appointment for dinner tonight at eight. Frosty had forgotten. He drinks the coffee. He plays Tekken for an hour on his PlayStation. He wonders what he should wear to meet his father. Making an effort will probably be the easier option in the long run, and so he puts on his Comme des Garçons suit, with a white shirt. Because the temperature is flirting with the minus figures, he pulls on a wool overcoat and sets off.

Virgin Records

Frosty gets off the bus at Oxford Street and goes into Virgin in search of some much needed new CDs. The time is seven-forty. The doors are wide open and snow is billowing inside, turning the ten feet of floor by the entrance into a slushy mess. The temperature inside Virgin is arctic: clouds of breath steam up from the sheltering customers and mini-icicles are hanging from the listening posts next to the door. A metal band is playing a set on the stage at one side of the store, and a sweaty scrum of fat goth kids are trying to get a mosh pit started. *Scooby Doo* is on all the monitors.

Frosty browses through the sales rack, dropping a handful of stickered CDs into his basket: Catatonia, Stone Roses, Grooverider, Space Raiders, Lo-Fidelity All Stars, Sebadoh.

'Frosty,' says Lee, his hand around Frosty's wrist.

'Hey . . . Lee,' says Frosty warily.

'Wow, neat coincidence seeing you here.' Lee worked for a firm of solicitors in the City but he stopped going in there a couple of months ago when the junk took hold. His savings have already gone and now he is into petty crime to support his habit. He has sold most of his clothes but still manages to look decent today in a Stüssy jacket and boots and a pair of Urban combats. His eyes are the calm, glassy eyes of the junkie. He looks diseased and he has a bad case of the shakes.

'I guess,' says Frosty, shuffling away up the aisle.

'Have you got any H on you?' Lee is pretending to study the playlist on the back of an REM CD.

'What do you think I am, stupid? In a place like this?'

'I'm like really in need of a fix. I mean *really*. Anything'd do.'

'I haven't got anything on me. Sorry.'

'Even Demerol? Morphine?'

'No and no. *No.*'

'Will you be at the flat later?'

'No. I'm busy.'

'Well, what the fuck am I supposed to do?' Lee says, panicked.

'Find someone else, maybe? Look, I'm sorry and everything but there's nothing I can do. Find someone else.'

Frosty walks away from the sales rack and heads down into the Dance section, dropping a Finitribe CD into his basket. A couple of Japanese girls are staring at a huge cardboard hoarding for *Plastic People* in front of the escalators: an eight-foot Vid Danton dressed in skintight shirt and trousers, looking darkly out into the store. Quotes from reviews saying things like 'inspired' and 'zeitgeist' and 'masterpiece' hang as banners throughout the store. There are no spare copies of the CD anywhere. Frosty thinks both Japanese girls are cute. They are pointing up at the giant Vid and giggling. Frosty feels like going up to them and saying 'I know him' and 'I could introduce you to him.'

Lee has followed him.

'Look, man, are you sure you haven't got any H on you? I've got plenty of cash.'

'You've never got cash, Lee,' he says, wearily.

'I've sold some Walkmans I lifted from Dixons to a bunch of junkies in Dalston. I'm pretty flush.'

Frosty turns to face him: 'Are you even listening to me? I haven't got any gear, Lee, OK, so just fuck off and find someone else and stop bothering me. I'm not in the mood.'

'Settle, dude,' Lee says. 'Jeez, whatever happened to customer loyalty?' Muttering, he heads away towards the Games section.

L'Odéon, Regent Street

Regent Street at night, and the snow is falling hard and steady and the buses and taxis are burrowing through with their headlights making little bowls of light in the flurries ahead. The festive lights have still not been removed, and glowing neon adverts for chocolate bars are suspended from ropes of lights looped across the street. The cold is numbing and sucks the warmth from Frosty's bones. He paces out the approach to the restaurant a couple of times, sheltering under the canopies of jewellers and tailors and experimenting with the cast of his face, straightening his tie, pulling out then tucking in his shirt, polishing his shoes against the back of his trousers, trying out a few greetings in his head. One, two, three, ready: smile; bigger smile; extend hand in greeting; smile some more; open mouth to speak; speak.

Hey, Dad, how you doing, you look, um, great, like, really together and sorted and the whole works. Oh and, yeah, I'm kind of low on resources right now. I don't suppose you could . . .?

Dad, hey, great to see you. Would it be, like, possible for me to get some extra cash because I'm, like, really short?

Dad, just love the suit. By the way, any chance of a loan to tide me over until the end of the month?

It's eight-thirty. Frosty is already half an hour late.

He checks his reflection in the window of a shop – 'World of Tartan' or something – selling Argyll jumpers and tartan everything else to crazy Jap tourists. He looks good: sharp aquiline nose and straight-ledged cheekbones. He practises a smile into the window and watches his dimples suck in. Inside, a Japanese woman reaches for her husband's arm in alarm. He eyeballs them both until they look away.

The cloakroom girl, who is Eastern European and cute, takes his coat and shows him up the sweep of stairs into the restaurant. A fine cloud of steam, rising off the damp clothes of the diners with reservations, also people who have come inside to shelter, glows in the lights. His father is already seated at a table next to one of the giant half-moon windows looking down onto the street and the snow. A copy of a Martin Amis novel sits on the table next to a half-finished plate of garlic bread with sun-dried tomatoes. He is looking out into the street; the glow of the streetlights flickering through the blizzard looks Christmas festive, only two weeks too late. The window-ledge outside is stacked up with fresh snow.

His father: taller than him; grey hair that actually suits him; tight forehead and sharp chin from the surgery last year; ultra-white teeth; always a tutorial in sophisticated dress. Today: grey herringbone suit from Aquastratum, two-tone grey shirt and tie combo, cufflinks with a silver dollar on the right and a golden pound on the left. His laptop is open and glowing on the table. The powder-blue light washes up onto his face.

'Hey, Dad.'

'Joseph.'

'Sorry I'm late.'

'How are you? Who'd've believed this weather? Here, sit down.'

'Nice machine,' Frosty says, sliding onto the chair.

'It's handy. I was just checking my mail.' He taps a key and the screen flickers out. 'Your sister says hello, by the way.'

'Great.'

'Aren't you flying out tomorrow? For the concert?'

'Yeah. Flying tonight, actually. After midnight. Should get there in plenty of time.'

'Pass on my regards.'

'Will do.' Frosty rubs his hands, trying to start some circulation. 'Like I say, sorry I'm, uh, a little late.'

'Hmm. Weather hold you up?'

'Um, yeah.'

'You look half-frozen. Let me get you a brandy. Claude, would you pour a brandy for my son? Warm him up.' The waiter glugs cognac into a glass. 'So, son, how are you getting along? You haven't been around to take my calls much. Busy?'

'Always busy, Dad. Phone never stops ringing. Ringing off the hook.'

'Doing what? Go on – down it. I'll get you another.'

'You know – busy stuff. Stuff keeping me awake at night.'

'Really?'

'Yeah, really. I mean *big* time. I'm so busy I don't even know what day of the week it is, man.'

'So I should be grateful you remembered to join me?'

Frosty is flipping through the menu. 'Like I'd *forget*.'

'Quite.' His father sighs.

The second brandy is poured. Frosty drinks it. 'God, I need a beer. Or a glass of carbonated mineral water with a hint of apple.'

The waiter, Claude, arrives and silently takes their order.

'Could you, like, do something about this music?' asks Frosty.

'What would you like me to do with it, sir?'

'Come on, Joseph,' says his father, arms apart, with palms upwards.

'Like, *change* it or something. I mean, don't you guys have this reputation for being this trendy hangout? I don't know if you guys noticed, but you're playing *Marillion*. Uh? Hello? Go and root around. Find something else.'

'It's really not important,' says his father to the waiter, apologetically.

'I've got a bag of CDs downstairs if you can't do any better,' Frosty offers.

To his father: 'It's no problem, sir. I'll see what I can do.'

Frosty takes a slice of garlic bread and peels off a sun-dried tomato. 'Look at him: sneering all the way back to the kitchen. He's going to spit in my soup now, I reckon.'

'That wasn't necessary,' his father says wearily.

'Matter of opinion.' Frosty drops the slice of bread into his mouth, whole.

'Look, can't we try and just have a nice meal for once? No scenes?'

'If they change the music I have no problems. I'll be as cool as a cucumber. I just can't eat to *this*.'

The starters arrive. Frosty has a cold carrot soup and his father a concoction involving chicken, bacon and crème fraiche.

'So, what are you doing with yourself?'

'Still looking for a job,' he slurps.

'You've been looking for *months*. Isn't it about time you found one?'

'Gotta get the right one, Dad. I'm not going to sell myself short.'

'And what would the right one be?'

'Something revolutionary. I'm tapping into the zeitgeist. I'm on the cutting edge.'

'Is that right?' the older man says.

'Oh yeah. You're cocking an eyebrow sceptically, but I've got big plans. I'm going to shake up the world.'

'Come on, son. You're not fooling anyone – least of all me. And it needn't be as hard as this. Listen, I've been thinking – I could get you something without any problem at all. A *good* job that pays a good wage. I mean, Glynn

Williams at that new news channel owes me a favour. I could get you something there. It'd only take a phone-call.'

'What, like as a researcher or something? No thanks. Not for me.'

'OK. How about something in the City? You've heard of Michael Bratsky, the American financier? No, probably not. He's putting together a rights issue for the company. He owes me.'

'The City? No thanks.'

'The money's great—'

'I'll never want a job that forces me to wear a tie. Some things I *will* not do.'

'You can't live off the trust fund for ever, son.'

'That reminds me—'

'The answer is no.' His father frowns.

'No?'

'No more money.' He is shaking his head, a piece of chicken skewered on his fork in mid-hover over his plate. 'Your allowance is sufficient for your expenses. It's plenty enough. I'm not going to increase it.'

'It's my car. It's broken. I need another.'

'Get the bus.'

'I did. I got it here. It was *horrible*. I wouldn't have been so late if I had a car that worked.'

'Then get a job.'

'Come on, Dad.'

'There's no more money. Final.'

There is an awkward silence. A bus rumbles past outside, the squares of light from the top-deck windows melting together into an amber swipe. 'How can you sleep knowing your only son is broke?'

'You're not broke. And I lose sleep over you for reasons entirely unconnected with your financial well-being.'

'I'll just blitz the credit card then, shall I?'

'Fine. Do what you want.' His father looks up sadly, glances over to the bar, back down at the table.

Frosty looks away, busies himself with his steak. He mutters something about being unloved.

'Who's that person over there?'

'Where?' asks Frosty.

'That young man staring at us. Over there, in the terrible suit. He's coming across – you must know him.'

'Oh God,' says Frosty.

'Hi, Frosty,' says Crumb with a big, inane smile. He is wearing a cheap blue nylon suit with horizontal red pin-stripes and a scuffed pair of white Reeboks. He can only fasten one jacket button around his girth; the jacket itself is stretched taut like a drumskin, or a girdle. 'Didn't expect to see you tonight.' He turns to Frosty's father. 'Nice one. You know Frosty too? He's my—'

'Excuse me, Dad,' Frosty cuts in breathlessly, taking Crumb by the arm and tugging him down the slope leading to the toilets.

'What the *fuck* are you trying to do to me?'

'I just wanted to say Hi. OK?'

'No, not OK. Definitely not OK,' Frosty hisses. 'I can't be seen with you tonight. Just do me a favour and eat your dinner and then go. Or just stay over at your table and ignore me.' He pauses. 'I'm assuming you're with the girls tonight?'

'Course. Amy and Pepsi. I thought I'd take them for a late Christmas treat.'

'Christ.'

'Are you carrying?'

'Fuck me, Crumb. *No.*'

'I was just asking. We're looking for a good apéritif. Something *punchy.*'

'Don't even look my way again.'

Still on edge, Frosty goes into the toilets and does a line from his own personal supply. This rush should last twenty minutes. One more line ought to do it.

His father is mopping up a slick of onion gravy with fluffy forkfuls of mashed potato. 'Who was that?'

'A friend,' he answers. 'Well, *kind* of a friend – more an acquaintance.'

'Why did he call you "Frosty"?'

The Rolling Stones start up on the stereo, Jagger singing 'Brown Sugar'. An improvement, Frosty thinks.

'It's a nickname. Dunno what it means. Maybe 'cos I like this kind of weather?'

His father pushes away his plate and starts to skim through the sweet menu. He looks up, his forehead creasing.

'Son, are you sure you're OK?' He fishes his glasses out of a pocket and puts them on.

'Of course I am. What do you mean?'

'I mean, are you OK? I mean, *really* OK?'

'Shit, Dad, I'm *fine*. Never better. I'm hale and hearty and fighting fit. Ready to go.'

Chips of light glint in the corner of the lenses. 'You just look so pale and thin. You hear so many stories about kids these days getting involved in all sorts of unpleasantness.'

'It's the demon drugs, Dad,' he sighs. 'They're controlling me.'

'You shouldn't joke about things like that, Joseph,' he says.

'Dad, do I look like the kind of guy who'd be into drugs?'

'You know that, um, if you ever get into anything like that, you've only got to let me know.'

'I don't do drugs, Dad, OK? You want to inspect my arms? Relax.'

'Will you look at something for me and give me an honest answer?'

'Sure. Course. What is it?'

His father reaches into an attaché case under the table and brings out a tan folder. He delicately slides a black-and-white photograph from the folder, an eight-by-six blow-up with a glossy sheen. The picture has been taken with a telephoto lens from a flat in the tenement opposite the squat in Bethnal Green. The quality is grainy but Frosty sees himself, at full zoom, fiddling with the locks on the door. He recognizes Zorba, his wide back to the camera. The date and time burnt into the corner of the print say this photo was taken yesterday afternoon.

'And these,' says his father, dealing out other photos onto the table like a croupier: Frosty opening the door and stepping inside; Damon pulling open the gate; Vid with his mouth lowered to the intercom, an angry frown creasing his brow.

'And this,' says his father, sliding a video cassette across the table. 'The same as the photos, but on actual video tape.'

'That's not me,' says Frosty, pointing at the fuzzy pictures. 'What are these?'

'No? What about this one? You're wearing a very fetching leather coat. A bit too fascist for my tastes, perhaps.' He flicks over another photo taken from a different angle. Frosty is staring straight down the lens, a cigarette dangling from the corner of his mouth and his mobile pressed to his ear.

'I can't believe it. My own father has been fucking spying on me,' Frosty says.

'Keep your voice down,' the older man mutters.

'I can't believe this.'

'I didn't have these taken. They were sent to me.'

'Oh right, of course.' Frosty pushes the pictures away. 'Well? What do you want me to say?'

'Let's say these pictures put me into a difficult commercial position, OK?'

'Meaning?'

'If a competitor was to get these, or the papers . . .'

'Yeah, yeah,' says Frosty.

'Um,' continues his father, 'what were you doing going into a place like' – he gestures at the photos distastefully – '*that*?'

'What can I say? One of my friends lives there, OK? My good friend Nigel. I went round to play on his Nintendo or something.'

'And these other people?'

'They came to play Nintendo too. We were playing Mario Kart. We had a tournament.'

'Really?'

'Yes, really.'

'I don't believe you.'

'Tough luck. It's the truth.'

'What if I was to tell you that flat is being illegally squatted? And that the police believe that it is being used to sell prohibited substances? Drugs.'

'I'd be shocked. It's a lovely place. Nigel's very, like, houseproud.'

'Is that so?'

'Yep.'

'Son, I hardly need tell you this, but I can't afford to have my name associated with anything unsavoury. You know what happened the last time that happened. The share price just got *blasted*.'

'I might have known. All that stuff about worrying about me – that's just bullshit, right?'

'You know that's not true.'

'No, it's just bullshit.'

'I'm not trying to *blame* anyone here. I guess what I'm trying to say is, if you've got yourself into any, um, trouble—'

'Jeez – I'm fine.'

'—if you've got yourself into any trouble,' his father

repeats, 'I want to know about it. I want to *help*. We'll sort it out. If the press get hold of anything, it could make things difficult for the company. I've already got a team working to keep this stuff under wraps. We may have to make a payment—'

'Dad, please. I'm *fine*. I told you already, I don't *do* drugs.'

'I know, I know ... It's just, well – your mother and I both worry about you.'

'Yeah yeah, I know. Look, can we just have our meal? Please?'

Shoreditch

Frosty dials Curtis and tells him they have to close the Bethnal Green squat. Curtis says he will make a visit later and remove the stash. Curtis then asks why they are doing this. Frosty tells him not to worry. He changes into a T-shirt and combats, picks up his suitcase and catches the tube out to Heathrow.

Alex

5 January
Las Vegas

'Vid,' says Alex, cautiously. 'Could we, like, have a word about something?'

'Why not,' Vid says in a dead voice. 'I'm going out of my mind here.' He has made a paper aeroplane out of a page from the *Las Vegas Tribune*, and is fiddling with the angle of the wings.

'Let's get something to eat. I know a place.'

Vid flicks the aeroplane out of the open window of the hotel room. It catches a hot shaft of air and rises up, before gracefully circling down to the sidewalk below.

'Look at that,' says Vid. 'I should like be in aviation, or something.'

Cornucopia

Cornucopia, the restaurant that opened last week just off the Strip and Paradise, and about which the *Tribune* said 'Dining here is paradise, like eating in an arboretum.' There are trees and shrubs everywhere, and there are parrots and macaws in aviaries around the perimeter of the dining room. No music, just piped birdsong. The ceiling is a tinted-glass dome, like a blister, and the sun is a burning blur spreading out like spun gold over the glass. The air-con is at full power, the air jetting into the room in muffled gusts. Because of the greenery and the birds, it is impossible to see more than a couple of other tables from each seat. This is why Alex chose it.

'What do you think?' he asks, as the waiter shows them to their table.

'I . . . can't . . . see . . . anything . . . man,' says Vid.

'You've still got your Ray-Bans on,' Alex says, tapping on a lense.

'Shit, yeah,' says Vid, not taking them off. 'I'm feeling kinda spacey right now, kind of not in the loop.'

'You want a Halcion?' asks Alex.

'Yeah. You got any?'

They order. Vid takes two Halcion with a Mexican beer that costs $7 a bottle. Alex hopes his memory of maxing out his credit card is a false one.

Stay calm, he tells himself. *This is the moment. The* moment. Everything he has ever done has led him to *this* point. How he handles this conversation will define every-thing, for the rest of his life. He could go up and up and keep going, or just skim along the surface for another year or so, losing momentum and then sinking back down under the waves. Back to the City and the Law. Back to drafting the same documents again and again, each day bookended by hellish commutes. That can't happen.

If he gets this right, dining out at a place like this would be the norm.

And it's just Vid. *Vid!* Jesus. The day he worries about dealing with Vid Danton will be his last in this business. He may have been blessed with some arbitrary stroke of super-charged fate, but it's just Vid. A shelf-stacker. An intellectual pygmy. Alex's bright sparkling intellect ought to run rings around him.

Just stay composed.

'Vid,' says Alex carefully, after their food has arrived. 'You remember when we played that Kitchen Bitches gig in Manchester? Last year, in April? You remember that one?'

'Nope. I have no clue,' he says. 'I'm feeling kinda hazy right now. I'm here and I'm not here, man. My long-term memory is a figment of my imagination.'

'The van broke down on the way?'

'Hmm, oh yeah, I remember. Hey, garçon, black pepper over here.'

'And do you remember the conversation we had after the gig finished? Outside the toilets, I think.'

'Nope,' he replies, scooping out shovelfuls of parmesan and sprinkling it over his pasta. Alex sees black olives glinting out of the strands of spaghetti. 'Have you got any blow?'

'I told you then that you had a great future in this business. And that I thought you could go right to the top. Remember?'

'Kinda,' Vid sighs, absently winding his spaghetti around his fork. 'I was pretty drunk, though. I need some blow – do you have any?'

'Yeah, well, that's what I said. And I've been thinking

about that a lot lately, and I don't think I did you justice. It was pretty faint praise, actually.'

'Yeah?' A blonde in a yellow top and red skirt sits at the table opposite them.

'Let me put it another way. All the people coming to the gig tonight, all the thousands and thousands of them – they're not coming to see Jared or Astrid or Damien. They're not coming to see the band. They're not really even coming to listen to the songs. Do you know why they're coming tonight, Vid?'

He is smiling at the blonde: a knowing, feral smile. 'Uh, nope,' he says after a pause. He is fumbling in his pockets for something.

'They're coming to see *you*, man. *You*. Without you this band is history. No one is even remotely interested unless *you* are on stage singing the songs.'

'You think? That sounds, like, pretty far-fetched, Alex. I can't even play my guitar properly, man.' Then, a hushed whisper: 'Have you *seen* that chick over there? You reckon she's recognized me? You think I should go over?'

'Vid, *concentrate*. This is like *really* important.' For me as well as for you. 'It's not the music, man. It's *you*. Vid Danton *is* Dystopia. *That's* my point. And my next point is this: you don't get nearly the *credit* you deserve for that.'

The blonde has been joined by an All-American proto-type quarterback who looks like Ricky Martin on steroids. His torso, steam-packed with muscle, is like a warped hall of mirrors reflection in comparison to Vid's skinny junkie frame.

'Did you say *credit*?' he says. He is definitely listening

now, taking off his glasses. He is sipping beer from the bottle, but he has Alex fixed in the whirls of his green-dark eyes. Alex can see his reflection painted onto the irises.

'Listen. I've got something pretty important to tell you. I've had an offer from a big – and I do mean *big* – record company. Let's just say they're pretty famous all over the world for producing games consoles and other shit like that. You're nodding somewhat dumbly but you know whom I'm talking about. They would like you to consider leaving Dystopia and going to work for them. As a solo artist, as "Vid Danton" – not "Dystopia", not even "Vid Danton with Dystopia".'

'Whoah,' Vid puts his beer down, suddenly lucid. 'That's pretty, um, heavy. Pretty serious.'

'I know it is, Vid. That's why I've given it plenty of thought. Before I bothered you with it.'

'What you, like, reckon – speaking as my trusted friend and, like, numero-uno adviser?'

'Well, we may as well pass over the money, because I know that's not what motivates you—'

'Um, how much? Just out of, like, interest?'

'The company'll increase your salary by ten per cent, minimum. They'll increase your share of the royalties by the same amount, too. I mean, the financial package is just awesome, man, but you wouldn't make a decision based on that alone, right? Am I right?'

'Yeah, course not.'

'You've got your artistic credibility to think of too, right?'

'Yeah. Right.'

'What the label can offer you, money aside, is the chance to carve out a name for yourself. You could be a big star, man, bigger than just about anyone else out there right now. Look at the market: where have all the big stars gone? They're all *too old*, man. Trent Reznor's thirty-five, for Christ's sakes, and he's so past it, it hurts. How old are you?'

'Twenty-five.'

'Precisely. And you've got it all. Just think about it, man. I know you hate it when people don't give you the credit you deserve. You can stop that right now.'

'I can't get this all, like, straight in my head. What do I do, man? What am I supposed to *say*?'

'I'm not choosing for you, Vid. This is *your* future. *You* have to decide.' That's it, Alex, lay it on nice and thick. He's taken the bait – now you just have to land him. 'But if you want a recommendation – well, I'd take it. Offers like this don't come around every day, not even every lifetime.'

'What happens to the others?'

'You all go your separate ways. The company isn't interested in them. It only has eyes for *you*. At the end of the day, man, this is just business – just like any other business. People split to do their own thing all the time.'

'Yeah.'

'Listen, think of it this way. How would you fancy coming back here in six months for the first gig of the Vid Danton World Tour? You could have that, if you wanted it. All of it.'

Spin

5 January
Plane

The turbulence comes without warning, shakes the plane violently for thirty seconds, then leaves just as suddenly. The stewardesses soldier on, fixing reassuring smiles whilst gripping onto seat backs for dear life. Spin isn't fooled: their eyes are bright with fear and their knuckles are white. Drinks are spilled, tepid airplane food slops to the left and right, luggage tumbles down from the overhead bins to snap open in the aisles. The baby in front of him wakes and starts up again with its interminable wailing, and then its mother starts screaming too. The passenger beside him squeezes his eyes shut and mouths the words of a silent prayer to whichever deity he hopes is watching over him. Spin remembers Vid's theory of flight and wonders if it is too late for supplication.

As the plane loses altitude, Spin has a vision of the immediate future: a blip disappearing from a radar screen; the arrivals board at Chicago flicking up DELAYED next to their flight number; a sombre airline official announcing to a TV camera that the flight is missing, presumed lost; boats laden with sonar equipment scouring the Pacific for wreckage; personal artefacts washing onto the white beach of an atoll, melancholy reminders of loved ones sunk under the sea. His precious records, floating in a lagoon like wax lilies. A dismal hangar somewhere in the Midwest, and bits of plane reassembled like a mammoth jigsaw with a million missing pieces. This staccato rush of images is replaced by Mary's smiling, beatific face. Spin knows they will be fine, and then the plane levels out and the juddering stops.

They pass safely through the disturbance and the plane gently regains its composure and nudges back up to its cruising altitude. Those passengers who had been holding their breath exhale collectively, and the nervous joking starts. The captain, laying on the equanimity a little too thickly, explains that they have just passed through a patch of clear-air turbulence and that, for everyone's safety, he is going to leave the Fasten Seatbelts sign on for a while, until everything gets back to normal. Spin doesn't mind. He's not going anywhere.

Spin can't relax on flights and so sleep is not a viable option for killing the time. Even when he is dog-tired and riding the red-eye, like now, there is no option but to hunker down and sit it out. It is not the improbable act of flying that bothers him, although he still gaped in bewilderment while he was waiting at Chek Lap Kok as the gargantuan 747s lumbered down the runway and heaved themselves up into the twilight over the sea. He can accept these little miracles. His inability to relax stems instead from the plane's myriad vibrations that generate a burr of resonance inside him, a stew of nervous energy with no means of release. The only way around this is to drop a couple of Halcion and cast himself adrift but he can't afford to do that; he can't afford to feel drowsy when he lands. He will need all his resources just to fight off the jet lag, without chemicals riding towards him over the horizon like sleep's cavalry. And he needs to be at his sharpest for this gig. This is the big one. The biggest of big enchiladas.

A jumbo spliff would be heavenly, but he dared not risk running weed through customs. Deportation for possession, and the inevitable stamp on the passport forbidding re-entry to the States, would cripple his most potentially lucrative market. He has a box of menthols in his pocket, but unscrewing the smoke detector in the bathroom, and then sitting there on the smeared metal toilet in that foul-smelling closet, waste swilling beneath him, is more than he can stomach. He tries the headphones and thumbs through the channels but all he gets is bad comedy, bad jazz and crushingly bad chart pap. Fucking great.

Spin rootles around in his bag and wonders which of the biographies he bought at the airport he will start on first: the slim volume on Duke Ellington or the fatter volume on Napoleon. Napoleon gets the nod.

Another day, another continent. He runs through the past few days again.

Spin had travelled early to Hong Kong so he could take time out to see the sights. He missed the old Kai Tak airport with its shuddering descent so close to the old, cankered apartment blocks of Kowloon. You used to be able to see the washing hanging to dry on the dirty roofs fluttering in the filthy wake of the engines. He missed the jarring wrench of the hard right turn as the pilot aimed between blocks to find the runway. He missed the short flat drag of touchdown, and the plane skidding to a halt seemingly inches before the green waters of the bay. This new landing was efficient; drab by comparison.

He picked up the late edition of the *South China Morning Post*, boarded the downtown Metro, immaculately kept, and watched the stations flash past.

The promoters had rented a huge apartment for him in the Central district, near to the Botanical Gardens. He felt like a lonely wraith floating around the wide-open spaces of that apartment, a *gwei lo* – like the locals said, a white ghost. Gazing out of the twenty-first-floor windows into the canyons created by other apartment blocks was too otherworldly. Eagles swooped past the windows, over the cyan squares of swimming pools a hundred feet below. How could people live like this? He wandered around the island and did the things that tourists do.

He took the funicular railway up Victoria Peak and looked down on the grey skyscrapers jostling for space before the wide green-and-blue palette of the sea. He crossed the harbour on the Star Ferry and explored the wide thoroughfares and crowded alleys of Kowloon. He watched a Bruce Lee marathon in a seedy cinema in Wan Chai. He ate sushi and drank green tea. He stocked up on retro toys and cartoon *objets* for the flat back home, things Lucy would like: a model of Godzilla in ductile green rubber for the bathroom sink; a set of *Battle of the Planets* figurines for the telephone table. He bought a necklace for

Mary from the jade market crammed under the flyover on Gascoigne Street. He spent hours talking to her on the phone.

The gig came and went. He put in a perfunctory performance, his mind elsewhere, the kids aping the industrial scene with almost religious fervour, dressed in black leather trousers, black T-shirts, and with multiple piercings like human junkyards. Spin thought it a shame to see the legion of identikit acolytes had spread this far east; he admires the oriental sense of style, always one step ahead of the West, from wide-eyed manga fashion to grungy lo-fi revival. Always setting the trends, he thought, and now they had slipped into mimicry. It didn't seem right.

The night was held in an ancient ice factory near the docks. The ice was gone, and the redundant machines loomed darkly up out of the gloom like ghost ships. The theming was clumsy and inexpert but Spin reminded himself that the scene was still fresh here, that this amateurism was preferable to the corporate vultures who had railroaded the underground spirit in London and New York, channelled it into megaclubs and into a licence to print money. He was the main attraction for the night, and he played for an hour. Just one hour, after travelling for eighteen times longer than that to get there. He was paid £10,000 for the privilege, an amount of money he found obscene and embarrassing, given that he was doing something he loves. He earned half his father's annual salary in an hour, just like that. And he would have done it for free.

The crowd went mental and he was only on cruise control. His playlist was deliberately retro, throwing in old

Manson, some classic cuts from KMFDM, Coil, Foetus and the like. Then he layered in little treats here and there to keep them guessing: The Jackson Five, The Monkees, all textured with the crushing syncopation that turned the fey chorusing into a dirge. And when he played his mix of 'Power and the Glory' the place exploded, strobes and arc lights burning up the dark. Dystopia are a hot property in the Far East. Their tour sold out in minutes. *Plastic People*, still only available on prohibitively expensive import, cannot be found anywhere.

'I like Vid,' a wide-eyed girl told him. 'He *so* gorgeous!'

The groupies gathered around his booth like black moths around a flame. He hardly noticed them during his set; when mixing, he zones out and nothing reaches him (he once played on in a burning club in Miami as the place was being evacuated). They waited patiently until he finished the set, fighting their innate politeness not to interrupt but ultimately cowed by stories of precious Western deejays who did very bad things to kids who disturbed them mid-set; very very bad things to kids who had the audacity to request songs that would ruin carefully crafted playlists.

'You sign?' asked a staggeringly beautiful girl as he lumped his pilot case onto a table. She had raven-black hair and mesmerizing dark eyes. Without a trace of reticence she pulled up her T-shirt to reveal the twin overhang of perfectly symmetrical breasts. Spin took her marker pen hesitantly and signed his name above her navel. He let her kiss his cheek.

*

Back to the plane. The in-flight movies have been chosen with the median viewer in mind. Middle-of-the-road rites-of-passage movies, romances, one tepid actioner with lame dubbing erasing even the whiff of controversy ('*Fun* you, muther*funner*'). He cannot even find the enthusiasm to play Mario Kart on the Nintendo fixed into the back of the seat in front. He pushes up the blind and watches a crimson dawn break over the Pacific.

As gigs go, Hong Kong was profitable. Ten thousand in the bank and a free holiday, such as it was. This current gig will not be profitable in the short term. He is doing it as a favour to Jared and the others – for kudos, no charge. But if he performs well, he knows that he stands a chance to really break into America. He has remixed a handful of tracks for Marilyn Manson and Ministry and Coal Chamber, enough to sink his name into the melting pot of British talent so in vogue at the moment, but now he needs something to pull himself from out of the homogenous mush so that the big labels really take notice. Providing the warm-up for Dystopia is a perfect opportunity. He knows a lot of label heads are going to this gig. This is the main chance. He will seize it.

Chicago, waiting lounge

He has three hours to kill between flights. Not long enough to go into town, too long to spend at the airport. He grabs a Fatburger and a carton of protoplasmic fries, and sets about them over a copy of the US edition of *Mixmag*.

He watches people wander into the departure lounge, congregate under the big departure monitors, and wait for the signal to move on. He wonders where they are all going, who they are going to see, why they are travelling. He thinks about calling London, but it is still the middle of the night there. He'd only wake Lucy.

Las Vegas, Immigration

Spin thinks American immigration officers must be paid to ensure visitors are held up in queues for the longest possible time. This process, with its officials in their pseudo-military fatigues and hard unsmiling faces, is alien to the smooth, polite efficiency of disembarkation at Hong Kong. He is shuffled slowly towards the front as the queue advances, watching travellers pleading with the officials that they should be allowed to enter this great country. When it is his turn he nervously pushes his passport across the plastic buttress separating him from his inquisitor, and waits as she compares him with the five-year-old picture inside.

'This doesn't look very much like you, sir.' She is right. He was twenty-two in the picture, and tentatively taking his first steps into the big wide world. He was training to work with computers in a City bank and wore his hair cropped short and his suits crisp and clean, the perfect corporate puppy. Now, his hair is screwed into white-boy dreads and the bottom of his face is adorned with a beatnik goatee. His suits have all been given to charity and today's

T-shirt bears a picture of Marilyn Manson, looking especially androgynous, with the slogan 'Fucked up and Dead to the World Tour 98'.

'I know. It's an old picture. I'm sorry,' he says. Why is he apologizing? She flicks through to the back of the passport and studies his stamps.

'You've come from Hong Kong?'

'Yes, that's right.'

'Via Chicago?'

'Yes.'

'And you've been to Mexico City? And Miami?'

'Yes. I was working.'

'I see. And what is your business in the United States now?'

'I'm a deejay. I'm playing some records at a concert tonight.'

'You only have a tourist visa, sir. I'm afraid it is not permissible for you to work here under that visa.'

He scrabbles in a pit of white panic for a moment, before Inspiration tosses down a rope and he clambers out: 'I'm not being paid. I'm doing it for free.'

'That sounds unlikely, sir.'

'I'm doing it for some friends. They're in the band. You might have heard of them? Dystopia? No? I have a number here if you need to speak to them.' He fumbles in his 501s for the torn fragment from the fax Alex sent him. He can't find it.

'*Dépêchez-vous!*' says the father of the French family behind.

'*Je fais aussi vite que possible,*' Spin replies.

'What's in the case?' the official asks.

'My records,' he says, 'for the concert. Do you need to see them?'

'No, sir, that won't be necessary. Welcome to Las Vegas, Nevada. Have a pleasant stay.'

He struggles through the gate before she can change her mind.

Taxi

Las Vegas cabs carry large triangular hoardings attached to their roofs. These boards advertise local casinos, strip clubs, sports bars and other diversions and the cabs look like mustard-coloured sharks as they swim through the cluttered streets. Spin watches the casinos passing through his own partial reflection in the tinted window. He looks half-dead. He needs sleep.

The cab driver brings the car right up to the carpeted entrance of the hotel and opens the door for him. Spin reluctantly abandons the air-conditioning as the heat wraps him up and squeezes him like a vice. Las Vegas seems to be a series of short hops between air-conditioned oases: plane to airport; airport to car; car to hotel. Even the outdoor escalators have dozens of tiny nozzles that spray fine mist onto the pedestrians being ferried along. Not even Nature can interfere with Las Vegas' perpetual routine. Less heatstroke means more gambling. Everyone wins.

'Good evening, sir.' The bellhop opens the trunk and takes out Spin's suitcase. Once this is secured on his trolley he tries to take Spin's pilot case from him.

'No way, man,' Spin says, cradling the battered, sticke-red case to his chest like an infant. 'These are priceless. I'll take care of them.'

Spin's room

'Spin, man, *great* to see you,' says Alex. Vid is with him, a can of Red Stripe in his hand. Spin always feels slightly on edge whenever Alex is around. He is a chameleon, subtly amending himself to suit the situation. And he works for the label, not for the band. He might have fooled them all with his act of chummy camaraderie, but Spin doesn't buy it. Alex is in this for the money, not the music.

'Hey, Alex,' he says, accepting the clasped handshake. 'Hey, Vid.'

The curtains are open. The desert wind is sucking them out into the hot night outside.

'Spin, man,' says Vid, downing the rest of his beer and tossing the can. He is wearing a wide-brimmed cowboy hat. 'How was the land of the rising sun?'

'It was cool. They love you guys out there. You'll have some *major* fun in Tokyo.'

Alex smiles. 'MTV Asia want to do a feature on us and *Rolling Stone* want one of their reporters to tag along for the Asian leg of the tour. They figure this is like the first crazy tour of the millennium. Kind of like Depeche Mode fucking with Primal Scream on acid. That kind of gig. I can see the renaissance of Gonzo journalism.'

'Cool. Well, like I say, they're up for it. Big time.'

'I can't wait to get acquainted with those Nip groupies,' Vid says, bored, dropping into a wicker chair. 'Fucking Chinks are dirty as fuck.'

Alex smiles grimly. 'Listen, Spin,' he says, 'I just thought I'd pop by and see how you were doing. Tomorrow's gig is going to be big. I mean *big*. I just wanted you to know that the band have got, like, total confidence in you. Total. You're the best there is. No one comes close.'

'Stop it, man. I'm blushing.'

'Yeah, whatever,' says Alex. 'You're too fucking modest, that's what you are.'

'You're, like, way too kind.'

'Whatever. Listen, anyway, I've gotta split but maybe you and me can get together for a beer later on? We could grab some sushi from Spielberg's restaurant?'

'I'd like that.'

'Great, pop by in a couple of hours. We'll go and hit the Strip.' Alex clasps him on the shoulder, 'Great to see you, dude,' and heads out into the corridor. Vid stays.

'Hey, man, I was just about to go and hit the Strip myself, anyway. You fancy tagging along?'

'I'd love to, Vid, but I'm pretty whacked. I haven't slept for hours – possibly days, I can't remember.'

'So? We only touched down a couple of hours ago. Anyway, the best way to beat jet lag is to batter your body into accepting the new hours you're gonna keep. If you go to sleep now, you'll pay for it tomorrow. Trust me, I have first-hand experience in these fields.'

'Vid, man, it's already' – he checks the clock – 'ten. That's a pretty natural hour to get some sleep. My body doesn't need to be battered into submission. It has already submitted.'

'No way, man, I'm just not taking no for an answer. This is Las *fucking* Vegas. Vegas, man! You don't just go to *sleep*. Not here. I refuse to let you cheat yourself. Dump those records and let's go. Just for a swift half.'

Knowing exactly what Vid's definition of a swift half will be, and hating himself for his lack of discipline, Spin locks his records in the room safe, then changes into a clean Psycho Puppies T-shirt, and follows him into the lift. Vid is already bellowing out the chorus from 'Viva Las Vegas'.

Caesar's Palace

It is the sound of the slot machines that Spin will take away from Las Vegas with him. The sound of reels turning, buttons being slammed, dollars being fed into the slots and occasionally spat out the other end; it all merges into a throbbing cacophony which drowns out everything else, even the traffic on the Strip. They pass dozens of fat, rich Americans as they stroll into Caesar's Palace. They waddle from point to point in garish Hawaii-print shirts the size of tents, and shorts exposing acres of white, puckered flesh.

The patriarch of one such family, a gargantuan blimp who appears to be made out of four short fat balloons attached to one larger fatter one, thanks him sweatily as he holds the door open for him.

'Fat pig,' Vid mutters as they pass by. Spin has no doubt the entire family heard him perfectly.

'What do you fancy?' Vid asks, sweeping the huge pit of the casino with an outstretched arm. 'Beer or bet? No, I know – both.' He grabs Spin's elbow and leads him from the periphery and deeper into the roiling throb around the blackjack tables. They stop at a table with a minimum bet of five hundred dollars a hand. Vid takes the seat offered to him by a waitress, and hands the croupier his platinum AmEx.

'Five thousand bucks on that,' he says. 'Spin, you wanna play?'

'This is a *little* too rich for me,' Spin says. The chips on the table, the thicker, more simply coloured chips that are currency for Vegas' real high rollers, would buy his London flat several times over. The croupier hands back Vid's card and slides across two stacks of blue chips. Five hundred dollars a piece. Vid gives Spin four of them. 'Sit down,' he says. 'You and me are gonna play.'

Spin has not played blackjack for years. The last time he can remember was on a train from London to Manchester for a versus gig with Oakenfold at the Hacienda. A bunch of squatters had busted inside and they revved the place up for one final Madchester revival. It was before Lucy was born, and Mary went up with him. They played cards for an hour or so to pass the time as the train cut its way through the green fields around the Pennines. He watches as the croupier spins cards off the top of the deck to the players. He gets a six, Vid a seven.

'Bad luck, son,' says an elderly man to his right, wearing an enormous cowboy hat and a Wild Bill moustache. His fingers are weighted with an ingot's worth of gold.

'Yeah, I guess,' Spin says, not knowing why this is bad luck.

They both hit their cards. Spin sticks on sixteen and Vid hits again and busts. The dealer gets twenty and silently shepherds away the losers' chips.

'You should always hit on a sixteen,' says Cowboy Hat. 'You ain't never going to beat the house with that.'

'Yeah. I guess,' repeats Spin.

'You know the house has to hit on sixteen, don't you, boy?'

'Sure. Course.'

The cards keep coming. Cowboy Hat's low-rise pile of chips stacks up higher. He exchanges a pile of orange hundred-buck chips for a single thousand-dollar chip and slips it into his pocket.

'That's me done for tonight,' he says, tossing the croupier his last orange chip. The croupier holds up the tip so his pit boss can take note of it, and drops it into a slot in the table. 'Good luck, fellas. Your luck'll come around. Just gotta ride it for a while.'

Within five minutes the croupier has cleared them both out.

'That's what I love about Vegas,' Vid says. 'It's the best

place in the world for spending serious money and ending up with absolutely nothing to show for it.'

'I'm pretty bad at card games,' apologizes Spin.

'*C'est la vie*,' says Vid. 'Can't win 'em all. Drink?'

Bar

Vid orders a bottle of JD and two glasses and they take seats in the VIP suite after Vid has flashed enough cash at the doorman. It is separated from the rest of the bar by a velvet rope, and it looks out onto the tables through wide smoked windows. Spin thinks Shirley Bassey is sitting with Tony Bennett in a booth on the other side of the room.

'Did you know it's snowing in London?' Vid asks. Spin shakes his head. 'There's this new weather channel that broadcasts on the internet and cable. I was watching it earlier on my laptop. You wouldn't believe how much snow they're getting. I could be 'boarding but I'm stuck in a desert.'

'Typical, I guess.'

'Yeah.'

The bar has monitors set into it, underneath waterproof cases. A couple of jocks are playing video poker against the computer. The TV screens overhead are all tuned to sports channels: college football on ESPN, NASCAR racing on ESPN2. The barman is running a mini-book on the outcomes. You can bet on anything here. If there were two dead flies on the bar, you could bet on which one of them would decompose first.

'Anyway, what do you, like, think of the new album?'

'It's great, Vid. I mean, *really* great. Some of the tracks just blew me away. I've already got most of them in my playlist. "Sound and the Fury" is just immense.' Spin watches absently as the quarterback of one of the college teams is body-slammed to the artificial turf.

'Jared'll tell you he wrote them all, but that's not true. You know about my input?'

'I know you wrote one of the tracks. "The Alone", yeah?'

The track is, by a considerable distance, the weakest on the album. It should only have been a B-Side, at the very best, and only the intervention of Damien's drumwork and Jared's distorted guitars save it from complete ridicule.

'Yeah. You like it? It's all about what it feels like to be me. It's pretty personal stuff. Straight from the heart. I kind of agonized whether it was, like, a little bit *too* personal, you know. We do it with acoustic guitars on stage, and Astrid has all this ambient shit going on. It's pretty spooky.'

'I thought it was really, well, kind of interesting.' This is not a complete lie. Spin is interested as to how Vid managed to get it past the band and the record company and onto the album. That is inexplicable. Perhaps Vid has acquired more influence than he is given credit for. Looking at him, nervously twisting a coil of hair around his finger, that is difficult to believe. 'It's really excellent, man. Your voice comes through really strong in the mix. The production is high class.'

Vid has picked up a coaster with the Caesar's Palace logo on it and is tapping out a lazy beat on the bar with it. He starts to softly sing the chorus to the song: ' "Standing there, the alone. Got no spirit, got no home. I'm crucified. I'm alone." '

'That's great,' lies Spin.

'Difficult to think of a rhyme to go with "alone". So I just repeated it. It's kinda like an echo. I wanted to make the point again. You know – reiteration?'

'Moan? Zone? Phone?' offers Spin.

'Nah. Kinda thought of all them. Bone. Roam. Tone. They just don't fit with the sentiment I'm trying to get across.' He sips his drink and seems to have sunken into a maudlin mood. 'It gets pretty lonely up there on stage sometimes – like being the only person on a deserted island. All those people looking up at you, most of them adoring you, and you know the only relationship you'll ever have with any of them is, like, completely superficial. You fuck a groupie and that, like, makes her whole *life*, but to you it just makes you feel cheap, worthless. It's *just* fucking, you know? I mean, I probably fuck more times a day than I eat. Those girls will never know the *real* me. I'm a pretty sensitive guy, you know what I'm saying? Do you feel that when you're playing?'

'Not really. But I'm not alone. I've got my records.'

'I guess. I've just got my guitar, and I can't even play that properly.'

'Listen, man, I think it's great – the song. You're a talented guy.' On the screen a car slams into the side of another and then spins into the wall. Flames lick from the crumpled bonnet. The wreck is replayed in super slo-mo from a dozen different angles.

Vid brightens. 'You think? Alex thinks that I could go a long way. You know, when the band finishes. He reckons I've got the brightest future. For a solo career, I mean.'

'You've talked about that? Do the others know?'

'I guess they do. But then I don't know what the fuck Alex talks to them about. He tells me I've got to keep a grip on things, not go too nuts on the drugs and the sauce and the groupies and shit. And I *do* try, you know, I really do. It's just it can get so difficult to ignore all these temptations everywhere. I feel like Jesus in the desert.'

'Not a good analogy,' says Spin with a careful smile. 'He resisted everything.'

Vid pauses, contemplatively. He looks vulnerable. Much more so than when Spin saw him last. He has always been delicate, with his skinny body and his tendency to mawkishness when he drinks. A complete contrast to the monster he becomes once he is high. He rubs his forehead, scrunching the skin under the heel of his hand, wiping fatigue away. His voice is distracted. 'That'd be so cool, man, a solo career. Hey, would you, like, deejay for me when I do my first solo tour? Man, that'd be so fucking *cool*.'

'Sure, Vid,' says Spin. 'I'd love to.'

'That's so fucking class, man. I really appreciate it. You're a good mate. I won't forget it.'

'Sure,' says Spin, sipping his whisky.

'Excuse me?' It is a teenage girl, maybe eighteen or nineteen. She is all blonde hair, flawless complexion, heavy breasts: the wholesomeness of a homecoming queen. She probably even comes from Kansas. 'Are you Vid Danton? From Dystopia?'

It is as if someone has pressed a button inside Vid's head. His loose comradeship – the unveiled vulnerability – immediately compacts into a tight wad of aloofness. His eyes become cold orbs. The corner of his mouth kinks into an indolent sneer.

'Maybe.'

'I'm, like, *so* sorry to interrupt but I'm going to the concert tomorrow with my friends. We've had tickets for months. I can't wait to see you guys live. I mean, like, I just literally *cannot* wait. Do you think you could sign our tickets for us?' She slaps the tickets onto the bar. The security hologram of the band wobbles as she pushes them at Vid. 'It would mean, like, so much. If you could.'

'Where are your friends?' asks Vid.

'They're waiting outside.' She points to the entrance. There they are: another couple of identical clones: blonde, big tits, ivory teeth, airbrushed complexion, rigid smiles. 'I had to *beg* with the doorman to let me in. We saw you on the blackjack table and just had to see if it was really you.'

'No kidding.' Vid turns away from her and hunches over his glass. He is watching the ice cubes turning slowly in the brown whisky. Her excitement is replaced by confusion and then awkwardness as she realizes he is ignoring her. Spin feels it too.

'So, can you sign the tickets?' she asks again with a nervous smile.

'Listen, I'll do you little starfuckers a big favour.' He is writing on the tickets. 'If you wait outside the entrance a couple of hours before the gig, I'll send out a roadie so you can come backstage. OK?' He hands the tickets back. He has written BACKSTAGE PASS across them.

'Wow,' she gushes. 'That is, like, so *cool* of you. Thank you so much.' Beaming with pleasure, she bounces back into the casino.

Vid goes back to his drink. He seems fixed into this new mood.

'Are you going to send someone out for them?' asks Spin.

Vid laughs. 'Fuck, *no*. Of course not.' He pours out fresh measures for them both. 'Alex wants me to go into detox again,' he says.

'I didn't know you'd even been in before,' Spin says, hesitating. He feels awkward. He hardly knows Vid; certainly not well enough to feel comfortable acting as his confessor.

'Yeah. I was at the Priory a while ago. It's been a bit heavy with horse, and I was mainlining three or four times a day, and getting sick when I didn't. I tried to come off it myself, you know, without telling anyone. Cooked up a big brew, and then every time I took a shot I'd put an equal amount of water back into the solution. Eventually I was going to shoot plain water – get the cure that way.'

'It didn't work?'

'Nah. You just find different excuses to explain the fixes that don't fit in with the schedule. I can score so easily, it's hard to cut off all the connections. The junk's too powerful. It's too fucking *despotic*.'

'You clean now?'

'Yeah, pretty much. The cure's pretty brutal but it works. They shoot you with Demerol for three days and then take it away and just stuff you so full of sedatives and antihistamines and shit, it starts coming out of your nose. It's fucking torture.'

Spin watches the ice cubes dissolving in his drink. He doesn't know what to say.

Vid is staring into his drink, too. 'I mean, I still do a lot of free-base, but who the fuck doesn't? Alex does more than me. I mean, Alex does lines for breakfast. Jared too. Damien is the only person I know who's clean and, I mean, we've only got his word for that. But I'm off the skag now. Completely. For sure. That's why I'm not going back into detox. If I go, they can come in with me.'

Sidewalk

Vid drinks most of the whisky himself. He takes the bottle with him when they leave the bar, tipping all the bar staff and the doormen with twenty-dollar notes thrown like confetti as they make their way back into the casino.

Outside, Vid pauses on the sidewalk. 'Listen, Spin, I'm going to go and buy a bike and head out into the desert for a while. I just need to get some space. All this hassle, it's kinda getting on top of me. You're welcome to come?'

'I've got to sleep, Vid. I'm wasted. But you go.'

Vid seems pleased. Maybe he wants some solitude. 'Sure thing. You do look tired, man. Listen, I really enjoyed tonight. You're a fucking great bloke.' He leans in and fixes him in a drunken embrace. Spin accepts it reluctantly, clapping him manfully on the back. Vid feels as gaunt as a skeleton through his clothes. Spin can feel the corrugated ridges of his ribs.

'Take it easy,' Vid says as he turns and disappears into the crowds.

Spin's suite

He wonders if he should stop at Alex's suite as he passes down the corridor. He checks his watch: 1.30 a.m. It is too late. Alex will have gone out and, anyway, Spin is tired and he doesn't even know where his suite is. He needs to sleep.

He lets his weight sink into the king-size bed and closes his eyes. The monster television is switched on with the sound muted. The changing pictures flicker against the wall and ceiling, colouring the room with alternate electric hues whenever he opens his eyes. He has been flicking through the *Las Vegas Directory*, the equivalent of the *Yellow Pages*. The entries under E include sixteen pages devoted to 'Escorts'. Escorts that will come to your room, escorts you can take out with you to parties and functions, trannies, dominatrixes, schoolgirls, pensioners, models, those specializing in oral and anal, escorts into watersports, fat escorts, thin escorts, amputee escorts. Escorts for every conceivable inclination or perversion. Spin stares at the pictures agape. The hotel left it in his drawer, next to the room-service menu and a copy of the Gideon's New Testament. Only in Las Vegas.

He reaches over until his fingers fasten around the telephone. The international operator connects him to the number, and he waits as the dialling tone – the familiar double buzz rather than the unnatural American extended hum – comes back at him.

Mary picks up on the third ring.

'It's me.'

'Where are you? I've been worried.'

'I'm in Las Vegas. I'm just about to get some sleep. I'm whacked.'

'How was the flight?'

'Oh, you know, pretty good. But long. There was a bit of turbulence that put the shits up everyone, but, you know, I'm fine. How are you?'

'I'm good. Work was dull. Pretty standard these days. What's Vegas like?'

'Weird. It's hard to describe. It's everything that's good about America and everything that's bad put into a pot and stirred around until you get this weird mixture. Some of the things are beyond belief.'

'Such as?'

'Oh, you know, there's a rollercoaster on the very top of this massive observation tower that is, like, a thousand feet in the air. And they've built a scale model of the Eiffel Tower in one of the hotel courtyards.'

Only in America. 'Yeah? You'll have to show me one day.'

'New York first – then Vegas. You need a frame of reference for this or you'll just go crazy. Listen, I've got to go. I'm drooling, I need sleep so bad.'

'You're not about to sleep with a beautiful blonde American prostitute, are you?'

'Not a chance.'

'You better not. Call again?'

'Of course I will. I love you.'

'I love you too. Lucy wants to know when Daddy'll be back.'

'Tell her soon.'

'I will.'

'And kiss her good night for me.'

He waits with the phone purring in his ear before he settles it back in the cradle.

Restaurant

Spin first met Jared at the Electric Ballroom in Camden a year ago. Spin was the deejay at Nocturnal, the Friday-night members-only angst-fest that drew in the capital's fashionably alienated from all points north, south, east and west. The club was an exercise in tackiness: the dancefloor was made up of a roll of linoleum that was unrolled when the doors opened and then stowed away again at four, to make way for the stalls of the market that took up residence on Saturdays and Sundays. Clones of Robert Smith and Andrew Eldritch letched after clones of Lydia Lunch and Siouxsie Sioux. Spin was still green then and learning his trade, but the club had a pair of Technics 1210s and a decent mixer and they paid him decent money, with free beer. He was being paid to hone his craft and he enjoyed himself there, most of the time.

On alternate Fridays the club brought in an unsigned band to play a set. These bands were usually *unsigned* for a simple reason: they were terrible. Spin would sit in his booth flipping though his record box and amending his playlist, sipping on a Diet Coke and smoking a fag, while they blitzed the speakers with angry, unlistenable garbage. More than one band was forced to flee a shower of glasses and bottles thrown by the regulars who wanted Spin back again.

The Indigo Violets were different. He is not sure quite what it was about them that caught his eye. They had a cocky swagger that almost defied the crowd not to like them. Damien, bare-chested, displaying his tattoos and his fuck-you demeanour, looked like more than just the drummer as he paced them from behind. Astrid hadn't joined the band then, and Vid was still stacking shelves in Safeway; Jared sang the vocals. His voice isn't as versatile as Vid's, and he doesn't have the stage presence, but there was something so honest about him that demanded you listen to him. Spin realized they had a chance. He and Jared got to talking as the lights came up at four, and they swapped numbers. As their reputation soared, so did Spin's.

This afternoon, Jared is wearing a silver shirt; sleeveless like chainmail, that forms a brilliant contrast with his dark skin. Rock stars are not supposed to look this good. They are supposed to look gaunt and ravaged and diseased like Vid does. Jared looks like a well-fed CK model. They have a table under an awning that looks out onto the Strip. The sky is as lifeless as the desert below. Perfect sapphire. It is hot with the desert's dry, weighty heat. Moisture is alien here.

'It's great to see you again,' Jared says, as the late breakfasts they have ordered arrive. 'It's really good of you to come over like this. Means a lot.'

'Listen, it's my pleasure. God, you've given me a great opportunity to break through over here, and you're thanking *me*.'

'Well, if this goes well we'll both break through.'

'You're already there, man.'

'Hardly!'

'Come on. Tell me how things could be much better? I mean, I've heard all about your video shoot next week.' Lars von Trier is directing the video for the next single. He's never been persuaded to direct for bands before; he's turned down both the Smashing Pumpkins and U2. And the rumour is that he approached Revolution Records to ask them if he could work with the band.'

'I don't know what to make of that. It's in black and white, of course. And Edward Furlong's in it.'

'Nervous?'

'About the video?'

'No. About tonight.'

'I guess. OK, yes. This isn't like Milton Keynes, is it? There are journalists out here who would just love us to fuck up. What with the bad press about Manson and KMFDM and all, the bar's been set pretty high. Still, we can do it. The album seems to be going down really well.'

'Yeah, well, you *could* say that,' Spin ribs. 'I mean, it's only been at number one for five weeks or something.'

'*Three*,' Jared corrects. 'And you're partly responsible. That mix you did for "Sound and the Fury"? MTV absolutely loves it. It's been on constant rotation – least it *was*. You heard Vid set fire to their sofa this morning?'

'Alex told me. He was wasted?'

'Who knows with him? He'd do it just because he thought it was funny. He's been pretty erratic recently.'

'He's an ambitious guy.'

'Vid, ambitious? No way. He doesn't look further than the next fix, man.'

'You'd be surprised. I had a beer with him last night. He's already thinking about his solo career.' Spin regrets saying this almost as soon as the words leave him. Jared's brows clench into a shallow V, like pointed wings.

'A solo career?'

'Yeah,' he backtracks. 'Ah, you shouldn't worry too much about it. He was just looking down the road. A long way down the road. Anyway, he . . .'

'He'd never make it,' Jared says, interrupting. 'I mean, Jesus, most of the time we're all covering up for his inadequacies. What are they going to do, get a team of session musos to do that for him? And who'd write his songs? He almost fucked up the album with that useless piece of shite he managed to squeeze onto it.' He skewers a waffle with his fork and smears it in syrup. His jaw juts as he munches down. 'Have you heard that track?'

'Yeah. It's not exactly great.'

'And he thinks he'd last five minutes on his own? He'd

just show himself up. The critics would savage him. Eat him alive.'

'He wasn't serious, man,' says Spin. 'Don't get worked up over it. It's nothing.'

'I know.' Jared stares out into the Strip. 'But it's pretty depressing to see all the coverage he gets, you know? Everyone seems to think this is *his* band. Vid Danton and, oh yeah, those other three. Just because he's the singer and he stands there with a guitar . . . You know he can't play guitar? It's not even plugged in most of the time.'

Spin nods.

'And why we give him joint credit for the song-writing, fuck only knows.'

'What would you do? If he did go solo?'

'Honestly? I don't know. I've no idea. It'd probably finish us off. We can't go back to how we were before. You can't ever go back.'

Spin's suite

The band has gone to the arena to soundcheck. Spin has asked Baxter to make sure the sound crew works over his decks, so he can stay behind to check his playlist again. He has spread his selections over the unmade bed and shuffles them into an order he knows will work. Spin will use vinyl for as long as he can. Deejaying with CDs is too easy; there's no skill in it. You can't crouch over the deck and watch the needle slide over the grooves. You can't drop a finger onto a CD and cue it up by hand. If one of his records is a half-beat out of time he can jolt it forwards by flicking a finger across the fat black plastic. He needs to be a *part* of the process. He needs to be able to touch his medium. CD players with their automatic beat-matching and super-accurate pitch control make the deejay irrelevant, take him out of the equation.

He takes a cloth from his case and wipes each record down, both sides, inside to outside. Nothing beats the sound lifted out of vinyl. He thinks of Mary, who considers his devotion quaint. She calls him a Luddite; maybe he is. But he won't change. He wonders what she is doing now. Probably just lifting Lucy out of her cot and putting her bottle into the microwave to warm. The surge of loneliness is sudden and acute. He is thousands of miles away. He is missing all the sudden jumps of progress as his daughter begins to assemble her own character.

Concert

The roar of the crowd shudders the darkened glass at the front of the booth. He pushes more juice into the amp and fights back, each pushing the other to double and then redouble their volume. His limiter is blinking amber. When it goes red, just before the automatic cut-in intervenes to stop the speakers from melting, he gives up the fight and nudges the levels back down to the safe levels. His monitor is jacked so high the bass is thumping him in the gut. His heart is just another beat to filter.

Spin batters the cross-fader, jumping from deck to deck,

taking competing sounds and melding them into a seamless aggregate. He fades down one of the tracks and lets the other, Trent Reznor singing 'Closer', drone out. Handling records is Spin's life, and he flips the disk off the turntable and drops it into its sleeve and into the flight box, all without thinking. He knows what he wants next, dips a hand inside and pulls out a rare Grooverider mix of Filter's 'The Best Things'. It's on the deck, needle applied, in one fluid motion. He stoops to read the tune out of the vinyl grooves, as intense as a master potter at his wheel, then presses his cans to one ear and lets the sound rush in. He filters out everything but the beat, lets it drum his fingers and duck his head until it has seeped down into his bones. Once he has it there he opens himself outwards and breathes in the noise from 'Closer'. Trent singing out his bleak vision. Fifty-five beats per minute, really slow, metronomic, hypnotic. He tweaks the pitch of Filter until the ugly doppelgänger discord of the two tracks narrows, the beats stuttering together, then dropping into perfect alignment. 'Closer' drawing to its crescendo; ten seconds left before it ends, suddenly. No room for error. The crowd froth. The drum beats spiking in his head, jagged rhythmic peaks. He ends 'Closer' with a flurry of spinback and with the slider pushed up to the max, Filter marches out clean.

The crowd goes ballistic. They recognize the track at once, despite the tranced-out take added in the mix, and surge upwards in a sea of flailing, punching, grasping limbs. Fucking A. He gets the buzz. Ten thousand kids going crazy because of a quartz needle skimming over a piece of cheap vinyl he liberated from a rack in a second-hand shop in Camden. He has powered them to this: *he* loves this song, it is his choice, and he loves it more because of them. This is better than sex. This is better than drugs.

The booth is built next to the mixing desk, halfway between the stage and the back of the arena. The crowd surrounds him on every side. Every fresh cheer is a visceral thrill. The walls shake from bodies thrown against them, hands slapping. He feels like a sailor awash in a boiling sea.

This set has never been tried before. Each track has been chosen to ratchet up the crowd's mania until, just when the tension is as taut as piano wire, it drops away into silence. And that's where Astrid, and then the band come in. The eye of the storm before the hurricane to follow.

The clock on the wall shows ten-ten, time for him to pass the baton. He cuts up the track and lays down a chunky slab of fat bass from the sampler, then the cheesy version of the *Star Wars* theme. This is the signal. He watches as Astrid slides out of the wings and takes her position behind her keyboards. The crowd sees her and a wave rolls back at him from the stagefront as kids already soaked with sweat and spilt beer crack open the energy, natural and artificial, they have reserved for the gig proper. Spin fades down his outputs and blinks away the arc lights that burn into the crowd. Astrid stands like an angel in the chiaroscuro.

Spin collects his records. The band are on the stage. The sound is physical now, something more than sound. He still has the buzz but the low is coming. He needs a beer and some company.

Gretta

6 January
Islington

The envelope has been left unopened – propped on the mantelpiece next to the expired plane ticket to Las Vegas and the band's framed gold disk for 'Sound and the Fury' – since it arrived on Friday, six days ago. It remains untouched, still with the same pristine creamy finish, no smudging, no postmark. This is pure ostentation – Tamara and Chloe have gone to the expense of having it hand-delivered rather than subjecting it to the usual ministrations of the Post Office. Gretta knows what is inside without needing to open it: an invitation for the party tonight. The sisters have called on alternate days for the last week, and twice already today, to check and recheck that she and Jared are still coming. Now Gretta is screening her calls. She would rather stay at home and brood but she has agreed to go, and no amount of mental investment has yet procured a satisfactory excuse for backing out. Gretta suspects that their constant beavering, the Chinese water torture she has been forced to endure alone since Jared left for America last week, has eroded her defences. Resistance is pointless. It will be easier to make just a brief appearance than to suffer their recriminations next week.

The sisters hold an annual dinner on the sixth of January. Today's has neatly coincided with the release of the low budget art-house film that Tamara has a cameo part in, *Vaudevillian*. Gretta didn't go to the première; she finds the use of the phrase 'low-budget' as a synonym for 'high-quality' misleading, and sitting alone in a cinema full of couples (even ersatz showbiz couples) would just have reminded her of her loneliness – and she doesn't need to be reminded of that, especially not today. Before it became impractical to do the things that normal couples do – go shopping, take walks in the park, eat out on the spur of the moment – they often went to the movies together. They saw a movie on their first date, three years ago today, sniggering at the blockbuster of the moment together. Not including the dreary glitter of premières at the Leicester Square multiplexes, they haven't been to a proper cinema for months. Sitting there alone in the lounge on the evening of their third anniversary, Gretta realizes how much she misses those small luxuries. She wonders whether the impracticality of Jared's fame has become an excuse to neglect the intimacy they used to share.

Tamara is Jared's acquaintance. To call her a 'friend' would be an exaggeration; they went to college together and Tamara rekindled their acquaintance when Jared became more famous than she is, which is not very famous at all. This rapprochement might be a happy coincidence but Gretta is familiar enough with Jared's new attractiveness to others to suspect otherwise. She and the sisters have met briefly and exchanged a few pleasant words but their relationship is no more familiar than that. She surprised herself a little when she elected to go to this party despite Jared's absence. Normally the prospect of glad-handing a room full of complete strangers would fill her with dread, like dental surgery without anaesthetic.

No. She is making a point by going alone. This is an opportunity to step outside of Jared's shadow and forge her own path. Whenever she appears in the papers it is on the periphery of the photographs or as an addendum to the articles ('**Jared Melchior** of **Dystopia** and **Iggy Pop** talked into the night about a collaboration insiders tells us is just waiting to happen. Jared's girlfriend [society girl Gretta Conway] and Iggy's latest squeeze [a mystery blonde] looked on aghast as **Vid Danton** caused a scene with **Bobby Gillespie** from Primal Scream and **Bez** from the Happy Mondays . . .'). Gretta is tired of being an accessory to Jared's fame: always on the fringe, always in parenthesis. This is how the record company wants it. Safe, stable relationships conducted in public are not what the image consultants who plot and graph Dystopia's popularity call 'brand conducive'. They live in a genre that demands sullen misanthropy. Pictures of beaming partners or, even worse, children, are disapproved of. Vid is the consultants' wet dream – his voracious appetite for drugs and groupies needs no spin from them. Astrid and Damien are single and Astrid's semi-overt lesbianism is almost a selling point. Gretta provides them with more of a conundrum. Most of the time, she is kept scrupulously in the wings. She feels like an embarrassment. This is the first opportunity she has had to demonstrate her independence. It is only a small gesture, but it is a start.

She stands and addresses her reflection in the mirror. She is not so plain. She is a tall, wispy woman, taller than Jared, and she wears her twenty-nine years well. Her skin is still tight and smooth over defined cheekbones. Her glossy black hair, wound into its natural coils, is worn combed back so that it spills down over her back. Balanced on her nose, scintillating restlessly, are the polished lenses and wire frames of her reading glasses, screening her delicate and restive eyes. She looks OK, she thinks. *Twenty-nine, and I still look good.*

'Things look very bad for the weekend,' says the presenter on the new twenty-four-hour weather channel that Gretta is using to fill the silence with companionable noises. 'Following the coldest Christmas on record, it looks as if it's more of the same for the whole of the country as we push on into January. This band of low pressure and the winds blowing in from Eastern Europe look like they will be bringing with them even more snow and winter weather. So wrap up warm if you're out and about over the next few days.' She speculates on the presenter's circumstances, on the life he will return to as soon as his broadcast has been completed. His expression is eternally reassuring, but she thinks more with the fey hopefulness of youth than through any grim experience. She wonders at his age; younger than her, she guesses, maybe twenty-five? She wonders whether he is in a loving, mutually satisfactory relationship or if he feels as if he has been cast adrift too. His ring finger, extended along the slim device he uses to trigger changes in the blue-screen behind him, is ringless. She clicks the TV off.

She collects the jumbo bar of fruit and nut she has been comfort eating and goes into the bedroom. The new iBOOK, still not on public release, has been left open and powered up and its innards are glowing green through the transparent casing. Michael Kaiser gave the iBOOK to them to celebrate Dystopia's first appearance on the cover of *NME* (Vid, white paint, black eye shadow, looming in centre-shot; the others fanned around him, coven-like: 'Take me to your Readers! NOTHING can stop Dystopia now!').

An icon is blinking that new mail has arrived. Has Jared sent an anniversary card by email instead? With an hour to kill before she needs to prepare herself for the evening's festivities, she slides out a cigarette from the almost full packet balancing on the keyboard, and lights it. She is down to a pack a week now, the best in months. This is her last packet, she tells herself. This one and then no more. The cold snap has crystallized London's smog – the atmosphere, acrid and choking, is the best reason to quit she has ever had. Three people have already had fatal asthma attacks. This is aversion therapy on a massive, inescapable scale.

A tap on the keyboard dispels the screensaver (the themed Damien Hirst artwork commissioned for the band's first five singles). As the browser fills the screen the computer plays a half-megabyte snatch from the album: the only track (title forgotten) that Gretta doesn't find depressing, just morbid. They have separate email accounts and she sees dispassionately that the new mail is for him, not her. The messages in her in-box are rendered in dull, demoralizing grey, already opened but not yet deleted. Probably, she realizes with a flash of self-insight, to hoodwink herself with the impression of popularity. At the top are her three most recent messages, each from Tamara, each exhorting her in increasingly zealous and frantic terms not to neglect the evening's appointment: 'You simply must *not* forget tonight. I've booked a car for you both. T.' Tamara is attacking on all fronts. Gretta has not mentioned that Jared is in America. Having the invitation rescinded because of his absence would be more than she could bear, whatever her opinions about the sisters and their hollow little party might be.

She closes the window and hovers the pointer over the shortcut to Jared's mailbox, bulging cartoonishly with mail. She double-clicks it open ('You have new mail,' the animated postman cheerfully reports) and, suppressing the guilty reprimand for this minor invasion of his privacy, scans the unread messages, all sixty-five of them, a thick wedge of blackened type. His user profile is customized to display the sender, subject and the first line of the mail. There are messages from Michael Kaiser at Revolution Records. There are a couple of addresses she recognizes as belonging to music journalists. Here's one from Trent Reznor; he has mixed Spin's version of 'Sound and the Fury' that MTV-USA has on heavy rotation. He has been bugging Jared to visit his studio in New Orleans to contribute riffs for his new record.

Gretta notices immediately that one of the unread messages is from DystopiaFan3@Hotmail.com. She swishes the cursor over:

From: DystopiaFan3@hotmail.com
To: RockGod4@hotmail.com
Date: Wednesday, January 5, 1.38 P.M.
Subject: Why so cruel to me?

*When I tried to send emails to your old address my delivery
receipts bounced.*

How has she found his address? (Force of habit reflexively
attributes gender to the androgynous correspondent.) Jared
has already had to close down three email accounts after a
hacker correctly attributed the addresses to him and then
published the details on the web. She understands, vaguely,
that software exists that is able to scan global email traffic
for the unusual combinations of keywords and circumstances that might indicate the presence of a particular
individual. On the previous occasions that his anonymity
has been compromised, Jared has been deluged with
incoming mail, some of it creepy. He has already had to
adopt three new cyber-personas – he is now RockGod4@
hotmail.com. (Gretta is not sure which is worse – the
name, or the fact that three others have staked previous
claim to it.)

Klaus, the stoical German ex-Stasi tech-guy who looks
after Revolution's IT, told them about these threats with
enough straight-faced gravity to suggest they risked their
physical well-being if they didn't follow his house-rules. He
visited the band to install matching facilities; ultra-high bit
transfer protocols so that they can compose together in
real-time wherever they are. He also set up supposedly

secure accounts and urged them to avoid using obvious keywords that might 'compromise' their cyber-safety: hence, they must substitute 'The Project' for Dystopia, 'The Record' for *Plastic People*, and so on. A 'safe' list of suggested synonyms has been stuffed into a drawer somewhere, discarded and redundant. Jared finds it all hilariously over-the-top, all very espionage, very Bond, and Gretta doubts he pays very much attention. *She* pays no attention.

Gretta wiggles the mouse hesitantly over the EXPAND button for Hi!, and then with a jab of her finger she whooshes the cursor to the bottom of the screen, hits the START button and then selects SHUT DOWN. She pushes away from the desk and stands up, heading into the bathroom to run a bath and prepare herself for Tamara's party.

Street

The remote control prods the security computer to fasten the locks, activate the burglar alarms and establish a connection with the security company's new residential security mainframe. The connection secured, it triggers a net of infrared motion detectors that criss-cross the empty house. The system is called Cerebus, which Gretta finds rather pompous, and it cost twenty-five thousand pounds to install, or the price of a small terraced house on the island where Gretta grew up. This is another of the record company's little presents, although Michael Kaiser describes it as 'investment protection, more for my peace of mind than for yours'.

The weather has been wintry for days and now more fat flakes of snow begin to fall. Over the city a vault of winter clouds as cold and grey as limestone. The street is far enough from the main roads to be quiet and the snow deadens the urban hum to a murmur. The wind picks up, whistling through the street, arctic. She wraps her coat around herself tightly and negotiates the narrow flight of steps down to the pavement.

She has accepted Tamara's offer of a car rather than struggle across town on the Northern Line or by taxi. Seeking to ameliorate her indolence, she has asked the driver to pick her up on Upper Street, a brisk five-minute stroll away. The snow begins to fall more heavily as she sets off, settling on the bonnets of the BMWs and Mercedes lining the road. She feels a jolt of unexpected optimism. She enjoys Islington, with its quaint streets of distinguished terraces, the well-painted railings, uncurtained windows revealing freeze-frame dioramas of other people's lives. It is comforting to confirm that the ordinary world is continuing without her, that if her temporary dislocation from the everyday run of things should come to end, it will still be there, just as she remembers it.

She cuts across Prebend Street and passes the Catholic school where the playground is marked out with the concentric circles and gridlines of children's games. The snow is settling. A thin shroud already covers the streets and the doleful sky promises worse. The world seems muffled, deadened. Snow has always been an otherworldly phenomenon for her, bringing with it the languor and lethargy of afternoons spent in front of the hearth. It has always been a trigger for her memories. Her childhood: gazing through a circle swiped in the frost of the dining-room window and over the snowy field to the lake where the ferry is crossing to the mainland. The boat seemingly gliding over the white ice and only the thin channel of steaming water proving otherwise. A final journey before the water freezes solid and the ferry has to take the longer route, until the spring thaw.

A woman walking in the same direction towards Upper Street breaks into a trot and crosses the road, aiming directly at Gretta. She is in her late twenties or early thirties, well dressed but entirely unremarkable: the kind of face that will naturally submerge into a crowd, a face that will prove difficult to reconstruct after the event. Gretta turns as the steps quicken, muffled by the snow.

'You *bitch*,' screeches the woman, bug-eyed, accelerating towards Gretta and then raising her hands. There is a glint, something metallic – only a bangle – Gretta raises her arms, warding the woman away. 'You bitch!' she snarls again, terminating her headlong plunge with a double-handed shove to the sternum that sends Gretta lurching against the cold railings overlooking the basement windows of the flatlet below. The woman has stumbled with the impact and, as she rights herself, palms in the patchy snow, a tightly wound coil of copper hair brushes against Gretta's nose.

'I know who you are,' she hisses, drool spilling from her faintly moustachioed lip onto her downy chin. 'Just

remember that, you slut. You don't *love* him, not like I do.'
She gives Gretta another double-handed shove, winding
her, and bounces away like an errant atom impulsed into a
fresh trajectory. She pounds towards Upper Street, her
shoes (red DMs, Gretta notices absently) leaving thick
treads in the snow.

Gretta stops to catch her breath and fumbles for her
mobile. As she feels the phone in her palm the woman cuts
sharp right into Essex Road and disappears behind the
trees and parked traffic. Gretta leaves the phone in her
pocket. There is no reason to call the police. She is unhurt.
Nothing has been taken. It was random, senseless and
motiveless – the woman is probably disturbed: a day-
release victim wandering the streets. Gretta imagines that
the police have more to concern them than push-and-runs.
And Gretta is already wiping out her assailant's details, the
face, the clothes, the shape, airbrushing them away. She
erases everything but the eyes – the paradox of atavistic
ferocity and blank lifelessness – and the mouth with its
thin masculine lips.

She rearranges her coat around herself and follows the
woman's tracks towards the clamour of the junction, until
they branch away. The sky is blackening. It looks like a
blizzard is coming.

Limo to the party

She sits pensively in the back, feeling isolated and
uncomfortable, as the driver cuts their way through the

dwindling nighttime traffic. Gretta is still shaken from the incident in the street – she needs a cigarette but she didn't bring any. A packet, still in its cellophane wrapping, is wedged into a trough behind the handbrake. She doesn't want to start a conversation to ask for one, and so she makes do with a stick of gum. Bars of golden light from the streetlights overhead roll over the car from front to back and Gretta sits, her neck supported by the leather neck-rest and her eyes aimed skywards, to watch them ripple like waves over the tinted rear windscreen. She tries to focus on individual flakes of snow floating down through the golden light, but they merge into a homogenous white morass and she gives up.

As they wait for the lights at Highbury Corner to change, a huge three-in-one hoarding fixed to the side of an office block snags Gretta's attention. Liz Hurley in a spray-on bikini (the judder of self-loathing that follows the automatic comparison is mercifully brief) disappears as the hoarding's rack of triangular Toblerone bars revolve to fill out *Plastic People*'s ubiquitous cover shot – the four of them sulking into David Bailey's grainy camera, the epitome of contrived alienation. Market-friendly enmity. Gretta looks up at Jared, his brown skin darkened by the eye-shadow circling his coal-black eyes, and wonders where the emptiness has come from. Why is she so maudlin? Her mood dampened, freshly pensive, the lights flicker green and the car judders and draws into the delta of traffic.

'You OK?' asks the driver. 'All strapped in nice and safe?'

'I'm fine,' replies Gretta, curtly.

'Better safe than sorry.' She says nothing. The driver is young, probably still in his early twenties. His fingers, wrapped around the leather-sheathed steering wheel, are heavy with fat gold rings.

'This weather,' he offers.

She says nothing.

'You know who I think you are?' he says after a pause, swivelling to look at her directly. He looks like a toy soldier in the limo company's sharp livery.

'Nope,' says Gretta. This is the last thing she needs now. 'I'm nobody.'

'No – I'm sure I've seen you before. Sure of it.'

'I doubt it.'

'Listen – I don't mean to pry. If you want me to, I'll shut up.'

'Please.'

'OK, sure, no problemo.' He busies himself with the driving, but Gretta watches his eyes flicking up, lizard-like, to the rear-view mirror and flicking back down again when he sees that she notices him. He clicks on a radio, dials through the static, clicks it off again.

'But you *are* who I think you are, aren't you? You're going out with that guy, you know, that guy from the band? The, like, gothic band? I listen to them on the radio sometimes. My nephew's got their album. Wait, wait – here, this is you, right?' Driving one-handed and half out of his seat, he has leant across to the passenger side and produced a folded copy of yesterday's *Standard*. He hands it to her. 'I've got you, right? That's you?'

There is a picture of Jared and Gretta, him glowering, nurturing the brand, her staring blandly, vapidly. She remembers the picture. It was the day before he flew out. They had been fighting, not that it was obvious from a picture that looked just like all the other pictures that beat the record company's embargo and included her.

'You got me,' sighs Gretta. 'Could you just drive the car, please?'

'Sure, sure. I just had to know? OK? My curiosity just got the better of me?' He speaks in questions, the end of his sentences fluttering quizzically up half an octave. 'I've had famous people in this car before, course, all kinds of stars and such like. Martine McCutcheon, Prince Naseem, that girl from *Wheel of Fortune*, the boy band doing so well – what's their name again? – and Geri Halliwell, Les Ferdinand and that bird off the telly he's seeing – Dani Behr, that's it? Watch where you're going, love! Women drivers, no disrespect intended of course, but she was more interested in her reflection than the state of the road. The three Fs: focus *fucking* focus. That's my motto, my road rules. Where was I? Jeffrey Archer left a manuscript in the back that I've still got in my flat; there was that Trevor McDonald, Alan Sugar, Ofra Hazel, David Essex. That's one of the perks of the job, driving people like that, you know? The rich and the famous. I'd love it if you'd just sign my logbook before you go, if it's all right, not too much trouble? I'll understand if it is, too much trouble that is, course, but it's just one of my little habits, you know? A foible. Makes the job more interesting. You won't mind, will you? And it's, like, company policy that I get you to sign to make sure you're happy with the drive and the service and all that.'

'No. I mean yes, that's fine. I'll sign whatever you want.'

'I'll add you to the collection.'

'You do that.'

The Boltons

Tamara and Josh have a large house in the Boltons. Tamara used to live with Chloe before her marriage. Their palatial apartment was a hub of high society but now Chloe lives there alone. These small details Gretta has absorbed, more by osmosis than any concerted effort to educate herself, from the society pages in the appropriate newspapers and magazines.

The blaze from half-a-dozen windows on the first floor casts warm squares of light on the snow as the driver draws up beside the entrance gate. To one side is a concreted area where an Aston Martin, a Jaguar and two BMWs have been tightly parked. She is pleased now that she accepted the offer of the limo. Stepping from the back of a London cab would have been an inauspicious entrance amidst such a public display of wealth. She tips the driver with a five-pound note and signs his papers.

The door opens as she approaches and a doorman dressed in an immaculate three-piece tuxedo removes her coat. The downstairs lounge has been converted into a temporary cloakroom. The tiles on the hall floor are wet with melting snow carried over the threshold on the shoes of other guests. An attendant is wiping this slush away with a mop. The muffled thump of music is audible from upstairs, punctuating the murmur of conversation.

'Am I late?' asks Gretta, anxiously.

'Not at all,' the man says, folding her coat across his arm. 'The other guests are upstairs, Miss Conroy.' She is impressed that he knows her name. She doesn't realize that he has a list of all the guests, together with their pictures, and has already matched her likeness with the grainy CCTV image fed through to the monitor in the cloakroom. 'Andrew will show you up.'

Andrew, similarly immaculate in appearance and bearing, leads the way up the broad flight of stairs towards the source of the music. Gretta pauses, asks for directions to the toilet. He makes a silent diversion, leading her instead along a quiet corridor onto which a number of closed doors abut.

She locks the door behind her and runs the cold tap. With her forehead pressed against the icy glass of the mirror, she lets the water gush over the backs of her wrists, trying to cool her hot blood. She is suddenly nervous. She eschewed the première because she would have to go alone. Why did she think that a dinner party would be any easier? It will be worse – she will be the only guest without a partner. Her intention to strike out for herself seems foolish now, a foolish decision driven by narcissism and conceit. And that lunatic woman in the street has got under her skin. Gretta is on edge. She needs a drink and a smoke badly. She spills out the contents of her bag and finds her

Librium. She swallows the tablet with a mouthful of water, braces her hands on the wall, and works to regain control.

Andrew is waiting for her a discreet distance along the passage. He leads her to a doorway filled with the light from inside the room. 'Just a moment,' she says, using a fumble inside her bag as an excuse to delay her entrance. Her heart is fluttering and she takes a deep breath, still rummaging, until she feels she has herself back under control. She listens to the music and the burble of conversation. This was a terrible idea. What possessed her to think that she belonged in company like this? The evening will be excruciating.

'Gretta Conroy!' bubbles Tamara enthusiastically.

They are in a large room, well lit, with a dozen people either sitting on or gathered around two vast sofas in the centre of the room. The usual, natural divisions are beginning to form: friends congregating with other friends, falling back upon old acquaintance, whilst they drink enough to brave strangers they have yet to meet.

Tamara must have been standing just inside the door – there is no one else with her and Gretta suspects that she was waiting. This is not arrogance on Gretta's part – she has heard that hostesses have started arranging for their doormen to page them as guests arrive. Although she cannot actually see the telltale nugget of a pager bulging against the line of the daring Ocimar Versolato dress Tamara wears, Gretta is not about to rule out that possibility. Tamara is, if nothing else, an avid follower of fashion.

'Fabulous you could make it,' says Tamara. She fixes

Gretta in her high-beam smile, temporarily overlooking Jared's absence. It can only be a temporary reprieve. She is a good-looking woman, late twenties, tanned from frequent modelling trips abroad, hair left to hang straight and long, fine features rumoured to have been surgically enhanced.

'It was nice of you to invite me.'

'Oh, *really*! You and Jared were the first names on my list. You're my favourite famous couple.' Gretta swallows down a surge of irritation. She cannot stand insincerity, and she can see that this false bonhomie is going to grate. She smiles thinly, allowing Tamara to take her by the arm and guide her further into the room.

'Try some sushi?' asks Tamara, half-turning to attract the attention of one of the waiters working the room.

'I'm on a diet,' lies Gretta, patting her midriff.

'Oh, *no*! Nonsense!' Tamara squeals, taking Gretta's wrist. She is wearing an enormous diamond studded bracelet. It is the most hideous piece of jewellery Gretta has ever seen, and probably the most expensive. 'You're the absolute last person I know who needs to diet. Look at you! Look, here – look at your wrist. It's stick thin! You're so *perfect* you make me green with envy. And the sushi is just *so* delectable. I'd hate for you to miss out. Especially the nori rolls with pickled ginger and soy sauce.'

'It's a step up from cheese straws and sausages on a stick.'

Tamara is momentarily caught off guard, wrong-footed. Gretta winces inwardly – it was not intended to be a slight.

But Tamara has recovered: 'Are you sure I can't tempt you?'

'Maybe later.'

'You promise me you'll eat something?'

Gretta promises Tamara that she will eat something. She promises to herself that she will leave as soon as she can make a discreet exit.

'And where is your talented other half?' she asks. 'I saw him in the papers this week.'

'Jared's in America – touring. Didn't you know?' A flicker passes across Tamara's face – confusion? – before she smoothes it away, almost before Gretta can notice. The woman is a skilful dissembler. 'It was on the television? You didn't see it?'

'Gretta, my dear, you absolutely know I don't watch television these days. It's all so *phoney*. I stopped after those hurtful stories came out. Oh, and by the way, thank you so much for your card. *So* sweet of you both. It meant such a lot to me and Josh to have your support.' Tamara was rumoured to have been checked into the Priory six weeks ago to dry out a drink problem. Gretta didn't send a card but decides she can't be bothered to correct her. Tamara scowls for a moment, diverted from her rehearsed conversation, before finding her bearings. She frowns afresh. 'And I had absolutely *no* idea about Jared. That's *so* unfortunate. I was rather counting on him being here. There are all sorts of people here who'd love to meet him. You should have mentioned it.'

'I thought I did. It must have slipped my mind.'

'It doesn't matter. The others will be disappointed, naturally.'

'Well, these things can't be helped.' *And what about me? I'm here, aren't I? I'm braving this hypocrisy fest although I have no idea what for, exactly.* 'I thought I'd come along anyway.'

'Well, yes, I'm glad you did.' Tamara is floundering a little, diverting resources to an internal recalculation of the geometry of the party, and the consequences Jared's failure to attend might present.

'You don't mind?'

'Don't be silly,' she answers, the mask replaced. 'Another time.' Tamara's eyes wander uncomfortably and she fingers the stem of her glass. Here it is, right on cue: the first of the evening's awkward pauses. 'Listen,' she continues. 'Let me introduce you to the others. There are some interesting people here tonight.'

She leads her guest to one of the sofas, where sit five people, four of whom Gretta has never seen before in her life. 'Everyone, this is Gretta Conway – Jared Melchior's girlfriend. Jared couldn't make it tonight. Gretta tells me they're touring. Gretta, let me introduce you. Over here is Clive, here's lovely Owen, you know my sister Chloe of course, this is Marcel and this is Antonia. Most of them work in the movie business, but they can now give you all the glamorous details because I have to make sure that the food is ready.' Despite herself, Gretta wants Tamara to stay with them – the woman being her only anchor in a sea of unfamiliar faces, and without a means of inclusion in whatever they are discussing Gretta risks floundering. With perfect timing, a waiter appears with a tray bearing flutes of champagne. Although she dislikes champagne, she takes one. At the very least it will serve as a prop to occupy her hands.

After the opening small talk, Gretta allows herself to drift out to the edges of the conversation. The four of them are evidently familiar with each other and, once they sense their duty to include Gretta has been absolved, they revert to the knowing gestures and verbal shortcuts that all friends rely on. They are talking about parties they have been to recently, bitching mostly, outdoing each other with their horror stories. Clive describes a party he went to where the music was provided by a troupe of buskers gathered up from the tube stations where they usually perform.

'It was horrendous,' he says. 'Ten competing versions of *Hey Jude*, and none of them any good.'

Gretta nods and smiles in all the right places, but she isn't really listening. She is wondering what Jared is doing, why he hasn't been in touch on their anniversary, whether his silence surprises her, whether she is really all that concerned. She remembers the row they had before he left for the airport. It was petty – all their rows are petty – and she shrugged it off without effort as soon as he got into the car to leave. The rows don't pain her any more, not like they used to; they just wear her down. Now she wonders if he is ignoring her because they parted badly. Is he trying to punish her?

'There're a couple of others still to come,' says Tamara, returning. 'But I think we should start now anyway.' She shepherds everyone into another large room, dominated by a long dining table and chairs. A fat brown turkey, skinned and basted, sits at one end of the table on a silver platter. At the opposite end of the table is a hunk of venison, sitting in a deep tray with its juices soaking back into it. The path between these two offerings is lined with a selection of starters: Sydney rock oysters on the half shell with fresh lime wedges; kangaroo swaggies with Illaware plum sauce; spinach and pinenut tartlets; curried vegetable puffs with coriander chutney. There are dishes of potatoes, some mashed with mature cheddar, some roasted, some boiled with parsley. There is sweet-potato pudding and cranberry consommé. There are sprouts, carrots with melted butter, bowls of shelled peas and cauliflower, and china jugs full of gravy. A separate platter holds the vegetarian options: spanakopita, eggplant casserole, ricotta dumplings with asparagus.

A fruit-stand holds pyramids of apples and oranges and a glass vase holds long stalks of celery. The sweet trolley is jammed with pecan strawberry shortcake; apple dumplings; cinnamon apple rolls; poached pears in port sauce; banana nut bread; banana and pecan beignets; and frozen boysenberry compote. There is Kir Royale sorbet; White Russian sorbet; rainbow daiquiri sorbet; lime margarita sorbet; mai tai sorbet; mint julep sorbet. The guests murmur appreciatively as they file into the dining room.

'I can't claim *all* the credit for this,' says Tamara, directing them to their places. 'Although I do admit to the glaze on the venison – one of my mother's hand-me-downs.' Gretta is seated between Josh, Tamara's husband, and Clive who earlier recounted the anecdote about the buskers. Clive and Josh talk around and over her about football, a subject in which she is utterly unable to muster even the slightest interest. Three waiters, in matching white shirts and black waistcoats, emerge to take their places hovering around the table.

'Josh, darling,' says Tamara, 'I think we're just about ready. Would you do the honours?' She has a long carving knife in her hand and indicates the turkey. Josh excuses himself from the conversation and takes his position by the bird.

Memory

Gretta will only remember excerpts from the dinner that follows. Swathes of conversations she will have, or over-hear, will be blended together into a homogenous mush. The tedium, the alcohol, the Librium, the two lines of coke she will do in the toilet, the events after she leaves the party – all will collude to fuse her recall of what was said and done, into a seamless aggregate. When she reviews the evening's events occasional globs will bob to the surface, twitching there before submerging back into the ooze.

'Quite a spread,' says Gretta lamely, feeling completely superfluous.

'Tamara usually pushes the boat out for this dinner,' says Clive. 'You haven't been before, have you?'

'No, this is my first.'

'This turkey is *good*.'

'It is. Juicy.'

'What was your name again?'

'Gretta. Gretta Conroy.' Clive apologizes, says he has a terrible memory for names. 'Did Tamara cook all this herself?'

He laughs, then checks that Josh is otherwise occupied. He is. 'God, no! They hired caterers. I'd be surprised if she even shelled a pea.' Another serving of turkey is slopped down into the gravy on his plate. 'Pass that cranberry sauce?' he asks, chomping down noisily.

Gretta, drinking because she needs something to do during the silent pauses that drag on for ever. Waiters patrol the table silently, armed with bottles of vintage wine. Her glass refills magically and she has lost track of how much she has had already. The Librium has dulled the edge of her anxiety, but she is still drinking hard.

'Who's that?' Gretta asks Clive. A guest sitting opposite Gretta is drinking straight from a bottle of JD. The bottle was full when he sat down for the meal, but he has finished half of it and now he is slugging from the remnants. He is wiry and agitated, late teens or early twenties, T-shirt bearing a picture of Kermit smoking a crack pipe, rings through both eyebrows, nostrils (both) and ears (multiple, like a coiled spring), plus a bar through the fleshy bridge of his nose. He reminds Gretta of Quentin Tarantino, only punier and with a bigger nose. He is bugging Chloe, leaning towards her, gesticulating expansively, leering.

'Who?'

'Him' – she points – 'the drunk.'

'That's Muppet, Tamara's dealer,' he answers matter-of-factly.

'Tamara's invited her dealer?'

'No party is complete without charlie. Didn't you know? Everyone does it.'

'Is he dealing tonight?'

'Of course.'

Gretta, on her knees, jack-knifed over the toilet snorting up a line of coke she scored from Muppet. A drop of blood on the rolled twenty. She slumps back against the wall and spreads her arms like Icarus soaring into the darkness. For a few exquisite heartbeats she is omnipresent and omnipotent. The cool sting of the coke burns her nostrils. She pours the rest of the wrap onto the toilet seat, and chops and scrapes another line with her credit card. As she lowers her head, there are a few light taps against the pane. She turns to the window. The flakes, silver and dark, falling obliquely against the lamplight outside.

'Have you seen Tamara's movie?' she asks a bald guy, a six-footer dressed in a black polo-neck and white Levis. He says he produces movies, movies and adverts, although mostly adverts.

'*Vaudevillian*?'

'Is that what it's called?'

'Yeah. Like, what does that even mean?'

'Have you seen it?'

'I went last night. It's shit. It's embarrassing, turgid, worthless shit.'

'Is it?'

'Trust me. I've seen my share of turkeys, but this . . .'

'I heard it was good. I mean, I heard it wasn't shit.'

'Trust me, OK? Life's too short to waste time on it.'

'What does *she* think?'

'Who? Tamara? She loves it, of course. It's her "vehicle", she says. She says it'll lead on to better things.'

'Will it?'

'Oh, sure. Tamara has a rich and prosperous career lined up in the world of television adverts and late-night presenting. I mean, she couldn't act her way out of a paper bag. She's completely devoid of talent – *completely*. I'm not even sure why I bother coming to these things. I mean, it'd be understandable if there was major-league talent to be unearthed or if Tamara had a shred of influence or one, just one, decent contact. But the reality?' He throws up his hands.

'But I thought she was doing well?'

'Listen, she calls herself an "actress" but you want to know her justification for that?'

'She appears in movies?'

'*Anyone* can appear in the movies. If *you* wanted to be in the movies, I could get you a part, with lines, just like that.' He snaps his fingers. 'Her whole career is based on a total of two minutes fifty-two seconds' screen time in *Scream Harder* last autumn. *That* is what makes her such a big-time actress? Big fucking deal. Did you see that movie? She pouts. She flounces a bit. She screams – badly I might add. And her one line: "Ohmigod, that's a knife!" I mean, Jesus, I've seen dead people with more inflection. I don't know what Williamson was *thinking*, casting her.'

A pause. Gretta needs to fill it: 'Did you go to their wedding? Josh and Tamara's?'

As Tamara flounces past, he lowers his voice: 'Don't get me started on *that*. What a fucking orgy of bad taste that was. Essex bird and boy racer with unlimited funding – a recipe for disaster. You know they dressed their little boy up to look like an angel? Like, calling him Trooper wasn't enough of an insult to the poor little bastard.'

Talking about the layer of snow that is piling against the house outside, someone tells her that the natural state of the Earth is glacial, and that, historically, periods of relative warmth have only been sustained for ten- or twenty-thousand-year stretches. These pale in comparison with the million-year epochs of cold. This person suggests that human civilization has sprung up during one of these fleeting thaws, and that it must be nearing its end since we are still in the midst of the most recent ice age, an especially severe one, which set in some three million years ago.

A banker (she thinks), all in black, with goatee beard and a ponytail at the back: 'So, you're here all on your own, then?'

'Yes.'

'A free agent?' he asks.

'No.'

'You unattached? You're way too pretty to be unattached.'

'*No*, I have a boyfriend.'

'I don't see him.'

'He's in America. He's touring. He's in a band.'

'Wow, really?' He takes a cigar from the maplewood humidor, lights it, swigs from his cognac.

'Yes, really.'

'You know they have twelve bedrooms here?'

'Really?'

'You want to investigate one with me?'

'No, I've got a boyfriend. Are you even listening to me?'

'Hey, take it easy.'

'Does your girlfriend know you're hitting on me?'

'I'm not hitting on anyone, baby. Get *over* yourself.'

'Just fuck off back over there, OK, or I'm going to tip this glass over your head.'

'And that's not my girlfriend, OK?'

'Whatever.'

A pause. 'What band is this mystery boyfriend in?'

'This conversation's over.'

He shrugs, walks away.

Tamara: 'Why didn't you *tell* me that Jared wasn't coming tonight?'

Gretta: 'I thought I did.'

Tamara (slurring, drunk): 'You didn't. No. I would have remembered.'

Gretta: 'I'm sorry? OK? I *apologize*.'

Tamara: 'Oh, shit, it's not *your* fault. It's just Jared would have been perfect tonight, *perfect*, everyone knows him, he's so fucking famous, a *celebrity*, you know, a proper celebrity, like he's on the cover of every magazine right now, and the papers, the papers love him, and it's just so weird that I've known him for, like, *ages*, back in college, before *you* knew him, way before, and I'd love to ask him: How has this changed you? Are you a different person?'

Gretta: 'I didn't have to come.'

Tamara: 'I know. I'm grateful. It's been great to see you again. We should have lunch or something.'

Gretta: 'Yeah.'

As the plates from dessert are being cleared away, the door from the hallway opens.

'Everyone,' says Tamara, wedged between the tall, tanned man and his slight, dark-haired companion, 'Michael Bratsky and Caitlin are here.'

'Sorry we're so late,' says Michael, his accent thickly American. 'There's a big-time blizzard going on outside like you would not believe. The roads are terrible.'

Conversation starts up afresh as Michael and Caitlin sit down with their drinks. Gretta pays no attention. Her eyes are fixed on Michael's face. The new arrivals are placed next to Muppet, one on each side of him. They start talking earnestly, and Muppet switches between them like a spectator watching tennis. Gretta doesn't think he has noticed her yet. She wonders whether to excuse herself and leave but before she has the chance he looks up, catches her eye and waves. She smiles back, the corners of her lips curving up reflexively as he winks at her. He is tall and tanned, wearing a black suit with wide lapels and a white shirt, no tie. He looks just as he did when she last saw him, eight years ago. He hasn't changed a bit.

She is unable to concentrate as she drinks down a cappuccino. Michael is still talking with Muppet and the woman, Caitlin. Gretta looks over at his companion, assesses her – Caitlin is as thin as Muppet, with an emaciated Ally McBeal gauntness. Her skin is so pallid it looks almost translucent. She is smoking Lucky Strikes – the white of the cigarettes contrasts with her nails, painted black. He concludes something with Caitlin, who nods, and then he stands, clanging his spoon against Muppet's empty whisky bottle.

'Ladies and gentlemen.'

The conversations peter out and the guests turn to look up at Michael.

'Ladies and gentlemen,' he repeats. 'Firstly, I apologize

again for my quite unforgivable time-keeping. As I alluded to earlier, Caitlin and I were rather waylaid by your English weather. I'd always been led to believe that your country enjoyed a mild climate. I feel bound to say that, on tonight's evidence, quite the opposite is the case. This is more like Montreal! But, by missing out on the feast I am sure Tamara has treated you with, our punishment has already been a severe one.'

'We've made you both doggie bags,' Tamara chirps, to polite laughter.

He smiles. 'This is the tenth of these dinners I have been fortunate enough to attend. I wish that Tamara and Chloe could be persuaded to hold them more often than once a year, but they seem absolutely determined to ration them so as not to dull the thrill of expectation we all have as the turn of the year approaches. I feel sure that if the dinner was held every weekend I wouldn't tire of it, but we must bow to the wishes of our gracious hostesses. Here's to the next decade.'

He salutes them with a raised glass and then sips from the cognac.

'Now, ladies and gentlemen, unaccustomed as I am to public speaking' – he clears his throat, a peal of polite laughter – 'I will only intrude briefly upon this evening's festivities. As we are all well aware, our inestimable hostess has recently finished her latest film, one that I have been fortunate enough to finance in my own modest way. Indeed, many of us were fortunate enough to attend the première last night. For those that were unable to attend, I urge you – no, I *implore* you – to go. I feel bound to say that the film is a complete triumph. It is a film I have no doubt will perform spectacularly with the critics and at the box office. In particular, I would direct your special attention to the scene in which Tamara makes her entrance. I understand that it's often the case that a cameo steals the show. After watching Tamara act her co-stars off the screen last night, I have no doubt that there is truth in that rather clumsy generalization. Congratulations, then, Tamara, for a fantastic performance. May your agent reap the rewards for many years to come!'

The table claps, at first politely and then, when it senses that more is expected, vociferously. He clangs the bottle again.

'Ladies and gentlemen, allow me to finish by thanking Tamara and Chloe for their hospitality once again, and by sincerely hoping that the next year's meal comes around again quickly.' He hoists his glass into the air. 'A toast!' The table follows suit, a dozen raised glasses catching the light. 'To Chloe and Tamara.'

'To Chloe and Tamara,' chime the guests. Gretta joins the toast, still dazed to see him again and wondering how he knows Tamara or Chloe well enough to give this speech. He has grinned at her several times during his performance, and she has reciprocated shyly, embarrassed at her weakness, especially after such a span of time. She wonders again how much she has had to drink.

The table disbands and they reconvene in the drawing room. A trolley of spirits appears. Gretta takes a whisky and tries to act nonchalant as Michael, Caitlin and Muppet approach.

'Hi,' she stutters, feeling herself blush, embarrassed at her lack of poise. 'Michael, my God, how are you?'

'I'm good,' says Michael, smiling a smile that Gretta is dismayed to find she remembers easily. 'I'm real good. And you . . . *look* at you: you look a million bucks, Gretta.'

'It's been a few years.'

'Five years?'

'A long time,' Gretta says, unable to hold his gaze and hating herself for her weakness.

'Wow,' Michael says. 'It's so great to see you. I mean *really*.' She smiles. 'Listen, Gretta, let me introduce you to my friends. This is Muppet.' Muppet staggers against Caitlin as he snares another drink from a passing waiter. 'And this is Caitlin. Guys,' he takes Gretta's hands in his, 'this is the lovely Miss Gretta Conway, a very dear friend of mine.' He raises her hand to kiss it – his lips brush her knuckle, the middle one.

'And what do you do, Miss Gretta Conway?' asks Muppet, with a sleazy insouciance that makes her wonder if he is older than he looks.

'Muppet's drunk,' says Caitlin.

'I am not,' he responds.

'Journalism,' Gretta stretches the truth. '*Time Out*.' She hasn't been near the office for weeks, not since she found it impossible to reconcile the small fortune in her bank account with her friends sweating shit to pull down their meagre fifteen-thousand-pounds-a-year salaries so they could hold on to their dinky flats in Hampstead or their boxy maisonettes in Archway. With them she felt like an anthropologist observing captive primates, dimly embarrassed that this was her own origin, and hating herself for it: a hypocrite of the worst, most contemptible kind. She always said that money wouldn't change her, and now she knows that isn't true. She can never go back there, that much is certain. *Too much* has changed.

'Gretta was the great white hope of the features desk.'

'Was?' asks Caitlin.

'Alas, I hear she has ignored that well-worn axiom: never take work home with you.'

'You're screwing someone you interviewed?' Muppet asks, impressed. 'Nice moves.'

'Ignore him,' Michael says, clipping him on the side of the head. 'He gets excited when he meets new people.' Gretta smiles tightly, embarrassed for the wrong reasons, and suddenly unsure of herself again.

'How do you two know each other?' Caitlin asks, her accent a more tuneful rendering of Michael's brash drawl. Gretta notices that her tongue is pierced – a stud gleams against the moist red.

'Gretta did a story on me five years ago. Or was it six? Christ, the years go by so fast, I can't keep track.'

'Eight years ago,' Gretta corrects. 'Just after the recession.' Gretta was doing a feature on the new wave of cocky, well-educated City traders earning stratospheric salaries despite the shiny new attitude of fiscal prudence in the wake of the recession. Michael was trading in the pits at the Stock Exchange. Harvard-educated, including a Rhodes scholarship at Balliol, a powerful father (the CEO of Glaxo Wellcome's US operation), impeccably mannered, always beautifully dressed in bespoke Ozwald Boateng suits and

Oxford cap shoes, he was the golden boy of the trading floor. He was the first trader to pull down a seven-figure salary, made largely thanks to his then-pioneering trade in obscure internet and biotech securities, before the media and the market inflated their prices beyond sustainable levels and started the feeding frenzy. He was The American – he achieved iconic status for his wide-boy Essex colleagues and became the darling of the media, the acceptable face of corporate avarice. Gretta heard that he stopped trading two or three years ago to transform himself into an asset manager, pooling multi-billions of other people's money in pension funds, and investing on the strength of his market hunches.

'I was a great white hope myself back then,' Michael says, with mock artlessness. 'Back in the good old days before computers took over the markets, when all this newfangled nonsense was but a distant speck on a beautiful horizon.' He sighs theatrically. 'But these things happen to the best of us. We move on.'

'Poor love,' Caitlin says soothingly, grinning. She pats his hand. 'Losing a zero off that eight-zero salary must have smarted.'

'It is a struggle, my dear, a daily struggle. An ordeal, even.'

'Michael's just had his car shipped over from the States. You don't want to *know* how much it cost.'

'It was worth every nickel and dime. They can insist on making us drive on the wrong side of the road, but they will *not* force me to shift gears with my left hand.' She is fixed by his eyes as he speaks. 'But look at me: you've finished your whisky and I haven't found you another. Which is shockingly remiss of me. Another gin and tonic for Caitlin, I believe, and an orange juice for the young pup.'

'Fuck you,' says Muppet.

'Sorry, my mistake. A *fizzy* orange for the youngster.'

Muppet gives Michael the bird, leering. Michael attracts the attention of the waiter. 'Excuse me,' he says. 'I'll be back in a moment.' He heads over towards Tamara. Caitlin follows him. Gretta wonders: *Is he trying to set me up with Muppet? This sappy, sodden adolescent?*

'What do you do?' she asks him without thinking, only taking her eyes off Michael to ensure the question is properly received and not lost in the static of the party.

'Like you don't already know. You've already sampled my main product. It's the import/export business,' he says, grinning, leaning in conspiratorially. 'Well, the import business, mostly.'

'What kind of merchandise?' she asks vacantly, distracted.

A frown flickers across his brow. 'Certain illicit products. Powders, for example. Pharmaceuticals. Pills. Like, you know? You *enjoy* the sample?'

'Oh, I see. How interesting.' Michael is talking to Tamara, who is politely protesting at whatever it is he has told her. Gretta is flooded by flashback. She can barely bring herself to look at Muppet.

'There *are* perks. Products have to be sampled for quality – that sort of thing. I'm doing some more sampling later, if you're interested.'

Michael returns. 'Listen, sorry to be a killjoy,' he says, 'but Caitlin and I have some business to attend to. It's been great to see you again, Gretta, really great. We mustn't leave it so long next time. Here, take this.' He presses a business card into her hand. 'And call me? We'll meet up in the City for lunch sometime. I know a place.'

'Sure,' she says, her heart sinking. 'We must do that.' She takes the card and slips it into her purse. Michael kisses her on the cheek, brushing the corner of her lips. Caitlin says goodbye and allows herself to be taken by the hand and led towards the door. Gretta bites her lip and tries to maintain her composure. Muppet is still at her side, although he is scanning the others restlessly.

'What's the deal with them?' Gretta asks him, striving for innocuousness.

'Beats me. They fuck like rabbits, I know that much. But as for the rest . . .' He shrugs expressively. 'Who knows? Listen, it's been great to meet you, but I've got to run. I'll see you around.'

The Boltons, exterior

She looks again at the business card, still clenched in her cold hand. 'Michael R. Bratsky', it says, 'Senior Partner, The Pound Machine – Fund Analysis.' And underneath the small-print contact details (phone, fax, homepage, email, v-mail), in handwriting: *'Be outside – street – 1.30 a.m.'*

It is 1.40 a.m. Gretta is waiting in the road outside the house, far away enough to be sure that she can't be seen from the windows, as the muffled sounds of the party continue unabated. The music has been turned up. The dull thud-thud-thud of the bass line gently rattles the windows in their frames. A scrawny cat, filthy and shivering in the cold, slinks from behind a row of parked cars and, keening softly, continues to search for scraps. It is difficult to rationalize why she is waiting here, in the freezing cold, for Michael to pick her up. Her feelings are imprecise, scrambled, and she cannot discern a sensible justification from the drone of static that fills her head.

The snow has been falling all evening, judging by the foot-thick carpet that has settled over everything. The tyre treads from limousines and taxis have compacted the snow on the road into a grooved, hardened, icy whiteness. A black cab, its motor chugging idly and dense clouds pumping from its exhaust, waits by the entrance. The jaundiced yellow glare of the headlights picks out fat snowflakes that spin and turn within the twin beams. The cold is compressing, drawing in on itself, and in its pithiness it seems almost solid. A sympathetic knot of fear or anticipation forms in the pit of her stomach.

Car

'I'm glad you're here,' says Michael, resting a hand on Gretta's knee, squeezing it. She says nothing, ignores the shiver of electricity, and stares unblinkingly at the white cityscape slowly passing by on either side, as he guides the big American car gingerly through the treacherous streets.

Islington

A microwave signal is beamed from a mobile phone in the Nevada desert, on the outskirts of Las Vegas, to a mobile telephone switching office at Barstow. The signal is digitally compressed and, combined with millions of other signals, bounced off a satellite in a geostationary orbit over the Atlantic and aimed at a station in Hampshire. It travels by fibre-optic cables to an exchange in Camden, and then by copper wire to the flat in Islington.

The answerphone picks up the call after three rings. The digital recording of Vid and Jared's jamming session plays back and, when it finishes, the beep is longer than usual; Gretta's mother has left a message and she tends towards prolixity even when her daughter is out. As the answerphone begins to record, the only audible noise is the crackle and hiss of solar interference and – *there* – faint laughter from a group by a blazing fire in a desert.

'Hi, Gretta, it's me. Pick up. It's, what, nine your time? Where the fuck are you? Pick up?'

The message ends. The flat is quiet again.

Millbank

Michael has a penthouse on the top floor of a new high-rise on the north bank of the Thames at Millbank. She remembers enviously reading a double-page feature on the development ('Upper West Side Living comes to the North

Bank') in the *Observer*'s Life supplement a month ago – the basic duplex flats were fetching £250,000 each and Michael's apartment covers half of the top floor, fifteen thousand square feet's worth of prime London real estate. God only knows how much it cost him.

The lounge is sparely populated with furniture from a selection of contemporary designers. As he collects crystal tumblers from a vinyl-and-chrome 1950s-style bar, he brusquely points out an Arne Jacobsen chair, a table by Jørgen Gammelgaard, a Castiglione Boalum cantilevered lamp, authentic signed Rothko prints of the Seagram Murals. An exquisite bonsai Juniper in a terracotta pot sits alone on a Saarien hand table. Music (Simply Red, which she loathes, but at least his taste is flawed) faded up discreetly when they entered the flat, triggered by the severing of an electrical relay when Michael opened the door. Hidden lights in the ceiling and behind wall sconces were also triggered, and are slowly blooming around the room. The tiniest details are perfect, just so – the minutiae that cost the most to get right – and everything drips, *oozes*, the kind of serious money that puts Jared and Gretta's good fortune into the starkest of reliefs. She suddenly feels foolish and arrogant.

'This was all just a shell five months ago,' Michael says with an expansive gesture as he disappears into the kitchen. 'We ripped out the original fittings; they were rather crass, unfortunately. Wine or whisky, whisky or wine? Do I have a bottle? Yes, praise the 7-Eleven, a bottle of rather vulgar JD. That do for you?' A bottle is unscrewed and the contents poured. 'I had architects, builders, the whole shooting match in here for, like, *months*. It's only just ready for public inspection. You're my first visitor.'

'Caitlin hasn't been around?'

'Do you know, I don't believe she has.' He is still fiddling in the kitchen, prising the lid off an airtight container.

The lounge is a forty-foot-by-forty-foot expanse of Canadian oak floors and exposed limestone brickwork ('individually selected from the nave of a Neapolitan chapel shelled by the Allies in 1945'). One wall is taken up by a wide span of window with a sheer view across the sleeping city. In another large window is inserted a door that opens out onto a thousand-square-foot oriental garden dug into the roof terrace. A fu dog guards the entrance, snow piling on his snout. Gretta pushes back the sliding door and steps outside.

Camellia and hydrangea have been planted on either side of a gravel path that leads to a glass-fronted balcony thirty storeys up. There are flourishing clumps of calanthe, white chrysanthemum, groomwell and peony sprouting from narrow clay trays angled back from the path. Gretta stops to brush the snow from an azalea bowed under its winter freight.

'The Japanese call them Satsuki,' says Michael, indicating the shrub. 'They produce dwarf hybrids for their bonsai and ikebana. That one's a more traditional breed. And see this tree, here? It's a Japanese plum-yew. Fairly hardy, strong enough to survive the shitty atmosphere up here. The Japs use the wood to make their Go boards. You remember Go?' He smiles warmly, knowingly.

She remembers. She remembers playing game after game throughout the first night she spent with him, passing the time as both of them danced around the real reason she had invited him to her flat, both of them figuring out whether the attraction was mutual before they finally slept together. Inexplicably, she notices a tear forming in the corner of her eye. She blinks it away.

'Do you like it? The garden?'

'It's beautiful,' she says. 'Like an oasis.'

Gretta can see the spotlit mass of the Tate Gallery, and the Vauxhall Bridge reaching across the black water of the river to Lambeth and Southwark. To the north, the minarets and ziggurats of the Square Mile are lit up with myriad sparkling lights. This stunning vista is cloaked with a white mantle, every building, every road, every passing vehicle that shudders through the night sheathed by snow. The glow of the streetlights casts amber circlets of warmth, an incongruity given the plunging temperature. The sounds of the city, the hum of metropolitan activity that is always audible, even at night, is muffled. Gretta feels like she did when she once stood at the top of the Empire State Building; the buzz of the city is the same, and she felt just as dissociated and faraway then as she does now.

'It's beautiful, isn't it?' says Michael, handing her a whisky and slowly kneading away the tension in her shoulders and neck. He continues to talk, his tone matter-of-fact, a counterpoint to her edgy thrill. 'I prefer it to Manhattan, in a way – the river, the architecture, the sheer *history* of the place. People forget Manhattan was a muddy swamp a hundred years ago.'

261

'The snow makes it look ... sterile,' Gretta murmurs, hanging her head languorously so his hands can move up the nape of her neck towards the base of her skull. That far but no further. 'Dead, in a way, like everything is suspended. It reminds me of those snowstorm ornaments, the ones with water and tiny particles that look like snow when you shake them up?' The ice cubes rattle as she brings the tumbler to her lips. She does not taste the colourless, odourless, two-milligram dose of flunitrazepam Michael has dissolved into the whisky. The tablet, marketed as 'Rohypnol' by Hoffman La Roche, is part of a shipment Michael secured from his dealer in Mexico City, where the drug is available cheaply and plentifully. He needed a stockpile before Hoffman La Roche re-engineered the chemical compound so that a blue warning marker is left when it is dissolved.

'It *is* beautiful,' Michael says again, missing the point, his attention snagged by the bead of spiked whisky on her lower lip. He wipes it off with his finger and gently inserts it into her mouth. She sucks the finger dry. 'Come on inside. It's freezing,' he says, leading her to a Russel Wright leather sofa that sits marooned in the centre of the room. Gretta is feeling light-headed, vertiginous, and she is not able to focus her mind. Streams of data are incoming from all directions and she is overloaded, unable to decipher the signal from the background fuzz.

'Let me play you something,' he says, stopping the CD. 'I think you'll remember this.'

A moment of silence then the first chords of a song. A guitar strummed to a downbeat tempo. The recording is scratched – it hisses – is he playing it from vinyl? Hank Williams's voice, deep yet still reedy, old beyond its owner's years, starts singing 'My Heart Would Know'.

Their song, from the album he Fed-Exed to her from Tokyo, after he left London to work there for six months. It made her cry then. She played it for days. It made her maudlin, made his absence melancholic yet bearable, a bittersweet reminder that he was still thinking of her. Their relationship died eventually, the distance and the distractions slowing and then halting its momentum until it ground to a halt. The words of the record are faint and dim. It is as if she is listening to them underwater. Her eyelids are heavy.

'Tell me about your new boyfriend,' he coaxes. 'You haven't mentioned him all night.'

'He's not a *new* boyfriend,' she slurs, tripping over each syllable. Her thoughts seem coated in grease. She cannot fasten onto them. 'I've been seeing him for two years? Or three?'

'Oh, I *see*. I just found it, well, a little strange that it's now' – he checks his watch – 'two-forty-five and you haven't mentioned him – not once. Not even given our history.'

'It's our anniversary today.' Her muscles feel torpid. He smiles and strokes her hair. 'Are you seeing Caitlin?' she murmurs.

'Caitlin and I are *compatible*,' he says slowly, 'but not a couple. Caitlin doesn't believe in relationships. She's rather nihilistic when it comes to those sorts of things.'

'You're not sleeping with her?'

'I didn't say that.' She doesn't comment. 'We fuck occasionally – socially.' He is not embarrassed or shy – he looks directly into her eyes as he slides his hand across the leather and up onto her thigh. He brushes the hem of her skirt with his finger. 'These are liberal times we live in.'

Through the static the record continues.

She thinks of Jared. She tries to picture his face, but all she has left is a faded copy, the edges blurry and indistinct. She doesn't miss him. Their relationship has waned too, just like it waned with Michael eight years ago. All it has taken for her to admit it is his absence, and this dead singer singing an old-remembered song. She doesn't want to be here any more.

'I feel woozy,' she says.

'It's late. You're tired.'

'Hmm,' she murmurs, unable to object as he slides his hand up the inside of her thigh, and upwards. His fingers are icy. His face looms over hers.

She allows herself to be pulled to her feet. Volition, like clarity of thought, cognition and memory, has been temporarily suspended by the drug. She feels as if she has been cast into heavy gravity or a sea of oil; her limbs only reluctantly obey her demands, and what she should be demanding is harder and harder to ascertain. She should be at home.

She is arranged face up on a wide bed. Her dress is removed deftly by a second, more slender pair of hands, and a black-painted nail traces the contours of her breasts. A tongue slides up her ribcage.

'I've missed you,' says Michael, but she doesn't hear

him. Her lifeless eyes are on the dark windows where the snow has started again. She watches sleepily the flakes, falling like static, floating ponderously, gusted against the glass by the winter wind, piling up on the windowsill, piling up in the streets below, choking them, covering the city with an inert, numbing blanket.

Vid

Mojave Desert

The hot rush of the wind stains the damp sweat into Vid's shirt and trousers as he guns the bike through the gloomy desert. Without a helmet, his dank hair is drying into dirty plaits in the sandy gusts, and motes of grit are punching through his meshed lashes to sting his eyes. He feels soiled, covered by a sheen of other people's sweat, and his muscles are cramped and tense. The clamour of the concert still clatters in his ears, louder than the bike itself. The effects of the last E have long since worn off and now he feels as dry as the desert.

Dunes and sandbanks rise and fall on either side of the highway, the dim lines sometimes broken by the fuzzy lattice of mesquite and creosote brush. The headlight stains with amber a mangled Joshua tree at the side of the road. A coyote slinks on its belly into the scrubby furze, as he passes. Vid pays no attention to these distractions. His attention is focused on the white lines disappearing beneath the thick tyres of the bike; he opens out the throttle even more to try and merge the paint into a blurred, unbroken swipe, evidence that the miles are passing. The engine howls louder and the jarring, juddering exertion of hanging aboard intensifies. In his mirrors, he checks backwards along the road. The multicoloured luminescence of the city still floods out behind him like radiation, staining the dark. He needs more distance; he needs to put the horizon between his back and the city.

After thirty minutes, a glow of neon sparkles out of the blackness ahead. A sign on the side of the road: TRUCK STOP – AHEAD 500 YARDS. The letters are formed by fizzing bulbs, some of them flickering or burnt out. The thought flashes across the throbbing discord in his head: he is thirsty and hungry. He bleeds off the speed and steers the bike into the dusty fenced-off square of desert that serves as the diner's car park. Chequers of light are cast from the windows of the low-slung building. A single petrol pump stands watch and a mangled Buick has been left to the desert's mercy. A lizard scurries out of the broken windshield as the bike growls alongside. Vid pauses to look at his reflection in the glass pane of the door. His shirt is ripped to the navel and it flaps open in the breeze. His skin is ashen, the colour of decay. Sand and the sediment of dry ice have muffled him and painted on a grimy carapace, like a rind. His eyes burn brightly from within this dun mask. A darker-red stain is crusted around his nose and lips.

Diner

Inside, the glare from the striplights is harsh and Vid squints until his pupils contract. He takes a seat at the back and looks through the bland menu. The room is empty save for the waitress, reading a trashy novel and unwinding spirals of smoke from a cigarette. She is on the cusp of middle-age, battling to preserve the evidence that she was once pleasing to the eye. Her face is caked with make-up but Vid can still see the roadmap of creases and grooves, the striation of age. Her hair is tied into a tight bun and jacked up behind a peaked cap, part of her homey uniform. An enamel badge identifies her as Sandy. The Stones are playing on the radio.

'Jeez,' says the waitress, munching on a wad of gum. 'You been out riding on the dunes?'

'Yeah,' says Vid. 'Something like that.'

'You wanna clean up? We got a washroom out back.'

'I'm fine.'

'Suit yourself. What're you having? The pancakes are good.'

'A Diet Coke. And, um, a hamburger.'

'Sure.' She pauses. 'Say – what happened to your face?'

Vid dabs his fingers to his lip – flakes of dried blood crumble away from where Jared punched him. His nostrils are caked solid. He frowns, trying to remember why Jared did that. They were arguing about something. The gig? Jared has been so *temperamental* lately. Vid laughs skittishly, without really knowing why.

'It's nothing,' he says when he notices that the waitress is still there. 'I had an argument.'

There is a deep bass rumble: the salt shaker and the plastic sauce bottle shaped like a fat tomato start to tremble, then shake. The walls buzz and vibrate as the bass deepens and broadens into a throaty roar. The sepia pictures of the desert on the walls jangle from their hooks and jolt further off the horizontal.

'It's the airport,' shouts Sandy, pointing up to the ceiling. 'We're right under the flightpath for McCarron.'

'Maybe it's aliens,' hopes Vid, 'come to take us away.'

'Ain't no aliens want to stop here,' Sandy yells.

The rumble evens out, and then tapers away as the jumbo heads onwards.

'They pass over every ten minutes or so,' she says.

'Why are you out here?' asks Vid.

'What do you mean?'

'Working out here – in the middle of nowhere?'

'Why not? It's a job. We all got bills to pay.'

'I haven't,' says Vid morosely. 'I was a millionaire before I was twenty-five. I've got more money than I could ever spend.'

'Lucky you,' she says, distracted, thoughtful. 'I used to think that. Back when I worked on the Strip. The shows paid good money, got my room for free – and bumped up the cash with escorting on the side. That was a good life.'

'You were in the shows?'

She hesitates. 'Kind of. Well, yeah, the titty shows off Fremont Street.'

'And now you're too old.'

If she is offended, she hides it well. 'Gravity takes it toll, baby. Looks never last. We all start to rot away, slowly at first, then faster. You can only hide it for so long, you can't fight it. And then, one day, that's it' – she clicks her fingers – 'all gone. You scrape around as best you can after that.'

'Everything falls apart,' offers Vid.

Sandy shrugs sadly and heads towards the kitchen.

'Champagne Supernova' by Oasis is playing. Sandy has been gone for ten minutes, but it feels like longer. He takes a pen from his pocket and tries to fit words to the chord progressions that have been playing in his head. He scribbles words onto the back of the menu card – '*empty*,' '*blank*,' '*vanished*,' '*extinct*' – but they are just random words, he can't trace the pattern between them. How does Jared do it? There must be a technique. Jared has already written two songs since they've been here. Vid gives up.

He feels the need to speak to someone. A fly has settled onto the crescent of strawberry cheesecake someone has left on the table opposite. It is looking at him, snickering, with gobs of gelatinous goop on its mandibles. Vid shudders, then takes his mobile out of his pocket and flips the lid back. With one eye on the fly, he scrolls through the memory, and then presses SEND at a random entry. The numbers click as the phone dials them, then comes the hiss of static and a dialling tone. Frosty answers after four rings, says he is at the airport, getting a car to the hotel.

Vid only indifferently observes their conversation. He is fumbling in his pocket for his snuffbox, watching the fly trample about on the cheesecake, saying something lukewarm about the concert, Frosty apologizing for not being there (his plane was late or something), prising the snuffbox open with his fingernail, listening to Frosty's buzzing insect voice saying nothing, tipping out the snuffbox's contents, Frosty asking if he is OK, measuring how much he has left, apologizing to Frosty for calling, brushing the brown powder back into the snuffbox, pressing CANCEL. He drops the phone into the ashtray and his last E onto his tongue. The buzz shudders up at once. The E completes an electrical relay, the missing ingredient in his chemical soup. A blue charge arcs across his brain, sending forks of lightning down his spine and out across the branches of his nerves. The rush makes his fingers tremble, then his arms. His mouth feels as if it has been coated with sand.

'Here's your hamburger,' says Sandy. She blurs through his vision, dancing through the rainbow spectrum of colours refracting out of the glare of the lights. Reds, yellows, blues, greens. Sweat is already running down into his eyes. He can taste it and smell it. The grime starts to run and smear in muddy tracks.

'Are you OK?' she asks. 'You're sweating like crazy.'

'That fly's been watching us,' says Vid conspiratorially.

'No. Really?' she says.

'Yeah. It's planning something. With its friends. They're telepaths.'

'We'll be just fine, honey,' she soothes, pointing back at the electric blue glow of the insectocutor fizzling over the entrance to the kitchen.

'I'm too fucked up to care any more,' he says. His voice is distant and distorted, as if he was shouting into a canyon.

'Sorry?'

'This whole mess. I don't give a fuck about it any more.' His head feels stuffed full of sand. 'My head is stuffed full of sand.'

'Right,' she nods, but Vid knows she is thinking here's another crazy. Another loser on the run from Vegas.

'It's, like, I should point the bike into the desert some-where, nowhere, and just like ride it until the petrol runs out and then just lie down in the sand and let the insects bury me; *they'd* make me disappear and that's all I want, really, I just want to like disappear – vanish. That's all I want. Can you like dig that? What it's like to vanish? Don't you wonder sometimes?' The words bubble up unbidden.

'Uh-huh,' she says with an edgy smile. Her eyes are clouding over: doubt or fear? 'Enjoy your burger.'

Vid takes a bite out of the bap. The meat is blackened and burnt and he can't swallow it, gagging. He finishes the tepid Coke in one long draught, feeling the fluid chugging out of the can and down his throat. He needs more.

'Um, actually,' he says, 'I *will* use your washroom. Where is it again?'

'Through back,' says the waitress, pointing.

The washroom is small and seedy, a puddle of dirty water gathering under the leaking pipe that snakes beneath the urinal and into the wall, and with a cloud of flies infesting the cubicle, an audible buzzing. A leaking tap drips into a single sink underneath a greasy mirror. The only striplight flickers, shadows dancing with each fresh fluctuation. There is a lock on the main door and Vid slides the bolt through.

He tips a third of the heroin he has left into the bowl of a spoon he has taken from the table, and next drips in enough citric acid and water to form a thick paste, then cooking up with his Zippo, a difficult process, holding the spoon in the flame until the metal blackens, then glows red with heat, and the paste deliquesces into the delicious clear brown liquid. A plane rips overhead and the light dims for ten seconds until it passes.

With the shot in front of him, primed and ready to go, his defences collapse and the junk takes over. He knots his belt around his arm and pulls it tight until he can feel the blood throb. He finds a fat hungry vein on his wrist and slides his needle in, drawing the plunger back a touch so that threads of his blood unwind into the barrel. He watches his face mutate in the mirror: teeth bared and eyes rolling back, feral rapture.

It starts on the back of his legs, slackening the tight muscle with waves of relaxation, then it eases the back of his neck, seeping down into his shoulders and the tops of his arms and then washing into his chest and down his spine, stroking his hips and pelvis, working on a molecular level, infiltrating his cells, adapting his DNA to fit its own tranquil pattern. He feels the familiar sensation of floating inside a dark and warm flotation tank, smooth fingers stroking him lovingly, the pain assuaged. Dark shadows gather at the edges of his vision but the fear passes painlessly enough and the fragments of his dreams begin to coalesce, pieces collecting and binding like film of a china plate breaking being played back in reverse, a galaxy of stars sprinkled into the darkness like dust. This must be what infinity looks like.

Vid shuffles back into the diner as another plane roars overhead, shaking the ground as it passes. He leaves the notes and coins in his pocket on the table, around two hundred dollars and change, and goes back out to the bike. The shot will last him until he gets back to his hotel room.

Back in the diner, the phone chirps in the ashtray. Vid has programmed it to play the first few bars of 'The Alone'. Sandy, shuffling the wad of notes that Vid has left her and wondering whether she should stop him to ask whether it was a mistake, picks up the phone. The display glows green, like kryptonite. EVIL CORPORATE STOOGE say the black letters on the caller ID. Alex is calling. The deejay on the radio is playing Dystopia.

'Hello?' she says.

'Vid?'

The fly buzzes into the air, circles a few times, sweeps over to investigate the glowing blue light, and is incinerated, a crackle of electricity reaching out to greet it like a solar flare.

'Uh, I think he just left. He left his phone.'

The line goes dead.

Vid has already turned around and is following the lights of the jumbo back into the city.

Spin

Party

Alex is wired to the eyeballs. 'Spin, *fuck*, Spin, you're a fucking hero! That set – Jesus, man, that was awesome. No, I *mean* it.'

He is with two girls, both out of their heads on whatever it is that has also juiced Alex. Damien wanders over with a bottle of Becks.

'I thought it went well.'

'Jesus! They said you were modest but, man, they weren't kidding. Listen, I was with Mike Kaiser while you were on. You met Mike? He's the head of Revolution Records. We're talking about a seriously important *fromage* here. A *grand fromage* of the highest order: the top dog. Mike says to me, "Al, who the *fuck* is the deejay tonight, 'cos by *fuck* I need to meet that guy."'

'No?'

'Straight up. I says, "Mike, that's only Spin, the band's favourite fucking genius deejay." He's going to be coming around tomorrow to give us a send-off for the rest of the tour. He said he'd really appreciate it if you could be around at the photoshoot tomorrow to, like, have a word. He's probably going to make you an offer. One of the "can't refuse" variety. This guy has some serious money to back up his offers with.'

'What can I say? Thanks, man. It means a lot.'

'Fuck that, man, I didn't say jack shit to him. It was all you, Spin. You're a fucking *demon*.'

'Spin,' says Damien, 'tell Alex that story about you and dancing and shit. You know the one I mean.'

'Damien . . .'

'No, this story rocks, really. Seriously. Tell it.'

Spin tells them about the time he was deejaying at Nocturnal, early on, and the set was going down just about as perfectly as a set can go down. He decided to chance his arm, and segued into the risky ten-minute ambient mix of 'Tower of Strength' by The Mission. He let the tune take over and, finding the booth too confined a space to sway with the tune, he went out onto the dancefloor and joined the euphoric crowd. He lost track of the time in the trancey ether and only came around as the final bars were fading down. He skidded back to the booth, the next mix ready in his head, only to find that he had locked himself out. The place was silent for five minutes until the bouncers battered down the door so he could spin another tune. It was the most embarrassing five minutes of his life.

'*Un*-believable, man,' says Alex, nuzzling the neck of one of the girls. 'Just as well you didn't do that tonight. We'd have had you shot and buried in the desert some-place!'

Spin laughs, a little nervously. Alex is always difficult to gauge.

'Do you want an E?' Alex asks. 'High quality, straight out of a mafia laboratory in Amsterdam.'

'No thanks. I don't do drugs.'

'You don't do drugs?' Alex has a handful of pastel-blue tablets in his hand. They have lovehearts imprinted on one side. The colour is leeching into his sweaty palm. Alex's forehead is slick with sweat and his eyeballs are pinned.

'We don't all have appetites like you, man,' says Damien.

'I do some weed occasionally, socially,' says Spin, 'but that's about it. I don't need it.'

'Whatever you say, man. Whatever.' Alex pops one of the pills and then drops one each onto the ready tongues of both girls.

'Whoosh,' he says.

Desert

The firelight glows orange against the dark horizon and Spin keeps walking, putting it further behind him. He is walking away from the noise and hustle of the party, looking for a quieter spot. He passed several couples fucking on the outskirts of the gathering, where the gloaming flickers out into the gloom. Roadies released on the devoted like hungry dogs, and the devoted happy to take whatever they can get. If they can't get to the band, then they'll take an association with them. Spin needs some space.

The desert reminds Spin of the moon and the city, with a bowl of light glowing over it – a moonbase. He sits down on scrubby vegetation and looks up into the sky. The stars seem brighter out here.

He takes out his mobile and the scrap of paper he tore out of the Las Vegas *Directory* in the hotel yesterday. He punches out the number. As he waits for it to connect, a bike passes on a road two hundred metres away headed back to the city.

'Oh, hi,' he says.

Spin's suite

He has thrown off his drenched clothes and showered by the time that she arrives. He knows what to expect; he has been in this situation so many times before that the rituals have been etched into his muscle memory. Alone in a different hotel room in another different city. His family might as well be on another planet. Vid doesn't know what loneliness means. He can't even *comprehend* it, not in its purest form. Spin can. It is standing alone on a peak in Asia before a stupefying view. It is freezing in the cold breeze gusting around the top of the Empire State Building without anyone to drink in the atmosphere with you.

She taps softly at the door, three times. He checks that the champagne is cooling properly in the ice bucket, then lets her in.

She looks taller in real life than in her picture. She has the full figure that he likes and red hair that falls across her shoulders. She is wearing a ruby-red leather skirt, a black blouse under a leather jacket and biker boots dyed the colour of tomatoes. He doesn't know her real name but she advertises herself as Poppy.

'Hi,' he says. 'Poppy?'

'Hi.'

'Come in.'

She takes off the jacket and folds it across the back of a chair. 'OK. You tell me what you want, we sort out the payment first, up front, and then we do it. Then I go. You understand?'

'Sure.'

'Well? What do you want?'

Spin is on the bed. He watches as she stands before him, hands on hips. 'I want you to fuck me,' he says slowly.

'Two hundred bucks, up front.'

Spin finds his wallet and counts out ten twenties. She checks them and folds them away in a pocket.

'On top.'

As she falls on him, Spin's gaze wanders up the wall and out into the sky. The thousands of cubic feet of neon are bleeding into the night and staining it with colours that switch on and off with the bulbs. The blackness is just another canvas to be exploited. His focus breaks up as she slowly works down his body with her tongue. He watches them from above, watches himself pinned to the bed, and then she slides herself over him and him into her and starts to push.

*

The sound of water plashing into the basin.

Spin feels the cold grip of a panic attack fasten a clammy fist around his heart. What the fuck has he done? Why can't he just fight the urge down? His breathing is ragged and he hardly recognizes his reflection: the red furrows of her nails across his cheek, the glassy eyes shot through with blood, teeth bared like a werewolf's. His chest is punctured with four florid incisions where she sank her cherry-painted nails; it looks like a join-the-dots puzzle. He dunks his head into the full basin. He has tipped the ice cubes into the sink and they clunk around his head, burning cold as they jostle his temples.

Spin washes the wet blood off his knuckles. The cold water stings in the cuts on his forearms. The water stains. She struggled hard, digging her nails in, until he caught her under the chin with his elbow. She is still in the bedroom, unconscious; her body shutting everything down to absorb the punishment he meted out. Her breathing was faint and shallow.

He remembers that change in her eyes when he threw her off him and cocked his fist: the woman looking weary, almost resigned to a beating, something that has to be endured in this line of work. He was overcome with fury, possessed, and punched and punched until she went limp and fell across him on the bed. He left her draped across him as he lay there gasping, reasserting his self-control, fighting the dark thoughts. She was warm; he thought of Mary warming the bed for him at home.

He has long since rationalized this behaviour, this impulse. He knows that it is wrong, perhaps even an illness, but there is no point in fighting it. The urges are too strong. The first time he succumbed was in Paris six months ago. That first time, Mary's birthday, he felt empty and utterly alone. He had already ordered the biggest bouquet of flowers he could find, and had hidden love notes around the house that she would find while he was away. He found a whore near the Palais de Chaillot and took her back to his hotel room and asked her to fuck him. He felt sick to the pit of his stomach as soon as he came. Habit has not since neutered his self-loathing.

Mary has never complained about the lengths to which his work takes him. It's good money, after all, and with another mouth to feed they are not in a position to turn it down. And they both know the transience of the market-place. He is in vogue at the moment, but Spin knows dozens of deejays who had their fifteen minutes and then shuffled off to present the graveyard shifts on local radio stations. Not for him. No way. He wants to make a bigger breakthrough, and get them some proper security. To do that, he must do this. And everything that comes with it.

He usually asks the girls to fuck him on top so he can squeeze his eyes shut and think of Mary and wait for it to be over. He is polite; he tips them so they will leave him the sooner. The urge surprised him with its power this time. It battered his will like a typhoon. For a moment she embodied all his weaknesses, everything he hates about himself.

'Listen,' he calls from the bathroom, trying for an everyday inflection. 'I'm really sorry ... about all that. I just got carried away, I guess. I've got about a thousand dollars. You can have all of it, OK, as long as you were never here. You understand me?' She doesn't answer. She must still be out cold.

He puts his clothes back on in the bedroom and dabs at his thick lip with a piece of ice from the bucket. She is lying amongst the crumpled sheets. Her flesh is infused with ripening bruises: blue to brown to black. Blood has crusted at the corner of her mouth and under her nose. He nudges her. She doesn't stir. Fuck, this might be more difficult than he thought.

He can hardly bear to look at her, but he knows what to do. Jared has told him about Vid's horseplay with groupies before. He is always beating them, he said, and all it takes is a phone call to Alex to have the roadies sort the problem out. They'll take her somewhere quiet, give her a few hundred dollars, and let her out onto the street. He collects her clothes and piles them on the bed. This will be embarrassing, but maybe he could say she was trying to rob him? Yes, that's it. He'll dress her first. Or that she went crazy on him and he had to protect himself. Self-defence. He can sell that. And Mary need never know.

He stoops over her face. She isn't breathing.

Fuck.

He checks again. Nothing. He feels for a pulse in her wrist, then her neck. Nothing.

Fuck! FUCK!

He shakes her, gently at first and then hard enough to slam her head back against the headboard. Her joints are loose with a rag doll's slackness. He slaps her across the cheek. Her head lolls with the impact. No response. He covers her nose and prises open her mouth, blowing stale air down into her lungs and pumping on her chest. *Come on. COME ON.* Her mouth tastes strange: champagne and something else, something acrid with a tang like oysters. Unbidden, he remembers something that a girl in Cleveland said to him once, as she was unrolling her tights up her sticky thighs: *It's really not so bad once you've gotten past the taste.* He retches, hacking up the pancakes he had with Jared for breakfast. The puke splatters chunks over the sheets.

Don't panic. Don't panic. Don't panic. If you just stay calm, everything will be fine. Everything will be OK. There's a way out of this, there has to be. You just need to be *calm* to find it. It looks worse than it is. *No!* How can this be any *worse*? *There's a dead whore on your bed!* How did this happen? Wait. Breathe. Concentrate. It was an accident, yes, that's it. She came on at me, she went crazy, the fucking bitch, I hit her once to defend myself and she just fell. She just went down. Her legs just buckled. A blood clot maybe. An aneurysm. That happens, doesn't it? A thin skull, just bad luck. She cracked her head on the side of the bed. I tried to bring her around, but it was too late, she was already dead, already gone. What more could I do? I did all I could.

He has *killed* her. Sweet Jesus.

What if Alex won't help him?

He reaches for the phone, then replaces it. Can't call the police. They'll arrest him. They won't listen to him. He'll have to stay here for months, waiting for a trial. And what if they don't believe him? What if they convict him? Does

Nevada still have the death penalty? Even if it doesn't, he'll still get fifty years in prison. At least. The rest of his natural life. Mary will be devastated. It will finish her. She'll leave him. She'll hate him and he'll be on his own. He'll never see Lucy growing up. No, that's *not* going to happen. He can't call the police. Not yet. He needs to get Alex on his side. He needs his experience, a cool head. Alex'll work something out. Someone to provide some corroboration. A *witness*. Alex could say that he saw her acting weird, asking strange questions at the party about Spin. She was a fruitcake, see. See? She was a lunatic. It's going to be *fine*. Don't panic. This is going to be fine. Fine.

He stares at the phone. Fuck. What's Alex's number? He doesn't have it. Vid is next door. He'll go and ask him for it.

Corridor

He gulps a glass of cold water and heads into the corridor. The ice machine at the end of the hall is clunking to itself, dumping fresh ice into its reservoir. All kinds of debris litter the floor. A pair of unconscious teenage girls asleep in each other's arms against the wall. The fragments of a smashed bong have been ground into the stained carpet, and the smell of strong dope is heavy in the air. A fire extinguisher has been set off, and long tongues of foam stretch down from the ceiling like stalactites. A light fitting has been pulled out of its socket and it is hanging from its cord. Beer cans, bottles and cigarette papers are strewn around like confetti. Spin steps through the mess gingerly and taps softy on Vid's door. There is no reply. He tries the door, and opens it.

Vid's suite

Vid is lying face-up on the floor, with his fingers plucking dumbly at a syringe stuck into his arm like a dart. He is naked from the waist up and a belt has been looped around his arm. A blackened spoon and two bags of differently coloured powder, brown and white, lie at his feet. His lips are black and his eyeballs are bulging. His make-up is running: a streak of inky eye-shadow looks like a tear. Foam flecks his lipstick. Spin knows enough about drugs to recognize a speedball overdose.

'Fuck,' says Spin, kneeling at Vid's side. 'Vid, man, are you OK?' Vid looks up at him helplessly through filmy eyes. He mouths a sentence but no words come: he is as silent as a ghost. His pupils are tiny twitching pinpricks. Vid brushes the syringe again with his fingers, jacking it further into the vein; it is already full of his blood. Spin presses the hand away and pulls the needle carefully out of Vid's arm, holding the barrel of it with Vid's discarded T-shirt. A tiny bubble of blood bursts as the hole in the vein is uncorked. He pulls Vid's dead weight into a sitting position against the bed. He checks his airways are clear. Vid faints – out cold. His head lollops onto his chest.

Spin paces the room anxiously. He needs to find Alex. He goes to the window and gazes into the darkness. The tail-lights of a plane blink as it rises up from the airport and curves into its trajectory. It looks like a tiny fragment of the city's fulgent glow has broken free and floated away like a child's balloon. He watches as it adds altitude, fading into the darker blacks of the troposphere. After five minutes, another plane follows it up, and then another. In eight hours, Spin wants to be on a plane aimed back home.

An idea – no one has seen him with Poppy. He didn't tell her his name. He just gave a room number. Maybe she didn't tell anyone else where she was going. She isn't wearing a wedding ring, and she probably works from home. Vid won't remember seeing him right now. Vid probably won't remember anything about the whole evening. Vid might die. And Spin is booked onto a flight back home tomorrow. He'll be gone and safe. And Alex will have to protect Vid, if he lives. The band will depend on it. He'll have no choice. There's a chance that Alex would choose not to protect Spin; he is just the deejay, after all. But not to protect Vid? That couldn't happen. He is too important.

Spin goes back to his room and shakes out the contents of her handbag. Her passport: Jane Delacroix; French-Canadian descent, formerly of Montreal; date of birth 25 November 1968. An asthma inhaler. A bottle of Halcion, half empty. Make-up, tissues, a packet of Luckys, some keys. He takes out the two hundred dollars and stuffs everything back. He finds a large sanitary bag from the bathroom and stuffs the handbag inside that. He dumps the package down the rubbish chute at the end of the corridor and waits until he hears the bag splash into the trash at the bottom. Perfect.

With her clothes under one arm, he slings the girl over his shoulder. The corridor is silent and empty as he carries her into Vid's suite.

Suzy

From: DystopiaFan3@hotmail.com
To: RockGod4@hotmail.com
Date: Friday, January 7, 1.59 P.M.
Subject: The real U

I know all about U now. I know everything about U and I can't believe I have been so STUPID to waste my time liking U and your pointless music. I feel stupid + used by U and the way U have treated me is nothing short of DISGUSTING. If the papers were interested in the stories that the little people like me have to tell I would write to them straight away and tell them exactly what kind of person Jared from Dystopia really is.

In case U were wondering, I waited at Aroma until seven when they closed and I had to leave. I must have had about six coffees. Then I waited outside in the freezing cold for another hour just in case U had been delayed and were still trying to get there. I was there for four hours in total, on my own I might add, and then it started snowing so heavily I couldn't see in front of me. Typical – it doesn't snow at Christmas and then it comes down just when I am feeling as sad and low as I can remember. Loads of people came and went but not U. Oh no. U didn't have time to spend five minutes with your most dedicated fan, did U? U were too busy fucking that airhead girlfriend of yours, weren't U? U see, I know all about Gretta Conway. I know everything about her there is to know. Did I tell U that I work as a researcher? Digging up dirt on people is what I do for a living and for such a supposedly BIG STAR U have been easier than I thought. I have been able to find out all about U + Gretta Conway and I have been able to find out stuff about Gretta Conway that U don't even know, stuff that is going to really hurt + upset U. It might make U feel the way I'm feeling now but that's not why I'm going to tell U. I am a nice person, ask my friends and they will tell U, and I don't think 'revenge is a dish best served cold' or anything like that at all. What I am going to tell U now is for your own good, a friend who U have fucked around still proving that she cares about U, although she wonders why she still does.

I know U live at 92 Prebend Street, Islington. Your house has a shiny black door and a little flight of steps that leads down to the pavement. The number of the house is fixed on a board to the left of the doorknob. U haven't picked up your post for a while – there were about twelve letters on the doormat. One of your neighbours thinks U R 'a nice couple'. How did I find out where U live, U might ask? Simple – all I had to do was ring up Revolution Records and pretend to be a journalist who was going to interview Gretta Conway for a newspaper article. I told them I had arranged an interview but that I had forgotten Gretta

Conway's address. And they gave it to me, easy and with no questions. Everything was easy from there.

I drove to your house. Eventually Gretta Conway came out, looking all prim + proper with her fur coat and her fancy hundred-pound haircut and everything else that U have probably bought her from the money your loyal fans have given U (not knowing how cruel + selfish U really R).

Frankly, I am disappointed with your taste, Jared. She is pretty (in a skin + bone kind of way) but then everyone says I am pretty too and the difference between us is that I am also smart + intelligent rather than a dumb bitch and that is exactly what she is. She might have a perfect skin and a good figure but so what if all she has between her ears is empty space? They say 'beauty is only skin deep' and 'U should not judge a book by its cover' but I doubt U have ever even wondered what lies beneath Gretta Conway's pretty exterior.

Do U think U know everything about her, Jared? Do U think U know about all the skeletons in her cupboard? I doubt that very much. I think U know absolutely nothing about her at all. She has all kinds of dark secrets U have no idea about. For example:

(a) Did U know that she went to a party without U at a house in South Kensington belonging to Tamara and Josh Wilkins?

(b) Did U know that she left the party in a different car to the one she arrived in? A Jaguar registered to a Mr Michael Bratsky. U probably don't know Michael Bratsky, but I have found out all about him too. He

works in the city as a 'pensions fund consultant'. He
was one of the 'super-traders' in the 1980s and he
has been listed as one of this country's 100 most
eligible bachelors for six years in a row. He earned
over £1 million last year. He kissed Gretta Conway
on the cheek when she got into his car.

(c) Did U know that they went to Michael Bratsky's
apartment in Millbank and that they went into that
apartment together holding hands? This was at two
in the morning. Not the kind of behaviour U would
expect from a loyal + caring girlfriend, U might say.

U think that U know about her but U don't. I do – I saw
all this happen. I was there, outside. She is sleeping with
Michael Bratsky behind your back and U don't know a thing
about it. I took lots of photographs of them after the party on
Saturday, and I will send copies of them to U if U want
proof. If U don't, and unless U stop being so unkind to me,
maybe I should think about sending them to someone else
who might be interested? Like the papers? That is for U to
decide.

I hope U realize just how STUPID U have been.
Although I am seriously upset with U it gives me no
pleasure to tell U these things. I am not a vindictive kind of
person – I am a kind + caring person at heart. Even though
U have made a fool of me and made me feel really awful
about myself I am still willing to give U a second chance to
show me that there is a shred of decency in U despite
everything U have shown me to the contrary. All I want is
for U to meet with me and tell me that U R sorry. Is that so

much to ask? Although U R probably feeling bad now that U have realized what a slut Gretta Conway is U might look back on this and think 'Hey, Suzy Abbott has helped me out' as well as all the other ways I have helped out U and the band. I hope U think that and I hope U R ready to try and show me that U mean it.

U have stood me up once already so I am not going to suggest a place for us to meet so U can stand me up again. Email me with details for a meeting and I will see if I am available to make it. Please show me that U R the kind + decent person I once thought U were.

SUZY ABBOTT

part **Three**

Alex

The syringe empties, the milky adrenalin squirting into the same vein that Vid used. The plunger reaches the bottom of the barrel. Vid doesn't even flinch.

The ringing tone chirps from the mobile Alex has pressed to his ear. One ring. Another. The spaces between each tone are deep black abysses big enough to swallow him. Hot blood is pumping through his temples. A third ring. He is sweating despite the frigid air-conditioning.

Calm down, Alex. Let's just think about this calmly for a moment – another ring – *and rationally.* He concentrates on his breathing, long deep breaths, in and out.

A dissonant female voice is buzzing in his ear: '—what service do you require?'

Think.

'What service do you require?' repeats the voice. 'Hello?'

Alex stabs his forefinger on the fascia until he hits CANCEL. The dialling tone purrs.

OK. OK. Let's start from the basics. Vid is dead. Dead. He is lying there, propped up against that ridiculous water bed, and not breathing. The adrenalin has had no effect.

There is an empty syringe on the floor next to him and he has a belt fixed tightly around his arm. The skin below the belt is starting to turn a mottled grey colour, like damp cardboard or dirty slush. Vid is past resuscitation. If Alex is going to call 911, it is not the paramedics he'd want. He'd want the police.

Let's extrapolate: being dead, Vid will not now leave Revolution; he will not leave Dystopia, either; and he will not be joining the new company. As a result of this, Alex will not be paid the signing bonus he has been promised, and will not receive any of the other mind-blowing rewards that Bratsky has offered him. He will be left to manage a band without a lead singer, a ship without a figurehead cast adrift on a sea of apathy. They'll never play another gig like last night's. These are all *bad* things.

But, thinking rationally, is there not an alternative strategy? Perhaps even a way to take advantage of the twisted wreckage of circumstance? A way out? Yes.

It is still early. Save Jared, no one else is up – no one that he has seen, anyway. No one will know that Vid is dead. He has been propped up here ever since whatever drug it was that he shot into his vein finally broke his abused body. What's to stop him just hiding the body? He could get him in the back of the car without anyone seeing, just use the private lift down to the car park and sling him into the boot of his hire car. Have the car waiting by the door, put him in the back and go. Drive out for half an hour into the desert, find a lonely spot away from the road, dig out a shallow grave and bury him in it.

Could he do that? Morally? Ethically?

What're the downsides? If he was spotted, what would be the worst that could happen to him? Not a murder charge. It might *look* like murder, him disposing of the evidence of his crime. But, no, how could murder be proven? The forensic scientists would be able to figure out when it was that the fatal dose was administered, and Alex would have an alibi with the girl in his room that would prove without question that he couldn't have been here, in this room, then. Plus, what would it serve him to kill Vid, when he stood to gain so much by having him alive? He has a copy of the contract; Bratksy could testify for him. No, he'd get some sort of obstructing-the-course-of-justice charge, maximum, or whatever was the US equivalent, and do some minor jail time if he was unlucky.

But if he could make Vid disappear, do it successfully, he could say that Vid had absconded into the desert. Dozens of jaded rock stars have pulled that kind of caper before, disappeared for months, years even. In the meantime he would forge Vid's signature, tell Bratsky that the deal was on, and that as soon as Vid returned they'd be in business. Bank the money and go and live somewhere hot.

Just keep calm. If you keep your composure you can still make something out of this mess.

He surveys the room. Vid won't be heavy. But – ah, shit! Over by the wardrobe, the groupie. Forgotten her. She'll have to go too. She can't stay. The police would be involved and Bratsky wouldn't want to get involved with a suspected murderer – which is what Vid will be if he leaves her here. Bratsky would find some way to avoid paying him. So she comes too.

The dawn is dappling the brown mountains with purple as he draws the curtains together.

Bratsky

Bratsky's private office: half of the top floor divided into an enclave for work and a separate, generous space for a bedroom – the ultimate pied-à-terre. The cold dawn is seeping into the darkness over the ranks of buildings jostling on Bishopsgate. Bratsky is wearing a new white shirt, crisp French cuffs pinned by cuff-links shaped like crossed sticks of dynamite. He pushes back in the leather recliner, swooshes the cursor across the screen and left-clicks over the REWIND slider, spooling the footage he has just finished watching, back to the beginning. He finishes his orange juice and thumbs the intercom.

'I'd like a couple of rounds of toast,' he says. 'And could you have Supperstone and Brooks come in.'

Five minutes later Supperstone and Brooks are sitting before his wide mahogany desk as he finishes the last crumbs of his toast.

'I,' he says through a mouthful, 'have been given something rather interesting. I'd like your opinion.'

He left-clicks the PLAY button, and watches again as the image rolls forwards on the big twenty-five-inch plasma monitor. He tugs it around on its pivot so that they can see more clearly. The quality is grainy, at best; the footage has been shot from a static camera onto a standard video-cassette (the film was subjected to image improvement before being compressed and emailed to him this morning, but only so much could be done for it). The camera appears to be behind an iron grille or fencing of some description; a lattice of grid-lines obscures the view. In shot: a walkway, with doors set at regular intervals on the right-hand side and a three-feet high ledge on the left-hand side, its murkiness ameliorated by round lamps fixed into the ceiling of the walkway, some flickering intermittently.

'Here we go,' says Bratsky. 'Watch.'

A figure emerges onto the walkway from a recess on the right – maybe twenty feet along the walkway. His appearance defines itself as he walks carefully forward: medium height and skinny, wearing an ankle-length leather coat, a white T-shirt with an indecipherable slogan, camouflage-style trousers, and heavy boots. He stiffens his collar as if feeling the cold. The figure walks over to the grille, his face shielded by one bar of the grid and also by a pair of black wrap-around shades. He lowers his head to the wall and appears to be speaking.

'No sound, I'm afraid,' says Bratsky. 'Not that any is necessary.'

The figure recoils suddenly as an arm reaches up from out of the bottom of the shot and stretches towards him. A kick – sending the arm away. A group of children has gathered at the end of the walkway and one of them tosses something, a stone or a tin can. The figure straightens out as the grille judders, then rolls aside, out of shot. Vid's sharp features pass directly under the lens of the camera as he walks through the shot.

'Despite the shades, that's Vid Danton, right?' asks Brooks.

'Without question,' says Bratsky, left-clicking on PAUSE. He click-drags the picture back, bringing Vid's features into focus again.

'Where was this taken?'

'Bethnal Green, I believe. This is Steve Biko House, a block of council flats reserved for low-income families, mostly from ethnic minorities. This camera was placed outside Flat 27 to provide an early warning in the event that the police attempt to enter the premises.' Bratsky is fingering the back page of a contract he had miniaturized and sealed in a perspex block to commemorate his first deal – fifteen years ago last week.

'Drugs?' guesses Supperstone.

'The place is a well-known local venue for junkies,' says Bratsky, skimming through the detailed email which accompanied the compressed footage. 'The police suspect Joseph Kellerman is the pusher operating from that flat. Who is, incidentally, the son of Owen Kellerman of Kellerman Aeronautics fame, and the sister of Astrid Kellerman, the keyboard player in Dystopia.'

'A family in the public eye.'

'More so than they might prefer. Kellerman Senior is being blackmailed with this film at the moment. His son appears in shot several times later on. There are some conventional shots too, through a zoom lens or something. Someone's been very thorough here. There were rumblings that Kellerman Junior was involved with drugs a couple of months ago, but they were suppressed by the lawyers. I'd say this evidence might prove to be rather more difficult to suppress. The papers will be running the first pictures next week – although the segment you've just watched is likely to receive rather more coverage, I'd've thought, given Mr Danton's notoriety.'

'Hmm,' agrees Supperstone. Bratsky wipes the corners of his mouth with a napkin. 'Where'd *we* get this?'

'We bought it,' Bratsky says. 'Consider it due diligence. I'm not having a deal go south because we didn't cover our bases properly.' *Let them take that as a reproach for shoddy research*, he thinks. *Keep them on their toes.* 'The question is this: what do *we* do next?'

Brooks, taking notes, looks up. 'What drugs are we talking about? Do we know?'

'We suspect heroin.'

'Heroin,' muses Brooks, stroking his chin. 'Ecstasy would be no problem. The papers'd fanfare about it for a couple of days, parents of dead teenagers'd have their say, then it'd blow over. And cocaine we could probably ride out. Most people already know Vid has the taste for it. Might even add to his aura. Heroin is a different thing, though. Whether that'd stain him irretrievably, I don't know. Look at what happened to Damien's reputation; it could get just as messy.'

'Apart from the practical fact that he could OD at any time,' adds Bratsky. 'That's not a sound basis for an investment.'

'What do we do?' asks Supperstone.

Bratsky gazes out into the dawn. Men are sweeping the pavements below and the pigeons are already swooping. He remembers the eagles that glided outside his office window in Hong Kong.

'Bin him. I'm not taking the risk. Can we get out of the contract?'

She nods. 'No problem. Unless Vid's signed the contract already, there *is* no contract. We can just recall the papers. If he has, we can rely upon the termination provisions I put in. Hold on' – Supperstone flicks through her tabbed copy of the contract until she locates the clause she wants at the back – 'here. Clause thirty-nine, point one, sub-paragraph A: "Negligent Performance of Duties". And I quote: "Should the Manager fail to perform his duties with due care and attention with regard to the health, safety and well-being of the Artist, the Company will have the immediate and unfettered right to rescind the Contract and demand the immediate repayment of any financial remuneration previously forwarded to either the Manager or the Artist." Pretty clear-cut, I'd say.'

'Good,' says Bratsky. 'Call Alex. Tell him the deal's off.'

Sandy

7 January
Diner

She sees a sedan break off the main road and bumble and tumble down the dirt track leading to the car park, dust clouds billowing out from behind the wheels, the suspension jumping on the uneven surface. The bodywork of the automobile is coated with sand and dirt, crusting around the wheel arches and staining the wings. The sun is already hot and bright, the clear Nevada skies a cerulean canopy over the crinkled mantle of the desert.

Sandy welcomes the company; she has been on edge ever since the guy with the bulging, staring eyes left on his motorbike four hours earlier. It is not unusual for the diner to attract the patronage of misfits spat out of the casinos and clubs in the city; it serves as a staging-post for mad drug-fuelled odysseys across the blazing sands to LA and the rest of California. She has seen some real crazies since she started working here, for sure, but there was something about him that dug down beneath her skin: the feeling that she should recognize him, that she had seen him before; his nervous, jittery posture, hunched down over his burger; eyes bulging maniacally, ripe with paranoia. She was glad to see the back of him.

She put his wad of money on the shelf behind the cash-till in case he comes back for it. She has also checked that Randy's old pistol is loaded and within easy unobtrusive reach, should it be needed. And she stared at the minute hand on the clock, willing it onwards, faster; it unwound only slowly, the night mired in her nervous foreboding. Now, at last, progress has been made. Only another forty-five minutes to go until the end of her shift.

The car draws up next to the wreckage of Randy's old Buick, the driver stepping out and brushing dust from his shirt: medium height and build, if a little comfortably plump; wild tangles of uncombed brown hair; scrubby stubble laced with sweat; restive eyes. He approaches the door hesitantly, looks back up towards the empty road into Vegas. As he pushes the door open she notices that his trousers, from the cuffs up to just below the knee, are dusted with dirt. His sleeves are rolled-up to the elbows, his forearms also dusted with sand and dirt. As she hands him a menu she sees that his right hand is inflamed and raw, with cracked skin and incipient blisters. The left hand picks at dirty nails, fidgeting.

'Morning,' she says.

'Yeah,' he mutters, glancing back again at either the car or the highway. The sunlight is glaring off the car's wind-screen in concentric circles. 'C-c-coke,' he orders, faltering, 'and, yeah, and could I, uh, borrow a pen?'

She takes a cold Coke from the fridge and a spare biro from the plastic pot behind the counter. He grunts when she hands them both to him.

Sandy waits behind the counter as he fumbles in a folder

he has carried inside with him from the car, taking out a sheaf of papers. The menu has fallen onto the floor and he has made no attempt to retrieve it. Sandy turns up the griddle in case he decides to order something, and listens as the fat starts to hiss and spit. He flicks through his papers, spreading a fan out on the table, finding the document he wants, planting it with his elbow and lowering the pen. She feels the bass vibrations of the plane before she hears it, then crashing overhead with a deafening clamour.

'It's the airport,' she shouts as he looks up, startled. 'The flightpath's directly overhead. The noise passes.'

He mutters an imprecation, lowers himself back to the papers and then swears again. 'Have you got a washroom?' he asks, brushing a napkin over a dirty stain his palm has imprinted onto the paper. 'I'm covered in dirt.'

'Sure thing,' she says, pointing to the washroom in the back of the diner.

He thanks her, locking the door behind him. Sandy turns up the radio, an ELO song she likes, and checks that everything is in her purse: house keys, cigarettes, pouch jangling with loose change, her compact. She hopes that Danny will be on time to pick her up. He was late yesterday, thirty minutes late, saying something about the car stalling just inside the city limits. Does he think she was born yesterday? She is tired and grouchiness is crouching. She wants her bed. Clean, cool sheets. The last thing she needs would be to have to stand and chat with Rhonda until Danny arrives. Rhonda and her malingering husband – how many times has she heard a variation on that same theme? Manny did this, Manny did that, yada yada yada.

She decides to make herself a coffee, enough of a caffeine jolt to see her through the final – check – thirty minutes.

'What the fuck is *this*?' yelps the customer, flinging the door aside. 'Some kind of sick *joke*?'

'Excuse me,' she says. *Not again*, she thinks.

'In there,' he stammers, jabbing his finger towards the bathroom. 'The mirror.'

She looks into the bathroom. Written with thick, greasy swipes of black lipstick someone has written the words VID and DANTON across the scummy surface of the mirror.

Astrid

7 January
Mojave Desert

A flat escarpment hemmed in between rolling sand dunes, and Astrid sheltering in the back of one of the off-road four-by-fours they used to drive out here. The black-glass pyramid of the Luxor on the Strip half a mile away, absorbing the morning sun, and the motley architecture along the remainder of the Strip: a medieval castle; the New York skyline in hundred-foot miniature; a Moroccan souk; Renaissance Italy; a Saharan palace; a Caribbean island. A busy hum of activity outside: PR people chattering with each other, organizing photo opportunities and interviews; journalists from fifteen different newspapers and magazines scribbling out their questions, testing dictaphones and gabbing on mobile phones to their editors in London, New York, Munich; a clutch of photographers driving the legs of tripods into the sandy dirt, making minute adjustments to apertures and shutter speeds, loading and spooling film; Damien leaning back against the bonnet of another jeep, talking to the reporter from *Bild*; Spin, waiting for Kaiser, orbiting the edges of the gathering, haggard after last night. The sun is already hot and Astrid gazes out over the desert through the half-open door, sucking at a coconut-and-banana milkshake. There are little patches of vegetation clinging onto the thin soil, every now and again a tree or a larger bush; heat haze rising in undulating ripples from the hot asphalt of the highway. How much more different could this landscape be to the soggy wetlands of the Fens, her home? This is like another planet.

She can still hear the set from last night, compressed into an indecipherable dull clanging that echoes in her inner ear. This despite the sixteen-decibel earplugs she wears on stage; the sound has still squeezed through. Frosty is still asleep back at the hotel; he missed his intended flight in, so caught only the ragged end of the party, jet lag ambushing him almost as soon as he had said Hi. She was pleased to see him. He didn't look as bad as her father's email had led her to expect. A pleasant breeze picks up and blows fresh air into the stuffy jeep. She finishes the shake and moves outside.

A dozen planes have taken off from the airport since they stopped here thirty minutes ago. Astrid looks up at the sky and the fluffy white trunk of merged vapour trails, branches separating from it as the planes break away into their individual trajectories. She watches the white tracks laid down by the climbing plane passing overhead, at first neat lines from the edges of each wing, then breaking up into fuzzy funnels as the wind teases and tousles their edges.

'Where's Alex?' she asks Damien, still talking to the reporter.

'He left a message. Said he was running late and that he'd join us out here.'

'And Vid? Still sleeping?'

'No idea. I stopped by his rooms before we came out. A right mess, but no sign of him.'

'Which means . . .?'

'Yeah, another binge. Best not make any plans with him included in them.'

The cameramen have formed a line, like a firing squad, facing back towards the lunatic skyline of the city. Their PR girl, Yvette from Lyons, who Astrid thinks is cute in an inaccessible sort of way, asks them if they are ready.

'This is second nature now,' says Damien, sliding off the bonnet and leading them out into the desert.

They strike their stock 'disaffected' pose for five minutes while the cameras click and whirr. Someone asks them to smile; Jared tells him to fuck off. Astrid wonders where these images will end up, these pictures of them stuck on a Martian landscape, at ten in the morning but already wearing make-up and still groggy from a surfeit of stimulants and lack of sleep. The PR company routinely sends them clippings detailing the front pages they are appearing on. The most recent package, before they flew out for this tour, contained glossy spreads from *Today* in Brisbane, *Pravda* in Moscow, the *New York Times*, and too many European rock magazines to remember. Astrid still treasures the crumpled front page from the *Cambridge Evening News*, her home-town paper, lauding her as the community's most famous daughter when the band first hit number one. That seems like an age ago; it has only been six months. The speed of their ascent sometimes leaves her breathless.

Astrid watches Spin as they hold slouching pose after

pose. He is fidgeting nervously on the fringes of the group, every so often looking over at the airport and the city. He must be looking forward to going home, she thinks. He has a wife and a child. This life must be anathema to him. She wonders herself, sometimes, if it is all worth it.

Alex's hire car bounces over the dunes as he nudges it off the road towards them. The front of the car rises and falls like a ship breasting waves, every downward plunge sending up plumes of dust, not foam. He parks next to the four-by-fours and slowly unfolds himself from the driver's seat.

'Maybe he's been talking to Kaiser?' Damien suggests. 'About the new contract?'

'We're done here,' says Yvette as Alex shuffles over the scrappy mounds and hillocks to join them. His suit is creased and looks damp at the bottom of the trousers. Dirt is clinging to it. He is wearing his shades.

'Where's Vid?' asks Damien. Jared and Spin have both come across. The photographers are storing away their equipment, and the first reporters are driving back towards the city.

'Um, not sure,' says Alex, his beetled brows crinkling into tightly pressed furrows. He runs a hand through his untidy hair and scratches his scalp. 'He's not in his room. He's probably, you know, gone off on one of his benders. I've just left Baxter checking the police and the hospitals. No sign yet.'

'When are you going to do something about him?' asks Damien peevishly. 'He's never going to last the pace at this rate.'

'I'll have a word,' assures Alex. 'He's under a lot of stress.'

'He's not doing my health much good either,' says Astrid.

'When's the bus leaving?' Jared asks. He is wearing shades, too. Astrid can see her reflection in them.

'In an hour,' says Alex. 'So we better move. I'll leave Baxter here. He can fly on with Vid, whenever he turns up, and meet us later.'

'If he turns up,' adds Damien.

'He will,' Alex says. 'You know what he's like.'

'Is Kaiser around?' asks Spin, squinting sweat out of his eyes.

'He's, uh, already headed back,' says Alex. 'You'll be able to catch him in London.'

'I can't wait to get out of here,' Jared sighs. 'I'm tired of all this heat. All this neon.'

They file back to the jeeps and bounce back across the dunes until they reach the tapered edge of the highway. The big blue and grey tour bus, 'Dystopia' written along one side in five-foot-high script, is waiting outside the hotel for them. A small cordon of tourists has surrounded it, gawping.

Jared

Bus

He settles into a seat and opens out the newspaper he bought before he boarded. Here is another review to save for later. The bus judders as the engine turns over. It creeps out onto the empty street.

Jared wonders when Vid was discovered – probably when Alex did his morning rounds, making sure they were all ready for the shoot. Why would Alex pretend that he had gone missing? He imagines him panicking, seeing his earnings dive-bomb into more defensible but still obscene multiples of zero. He'd call an ambulance and then they'd call the police. Panic is one thing, but to pretend Vid has disappeared is something else. But maybe, Jared thinks, it wasn't Alex. Someone else perhaps?

As the bus draws into a fast-moving stream of traffic on the highway and aims out into the baking desert, Jared takes out the notebook and pen that he always carries with him, ready for moments of inspiration like this, and begins to download his ideas.

Suzy

From: Girl4Apogee@hotmail.com

To: RockGod4@hotmail.com

Date: Monday, February 14, 5.55 P.M.

Subject: Hi

Hi. How R U doing? It's me again, Suzy, and I know it's been a long time since I have written but things have been really busy in my life and I haven't really had the time to sit down and write. I know U won't mind. It seems weird but maybe I'm not so much into it any more.

U never responded to my emails, did U? I was in such a state last month after U ignored me and changed your email address, I didn't know what day of the week it was. And then when I found out all about your girlfriend . . . that was the last straw, I guess. I was so out of it then – I totally forgot that you were in America, so I guess I now feel pretty stupid that I tried to meet up with you. I think I was pretty upset by that but I'm not going to apologize cos U were pretty out of order yourself. I didn't want to come into work for the rest of the week but I had to, just in case U replied to my last email. U never did (of course). One night, after my flatmate had gone out with her boyfriend, I sat in the bath with a razor for hours until the water was freezing cold. I was just thinking about stuff, U know, the heavy things we all think about now and again. I thought what it would be like to slide the razor over my wrists, just slide it across and watch my blood turn the water red. I obviously didn't do it but I made a few little cuts in my arm, just to see what it would be like. I ended up with loads of little cuts up my forearms and on the backs of my hands. My doctor was pretty worried when I showed them to him and I've had to stay in the hospital for a little while, just 'under observation' they said. All I did at first was sit there, wishing I could get to a computer so I could tell U about what it was like and then just lying there watching the ceiling and taking the pills they gave me. My parents were really worried and Christie was worried and said that she thought U were really cruel + heartless for ignoring me like U did. I don't think I really felt anything at all about U then. Maybe it was the drugs, I don't know, but I just sat there and stared at the wall and let their voices wash over me. Even my boss and my flatmate came to visit me which was really good of them and pretty unexpected seeing as my boss and I don't always see eye to eye. Actually, it was my boss who bought me the Apogee album. U remember Apogee – they were going to be one of your support bands at the Las Vegas gig. U must know all about Apogee – they R the best band I've ever heard. I have to say that I think they R much more talented than Dystopia and they really pour everything into their songs. Sorry, but I do. They R really honest and when I come to think about it I always kind of thought U were hiding your true feelings when U were writing your songs. That's the last thing U could say about Apogee. They really bare their souls in that album. It's really moving. If U do know them and if U see them, Brian the singer in particular, it'd be really great if U could let them know that I am their biggest fan. I'd really appreciate that.

I hope Vid turns up. The papers have all kinds of theories as to why he has gone away. I guess he just got tired of it all. And I was sorry to hear about Gretta leaving U, even though U might find that hard to believe. But I guess these things happen.

I haven't attached a 'read receipt' to this email. I guess if U want to answer U will and if U don't U won't. But I really don't need to be checking my mailbox every hour to see whether U have read my message and then worrying for days afterwards that U don't want to answer. I don't think the nurse would let me do that even if I wanted to! Anyway, I'm waiting for a reply from Eric from Apogee. He read my third mail at 2.35 p.m. yesterday and as it is now past midday in Miami I'm expecting him to get back to me. So I'll leave U here.

I hope U R well. Maybe U will write back, maybe U won't. But don't worry if U can't be bothered. I'm not really all that bothered myself any more.

Suzy

part **Four**

Alex

15 August
Waldorf Hotel, London

Alex cautiously leaves the toilet cubicle, sure he heard Damien's voice outside while he was crouching over the gram of speed on the marble cistern. The room is empty save for the attendant rearranging the rows of complimentary scents next to the sink.

He lets the attendant pour soap smelling of eucalyptus into his cupped hands, then rinses them under the warm tap and lets the attendant dry them for him. The rush from the speed is still spinning his head, his first hit of the evening. He feels energized and powerful and happy with his place in the world. He almost forgets about Damien – and what Damien represents. He looks over the complimentary colognes on offer.

'Alex,' says Bratsky, surprising him, as he comes out of the cubicle next to the one Alex himself was using. 'Well, well, taking on fuel?'

'Mike,' he says, 'hi.' He savours the flippant contraction, the narrowing of the social divisions between them now that his career has accelerated.

'How are you?'

'Never better,' says Alex. He feels a flutter of tension, a

slight tightening of the stomach while he watches in the mirror as Bratsky takes the sink next to him. He has never been completely able to accept his deception of a man of such patent commercial acumen, despite the overwhelming evidence that his deception has been complete.

'You never return my calls,' Bratsky says, but with a friendly smile that softens the rebuke.

'I know. Sorry. It's just that, well, I've just been so *busy*. I've never had so much work. I'm having to turn it away.'

'I've heard you're doing well. You deserve it. You should be pleased.'

'I am. Thanks.'

'Still no sign of the prodigal Mr Danton?'

'Not yet. I haven't heard from him for a month or two.'

'He's still hidden in the desert, right?'

Alex's heartbeat races. He swallows hard, masters it. 'Who knows, he could be anywhere.'

'He'll turn up eventually.'

Alex forces another smile and tries to ignore the cool glint in Bratsky's steely eyes. He feels as if he is being appraised, but Bratsky could not possibly know the truth. 'Of course he will, and when he does he'll make us both a lot of money.'

Bratsky nods. 'But you've got other clients up for awards tonight, right?' He rinses his hands.

'Best Single, Best New Dance and Best Classical,' Alex says, glad to have the subject changed.

'Well, best of luck,' Bratsky says, drying now. 'Not that you'll need it. You probably know the results already, right? That's why you came? The losers never bother, do they?'

'Let's just say I have an idea.'

'Of course you do,' the other man chuckles. 'All the mock surprise you see at these things is all so, I don't know, so *insincere*, don't you think? Those tearful acceptance speeches – so fake, so artificial.'

'No one has ever accused this business of sincerity,' says Alex.

'Never a truer word said, Alex, and something I've learnt since that first meeting we had. I've learnt a lot since then.'

Alex searches Bratsky's face for signs of censure, but he is scraping at something lodged underneath a fingernail, looking down. The man finishes with his hands and straightens the fit of his waistcoat.

'By the way,' he says, 'before I go, I think we're going to need to have a conversation about Mr Danton in the next couple of days you and I. A proper one, not a social chat like this. There are some things we need to go over, get cleared up, know what I mean? But this isn't the right time. It'll keep.'

'Sure,' says Alex carefully. 'Give my PA a call and we'll sort something out.'

As Bratsky leaves, Alex considers their conversation. It is true that he hasn't been returning Bratsky's calls, although the last one he ignored was over a month ago. For even longer than that, he has not mentioned Vid's absence, although Alex is not naïve enough to think that someone as sharp as Bratsky would blithely write off the half-million advance he paid to secure Alex's services. Alex has prepared himself for the eventual inevitability of a legal challenge and has already had his lawyers at White Hunter examine the contract. According to them, as things currently stand, the legal obligations entered into by Bratsky are unambiguous and unavoidable. They were confident that the contractual bonds would stand up to his strongest legal assault, and would only be broken in the event that Bratsky could prove misfeasance or misrepresentation on Alex's part. Given that seven months has passed since Alex patted down the last dry shovelful of earth over Vid's shallow grave, sealing away his own deceit, he is confident that the evidence of his plotting will similarly never be revealed.

It wasn't always like this. So easy, so effortless. For the first few weeks he couldn't sleep. He had a recurring dream of a dead Vid sitting on the burning MTV sofa, but flanked by the red-haired girl, their skins the colour of damp cardboard and with dirt matting their hair. As the flames blacken Vid's naked skin, crusting it with soot, he accuses Alex of conniving in his death and disappearance to advance his own career. Then the dream segued into himself running away and them giving pursuit, jerking like stiff-limbed zombies but always keeping pace, always just a trip or a stumble from lunging onto him and tearing him to pieces.

This repetitive dream passed in time. He was on tranquillizers and sleeping tablets for a couple of months, but not any longer. Each day pushes the scene in the desert further behind him.

Addressing his reflection in the mirror, Alex breathes

deep and even, straightens his bow-tie and returns to the table outside.

'Where are we up to?' he asks, slipping down into his seat next to Roxanne, the bassist from his new protégés, Apogee. Alex got to know them when they supported Dystopia on the American tour. They showed a glimmer of promise then, and now, with Alex's careful nurturing, they are showing signs of tremendous potential.

'Best Video,' she replies, resting a hand on his knee. He places his on top of hers, and laces their fingers together. Roxanne is wearing a pair of arctic camos and jackboots that reach up to her knees.

He scopes the room and spots Bratsky talking to a slim man in a grey pinstripe three-piece suit. Bratsky notices his gaze and raises a hand in acknowledgement. Alex returns the gesture, smiling as naturally as he can manage.

'Dystopia are up for that too,' he says vaguely, watching Bratsky and the man examining a document that has just been removed from a briefcase. The document is slipped into an envelope, which is then sealed. 'And I almost bloody well bumped into Damien in the toilets. Could've been embarrassing.'

If Roxanne is listening, she doesn't answer. 'When's it our turn?' she asks. 'I need to practise my acceptance speech.'

'You're after Best Newcomer,' he says. 'Just don't get too excited, OK? I'm not guaranteeing you've won anything.' He smiles despite himself, unable to stop the corners of his mouth creasing upwards. His mask of studied innocence amuses him, and Roxanne catches the smile before he can smother it away.

'You bastard,' she laughs, squeezing his hand. The coil of rings on her fingers presses gently against the soft edge of his hand.

'Alex, man, you've got to do something about that freaky bitch outside,' says Eric, the lead guitarist. Eric has had his hair cut and dyed this afternoon: now he has it in long, angled spikes, bleached blond.

'I know, you've told me. I said I'd see to it.'

'Weirdo's found out my email address again and now I'm going to have to change it. *Again*. For the third goddamn time. And she's fucking psycho, man. She's, like, out there – a real kook.'

'Will you just relax? I'm onto it. I'll speak to the police or something. I'll take care of it.'

'It's your own fault,' says Brian, the band's singer, to Eric. 'You shouldn't have asked her backstage. You brought this on yourself. Personally, I've no sympathy for you.'

'I was just being friendly, OK? And anyway, I thought it might stop her pestering me all the time.'

'It's not like she's anything to look at, man. Wasting your time.'

'Yeah, well, we all make mistakes. I was just trying to be, like, friendly or something. I didn't *ask* her to stalk me, did I? I didn't *ask* her to camp out outside our hotel throwing stones at the window.'

'Or roses?' adds Brian.

'They're orchids,' Eric corrects, 'which is worse.'

'Well, I think it's sweet,' says Roxanne. 'Love's young dream.'

'Ha-fucking-ha, Roxy. She's all yours if you want her.'

'Not my type,' says Roxanne, squeezing Alex's hand again.

This is the first time that Alex has hosted his own table at these awards. Even when Dystopia started to garner a reputation, almost a year ago, he was only a peripheral guest on a table hosted by Michael Kaiser, and only invited because of his influence with the band. No one was interested in him outside of his relationship with them. How things have changed: everyone wants him now.

He calculates the combined sales of his guests at this table, applies his percentage take, and his ominous mood slips away. Apogee are just working with their producers to put the finishing touches to the new album, and basking in the critical acclaim for their UK début single, 'Piranha'. Their charming innocence, the desire to make music in a vacuum without interference from the material world, reminds him of Dystopia before their breakthrough.

He remembers the trip to Manchester in the van that always broke down, the appalling concert there, the dilapi-dated hotel. A flash of nostalgia ... quickly suppressed by the reminder that he has come further, bettered himself, succeeded. Now he has an accountant working for him to handle the chores of financial management, and a PA to organize his schedule and shield him from difficult callers, like Bratsky. He wonders if he can remember the combination of buttons he must have pressed to launch Dystopia into orbit.

Opposite him is Alicia, the stunning cellist who has just recorded an innovative recording of Vivaldi's *Four Seasons*. The statuette for Best Classical Recording is on the table, awarded to her for the performance of Britten's *Soirées Musicales* she released last year. Alex credits her looks rather than her talent, for her surprising popularity. When he finishes with Roxanne he could do far worse than to enjoy her for a month or so. He has no doubt that she would welcome the chance to bring herself closer to him, so as to focus more of his attention on her. The supposition that his influence is a guarantee for the furtherance of careers has been a powerful aphrodisiac, and his confidence has been bolstered by his run of successes.

Next to her are Gus and Adam, identical twins who have made a considerable name for themselves by dancing half-naked, exhibiting rippled, tanned abs and miming to plastic cover versions of eighties hits.

These are the thoroughbreds of his new stable, the management business born with Bratsky's money and nurtured by his own burgeoning reputation.

There are other clients; he has a whole roster of young talent waiting for the right moment to be revealed. As his reputation has grown, so has the number of artists desperate for him to manage their careers. He has enjoyed, and taken advantage of, that attention. The character trait in him that he admires most is his ability to seize the main chance. It has flourished. His ruthless streak, restrained for too long, has finally been let off the leash.

There can be no doubt as to the feat that propelled him into the hierachy of this business. The miracle he performed with Dystopia stunned the media world. That same world would be overwhelmed should they ever come to realize how profound the miracle really was.

Looking around him again, drinking in the glamour of the elite, and his new place among them, he can hardly credit his good luck. He recalls Dystopia's giddy ascent – so far and so fast. The chaos in America when it became apparent that Vid was serious about disappearing, and not just for an evening or two as he had done before. All the way through the aftermath of his vanishing, Alex repeated his manufactured story like a mantra, pounding it into his head until the lies and excuses became second-nature. He wanted to reach a state of being where it would be difficult to separate the truth from the deception and, through long and repetitive practice, countless regurgitated soundbites, he achieved that goal.

He wove fact and fiction together into a tight cord until it was impossible to tell the one from the other. The long drive through the desert as the dawn sun broke over the hills; the hour spent opening two shallow trenches next to each other; the shock of finding Vid's name written in black lipstick on the mirror in the truckstop: those memories have been buried deep under the weight of his manufactured statements, just as the evidence of his perfidy lies buried beneath a layer of dirt and scrub.

They cancelled the tour eventually. At first it was postponed, and Alex flew everyone to the Florida Keys and a mansion where they could sequester themselves from the rabid press speculation outside. The debate raged furiously, endlessly rehashing the reasons for Vid's disappearance. Alex played the reporters beautifully, he thought, wielding latent talents he always knew he possessed but had never had the opportunity to exercise. He sowed seeds of gossip in scripted interviews and then carefully cultivated them until the media were convinced that Vid was hiding out somewhere in the desert, subduing the demons that had so publicly announced themselves in Las Vegas. That clip of him setting fire to the sofa on MTV was ubiquitous for weeks – evidence of his descent into addiction – and he quickly became the poster boy for America's disenfranchised youth, and the *bête noire* of the religious right.

Sightings were reported in Mid-West diners and in dive bars off Times Square. His image appeared on the covers of magazines catering for every taste. Endless documentaries traced the genesis of his tortured modern genius, and favourable comparisons were made: he was Kurt Cobain remade, the reincarnation of Jimi Hendrix. The publicity was more than Alex could possibly have imagined, and copies of the album sold faster than they could be manufactured. *Plastic People* became the fastest-selling debut album of all time. It has been in the top ten for thirty-five weeks, and each single off it has punctured the charts at number one on both sides of the Atlantic.

After six weeks the first rumours that Vid was dead surfaced. Alex accorded them weight by denying them only when it became absolutely necessary. Eventually, after two months of silence, he was forced to contrive a thirty-second phone call from Vid, who had, he said, called him from Arizona to assure his fans that he was alive and well. This was a tool that would grow to become increasingly useful.

Bratsky couldn't hide his delight when it came to the contract, but that had not been his initial reaction. There had been an early conversation with his lawyers on the day they left Las Vegas, when they said they wanted to invoke a clause in the contract to terminate its legal effect. Alex had been furious and disconsolate but then, as he was secretly arranging a legal challenge to enforce the agreement, Vid's popularity went into overdrive. Everyone was stunned by the public's reaction. Bratsky called back personally, and promised him that the affair was simply a misunderstanding, crossed wires in his organization that had now been remedied. He was contrite and humble, but Alex let him hang for a day as he 'reconsidered his position'. As a penance and an inducement, Bratsky increased the signing bonus, and promised to renegotiate the contractual terms as soon as he returned to London. Alex eventually accepted the offer, although every fresh hour he waited to disguise his own desperation was a torment.

Feeling the need to secure his fortunate position, Alex invented a telephone conversation with Vid and recounted it to Bratsky. He suggested that Vid had called him from Goodsprings, a small town a few hours' drive from Las

Vegas. He had apologized for his behaviour but explained that he wasn't sure if he could handle the demands of the tour. He found the adulation disconcerting. Alex speculated that the pressure was proving too much, and that Vid would need time to himself to consider his new-found status. This was hardly unexpected.

Alex reminded Bratsky that, after all, Vid was young and only recently removed from the delicatessen counter at his local supermarket, plain Christopher Driscoll. Now he was arguably one of the most recognizable faces in the world. A reaction was to be expected: a period of reflection and adjustment. Vid also wanted time to develop some promising new material that Alex had heard before he vanished. The material, Alex said, had surprised even himself with its maturity. Bratsky was beside himself with excitement, buying every fresh new lie that Alex put together.

At the end of the first week in Florida, Alex told the others that Vid had called again to express a desire to leave the band. He wanted to go solo. That was the real reason for his disappearance. What was more, he had practically begged Alex to manage his new career and, after considering his position at length and with much regret, Alex had decided to accept the offer. He was no longer able to manage Dystopia. There were no hard feelings, he assured them; this was just business.

He knew they would react badly to the news, and they did. Damien was livid, and demanded to know where Vid was, why he didn't have the courage to tell them himself. Astrid left for London the following morning without another word. She would quit herself, within weeks. Jared was more circumspect, more measured in his condemnation, although he did not shirk in the criticism he showered on Alex for his desertion. Since leaving Florida, Alex has not spoken with any of them, not even to address the sniping that they have directed at him via the music press.

Back in London, he used part of the advance to buy derelict premises just off Berwick Street in Soho. The happiest moment of his life was the day the interior designers finished their work, finally transforming the barren industrial shell into a chic office that matched up well with the opulence of Bratsky's city headquarters. The feeling of satisfaction as Alex walked into the office for the first time was indescribable. After years of dissatisfaction, being forced to endure his position as a cog in a wheel, he had finally arrived. He *was* the wheel. No more arse-kissing, or brown-nosing with Bratsky and his kind. Now he was a player.

Dystopia sued him, not unexpectedly, claiming breach of contract. His lawyers made short work of their claim, aided considerably by an affidavit sworn by Vid in Tempe, where Alex said he was staying. Vid was fulsome in his praise for the band's ex-manager, ascribing much of their success to his astute handling of their nascent career. Despite the band's doubts as to the statement's authenticity, it was admitted as evidence and was crucial to Alex's defence. The court ruled in his favour. This legal game was easy, Alex thought. You could contrive evidence to support whichever argument suited you best. He couldn't lose.

He could also handle his conscience because he knew he deserved success.

There was no need to advertise for clients. He let it be known that he was looking to expand his roster, and within weeks he was in the happy position of being able to turn away talent that, short months earlier, he would have fallen over himself to represent. *The Face* ran an article on him entitled 'The Soho Svengali' and he was listed as one of London's most eligible bachelors. He made moves into the world of film, and forged contacts with hip new talents. Some inked deals with him. His empire expanded.

On stage, the presenters announce the contenders for the Best Video award. Dystopia have been nominated, but are not chosen. Alex looks over to their table, located away from him (at his request) across the room, and watches for signs of disappointment. Although they have done well from the sales of *Plastic People*, their careers have stalled after the announcement that Vid had decided to leave and go solo. There was talk of Jared fronting the band again, as he had once before, but the market research undertaken by Revolution Records had, Alex understood, not been positive. An album of new compositions was mooted, some with vocals provided by Vid before his disappearance, but Bratsky had his lawyers injunct its release to prevent his new client's copyright being infringed. Now the rumour is that they are about to be dropped.

In many ways, Alex would prefer them to slip quietly into obscurity. Although he feels no guilt for the course he chose to take in Vid's hotel room, they still remain an enduring link between his tawdry past and his glittering present. Despite the passage of time assuaging his fears that he would be found out, to have them vanish would remove a potent reminder of the huge risk he took that morning. And, more pertinently, a reminder that his life was not always as easy and successful as it has since become. Remembering the beginning with them brings back too many memories of ass-kissing and kow-towing, a side to himself that he would rather forget.

Astrid is not here tonight. She left the band after returning to London and has begun new projects. There is the new sideline in photography, and the exhibition of black-and-white nudes at a gallery in Mayfair last month. The reviews were lukewarm, Alex considered, and he wondered if her rich father had arranged the spectacle as a distraction. Anything to deflect attention, no doubt, after the family was shamed by her brother's conviction for drug dealing.

Jared and Damien are standing alone together on the periphery of the tables. No Gretta with Jared this year; Alex heard that she has left him, although the reasons for the split have never been revealed to him.

They are talking conspiratorially, Jared stretching to murmur into Damien's ear, and paying no attention to the proceedings on the stage. They ignore the video for 'Power and the Glory' as it plays on the giant video screen, nor do they react to the murmur of gossip that follows the clip finishing with a freeze-frame on Vid's face and the moment of silence it inspires in the crowd. Even now Vid is the band. He is the fulcrum. People are wondering where he is, no doubt, and what he is doing now. Alex feels the familiar quiver of nerves, but it passes quickly, invisibly.

He wonders how Jared must feel, to be upstaged even after seven months have passed since Vid disappeared. Alex appreciated Vid's charisma, his commercial appeal, but he was never in doubt who the most talented member of the band was. Alex was always impressed at Jared's patience, his self-effacement, his equanimity. In similar circumstances he has no doubt that he himself would be consumed by envy.

'Wish us luck,' whispers Roxanne, flicking her dyed-red hair as the TV crew position themselves so as best to catch the band's reaction as the award for Best Single is announced.

'You'll be fine,' says Alex, managing a wink.

Apogee win the award, as the organizers promised that they would, and make their way to the stage to accept their prize. Alex is about to move around the table to talk with Alicia, when the man in grey pinstripe who had been talking with Bratsky approaches the table.

'Alex Culpepper?' he says rhetorically.

'Yes,' Alex replies cautiously.

'My name is Anthony Rogers. I work for Pomeroy and Krill. We represent Michael Bratsky.' He places a brown envelope on the table between Alex's unused knife and fork. The envelope has Alex's name typed neatly on the front. 'Inside this envelope is a Claim Form commencing proceedings against you. The Particulars of Claim are endorsed on the reverse of the Claim Form. I suggest that you speak with your own solicitors as soon as possible. However, so far as this evening is concerned, you have now been personally served.'

'What are you talking about?' says Alex. Silence is spreading out from his table like the ripples in a pond. People are craning around in their seats to watch the spectacle. He tries a jaunty smile but he can't fake it. It comes out like a grimace.

'There's one other thing,' says Rogers. 'This afternoon my client sought *ex parte* injunctive relief against you in the High Court, and was awarded both a freezing order and a search order. You'll find both inside the envelope, along with the Writ. The freezing order has already been served on your banks and we will be corresponding with you tomorrow to tell you what you may and may not do without our consent. The search order is being executed at your business and domestic premises as we speak. If you ignore the restrictions placed upon you by the orders, you can be arrested and imprisoned for contempt of court. Again, we will correspond with you tomorrow to discuss these matters, but I thought it best to warn you in case you were worried that you'd been burgled.'

'What the fuck are you talking about?' Alex's slick exterior has been demolished and cold panic has a hand around his heart.

'I'm not here to discuss this with you, Mr Culpepper,' says Rogers. 'I'm here to serve you with the papers. Your solicitors have also been served. Perhaps you should speak to them.'

Alex takes his wrist before he can move away. 'What the

fuck are you talking about?' he says, his tone undercut by alarm, his calm breaking up like a cloud of smoke, an illusion. 'What has he done – Bratsky?'

'My client has brought proceedings against you for deceit. He is seeking the rescission of a contract between you both that he says was induced by your fraud, together with associated damages and costs. Alternatively, he is seeking rescission on the grounds of fraudulent mis-representation.'

Alex can feel hot blood pushing against the back of his eyeballs. White spots bubble across his vision. He tightens his grip on Rogers' wrist with his left hand and curls his right into an awkward fist. Nothing would suit him better than to drive his knuckles into the man's nose, splash some blood over his crisp white shirt, feel his bones crunch as they grind together. Then he notices the expectant faces ranged towards him, eager faces hungry for scandal, and meanwhile Apogee picking their way back to the table. He lets go.

'You'll be hearing from my solicitors,' he says.

'No doubt,' Rogers says. 'Good evening.' He moves back towards Bratsky. The nerve! Alex watches him until his gaze alights on the big American; he waves at him again, a smug smile on his face.

Alex cannot concentrate. His brain pulses with anger, fright, danger.

'We won,' gushes Roxanne. 'I can't get over it.'

Alex stares dead ahead, trying to force tranquillity into his thoughts.

'Alex?' says Roxanne, placing a hand on his shoulder.

'What?' He shrugs her hand aside and stands to leave.
'We won?'

'Yeah,' Alex says. 'Nice one. Excuse me.'

The Aldwych, exterior

While he is waiting for his car to be brought around, Alex
asks the concierge to draw some cash on his visa card. It is
a hot, sultry night, as close and foreboding as his mood.
The daytime heat, soaked up by the pavements and roads
and buildings during the day, is leaking back out again.
Alex loosens his tie, then removes it altogether.

'Excuse me,' says a girl. She has slipped underneath the
temporary barrier on either side of the red carpet leading
down to the edge of the pavement. 'Alex?'

Alex turns to face her. She looks as if she is in her late
twenties, with tightly bound ringlets of hair. Her eyes burn
out of her face with a bright, piercing ferocity.

'What . . . who are you?'

'Apogee's biggest fan,' she exclaims. 'I met Eric backstage after the concert last month. We had a drink together.
Look.' She shows him a tatty Polaroid. She has her arms
around Eric's waist. Her face is stained with red-eye while
he has a look of edgy concern. 'See? We had a great time
together. We talked about all kinds of stuff.'

'Yeah, that's nice,' says Alex. 'It's really great. But listen,
I can't really stop to chat right now. I'm pretty busy.'

'That's OK, of course, I understand. I just wondered if
you would pass this on to him.' She hands him a sealed

envelope. 'It's some poetry I wrote, and a couple of pictures of me. I'd really like him to have them.'

'Fine, fine, I'll pass it on.' The concierge has returned, and has a look of awkward discomfiture across his face.

'You don't know what that means to me,' she continues. A porter appears, and asks her to return behind the barriers.

'I'm sorry, sir,' says the concierge. 'I'm afraid your card has been cancelled.'

'Could you tell him my phone number is in there too?' she calls out. 'Ask him to call me? My name is Suzy, by the way.'

Alex ignores her. 'What?' he says to the concierge. 'There's plenty of money in my account.'

'Your bank has cancelled your card,' he repeats, obviously embarrassed.

'Where is it? Let me try.'

'I'm afraid they asked me to keep the card,' he replies. 'I won't be able to return it to you.'

'What do you mean?'

'They were most particular. Perhaps you should take it up with them?'

Fuming, and feeling heat burning down to his collar, Alex drives down the Aldwych until he finds a bank. He double-parks and tries another of his cards in the machine. After three attempts, it swallows it and advises him to contact his branch.

He gets back in the car and then drops the girl's envelope out of the window. It catches the wind, rises, and then slips away.

Soho

Feeling dizzy with anger, he reaches his office in fifteen minutes, driving at high speed through quiet streets shared with cabs and drunken pedestrians. As he nears the office he can see that the lights are on, spilling out through the plate-glass windows and onto the pavement. A white transit van has been parked up on the pavement next to the entrance, its back doors open. Alex slides the car into his space behind the building, and makes his way back around to the entrance. Standing outside to greet him is a stranger, of thin build and with a narrow aquiline face, dressed in pinstripe. A small crowd of onlookers has gathered, intrigued by the scene inside. Alex looks over the shoulder of the man and into the office's wide main room. A dozen others are swarming over the filing cabinets, removing files and folders and tossing them into a pile in the centre of the room.

'Mr Culpepper?' the man asks politely. Despite his apparent courtesy, Alex notices that he is pointedly blocking the entrance.

'Who the fuck are you?' Alex says. 'And what the fuck are you doing in my office?'

'I work for Pomeroy and Krill, solicitors. My firm has been appointed by Michael Bratsky to bring an action against you.'

'I know that. I asked what you were doing. Now?'

'We're carrying out the search order obtained against you in the High Court this afternoon.'

'What do you mean this afternoon? No one told me anything about it.'

'The hearing was without notice to you, sir. We felt there was a risk that you would destroy evidence if you were notified. The Court agreed.'

'I don't understand this.'

'My colleagues are inside at the moment. It's my job to make sure that a thorough note is taken of any items that they remove.'

The doors open and a box full of his confidential files is brought out and pushed inside the back of the transit van. He sees from the label on the top file that these are documents relating to Dystopia. The van is already half-full with cardboard boxes brimming with documents.

'What are you doing?' asks Alex, reaching for the box. 'Give that to me.' The solicitor carrying it struggles with him – each of them tugging at one end of the box. The solicitor is wearing latex gloves. Alex slips and the box is tipped out onto the road. The folders, together with a perspex box containing floppy disks and a shoebox full of demo tapes, crash onto the tarmac.

Alex notices that the circle of onlookers has grown in number. Now there is a throng of young clubbers, diners and drinkers forming a semicircle around him. Some are laughing, others watching the scene with mouths agape.

'If you impede our work, I'll call the police,' says the solicitor. 'It'd be better if you co-operated. Just leave us to it.'

'You'll call the police?' Alex blusters. '*You* will? You're stealing confidential documents from my office. *I'll* call the police.'

'This work is all under the auspices of a court order and is perfectly legitimate. Interfering is illegal. If you interfere I'll call the police and have you arrested.'

Alex stares as his personal computer, trailing its wires and cables like streamers, is slid roughly into the van. A trolley follows, stacked high with boxes of correspondence.

'What do you need that for?' he says, pointing at the PC.

'We will retrieve your deleted emails and documents. We'll copy the hard disk and return it to you.'

'What right have you—?'

'Why don't you go home? We'll inform your solicitor tomorrow about what we've taken.'

'Because you bastards are at my home, too,' Alex says, 'doing more of *this*.'

'Then perhaps you should contact your solicitors. The court papers were served on them this afternoon. They will be able to confirm the details to you – explain things.'

Car

On his way back to the Waldorf, Alex dials the home number for David Cohen, his solicitor at White Hunter. Cohen picks up at once.

'They've fucking *sued* me,' Alex says.

'I know they have, they served—'

'What do you mean you know?'

'—the papers on us two hours ago.'

'Why didn't you warn me?'

'I haven't been able to reach you,' Cohen explains. 'You've had your mobile switched off.'

'I've been busy.'

'Alex, listen to me. This is very, very serious.'

'I don't want to hear that. I don't want you to tell me it's serious. I want you to tell me we can fucking deal with it – that we can make this whole fucking mess go away.'

'It won't be that simple.'

'I don't pay you to tell me that, Cohen. I don't pay you to be so *negative*. I pay you to sort this out.'

'Vid Danton's body has been discovered.'

A surge of black ink washes across Alex's eyes. When his vision clears, the car is pointing towards the dark black space of the Thames, just off the Embankment. He thumps the brakes and wrestles the car back into a straight direction. A car behind sounds its horn.

'Alex? Are you OK?'

'Of course I fucking am,' he says. 'I'm fine.'

'He was found buried in a shallow grave just outside of a town called Goodsprings. It's about half an hour's drive outside Las Vegas, apparently. Thing is, they found the body of a young woman in another grave right next to his. They haven't identified her yet, but they were able to identify him from his tattoos. Some of those were still visible. Plus the corpse was wearing a crucifix that matched the one Vid was wearing when he vanished. The story is breaking on the television now – I've just been watching it on the news – but they found them both a couple of days ago. The American police decided to keep a lid on it at first.'

Alex pulls over next to one of the floating restaurants near to Waterloo Bridge.

'How did they find him?' he croaks.

'There was a quad-bike race nearby and the riders disturbed a pack of dogs or coyote, whatever they have there. When they investigated they found the bodies wrapped up in bed sheets. The dogs had dug them up and were eating them. It was pretty messy, apparently. Someone's obviously killed them. They were both wrapped in sheets belonging to one of the hotels on the Strip. The name of the place was embroidered on the linen. The Nevada police have set up a murder inquiry.'

'What will they be doing now?'

'The police? Who knows. But I'd guess they'd interview the hotel staff first, then check out the security videos, that kind of thing. They'll probably ask for you and the band to go back out there and give evidence. Did you see anything suspicious, did Vid have any enemies – you know. But that's not relevant to us now. Bratsky is the problem.'

'I don't believe this is happening,' mumbles Alex with his forehead resting on the steering wheel. A stream of traffic heading back into the city is released by a green light, and blends into a red-and-yellow ribbon, sucked down into the chute leading beneath a flyover.

'From what I can make out from the Claim Form and the other papers, Bratsky's had private detectives sniffing around there for the last couple of months. He seems to have come to the conclusion ages ago that you weren't telling him everything, and decided to find Vid himself. I say that because the Claim Form was dated back in February, so all the negotiations you two have had since you got back were just a charade. They've just been humouring you while they figured out exactly what was going on. And then the police tipped off his investigators yesterday – his lawyers must have worked through the night to amend the papers and get their applications ready. I've got to tell you, Alex, Pomeroy and Krill are the best litigators in the country. They're like a pair of Dobermanns. We've got our work cut out fighting this.'

A cloud of fuzz settles in Alex's mind. He knows he should be thinking with clarity, setting out the new parameters of the problem and working out what his options are, but he can't manage it. He is helpless with terror. Sweat washes down his back. 'I don't see the connection,' he says. 'Why is this bad?'

'You've told Bratsky that you've been in regular contact with Vid. Right? I mean, didn't you tell him that you spoke with Vid a couple of months ago about the new material he was supposed to be working on? That's just not possible, Alex. Vid's body was already seriously decomposed. The police haven't released the autopsy report yet, but from the sounds of things he died months ago. Probably right after he disappeared. That's, what, seven months ago? You can see how this looks really bad for you, Alex. The court had no choice but to make those orders. The judge concluded that you must have made up those phone calls and the letters. Bratsky's alleged that the contract is a forgery too.'

'They're already taking stuff from my office. And my cash cards don't work.'

'That's what's going to happen. The court is worried you'll destroy evidence, or move your assets offshore so that Bratsky can't get at them. So it says that Bratsky can take away the evidence himself and stop you from spending a penny without his consent. If you try anything stupid, he'll have his lawyers send you to prison.'

Alex does not reply. He feels numb.

'I'm afraid it gets worse. He's saying that the half-million is just the tip of the iceberg of the damages that he's suffered. He said that his company spent over three million preparing for Vid to come across to them: marketing, media handling, publicity, stuff like that. He's arguing that all of that is consequential loss. In other words, money he wouldn't have spent without you fooling him into entering into the contract. Alex? Are you still there?'

His eyes are squeezed shut. 'Yeah.'

'All in all, with interest added on top, they're claiming over four million.'

'One million, four million, what difference does it make? I can't pay anything like that much, not even close. I've spent his advance. It's all gone. Everything else I've got is mortgaged up.'

Alex listens to the sound of his own ragged breath.

'Listen, Alex, I'm going to go to my office. I think you should come in too. We need to sit down with a coffee and work out exactly what you're going to say. Unless we can patch a decent explanation together, Bratsky will apply for summary judgment next week and that means you could lose the case without it even going to trial, unless we can put a credible defence together. So you should come over now. We've got to get going. OK?'

'Yeah,' says Alex. He ends the call with a clumsy stab of his finger.

Waldorf Hotel

Rather than turn into the city and White Hunter offices, Alex follows the road back to the hotel. Crowds are emerging from the theatres nearby. Alex envies their peace of mind, their obliviousness. His success is starting to unravel, fraying at the edges, and he feels helpless to prevent the process. He feels like an observer watching his own ruin.

The MC is announcing the award for the Best Dance Album. Spin, the deejay that they used to warm up the crowd in Vegas, wins the accolade for his first album, released after Revolution Records signed him after the gig. Alex had offered to manage him, but Spin declined. Alex has never been quite sure why. Bad advice, no doubt.

Bratsky is not difficult to find. He is in conversation with a small group of record executives beside the stage, and as Alex approaches he turns and breaks into a big friendly smile.

'Everyone,' he says, 'this is Alex Culpepper. Alex managed Dystopia, before Vid Danton disappeared. And we should congratulate him on his new band's success tonight. Apogee, isn't it? They've got a bright future.'

The others pass on their congratulations. Alex ignores them.

'I need to talk to you,' Alex says. 'Now.' He has no idea what he wants to say, just that something should be said.

'Didn't I say that we would talk? I just don't think that tonight's the right time.'

'Tonight is the perfect time.'

'I'm rather busy, Alex. Really, I think you'd prefer it if we didn't do this now. I'd much rather not spoil the evening by talking about business.'

'Perhaps you'd rather I told your friends about how you like to *do* business?'

'Alex, please—'

'—How you like to find ways to wriggle out of perfectly good contracts when you find they don't suit you any more? How you lie and cheat and bully?'

Bratsky turns to his guests and raises his hands in a theatrical gesture of helplessness, excuses himself and, taking Alex's elbow, tugs him gently so that they face away. Drawing him close so that Alex's ear is next to his mouth, he speaks in a voice that no one else can hear.

'Listen, you little shit.' He smiles congenially at a passing guest who catches his eye but his delivery is taut, urgent. 'You took me for an amateur and I'm not standing for it. I won't settle for having the advance returned. The money is insignificant and you could make an offer to settle and I'll reject it. No, I want judgment. Something I can use.'

'Are you threatening me?' Alex hisses. He tries to shake his elbow free but Bratsky tightens his grip, his knuckles whitening with the pressure, but his face a picture of urbane, benign calm.

'I'm not threatening you, Alex. I wouldn't do that. I knew you were lying as soon as you came back from America. You were so fucking transparent, pissing your pants and telling me your useless lies. I only let you have the money so I could get the evidence I needed to make an example out of you. And now I've got it: taped phone calls, letters, everything I need. I'm going to paint you for the manipulative, deceitful little fuckwit you are. And when I've done that, I'm going to ruin you financially, professionally and emotionally.'

His warm breath whispers against Alex's ear. Alex feels nauseous. Bratsky releases his elbow and Alex jerks clear.

'There's one other thing, before you go,' he says in the same low voice. 'The Nevada state police are looking at some interesting footage from the security cameras at your hotel on the day you checked out. I understand it features a man looking just like you hauling two white bundles into the trunk of his car. I'm sure they'll be in touch, I just thought you should know. Now, if you don't mind, fuck off.'

He takes Alex's hand. Leaning back, beaming heartily as he pumps Alex's hand, his voice changes into a jovial boom. 'Now, you'll remember to call me tomorrow? We'll have that chat.' Then he turns his back to him and continues his conversation with the others.

*

Alex feels unable to go home for fear of meeting more solicitors inside his house, rifling through his things with their pinstripe suits and latex gloves. He considers Cohen's suggestion that they should start to prepare a defence, but the conversation with Bratsky has drained him of his stubbornness and exposed his ruthless streak for what it really is, a pale sham. He feels helpless, like flotsam pulled away by a strong current. What good would it do him? What would be the point? He feels transparent, completely exposed. His ability to direct his own future has been circumscribed. He wants to get drunk.

He leans against the bar for support and begins to work his way through a bottle of cheap scotch he bought with the last note in his wallet.

The images, restrained until now, break free and float back to the surface, bobbing crazily in his mind's eye.

The dirt had been loosened by the rainstorm they tailed when they flew in to Las Vegas. It was miles away by then, in a different state, but they followed the path it had taken, soaring upwards to escape the buffeting from the turbulence left behind. He remembers the lightning spreading out like veins in the black clouds below, the way the darkness was suffused with a silver glow. The soil was dark with moisture and the snow shovel from the back of the hire car cut into it with easy, smooth strokes. He drove the blade in with both hands and pressed it down with his heel, scooped out the dirt, repeated the stroke. The water table was high and puddles of moisture collected at the bottom of the furrows. He had to stand in them to find the best purchase and clay and sod stuck to his shoes and the fabric of his trousers. After an hour of hard, aching work he had excavated two narrow trenches and built up low mounds of dirt and scrub behind him. He remembered the fresh smell of the earth, the sweet, sickly tang of the soil and the acrid scent of his sweat. His hands bled.

Alex is still at the bar when Jared and Damien find him.

He can't bear to hold their gaze.

Damien points at the bottle: 'That because you've heard about Vid or because you've been exposed?'

'Leave me alone.'

'No, really – we want to know.'

'We've got nothing to say to each other.'

'No, we do,' says Damien, shaking his head. 'You remember we sued you? And you remember you produced that affidavit from Vid telling everyone what a fucking great manager you are? How good you were to us? How we'd have been nothing without you? Of course you remember. As soon as it's confirmed that Vid died before he supposedly signed that so-called affidavit we're going to appeal. We've just spoken to our lawyer. It's a clear breach of contract, she said, and we'll beat you. The only reason you won before was because the judge believed you. This time we're going to take every last penny you have and then we're going to fucking bankrupt you.'

'Join the queue,' Alex mutters. 'Although there might not be much left of me by then.'

He had driven for an hour before taking a slip road off the main highway and then bounced over the desert for half a mile until he was shielded on all sides by the raised slopes of a shallow depression. The horizon was the colour of marma-

lade, the dawn bleeding slowly into the retreating darkness. The air was cold. Big fat planes from the airport rumbled low overhead, and he hid from the first few in the car, fearful that he would be spotted.

'Once we prove that you perjured yourself we're going for contempt of court. You'll get six to twelve months, apparently, minimum.'

'I'm not sure if I really care any more,' Alex says. He is surprised to find a sense of relief welling up through the cracks in his composure. The pressure has been building and building, and he has only ever effected cosmetic running repairs. He had thought that his façade was impervious, but one leak like this, and the whole edifice, all the lies and the falsehoods, has started to collapse. He has grown so used to the pressure, driving down on his shoulders, that he hardly notices it. Now it is lifting. He feels an almost overwhelming urge to confess.

He had stuffed the dead girl into the trunk of the car head first, next to the emergency first-aid kit and on top of the spare tyre. When he finished digging the second pit he lifted her out, staggering under her unsupported weight, and laid her flat, face up, in one of the wet trenches. Vid was sprawled across the back seat, covered with a travel blanket. He tugged him out onto the desert floor by his ankles, and dragged him into the other trench. Both of them were wrapped in white bed sheets he had taken from Vid's room. He had fastened them tightly with a roll of black duct tape he found in the car's tool kit.

Jared is standing behind and to the left of Damien, half of his face obscured behind his shoulder. He says nothing, but has an expression that encompasses both perplexity and foreboding at the same time. Their eyes catch; they look away simultaneously.

'Is everything all right?' asks Roxanne, putting a hand on Alex's shoulder. 'What's going on? What do they want?'

'Here comes the next stooge,' says Damien. He turns to face her. 'Listen, I like your music. I really do. You've got promise, like we did. But if you want to get tangled up with a selfish prick like this, you've got my sympathy. We made that mistake, and he screwed us, just like he'll screw you.'

'You're just jealous,' she says, although there is uncertainty in her voice. Alex remembers how much Apogee respect Dystopia. That support slot was their first major break. 'I know about Vid. It wasn't Alex's fault the band split up. You can't blame him for that.'

'Roxy,' says Alex, 'just leave us alone, OK? We've got some things to talk about.'

'Come back to the table with me. Come on – you can talk to them later. We want to celebrate, and they'll just bring you down.'

He shakes away her hand. 'Look, just get lost, OK? Just leave me alone. Please, just go.'

Her eyes cloud with a moment's confusion and then flash with anger. 'Well then fuck you, Alex,' she says, backing away. 'I just wanted you to have a good time. We were going to go on to a club or something and get drunk or wired but, you know, if that's not good enough for you, if you'd rather hang around here with them, then, well . . . whatever.'

'Nice one,' says Damien as she walks back to the others. 'You've still got that same diplomatic touch.'

Perhaps burning the bodies would have been better. He had looked in the trunk for a petrol can or a hose to siphon fuel from the tank, but with no luck. This was probably for the best, he reasoned. He didn't want to attract attention to himself with a column of smoke, and he had no idea how long two bodies would have taken to burn. He wondered whether he should cut off their fingers, or multilate them in some way, so that identification would be impossible. But as he stood above one of the bundles with a wrench, addressing their teeth, he lost his nerve. He didn't have the stomach for such brutality. And why bother? They were in the middle of the desert. What were the chances of them being found?

'It's not what it'll look like,' he says quietly, 'when it all comes out. You'll think I did it, but I didn't.'

'Let's go,' says Jared. 'Leave him.'

'No,' says Damien. 'Not yet. I'm enjoying him squirm. I've wanted to see him suffer ever since Miami.'

Alex looks down into his glass sadly. 'It'll look worse than it really was.'

Filling in the trenches was easier than digging them. The soil was looser, and he loaded each fresh shovelful with as much as the spade would carry. He worked fast, tipping the dirt over the two bodies, a thin layer at first until the whiteness of the sheets was obscured. Then a second layer. All the while he expected them to twitch, clawed hands to break through the dirt, to rise up at him. He wanted to check they were dead but he dared not touch them. By the time he was finished his hands were shaking and the bleeding was worse with the effort.

'Are you saying you *didn't* forge the affidavit?' says Damien incredulously. 'Fuck off. You fucking well did.'

'Of course I forged it. I'm not talking about that.' *Why are they being so obtuse?*

'What are you talking about?'

'Vegas. I'm trying to tell you what happened.'

'We know what happened. You screwed us.'

They were not buried deep enough but he didn't have the time to do the job properly. He just patted down the loose earth with the back of the shovel, the shape of the flat blade printing a pattern in the damp muck. When he was finished, he could still see the rounded slope where the soil followed the shapes of their bodies. He threw rocks and loose scrub over them to disguise the graves.

He finishes his glass and pours another. He feels calmer than he has felt for months. The words are coming easily to him, each one lightening the load.

Damien looks at him quizzically. He sighs and shakes his head. 'OK,' he says, turning to Jared, 'let's go. Before I do something I'll regret. Fuck him. Fuck you, Alex.'

Alex stops him with a hand on his arm. The tattooed script on Damien's skin looks reptilian, scaled. 'I just want you to know that it's not what you might think.' He explains slowly, as if speaking to children. He drains his glass again. 'Despite what people will say, and whatever happens to me, I didn't kill him. I didn't kill either of them.'

'Come on,' says Jared.

'No, wait,' Damien says. 'What? What did you say?'

'He was already dead when I found him.'

He drove away as fast as he could, unable to stem the sobs he had been choking down. He drove for half an hour before he realized he was on the wrong side of the highway. He had to swerve to miss a truck. He stopped at a roadside diner to clean himself up. He wanted a shower, needed to let hot jets scour the grime from his skin. He saw Vid's name on the mirror: had he written it, or was it just a fan? He told himself he had done the right thing. Or, at least, that he had done nothing wrong. In time, he believed it. He still believes it.

'Who was dead?' says Damien. 'Vid?'

'Someone else killed him. I don't know who, but it wasn't me.'

'Come on,' repeats Jared, more urgently. 'I can't listen to this shit any more.'

Acknowledgements

Thanks to all the following: Mette Olsen, without whom you wouldn't be reading this. My family and friends. Mic Cheetham, my agent, for taking a chance on me, for her advice, and for the ending; and Simon Kavanagh for his good taste, and for the beginning. Peter Lavery for his editing and wonderful generosity in Hastings and Montisi. Naomi Fidler, Richard Ogle and all at Macmillan. Neal Doran, who really should write himself. Also: Sharon Sullivan, Tom Nicholson, Anand Siva and Peder Flarup. This is not an exclusive list – if you've helped, I appreciate it.